The Stolen Cascadura

by

Beverley-Ann Scott

authorHOUSE®

AuthorHouse™ UK Ltd.
500 Avebury Boulevard
Central Milton Keynes, MK9 2BE
www.authorhouse.co.uk
Phone: 08001974150

First published by AuthorHouse 12/3/2007

ISBN: 978-1-4343-3287-5 (sc)

Printed in the United States of America
Bloomington, Indiana

This book is printed on acid-free paper.

Cover Illustration by Djenessa Jean-Baptiste Joseph

Dedications

This book is dedicated to my father Trevor Scott, who, though blind, had better vision than any man I have ever known.

Acknowledgments

Many persons came together to help edit and refine this work. My mother Grace Scott, who was always the editor-in-chief, was a tremendous source of inspiration for this book. Without her support and encouragement this book would not be possible.

For reading the original manuscript and assisting with the editing I wish to thank *Catholic News* Editor June Johnston, Fr. Gabriel Julien, Mr. Everton Smith, Mrs. Judy Seepersad, Eurico Jardim, and Janice Samuel (St. Lucia). I am particularly grateful to my cousin Djenessa Jean-Baptiste-Joseph for the cover artwork and to Willie Chen, Indiar Holder, Wycliffe Roberts, and Annabelle Roberts for their feedback.

I want to express my deepest gratitude to my immediate family, my brothers Chris and Dave, my sisters Denise, Karen, Mariella and my nephews, Jason, Jalen, and Jonah whose hugs and kisses have been my refuge from many storms.

I would also like to acknowledge my extended family, in particular my aunt Betty-Ann Cumberbatch, who has been a mother, friend, and teacher throughout my life. For always looking out for me I wish to thank my uncles in the Scott family especially Hugh, David, Mervyn, Roger and Bentley as well as my aunts Helen, Jennifer, Kathleen, Donna, Judy, and Pearl. I am eternally grateful to my aunts Carol des Anges, Gemma Thomas and Allison Burke, the Thom family, the Cross family, the Thomas family and the Jean-Baptiste family.

I would like to pay tribute to the Searwar family of Guyana especially Dr.Honnett Searwar, Mrs. Indrani Searwar, Nelly Sanasie, Marcia and Christine Searwar, who continue to love and support me in all my endeavours. I say special thanks to the staff of Catholic News. In particular I would like to thank Fr. Michel De Verteuil (former editor of *Catholic News*) who gave me the opportunity to explore my writing ability.

I am grateful to all my cousins and friends especially Mary Pitman-Gilkes, Marilyn Ramsumair and the Ramsumair family, Alice and Herbert Wetchler (USA), Mandisa Abraham (USA), Kafi Rodney, Bro Toni Badri OSB, Julie Julien, Joan de Coteau, Gwenneth Graham, Nicola Joseph, Melissa-Jo Maharaj, Karen Harper, Lusan Thornton (Guyana), Myrna Mederick and family (St.Lucia), Alina Louisy (St.Lucia) and Geraldine Carasco (St.Lucia). For always pushing me to excel, I thank you Francis Robinson.

Finally I thank the people of the Beetham Estate who allowed me into their lives and experiences and you reader for choosing to read this book. It is my hope that it will give you much food for thought.

Beverley-Ann Scott

Foreword

The Stolen Cascadura is a truly West Indian work of fiction. The setting is Trinidad in the year 2003. The novel revolves around characters who come from different cultural, ethnic and economic backgrounds and who are brought together by circumstances which change the course of their lives.

The Cascadura is a much sought after fish in Trinidad and Tobago and is a rare and expensive delicacy. In Trinidad folklore, it is believed that those who eat this fish will end their days in Trinidad. This fish represents everything sweet, golden and unspoilt about the land we Trinbagonians call home.

The Stolen Cascadura looks at some of the harsh realities of our times and seeks to present some societal issues in a realistic and thought provoking manner. It does not seek to pass judgment on any of the topics that it deals with but attempts to hold a mirror up to these difficult issues in order to facilitate healthy discussion, dialogue and debate.

The characters are meant to speak to everyone. Their lives are opportunities for reflection, and their responses to the challenges they face allow us to embrace their humanness, their weakness and their strength.

There is weakness and strength in all of us. We all have had something precious taken away from us at some point in our lives. We all have had our 'Cascadura' stolen. Some of us have been able to reassemble our lives and move on, while others will forever mourn the loss.

It is my hope that this book will lead its' readers to introspection and challenge us all to examine our own individual and societal capacity to love and to hate; to be weak and to be strong.

Contents

1   Another Day in Paradise 1

2   Life in San Antoñio 7

3   The Best of Friends 16

4   On Opposite Sides of Town 20

5   In The House of Pain 41

6   Those Damn Politicians 62

7   Those Who Eat The Cascadura 81

8   Definitely Not A Laughing Matter 101

9   Stymied Plans 121

10   Fire On The Beetham 139

11   Mouth Open and Story Jump Out 156

12   When All Is Taken Away 171

13   We Turn to God and Other Things 190

14   Not My Chile! 208

15   Life and Death in the Balance 227

16   The Truth Be Told 239

17   The Feeling of Christmas 257

18   Unacceptable Behavior 275

19   Something Ent Right 293

20   A Mother's Love 308

21   It's a Boy! 327

22   Aids is Not for Me 342

23   When the Roles are Reversed 356

24   Unexpected Fortunes 372

Chapter One

Another Day in Paradise

She was late again. It was the third time this week. As her lanky legs moved at breakneck speed under her starched pleated navy blue skirt, Lisa was oblivious to the tooting horns, the black smoke rising from the mufflers of the many cars on Frederick Street, the looks of frustration on the faces of the motorists or the smell of urine surging like a wave from the corners of the concrete buildings she hurried past. All she could think of was the look on Sr. Monica's face that would greet her before she got to class. It was the look she knew would probably spoil her entire day but today was Wednesday and she wondered if she would get more than just a look of admonition from the goodly Sr. Monica.

Beads of sweat trickled down her face and under her shirt. She knew she'd look a real mess by the time she eventually reached the gate. She wished her bag weren't so heavy with books; at least she would be able to run faster. Lisa was tall and thin, her cocoa brown skin was flawless for a girl her age. Fortunately for her, she had been spared the acne attacks of puberty that many of her classmates suffered and though she didn't consider herself very attractive, she was.

"*Morning Has Broken, like the first morning, black bird has spoken, like the first bird........*" The singing to close the morning assembly had begun and there was no way she could avoid Sr. Monica now. A large wet patch on the back of her white shirt evidenced her run up Frederick Street. But what excuse could she offer? Ted her mother's live-in boyfriend had come home drunk last night again. "The fool," she thought. What did her mother see in him? Everything about the man was loathsome to Lisa and when he had too much liquor in him, the sounds of her mother moaning in ecstasy under the man who had just hit her on the head with a frying pan made Lisa's blood crawl.

"All Form Five students are reminded that there is a parent's meeting tomorrow afternoon at five p.m. in the auditorium." Sr. Monica's shrill sharp voice interrupted Lisa's thoughts of the night before. She turned around to see a few other students from the lower Forms joining the late line. Somewhat relieved that she was not the only one, she knew that Sr. Monica would have to spread some of her usual morning venom on the other late comers. The shuffle of feet had begun, morning assembly was over, and students were going to class. Lisa hoped that Sr. Monica would be distracted so that she could quietly join the line of her classmates on their way to class but there was no chance of it. When Sr. Monica alighted from the assembly stage, black veil blowing in the wind and began marching like an army officer toward the late line, Lisa knew her hopes were about to be dashed.

"Well, well well, what do we have here…..Mizzz Williams. You seem very fond of coming late these days. Not a good example for the younger ones." Sr. Monica glanced briefly at the tall sweaty girl with head bowed. Before Lisa could muster a reply she had moved on to the others in the line, and was ready with quick stinging jabs of her fiery tongue for each one. "Whew!" Lisa breathed a sigh of relief. She hoped that that was the end of her morning dose of the dragon but she was wrong. "Ok then girls, off to class you go. Mizzz Williams in my office. Now!"

"Fiiiiiiiiiiiveee Dollars, Fiiiiiiiiiiive dollars a pong fuh tomatoes. Yuh cyah go wrong wid dat. Only fiiiiiiiiiive dollars!" Ms. Janice, as she was fondly called, had just the right pitch of voice for selling produce in Port-of-Spain market. "Get yuh tomatoes here at Fiiiiiiive dollars!" Like a calypso cut short, her sweet voice drew glances and customers to her ramshackle stall where they could get not only tomatoes but ochroes, eddoes, sweet peppers, cheese, garlic, onions, bodi, and breadfruit which was in season.

The mother of five from Santa Cruz was determined as always to sell all her produce but today was a slow day. Things would pick up later she figured. She knew how to be patient and down town market dynamics required people like Ms. Janice to be patient. "Darling, doo doo. Boy ah real love dis red woman smile boy," Papa Netty joked as he approached Ms. Janice's stall bare chested and staggering. Papa Netty was a market regular. In a tattered pair of rust colored jeans rolled up mid-calf, he leaned over the colorful array of breadfruit, melongene, ochroes *"et al"* and blew a kiss for Ms. Janice. Often drunk and smelling of rum but quick-witted at all times, Papa Netty was the butt of many jokes. He'd come to the market to pick up bottles and sell limes, but Pinto's rum shop where he was sort of a permanent resident, was the major beneficiary of the money he made from his meager sales.

He was in love with Ms. Janice. He believed that one day he would marry "de ole lady" and she would take care of him in his old age. But Ms. Janice had no interest in caring for his "ole raggedy ass" as she so aptly put it. "Boy doh touch meh tomatoes wid yuh stinkin hands! Dat is fuh de customers." Ms. Janice was not joking this time. "Boy move from by meh stall! Mash!" Papa Netty staggered and stopped, not able to stand steady. He tottered forward and back as any man who had as many drinks as he had had that morning would. "Ah would love to touch yuh tomatoes. Dey lookin big and nice," Papa Netty croaked with a lustful gaze in the direction of Ms. Janice's bosom.

"Leave decent people alone ole man. Doh leh me call police fuh yuh," the husky voice of Ma Thomas from the neighboring stall threatened. Ma Thomas like Ms. Janice was a widow but unlike Ms. Janice she had never bore a child. She had strong coarse hands and chocolate skin roughened by sun and hours of planting. Farming had whittled away what was left of her finger nails and varicose veins bulged like blue-black worms at the back of her sturdy calves. Still, the seventy-two year old looked like sixty and she loved Ms. Janice like a sister.

Undaunted by the remonstrations of the two women, Papa Netty wiped the sweat from his brow and continued as if determined to convince them that he knew how to make intelligent conversation. "How is dat lovely little gyul chile of yours Ms. Janice? Dat is one pretty little gyul chile and she look bright too bad." "She bright yes! An if she have any sense she will stay away from de likes of no good drunkards like you." Ma Thomas' words pierced him to the quick and a strange expression came over his face. His sunken eyes glistened as he struggled to hold back his emotions. He wagged his finger at her wanting to respond but the words seemed to rest heavy at the back of his throat. Unable to bring them forth, he tottered backward and forward; then, with head bowed low, wove a silent zigzag pattern through the market crowd.

"Poor ole fella," said Ma Thomas. She felt a twinge of guilt about her last utterance and wanting to change the subject, enquired about Ms. Janice's daughter Jesse. "Oh Jesse fine. Dat gyul is a good chile yuh hear." Ms. Janice beamed as she sprinkled some sell water over her lettuce and tomatoes, wanting to remove any maljoe that Papa Netty might have left behind. Ms. Janice was proud of her Jesse and had great ambitions for the Sixth Form St. Joseph's Convent student. "She studying sciences yuh know. Teachers sayin she could geh a scholarship." Her eyes lit up when she spoke of her first child.

The year 2002 had been a tough one for Ms. Janice. After the land had taken her husband, the family had been hit hard financially but Jesse had been such a support for her, taking such good care of the younger ones so that the stall could still bring in some change at the down town market. As she looked at her dirty cardboard hands Ms. Janice took comfort in the knowledge that Jesse would never ever have to work the land or sleep at night in a market stall or deal with men smelling of piss like Papa Netty. A knowing smile came over her face. Jesse's life would be a different one.

Chapter Two

Life in San Antoñio

Brian hastily removed the starchy red tie from around his neck as he waited for his father's driver to pick him up. He had just come from Chemistry lessons with Mr. Lee Wen and he was exhausted. A-level classes had taken a toll on the QRC student. For him CXC exams had been a breeze but since he hit Sixth Form, he was having a much harder time adjusting. It didn't help that he had been made Head Prefect of the school. Balancing that responsibility, keeping up with football practice, while trying to maintain his cool image as the prefect who'd turn a blind eye to the transgressions of students while in uniform, had been too much for him.

Ever since his girlfriend Amy won a SAT scholarship for Howard University, he seemed to have lost the pleasure he used to find in doing simple things. He could still remember her face at the airport in Piarco. She looked so happy to go; to leave him. He couldn't get over that. She was his first girlfriend and he had secret dreams of the two of them doing A-levels together, spending time at the mall, parties at Pier 1, dinner with their friends and eventually going to the same university together. She had meant so much to him. And even though he told his friends that they had slept together, they hadn't. Although in his head he was able to rationalize why she had to go, he missed her terribly.

"Ah feel like meh head going to buss. Boy I hate Organic Chemistry and ah hate alkenes … Geez I just wish there was a way to remember all this stuff. To cram it in my head." Eddy thought aloud having just emerged from the hall where moments ago he had been struggling to focus on the many reactions of benzene. He too was beginning to feel the stress of all these extra lessons. He gave his best friend Brian a friendly tap behind the head. Brian shot back with a playful punch and Eddy turned aside to avoid the imaginary blow. At that instant a glimmering black BMW pulled up on Oxford Street. A whispy looking man in a white shirt jack and black pants emerged hastily from the vehicle and signaled to Brian who was only a few feet off. When the man opened the car door, cool sweet smelling air escaped and Eddy could see the plush grey upholstery inside. "Aye I riding out. See you tomorrow," said Brian as he bid his farewell and disappeared into the heavily tinted vehicle.

Eddy turned and began his long walk home. He felt like walking tonight instead of taking a taxi. Besides the Beetham wasn't a long walk especially for someone used to it. Eddy Torres was no rich boy but by QRC standards he was good looking, which meant he could be popular if he really wanted to be. His jet black wavy hair, light complexion, and hazel brown eyes led people to believe that he was of Spanish ancestry, especially with a surname like Torres. Nobody had to know that he never really knew who his father was and that his mother was a whore who had got pregnant for a white man tourist many Carnivals ago. So for all intents and purposes Eddy continued to acknowledge when asked, of his Spanish grandfather who came to Trinidad from Venezuela back in the fifties. He had also managed to keep the fact that he really lived at Beetham Gardens Phase Four a secret from Form One all the way to Form Six. As he reflected on that, a sly smirk came to his face. That was an almost impossible accomplishment in a society as small as Trinidad. He always used the address of one of his aunts in San Juan. Even though it could never compare to an address that ended in West Moorings, St. Clair, The Mews, or Goodwood Park, it sounded a whole lot better than Beetham Gardens.

He knew his friends like Brian Chow Fatt and Sean Mathias would never befriend him if they knew he was a Beetham boy. Eddy was one of the brightest guys in his class; he just couldn't let people associate him with the grim realities of his living situation. His secret was safe too because Sean and Brian had never traveled beyond the lighthouse in down town Port-of-Spain, except of course when they had to go to the airport for their Miami vacations and even then, they went via the Lady Young Road. Eddy didn't realize that he was almost home until that all too familiar smell greeted his nostrils. It was the smell of the Beetham that so many people complained about but for him it was not as unbearable as it was made out to be. He had grown used to it. It was the smell of home. Maybe tonight he would be able to get a good night of sleep. Last night his slumber had been interrupted many times by the sound of gunshots and his body yearned for rest.

It was Wednesday night and Jesse was helping her younger sister Rebecca with her homework. She had a lot of studying to do but she didn't mind helping the impish seven year old. Rebecca was her favorite. They shared a mutual mysterious admiration for each other but the awe weighed heavily on Rebecca's side. "Sit down chile, Settle yuhself and act like a lady." Jesse was losing her patience as she held the red glossy covered Caribbean Reader for Standard One students close to her chest. Rebecca seemed to want to push her luck tonight. She laughed as if being tickled by Jesse's growing irritation. "C'mon doh leh meh have to slap yuh little gyul." Becca stuck her tongue out. "Ah doh want to do it," she whimpered lips pursed and arms akimbo. "Yuh cyah hit me. Ah will tell Ma on yuh." A mischievous light emanated from her little brown eyes and the huge bushel of her fuzzy brown hair seemed in agreement with her defiance.

She stared at Jesse with a pleading look. Jesse heaved a sigh of desperation but Becca snatched the book right out of her grip and ran laughing in the direction of the kitchen. She didn't expect the painful yank of her hair which was followed by the heat of a slap to the arm. "Yuh will sit down now and do yuh work yuh hear meh chile." Jesse's face was red now and Becca's dramatic display of tears, snatty nose sniffling, sobs and spitty open mouth crying was having no effect. "How yuh expect to be anybody if yuh keep behaving like dat? Yuh want to grow up stupid? Eh? Yuh want to have to plant yams and cassava like Ma? Eh? Answer me?" Jesse shouted as she dragged the bawling child by her arm and sat her down. Handing her a washrag so she could blow her nose, she spoke now in soft apologetic tones. She loved Becca she just didn't want her to repeat Common Entrance like their brother Steve. She knew Becca was a bright child but like an untamed horse let out of the stable, Becca could engage in all kinds of wild and wayward behavior if left unbridled.

Leaning over, she pulled Becca close "Silly girl. Why yuh have to make it so hard fuh me? Ah just doh want you to end up doing bad in school. Yuh doh want to be able to buy nice clothes and look pretty?" Becca nodded through drying tears full of remorse. "Well then yuh have to put something in that fuzzy head of yours." Jesse patted Becca's bushy hair down and managed to get a dimpled smile from the girl. She opened the Caribbean Reader to page fifty-six. "We reach here in class," Becca announced, as the pair disappeared into the page.

It was not easy to be a farmer in Santa Cruz. Ms. Janice and her husband knew that only too well. Crops were always at risk from flooding, stray animals, bandits, locusts and within recent times the mealy bug. In a country where oil was the mainstay of the economy, agriculture was not something that governments took seriously. Despite the many challenges Santa Cruz farmers faced, they worked diligently in sun and rain as if the entire nation depended on them. For many, it was more than just a job or a way to put food on the table. It was a way of life.

There was something pristine and unspoilt about Santa Cruz. To own a piece of property in Santa Cruz was truly a blessing but to be a farmer in Santa Cruz was to know that of all the soils in the whole of Trinidad, you had access to the best. The people were simple but hardworking; not fussy or complicated. They'd say "Good Morning" to strangers as they passed each other in the street. From Cleroy the Express newspaper hustler who sold papers down in the Croiseé, to the parish priest of the small Santa Cruz community, courtesy was a way of life and it was not a put on. It was not that 'valley people' as they were commonly called were lazy but it was hard to take life as seriously as town people did after growing up surrounded by so much natural beauty.

In Santa Cruz the air was cleaner, the soil was richer, the grass was greener the cows had shinier coats, even the goats seemed healthier. It was as if all creation knew that Santa Cruz had received an extra special sprinkle of God's rain, air, soil and sunshine. The cocoa trees knew it, the horses knew it, the banana trees knew it and the 'valley people' knew it, especially those who lived by the land. It was their secret pride and one of the things they could use as leverage when they went to the Port-of-Spain market. Their produce was from the valley. And although price of produce drove the market, for some regular market connoisseurs, the tomatoes, lettuce and sweet peppers from the valley were simply better in quality.

Deep in the heart of the valley in San Antoñio it was as if time had stood still. Narrow dirt roads, donkey driven carts, old men on bicycles with grandfather hats were not uncommon sites. Like a page out of an old history book, San Antoñio was the last reminder of life in 1970. The industrialization from the Croiseé, the development of gated communities and residential areas, stopped two miles before San Antoñio, almost as if San Antoñio had an invisible sign hanging over it which read 'Do Not Enter'. The older folk who grew up there in the late thirties were walking history books; and over a beer in Boyo's rum shop or a cup of tea on Tante Eva's frail wooden porch, any of them could relate the history of San Antoñio with a rich and vivid imagery that would captivate any visitor.

Jesse's father Gregory was born and raised in Santa Cruz and had inherited the lot of land his family now owned when his own father died. As the eldest of seven siblings, Gregory inherited the largest lot but unlike his other brothers who had ambitions of traveling the world and living in America, Gregory's only ambition was to have a good woman at his side and to raise his family on the land where his navel string had been buried at the foot of a blossoming Julie mango tree.

It was in this valley rich in God's blessings, that Mr. GG, as he was called by his neighbors, put on his dirty rubber boots and straw hat and walked out everyday to till the soil, fertilize it, pull out the weeds and get ready for market day.

He was a family man who wanted more than anything to give his children a good education. He looked forward to the days when he wouldn't have to wake up so early or work so hard; when he could tell his grandchildren stories on cool afternoons in his hammock under the old Julie mango tree. He never knew that his cholesterol levels were high or that he had coronary artery disease. In fact nobody knew until that day when he lay in Port-of-Spain General hospital hooked up to a breathing device, his chest heaving and collapsing with each breath. At forty-seven he still had so much to do, so much he wanted to see his children accomplish, so much, so much, so much.........and then he stopped breathing.

Jesse was there. Her hand had been resting lightly at the side of his chest, as if she needed to feel every single breath to know for sure that he was still there. "Paaaaaaaa......Paaaaaaa!" Her screams pierced through the Intensive Care Unit as she collapsed in her mother's arms almost lifeless. Ms. Janice held her child close and buried her face in her hair. She was mustering all the courage she had. She could not bear to look at him. In those last twenty-four hours, she felt like Jesus in the Garden of Gethsemane. She knew he would never make it back home but in her heart of hearts she had hoped. She had prayed. Not her Gregory. How could she raise these children without him? How could she survive without her man? And as if the reality of her aloneness in the world had suddenly hit her, Ms. Janice released the most piercing scream from deep within followed by the words "Oh God" before she passed out on the ward floor. The day was June 20th 2001 but it had seemed like yesterday to Ms. Janice everyday since.

Chapter Three

The Best of Friends

"Jess, Jess…..!" Lisa was making her regular run toward Frederick Street when she spotted Jesse hustling across the Brian Lara promenade. She had to shout a couple times before Jesse turned around. Their mouths relaxed into smiles and their paces slowed on seeing each other. At least they would have some company to face Sr. Monica's wrath this morning. Lisa's sweaty run turned into a brisk walk as her friend waited for her. With hair pulled back into neat buns and shirts tucked into their well ironed skirts they seemed the image of deportment, except for the wet spots on their backs. "I didn't think I would catch up with you gyul. You doh see or hear nobody when yuh walking." Lisa had come abreast of Jesse now and the pair began walking in unison. "Gyul you think I like to deal with Sr. Monica ah what. She doh deal too nice yuh know. Ah well at least I'll have company in the line."

The two giggled as they continued their stroll up Frederick Street. They were already late they figured and didn't see the point in rushing. Besides they were sweaty too, this way they could cool down a bit. Lisa and Jesse were best friends who shared similar ambitions and dreams for their futures. But more importantly, they trusted each other implicitly. It was a trust that they valued more than any other aspect of their friendship, especially in a school where the goddesses of gossip and popularity ranked only second to boys and tales of sexual exploits. Confidences among friends were betrayed every Monday morning in exchange for the unofficial stamp of acceptance by the popular girls in their Form Six class.

Metamorphosis of body, mind and attitude had been an ongoing experience from the moment they had set foot in the walls of St. Joseph's Convent six years ago. However it was invariably the changing bodies that largely influenced the change of mind and attitude for many girls. Lisa and Jesse had been too busy dealing with other challenges in their lives to get sucked into the never-ending vacuum of materialism and superficiality that they were faced with by their peers. It was not that they were not aware of it but they were more keenly aware that their real life situations varied significantly from many of their peers on economic, social and moral levels. They knew this so instinctively that their image as Convent girls was one that they put on as soon as they entered the black iron gates of the school but were happy to throw off at 2.30 p.m. when the school bell rang. Then, the burden of the 'convent accent' faded and as they walked out the gate they could feel themselves becoming at home once more in their bodies.

From Forms One to Lower Six they had had each other and had survived scathing attacks on their friendship. Through growing breasts, knotty unmanageable hair, period pains and fellas, Lisa and Jesse had managed to weather the harshness of their real lives, the challenges of what it meant to be a Convent girl and still pass all their exams placing among the first ten every term in their class. "So what was the weapon of choice last night Lisa?" "Hmmm leh meh see. First it was de rolling pin, den de cutting board, den he jus res some regular ole hand on she but by de time he start to res de hand he fall down. He was too tired." Lisa was almost indifferent as she stared down at the sneakers she polished last night.

Jesse didn't mean to be cavalier about it but she knew that until they discussed that aspect of the previous night's events, Lisa wouldn't be able to focus for the rest of the day. It was a routine with them for the last three plus years. "Well at least he getting tired now. All dat drinking must be tearing up his liver. Remember de days when he had energy? He could go for hours." Jesse needed to remind her friend of how much worse it had been.

"True... Dat is true. I just want to do my A- levels and get a job somewhere. When I start to work for my own money ah could move out and rent a place or ah could go and live wit meh cousin Tricia down in Couva." "Yeah dat sounding good," and with her free arm Jesse gave her buddy a one arm hug.

"It only takes a spark to get a fire going. That's how it is with God's love..." Morning assembly was almost over. "I always like to hear dis song," whispered Lisa. "Me too," Jesse whispered back as she lifted her heavy knapsack off her back and set it down between her knees. The late line was short today but neither of them cared.

Chapter Four

On Opposite Sides of Town

On the busy sidewalks of Charlotte Street there was never much room for pedestrians. Today was no different, and as always, shoppers took to the road often to the annoyance of many motorists. In the blistering midday sun, with washrags nearby to wipe the salty beads of perspiration running down their faces, you could hear a myriad of items being advertised for sale. "Geeeeeet yuh leather wallets here…., Blank CDS, Blank CDS folks a dollar fuh one. Yuh cyah go wrong……Ladies bras and panties here…get yuh ladies bras and panties." The accents were mostly Trini but some were Guyanese and others were from Grenada. It gave the melee of voices a color and richness that you could only find on Charlotte Street.

But more than the diversity of sounds was the diversity of smells and sights which made a walk up or down Charlotte Street seem like a long tickle of the senses. The ammonic smell of urine mingled with the gases from rotting foods and a variety of body odors. Multicolored cloths, blue, red, orange and green shoes, clothes, hair accessories, caps, garbage, rotting vegetables were everywhere in varying amounts. Tommy, head bowed with his stick under his arm, moved at a labored pace towards Tamarind Square. It was 9.30 in the morning and he had collected enough for breakfast. Now he was looking forward to drinking his little tin of coffee ends with the remains of a cold KFC Cruncher he had discovered in the first garbage bag ripped open.

Oblivious to the horns of the motorists caught in the mid-morning traffic, Tommy crossed George Street and hobbled on to Tamarind Square. Bronzed almost naked bodies stretched out on flattened cardboard boxes, wisps of smoke from small garbage fires warming tins of coffee ends, feces smeared rags, crumpled sheets of blood stained newspapers and the smells of every imaginable bodily odor or secretion, was what Tommy had grown used to as a resident of Tamarind Square. His smelly flattened cardboard boxes were still there where he had left them. He glanced around before setting his stick down and stretching out on his cardboard bed. Opening the wrapper with careful determination he sunk his yellow brown teeth into the already bitten sesame seed bun and filled his mouth.

"Hmm peppah!" Whoever bought that Cruncher liked pepper because the sandwich was soaked in it. He reached behind him for his coffee ends. It was cold and stale but tasted good to a man like Tommy who didn't like pepper. His dark blue t-shirt and slightly oversized brown pants had not become too soiled overnight. In fact, except for the urine, he thought he smelt pretty alright. He was expecting a visitor today and he was glad that he had managed to get some clothes off of the St. Vincent de Paul shelter just in time. He finished his meal, threw the wrapper behind him, and turned over to lie on his back so that he could look straight up to see the sky. Tommy liked to look at the sky. It was only when he was looking at the sky that the voices in his head seemed to become quiet. They never liked it when he looked at the sky. Sometimes he saw Jesus on a motorbike riding around up there; other times he saw childhood friends playing. Sometimes he saw snakes, alligators and tigers and even the devil. Other times he saw a whole army of people fighting and jumping up and down but he usually saw that when he was hungry.

The residual effects of his high last night were still there so it would be a few hours before he would need his next fix. This morning his belly was relatively full and the voices in his head were quieting down so in a little while he knew he would see his favorite sight; Jesus on the motorbike. Sure enough, in a minute or two, there was Jesus on a motorbike riding around and doing wheelies. Tommy especially enjoyed the fact that the motorbike made no sound and Jesus always looked happy even when he fell down. The sight of Jesus on the motorbike brought Tommy a great sense of happiness and inner peace, especially because the voices in his head would shut up whenever they saw Jesus on the motorbike.

A warm yellow liquid was soaking up his brown pants and staining the cardboard underneath him forming a large radial wet spot. Tommy was dead to his senses whenever he saw Jesus on the motorbike. Later, after Jesus stopped riding, he would wonder how come he didn't remember wanting to pee and he wouldn't be too happy about it. With one hand in his matted dirty hair and the other resting squarely on his stomach, Tommy's jaundiced eyes smiled upward. The thirty five year old was Eddy's uncle; at least that was before he 'went off'. Eddy refused to acknowledge him and only Eddy's mother Lystra would look for him from time to time, whenever she was on that side of town. His partner Bullerboy, who also frequented Tamarind Square sometimes, had told him that somebody was asking for him and said they would come back today to look for him. Tommy didn't like Bullerboy that much but on occasion, usually late at night, they would share hasty moments of orgasmic bliss in the corner of a nearby car park or sometimes right there on a cardboard in Tamarind Square.

But it wasn't like he was the only one with Bullerboy. Bullerboy had in fact earned a reputation for himself all over downtown Port-of-Spain, from Woodford Square to as far as the Savannah and on almost every narrow alley and corner smelling of piss you could find. Jesus was coming off the motorbike now and disappearing and once more the voices started up in Tommy's head again. "Shut up Tommy! Shut up! Yuh is a damn fool!

F----king asshole and mother's c---t! Devil go bite yuh! Devil go bite yuh! Devil go bite yuh! Ah will kill yuh boy! Ah will kill yuh!" The five foot seven inch, one time basketball player, curled into the fetal position and squeezed his head between his hands.

On the other side of town, Mrs. Chow Fatt was getting highlights put in her already dyed, straightened and chemically enhanced light brown hair. She knew her hairdresser Gina for many years even before she and her family moved from Plum Avenue in Cascade to the much larger, Spanish villa style mansion on Columbus Drive in Westmoorings. As the wife of one of the most prominent businessmen in Port-of-Spain, Mrs. Chow Fatt believed in looking her best at all times. She was of Portuguese heritage, with jet black curly hair which she never ever let the world see. Her husband Matthew was Chinese and from a long line of Chinese immigrants who had come to Trinidad in the 1850's. After years of hard work and sacrifice, his family owned a virtual empire of restaurants, clothing stores and hardwares. Matthew had inherited two of the restaurants, one hotel, and two clothing stores.

Over the years, he had diversified the range of items sold at the clothing stores to include shoes, watches, costume jewelry, accessories for men and women, and other brand name items. All this in an effort to keep abreast with the changing styles and fashion trends of the young and the middle aged. One of the clothing stores he had turned into a variety store almost completely fading out the clothing department. The restaurants and the hotel however were his pride and joy. The customer base in both restaurants had almost quadrupled in the last three years and the hotel was the number two choice for conferences and business functions, second only to the Trinidad Hilton. He attributed the success of the restaurants to the fast emerging national trend of eating out and the fact that the average middle income home ate out at least twice a week. Still, Matthew was intelligent with tremendous business acumen and often gave motivational speeches at business and other functions.

The two time president of the Downtown Merchants Association was indeed a well respected man. His wife was aware of this and firmly believed that as a career house wife, her main responsibility was to always make her husband look good and she did this naturally by always making herself look attractive and worthy of him. She never said it quite like that but she truly believed this in the depth of her being. She had not 'come from money' as they used to say back in the 60's and 70's. All Sally had was looks, color and bold-faceness. She used all these to her advantage to land herself a good catch with the then ultra shy Matthew.

"Don't cut it too much in the back Gina. Matt hates my hair too short." Sally instructed as she sat shoulders upright in the black salon chair. There didn't need to be an occasion for Sally to make a trip to Gina's house/hair dressing salon on Louis Street in Woodbrook. The joy was in the visit, seeing the wives of other distinguished men in society and of course, on a quiet day, confiding all ones troubles in the highly trustworthy Gina. "There you go. I think you look fabulous," said Gina with a feigned excitement that almost sounded genuine as she handed Sally a large black handled mirror so that she could inspect her new highlights. "Do you think it's too bright? I wanted it to be noticeable without being loud if you know what I mean," Sally responded. She tossed her hair back with one hand while looking carefully in the mirror she held in the other hand. "Oh yes, I see them now...this will do."

Sally was satisfied and eased herself off of the black leather salon chair. She was of medium height and fashionably thin with small breasts that allowed her to get away without wearing a bra sometimes. It was rare to see her without make-up, nail polish or matching clothes, shoes and accessories. Her mother had always taught her from an early age that she should always look her best whenever she stepped out in public since "one never knew when one could meet one's future husband." "I think I still owe you from the last visit when I forgot my cheque book," Sally reminded Gina as she reached for her tan leather handbag. Gina actually had forgotten about that. It was hard to remember everything about her clients. Gina was a good listener but then again her clientele were usually always talking, often about the same things. Sometimes Gina got bored but was excellent at masking that boredom.

"How is Brian's girlfriend doing?" Gina asked while she washed her pale hands at the sink which moments earlier was full of shampoo suds. Amidst Sally's non-stop chatter, Gina had heard no mention of the girl that had a few months ago been causing Sally so much distress. "Oh Amy you mean. Thank God the girl got a SAT scholarship to go to Howard University. That is the best thing those parents could have done for her and me. My son could do much better than her. I mean the girl was very attractive true but her parents have no class. Very small minded people those Josephs. The father is a plumber and the mother teaches in a junior sec so you know they don't make much. If it wasn't for some proper Convent training there is no telling how that girl would have turned out. Brian can't see it now but Amy going away was the best thing to happen to him. At least now he can focus on school." Gina nodded her head in agreement even though her views on the subject were quite different. She knew only too well that in her line of work her ears were of much greater value than her opinion and her understanding and empathy were priceless gifts which helped her maintain her already exclusive clientele.

Sally was almost out the door when she handed Gina a cheque for three hundred dollars and bid her farewell. Her handbag complemented the tan linen sleeveless pants suit she was wearing and the gold accessories seemed to give some color to her smooth pale skin. The sun shone brilliantly off her designer shades and warmed her exposed arms made cold in Gina's air-conditioned salon. As she stepped into the driver's seat of the shiny black Volvo, she felt a sense of accomplishment. She had something to surprise Matt with later tonight. Happy that she had given her driver the morning off, Sally quickly turned the key in the ignition, put on her seatbelt, locked all the car doors, sat upright with her chin up and drove off. She was meeting Marlene Mathias for lunch at the Sans Souci, one of the family restaurants and she didn't want to be late because unlike her, Marlene worked.

It was midday now and Lystra was just reaching Port-of-Spain. Maxi taxi drivers on the bus route didn't like to pick up passengers on the Beetham but Lystra didn't feel like walking all the way to Morvant junction. "Betta ah did walk to town," she thought to herself after reflecting on her long wait for a bus route maxi. The bag under her arm felt warm and smelt of food. In it were two hops bread buns soaked with butter and an old styrofoam container with some rice, peas and a stewed chicken leg just the way Tommy liked it. Her sole reason for coming to town today was to see her brother. Somebody had told her they saw "a fella bulling him" late at night in Tamarind Square and she was worried that her brother might 'catch something'. "My brudder is not no f---ing homo yuh hear!" She had cursed out the neighbor who had brought her this distressing news but was grateful for the information anyway. "Poor Tommy" she thought to herself, shaking her head sadly as she made her way through City Gate. Tommy and Eddy were all she had left. She had already lost Tommy to drugs, she just hoped that Eddy wouldn't desert her on the Beetham the way her other children had.

Lystra didn't look like fifty; actually she looked like she was in her late thirties. She got pregnant with Eddy long after her other children were born. He was a mistake on a drunken Carnival Tuesday night with a stranger whose name or facial features she couldn't even recall. Twice she had tried potions to abort and almost lost her life. When those two attempts failed, her neighbor took her to a healer in Morvant, who made her take off all her clothes and rubbed down her whole body in olive oil. He told her the child in her belly was an anointed child of God who would deliver her from bondage. She interpreted that to mean that somehow the child would bring money to her. And although she was $150 poorer and smelling of oil after that visit, Lystra felt sure that the child, boy or girl, would be lucky with money in life. Even if he wasn't, as her neighbor pointed out to her, "at least de baby go have sorf hair."

Beetham Gardens, in the eyes of many of its residents, was not as terrible as people made it out to be. True there was drugs and poverty, many of the men in the Gardens were unemployed but the industrious ones worked in the labasse and working in the labasse was a lucrative business. From the labasse came every imaginable household item - clothes, shoes, diapers, book shelves, books, expired chicken from groceries, jewelry and a whole lot more. But by far, the glass bottle, scrap iron and rag industry were the most lucrative of all. These items disposed of had excellent resale value when recycled on the Beetham; and the men and women that worked the labasse could make as much as $250 in sales on a very good day.

For those who worked the labasse and those who lived there, some for more than ten years, there was no shame. It was better than being unemployed. There were other services provided at the labasse too of a more nocturnal nature and these were accessed not only by Beetham residents but by men whose wives and girlfriends knew nothing of their night time exploits. Some of the women who worked the labasse were on drugs, some of the men too, but there were many who had families they supported and children they sent to school from their labasse income.

Not all the houses on the Beetham were ramshackled either. There were some concrete structures, like the small Seventh Day Adventist Church that had been put up around the corner from the rum shop in Phase Two. Some residents had concrete houses that were painted, had porches with potted plants like petunias and poinsettias, kept their tiny yards free of rubbish and even cut the grass. The dilapidated galvanize walled homes with floors made from stolen pieces of wood were there too. However, one was not to be fooled by the outward appearance of these seemingly clumsily erected houses. Behind galvanize doors braced by wood, one might find an interior which belied the exterior, aptly equipped with fridge, stove and television.

Many residents stole electricity through the spider web – a network of wires that ran illegally to the homes of residents, from the legitimate electricity poles. Some residents still had outdoor latrines and bathrooms made of galvanize. Some houses had running water while others relied on the nearby standpipe for their water supply and it was not uncommon to see men, women and children of all ages bathing naked at the standpipe. You couldn't really hide much of anything in the Beetham. Your business was everybody's business and even if it wasn't, it was definitely the business of the men who would sit by the culvert near the little basketball court, where not only basketball was played, but drugs, guns and sex were exchanged for money.

The basketball court was the life of the Gardens. If you wanted to get a 'piece' you came to the basketball court. 'Piece' was a multifaceted noun. If you wanted sex, or a gun or a joint of marijuana or a rock of cocaine, you wanted a 'piece'. And if you wanted any of these 'pieces', you needed to check with a fella they called Cut Outta. Cut Outta was a wanted man. The police wanted him behind bars, the women of the area wanted him for his money, the pipers wanted him for their drugs, the bandits wanted him for their guns and Reverend Miller the pastor of the Seventh Day Adventist church wanted him to give his life to Jesus.

Cut Outta was only forty years old. He had served some time in YTC as a youngster and then later on in Golden Grove prison for petty crimes, robbery, aggravated assault and marijuana possession. He had been charged with rape on two occasions but both witnesses refused to testify in the end. Rumor was they had been threatened. He had also been charged with the murder of a Muslim fella up in Never Dirty Trace in Laventille, but an accomplice to the murder turned state witness succumbed to a mysterious illness while in prison which led to his sudden death. The coroner said it was some rare food poisoning but everyone knew that fella was a dead man from the moment he agreed to testify against Cut Outta.

In all the Phases of Beetham Gardens, the name of Cut Outta was both respected and feared. The wiry looking brown skinned man was not an impressive sight. At only five ft five, the man who had earned his name at sixteen when, with one seamless swoop of his knife he cut open a man's stomach leaving intestines dangling between the man's legs, was quiet and reserved. His right hand man Bellies was not only his bodyguard but the one responsible for most of Cut Outta's finances. Bellies was burly and muscular. Nobody wanted to be in a fight with Bellies. A blow from his fist could knock a few rotten teeth out of a piper's mouth. Bellies was good at beating people up. He did it with a callousness and heartlessness that only a man unchanged by fifteen years in prison could have. Death was not his enemy; neither was jail or those who threatened his life. His only enemy was 'Babylon', as the police were called. Babylon was always the enemy because Babylon was always conducting raids down in the Beetham.

"Like it doh have no udder part ah Trinidad whey people doing wrong tings ah wat. How police always inside here so!" exclaimed Uncle Tremble. He and his rum buddies were chatting when the loud buzzing sound of a helicopter flying overhead interrupted them. It seemed to be searching for someone or something. Sticking out the doors of the aircraft was a man with a semi-automatic rifle wearing a dark woolen vest and cap, with the word POLICE clearly painted over the front of the vest. After a few minutes of noisy circling the helicopter flew up and east, allowing Uncle Tremble and his buddies to hear each other once more.

Uncle Tremble was seventy-three years old and trembling before he retired from the postal service as a postmaster in the eighties. His voice was frail and the skin of his neck sagged and folded in a zillion places, but Uncle Tremble's eyesight was as good as any teenager's and he could hear a bullet zinging through the air before it reached its mark. With nothing to do all day but sit on the culvert and talk politics, cricket and sports, Uncle Tremble was just the kind of person that Cut Outta needed to have on the take; somebody who everybody liked to talk to, who seemed above reproach and best of all, who saw and heard all the goings-ons of the Beetham. Ever since Cut Outta got out of jail, Uncle Tremble's measly pension from the government had been supplemented with "news money" from Cut Outta.

Yes the dynamics of the Beetham were many-fold. From the garbage hustlers and pipers who waited at the nearby dump from as early as four o'clock in the morning, to dive barefooted and sometimes naked into the mounds of smelly refuse thrown off the back of incoming garbage trucks in search of "gold", to the mother and daughter prostitutes that worked the Beetham and went to town at nights, to those who had been saved from a life of "sin and debauchery" and prayed that the fear of God would be instilled into the hearts of the men and women in the community, the Beetham was teeming with diversity and the rawness of life. But the one thing that united saint and sinner on the Beetham regardless of age, color or sex, was the smell.

The smell which could "kill yuh nose" from Phases One through Four of the Beetham Gardens; the smell of feces and rotting garbage of every description mixed with water which came from the outhouses, sink basins and bathrooms of the residents, was the most unique identifying feature of the Beetham. The medium size drain which ran like a straight odorous line through the area was always full and stagnant with a dark green caked layer of sewage intermingled with floating sweet drink bottles, plastic bags, condoms and other non-degradable rubbish.

Many appeals had been made to the government to address this health hazard. The Environmental Management Agency had even done a report stating that the degree of air pollution on the Beetham was far above acceptable levels. For over twenty years, the people of the Beetham had lived with this smell. Older folks like Uncle Tremble had grown up with it and younger folks like Eddy were growing up with it. You see to live on the Beetham was to know that no matter what you made of yourself, good or bad, no matter how respectable you tried to become, unless you left the Beetham and severed all ties with it, you would always be considered the poorest of the poor, the lowest of the low and the least of the least in Trinidad society.

"Oh my goodness I am so full. That stuffed lamb was absolutely delicious Sally. I'm surprised I never tried it before in all my time of coming here," said Marlene Mathias as she daintily wiped the sides of her mouth with a red cloth napkin. She rocked back in the cushioned wicker arm chair satisfied with the meal she had just consumed. "You are so lucky that Sean isn't all that interested in girls just yet. I was so worried about Brian and this Amy girl," Sally frowned as she put the last forkful of fried rice into her mouth. "I don't know if Sean is just shy or a late bloomer but he's doing well in school, he's not on drugs, he's not in trouble and I'm not fussing. There is plenty of time for girls later," said Marlene.

She and Sally had only been friends for a few years but she appreciated Sally's good taste and company. Marlene and her husband were from old money. As the head of the Syrian-Lebanese Women's group, Marlene had many connections and Sally always felt honored to be considered her friend. Marlene's husband, Damien owned the Fabulous Fabric chain of cloth stores nationwide and Marlene headed up the Frederick Street branch of the operations. She didn't have much education but then again she didn't really need to in her world. Married at sixteen to a man twenty years her senior and the son of one of her father's friends from the old country (Syria), Marlene was content with her life. She had everything she could possibly need and working at Fabulous Fabric gave her a unique sense of fulfillment. It was a lot of responsibility too; monitoring the workers, receiving shipments, signing invoices, depositing money in the night safe wallets at the end of the day, Marlene loved it all.

"Anyway I really must get going. But before I go Sally don't forget the brunch on Sunday."

"What brunch?" Sally was lost.

"Oh Sally you really ought to put that fancy palm pilot of yours to some good use." Marlene laughed and passed her hand through her thick and wavy jet black hair. "The American Women's Society is having a brunch remember, proceeds go to the St. Dominic's Orphanage Building fund…ring a bell?" Sally suddenly remembered.

"Oh yes how could I forget?"

"Be there nine o'clock, Country Club," said Marlene in an almost admonishing tone as she rubbed some hand sanitizer between her hands and stood up. "Sorry I have to run lovie. Love the highlights. I'll see you Sunday. Thanks for lunch." She gave Sally a smooch on either cheek and walked briskly off with the poise and elegance that she knew the wife of a multibillionaire ought to have. Marlene was not at all thin. In fact she was heavy set. Her breasts were small but her hips were wide and she sought to hide the latter aspect of her physique by never wearing blouses that tucked into her skirts or pants.

Sally sunk back in her chair almost sad to see her go. Lunch with Marlene was the climax of her day and the emotional and psychological outlet she needed. Everything after lunch would be an anticlimax, even surprising Matt with her new hairstyle. She doubted he would even notice it or her. Their marriage had hit the kind of emotional, psychological and sexual wilderness that led couples before a judge seeking a divorce. Divorce! Just the thought of the word sent chills down Sally's spine. If she wasn't Mrs. Chow Fatt who the hell would she be? A nobody? No. Divorce was just out of the question.

It seemed that the only conversations of interest they had had in recent times revolved around their son Brian. As for sex, he hadn't touched her in months and it wasn't that she hadn't tried to make things exciting in the bedroom. She wondered once if he was having an affair but she knew her husband. His social skills though much improved since their marriage, were still not good enough to qualify him as a charmer. The thought of him trying to sweet talk a woman was hilarious in itself. Sally examined her hair once again in a little wallet sized mirror she kept in her handbag. She wasn't about to let all that money she'd just spent at Gina's go to waste. "Even if he doesn't notice my highlights, tonight he will notice me. I don't care how damn tired he is," Sally thought to herself. Her next stop for the day was Intimate Secrets, an upscale lingerie store in St.Clair.

Lystra had finally found Tommy and all at once was overcome with a mixture of joy, relief and sorrow. When she got to Tamarind Square a vagrant she assumed knew Tommy told her he had seen him earlier on Duncan Street. She had walked all the way up Duncan Street and all the way back down without any sign of her brother. So she was indeed relieved when she returned to Tamarind Square to find him there walking about restlessly, scratching and speaking to invisible adversaries. "Steups. Boy yuh know how long ah looking fuh you…eh?" She held his grimy arm firmly and stopped his restless pacing. "Tommy boy.

Ah talking to yuh. Watch meh. Watch meh good. Is me Lystra. Remember me?" Tommy looked her squarely in the eyes. He seemed to be squinting at her. "Lys, Lys oh God Lys, he covered his face with his now very stained dark blue t-shirt to hide the tears as he began to cry. " Sit down boy sit down. Look ah bring food fuh yuh. Doh cry, doh cry."

Lystra still holding his hand firmly took him to the short wall that demarcated the Square and sat him down. She reached in her hand bag for the food, she had prepared. It was cold now but at least her food was better than anything he could be fetching out of a garbage bag. Lystra was not ashamed to sit with him. He was her little brother; her little Tommy; she had practically raised him. Her eyes become full and the tears began to escape like a flood. She set the food down and reached in her handbag for the few blocks of toilet paper she always carried with her. "Look is yuh favorite, peas and rice with stew chicken," she declared as she wiped her tears and forced a smile. Tommy was still crying but in between sobs he blurted out "Ah sorry Lys. Ah so sorry. Oh God. Oh God. Oh God...Lys." It was a while before he was able to compose himself and see the food Lystra had set down. Yes it was his favorite food but the sight of his big sister had made him lose all his appetite.

Seeing her, brought back so many memories of his life before this death he was living. He still had his memory which jolted him back to reality from time to time. This was one of those times. He saw his life flashing before him as Lystra's mouth appeared to move noiselessly in front of him. "She still looking good. My sister. My big sister," he thought to himself. He remembered when he used to have a job with Bistro Tyre shop down in Barataria. He remembered Cut Outta and his boys giving him his first piece down on the basketball court. He remembered how Lystra had put him out after he stole and sold the refrigerator for a fix. "What again it have fuh yuh to tief and sell boy? What again? You will be de death ah me Tommy! Next ting yuh will sell me an all! Get out! Ah cyah take dis ting no more Tommy. Ah cyah take it. Why yuh ha to do dese tings Tommy? Why?" Lystra was angry the night she had put him out but she was more hurt than angry. She did not know the man her brother was becoming; a man who would think nothing of stealing from the sister that raised him.

"Tommy. Tommy. Ah talking to yuh. Whey yuh?" Lystra interrupted his flashback with her voice. She realized that he had just been gazing; that he wasn't really listening to a single word she had said. "Listen keep dis." She passed him a tiny black plastic bag with about ten condoms in it. "Somebody did tell meh dey see yuh bulling somebody out here. Well ah tell dem ah know yuh is not no f---ing homo and ah know if is anyting somebody was taking advantage on yuh. But if yuh cyah defen yuhself at least leh dey use dis. It ha all kinda diseases out here. Ah mean is true yuh not in a good situation right now but trus meh yuh doh want to dead with HELP out here," Lystra warned.

Tommy took the plastic bag still gazing and tears began to well up in his eyes once more. Lystra knew that she wouldn't be able to do much more for Tommy today. "Anyway ah gone. Eddy say to tell yuh hello."

Tommy heard that last lie and the thought of his nephew who had loved him so much was a deeply painful one. He had let Eddy down and he didn't know if he would ever be able to redeem himself in Eddy's eyes. A maddening silence filled his head as he watched his sister walking away with her hips swaying from side to side in her skin tight jeans and the long shiny weave that made its way down her back. All of a sudden getting high became an instant necessity.

Chapter Five
In The House of Pain

"Ma remember I have lessons today eh," said Krishna as he smoothed back his jet black hair. The voice on the other end of the cell phone sounded concerned. "So what time yuh coming home around eight o'clock?" Krishna confirmed he would be. "Careful how yuh driving eh. Take yuh time on de road," his mother warned. "Yeah doh worry nah Ma. Ah didn't buy meh driver's license." Krishna laughed bringing a dimpled smile to his mother's face. When the conversation was over he smiled to himself at the thought of being able to take extra lessons in Port-of-Spain. He had inherited his mother's dimples and his father's confidence and at seventeen was quite a good looking young fella. If nothing else he would be able to meet some "hot" Convent girls at lessons. He adjusted the rear view mirror of his Honda civic and rearranged his hair just a little.

He was grateful for the fact that he was a fair skinned Indian and did not have his father's dark complexion. That and the fact that he drove his own car should surely work in his favor and overshadow the fact that he attended St. Augustine Senior Comprehensive School. He had heard about Convent girls and their snobbish attitude but with his looks, he felt certain he would be able to pick up a really good looking girl, maybe even "a red ting" as one of his friends had teased before he left school. Glancing quickly at his watch, Krishna knew the traffic on the Churchill Roosevelt would be a killer but he was so hungry. "Aha a KFC Cruncher special. That should hold me until seven," he thought. He pulled into the KFC drive through in Curepe. Thankfully the line was short.

It was almost 3.00 p.m. The gates of St. Joseph's Convent Port-of-Spain and St. Mary's College opened and the "gaping," flirting and text messaging began. Lisa and Jesse bolted out the black iron gates and walked briskly down Pembroke Street. They were on their way to the recently opened public library (NALIS) on the corner of Abercromby and Queen Street. They were getting their library cards today and needed to borrow books and reach up to Oxford Street by Mr. Lee Wen at least half an hour before classes started. Most of the girls in their class took extra lessons in Physics from Mr. Lee Wen. However some of them never went to class in their uniforms. They would drive home, those who had cars, take a shower and get all dressed up to learn about Newton's laws of motion. "Yeah right!" Extra lessons always lent itself to the possibility of relationship forming and for those girls whose parents did not allow them to go to parties and have boyfriends, extra lessons was the one parent approved place where they had the opportunity to talk to and hang out with guys.

Mr. Lee Wen was in fact an entire organization of extra lessons, not just in A-Level Physics, Chemistry and Biology but Management of Business (MOB), History, English Literature and French. His wooden establishment on Oxford Street had been a landmark for more than a decade and many scholarship winners from, Fatima, St. Mary's College, St. Joseph's Convent, Holy Name Convent and QRC had taken extra lessons from the elderly Chinese man. His wife who was of East Indian descent did the financial administration, collected monies from students and their parents and monitored the other teachers that worked for her husband. They were a loyal bunch those teachers. Many of them had worked with Mr. Lee Wen from day one. They were well paid, received a percentage of all the money Mr. Lee Wen made from their classes, in addition to receiving a sizeable monthly salary. The prohibitive cost of renting office space in downtown Port-of-Spain and the paternal relationship they had with Mr. Lee Wen, made it almost impossible for these teachers to conceive of teaching on their own or with anyone else but the silver haired old man. It was even harder now that class sizes had grown and become more diverse with students from government secondary schools in Belmont, Woodbrook, St. James and even as far as St. Augustine.

"We better start walking up now yuh know Lisa," Jesse said with a frown of concern on her face. It was already four o'clock and although the cool air conditioned library had successfully removed all patches of sweat from their off white shirts, Jesse knew that if they didn't leave the library soon they would find themselves rushing up to Oxford Street and sweaty all over again. "Alright, alright. Doh worry, classes doh always start on time," Lisa winked back. She had been chatting online at the library for the last ten minutes with some fella named "True Trini" in a chat room she had entered and she wasn't too keen on ending the conversation.

Today was Jesse's first day of extra lessons with Mr. Lee Wen. Her mother had made all the arrangements with him over the phone and had given Jesse the three hundred dollars for the first month of classes in a carefully sealed envelope. Jesse knew that three hundred dollars represented a lot of days of hard work in the market hot sun. She had pinned the envelope carefully to the inside of her skirt pocket and was anxious to hand it over to its intended recipient. "Do yuh best eh chile. Ah know yuh is a bright girl." Jesse could not forget the look of hope in her mother's eyes when she gave her the envelope and gently pushed a strand of her curly brown hair off her face. It was as if all her mother's hopes and dreams had been placed in that envelope and on Jesse's shoulders. All her father's hopes too. She had hugged her so tight. Like she did the day her daddy had passed away. Jesse knew she couldn't let her mother down and she was certainly not going to let Lisa make her late on the first day. Before Lisa had the opportunity to sign out of the chat room, Jesse was already half way out the door. "Eh gyul wait fuh me!" Lisa shouted. She picked up her knapsack and ran as fast as her long brown legs would carry her.

Tommy had not touched one bit of the food that Lystra had left him. He had been able to sell the food for $4 and all the condoms for $3. That was enough to get him something that could get him high for a few hours, even if it was just a bottle of Bayrum. He returned to Tamarind Square to find his cardboard gone and he was 'damn vex'. "One setta f----ing tief in dis place. Ah go buss somebody head! Ah go kill somebody! Allyuh betta fraid me yuh know. Blasted tief!" He didn't go on with his tirade for too long because he was anxious to dig into his bottles of Bayrum; but he felt satisfied that he had let the world know he was not going to be taken advantage of easily on Tamarind Square, regardless of whether he was a new resident or not. "Two bottles should do," he thought, as he sat down to enjoy them. Bayrum didn't taste too good but it was better than nothing and the drink of choice if you couldn't get real alcohol or drugs in Tamarind Square.

Tommy's brown pants had since collected many stains, mostly of pee and from him lying on the ground at different places. "Aye leh meh geh a lil taste nah." He had no idea who this stranger was behind him that was asking for some of his precious rum. "Hawl yuh mudder's c---!" Tommy blurted out. "Whey meh

45

cardboard? Yuh is a blasted tief!" shouted Tommy as he spit on the ground in the direction of the stranger. Suddenly everything went black and all Tommy could feel as he fell forward was a sharp pain at the back of his head and a warm liquid running down behind his ears.

"Okay then ladies and gentlemen, today we will be looking at the laws of momentum," Mr. Lee Wen said with a wicked smile. The room seemed to be getting hotter even though there were three standing fans circulating the hot air. Jesse and Lisa had their books open and were already armed with pens in hand to take notes. "For those of you who are joining us for the first time, I say welcome. You might find that you don't want to take notes while I am writing but it is up to you. Whatever makes you feel most comfortable." Mr. Lee Wen glanced in the direction of Jesse and Lisa and smiled before launching into the laws of momentum. Two rows back, Brian Chow Fatt could not take his eyes off of the back of Jesse's head. He hadn't heard a word that Mr. Lee Wen had said. He was just wishing that the brown haired beauty would turn around so he could get a good look at her face. He was mesmerized but he wasn't the only one mesmerized.

Krishna who was three rows back and to the right of Lisa and Jesse couldn't stop glancing to the left. He could almost see the side of Jesse's face and the long bushy wad of Lisa's hair. He was nervous. He had come in late on his first day of class but was hoping to make eye contact with at least one of them. Perhaps in the ten minute break he would get a better look. Five minutes into the class, the door to the class room squeaked open and in walked Cindy Sawh. Cindy's family were multimillionaires and Cindy made no point of hiding the fact that her parents were rich and had set up a trust fund for her to inherit when she turned twenty-one. Ever since the day when she declared that Catholicism in her view did not encourage people to be rich Lisa had despised her.

"After all, what was Jesus really trying to say when he said it is easier for a camel to enter the eye of a needle than a rich man to enter the kingdom of heaven? That is just ridiculous." Cindy had argued. Mrs. James the Religious Instruction teacher was not impressed. But Cindy's parents even though they were Hindu, were one of the biggest financial benefactors of St. Joseph's Convent and it was a sort of unwritten rule among teachers that donor's children were to be left alone no matter what. "Sorry Mr. Lee Wen," Cindy whispered as she grabbed a seat at the back. Lisa rolled her eyes up in her forehead at the sight of her arch enemy.

Cindy was the epitome of Bollywood beauty with thick black hair which ran all the way down to the middle of her back. She would have dyed her hair red if it were not against the school rules and if her parents would let her. She had light brown eyes and what most girls wished for, the Coca Cola bottle shape, curvy hips, medium sized breasts and a sizeable butt. Krishna was in awe. She had sat right next to him and he could smell the scent of her perfume. She was a goddess. He couldn't think straight but he was so glad that he wasn't wearing his school uniform and had changed instead into a pair of jeans and a red Polo t-shirt. He turned his head and smiled at her. The fake smile she used often was all she was prepared to give him. Intoxicated by her perfume Krishna was in heaven.

Down at the Port-of-Spain market Ms. Janice was getting ready to pack up. Today had been a slow day but tomorrow was fortnight Friday. Things would pick up. "Ah ent see Papa Netty some days now. Ah wonder wha going on wit he?" Ms. Janice asked Ma Thomas. "True. Ah really ent see him yesterday gyul." Ma Thomas, back turned and bent over a nearby drain was rinsing off her hands with some stale water she had in a sweet drink bottle. "Ah hope nuttin bad eh happen to de ole man." She didn't like Papa Netty that much but she had grown used to him and she wished him no ill. "Ah wonder if he have chilren. Ah never really hear he talk bout any chilren he have yuh know. But ah sure if he ha chilren dey wouldn be happy bout seeing him looking how he looking now."

Ms. Janice began to pack up her produce satisfied that she would not be making any more sales for the day. "Gyul......chilren is a funny ting yuh know. All yuh could do is do yuh best fuh dem an try an give dem a decent education an a chance in life. But no matter how big dey get dey is always yuh chile. Once a mudder, always a mudder." Ma Thomas shook her head in agreement, even though she knew she couldn't fully appreciate the last few lines Ms. Janice had uttered. Ms. Janice began to put away her lettuce bundles, tomatoes, ochroes, mauby bark and potatoes. She didn't have that much left over today. It was enough to fit in Old Jane, the yellow rust ridden station wagon her husband used to drive. "When las yuh geh dat car inspec Janice?" Ms. Janice looked quizzically at her friend.

"Inspec? Wha yuh mean?"

"Inspec. Remember two years ago govuhment say how if yuh have a car so much years ole yuh must geh it inspec to be able to be on de road? When it inspec yuh does geh a sticker. Yuh eh know dat?" Ma Thomas stared at Ms. Janice in disbelief. "Look an see if yuh have a sticker." Ms. Janice obediently walked a few yards away to the old station wagon and checked the front windshield. "Yeah ah see a sticker dere. Mr. GG probably used to get it check out," she reported on her return." Well is time fuh yuh to get a new sticker because ah sure yuh eh change dat sticker since Mr. GG gone and police stopping people on de road now. Yuh real lucky yuh ent geh ketch yet." Ms. Janice was really concerned now. She had never really paid attention to the little oblong shaped sticker at the front of the car. It had managed to hide in between the stickers that read "Jesus Saves," "Men against drugs" and "Join the fight against HIV."

"So how yuh does geh de sticker? Ah have to carry it in a garage?"

"Yes gyul and yuh better have money to pay because dat car lookin like it eh fit to be on de road," said Ma Thomas. "Hmmm is a good ting ah does always take de back roads to get home anyway," said Ms. Janice as she slammed the back door of the packed station wagon. She bid her farewell to Ma Thomas and like a pregnant cow the car lumbered slowly out of the Port-of-Spain market onto the Churchill Roosevelt highway.

A thick cloud of black exhaust fumes rose in the air behind the wobbly vehicle. She merged with the rush hour traffic. It would be a little while on the highway before she could get on to the main road. Her thoughts wandered to what she would cook later for those loving brats. She wondered how their day had been and she would look forward to Jesse's report on her first day of extra lessons. She loved all her children dearly. Jesse, Steve, Becca, and the twins Joan and Jacob were all very special reminders of the love she had for Mr. GG. Poor GG if only he could see how big they had grown. He would be so proud of them.

"Wow I am just exhausted." Sally stretched out on the queen sized mahogany bed she shared with Matt and wondered when he would notice the enticing lace nightgown she was wearing. He had just come out of the shower in his favorite dark blue bathrobe and was toweling his hair dry. "Oh I had lunch with Marlene today. She says Hi," said Sally. "That's nice," Matt grunted back without wishing to probe further. He was hardly concerned with his wife's daily outings. He knew that there were only so many places a woman like Sally could shop, eat, get hair, nails and face done and Sally had exhausted them all. He remembered when they first met. It was at the St. Ann's parish harvest and Sally was working in the sweets stall. She had the cutest little smile and he had never seen a creature as beautifully formed by heaven's hand as Sally. Had he known in his hormonally charged state that behind the wistful curls lay a vixen that would stop at nothing to marry money and class, the decision he made twenty odd years ago might have been different.

Thank God for their son Brian. At least having him made their marriage bearable. Between child rearing and work, family gatherings, business meetings, and hanging out with the ole boys at the Queen's Park Cricket Club and Smokey's and Bunty's, Matt had survived the biggest mistake of his life. He had had a few flings, and some one night stands but Matt was very discrete and Sally was too daft to suspect anything anyway. She was too caught up in herself and her world to realize that something was missing in their relationship and she still saw elements of that shy young man, nervous around the opposite sex. The irony of it all was that Matt knew Sally loved him. However, he often wondered whether she loved him for who he really was or Matt Chow Fatt multimillionaire and businessman. He already knew the answer to that question but sometimes when he was making love to her, she would look into his eyes as if he were her whole world and for a brief moment he would doubt that she was the power and prestige hungry woman he knew her to be.

Matt had slipped into his pajamas and crawled into bed with the crossword puzzle. His spectacles perched below the bridge of his nose, Matt had not even turned in Sally's direction. Sally drew closer under the polyester sheets, wrapped an arm around his soft belly and placed her head on his hairy chest.

"What's the matter Sal?"

"Nothing. Can't I snuggle with my husband?"

"Not when he is trying to finish his crossword puzzle," said Matt irritated. He took her arm from around him and gently shoved her off. Sally exploded. "Damn you. What are you trying to do to this marriage? You haven't touched me in months!" she screamed, snatching the sheets off of him and knocking the crossword puzzle out of his hands. "I spend all day getting my hair done and buying this expensive nightie and you don't even look at me. You don't even want to touch me......" Sally's face was red. She was breathing hard and heavy as the tears rolled off her face. "Who are you sleeping with Matt? Answer me you son of a bitch!"

Matt looked at her stunned at this dramatic outburst with eyebrows raised. "Sally don't be ridiculous. What nonsense are you talking about? You fail to realize how hard I work every single day so that you can get your hair done and your eyebrows waxed and your facials, your manicures, your pedicures......" Matt was getting louder and louder. "Did it ever occur to you that perhaps at the end of the day I just want some peace and quiet? Have you any idea what it takes to run up the businesses we own? How could you? " Matt shouted as he stormed into the walk in closet and grabbed down a pair of jeans. Sally refused to be phased. Wiping her tears she followed him to the closet. "I'm no fool Matt. I will not be made a fool of. Where are you going?"

Matt ignored her as he slipped his green polo T-shirt over his head and tucked it in his waist. Sally cuffed him hard and suddenly in his back. "Where the hell are you going at this hour of the night?" Matt stopped dressing and turned around to face Sally. With an almost soothing voice he said, "Sal if you think I am cheating on you after all these years and after everything I have done for you, then I must have done something terribly wrong." Matt's beady eyes looked sadly at her in her black lace nightgown. "I need some fresh air," he growled; and in a flash he had picked up his car keys and was gone.

Earlier that evening the hormones of at least three young men were racing through their hairy little post-pubescent bodies. Matt, Krishna and Eddy were clearly in lust. Lisa and Jesse had managed to struggle through Mr. Lee Wen's class. During the intermission they had observed, commented and giggled about almost everybody in the class. Class was over now and the clatter of books closing and chairs being pushed aside seemed like a joyful sound. Lisa and Jesse weren't the only ones happy to be released from the clutches of the laws of momentum and its many applications. Brian had not been able to concentrate for the entire class. He had to meet that girl somehow and the opportunity for an introduction came as she waited at the end of the wooden staircase that led away from Mr. Lee Wen's "House of Pain" as it was nicknamed by the students.

"Is this your first class?" Brian asked the shy looking girl he had just stood next to. "Yes," Jesse responded nervously. "Well if you need any notes or anything like that just let me know Ok. I take very good notes. We did Newton's laws of motion last week. But that wasn't too bad. Oh by the way, my name is Brian," he said as he reached out to shake her hand. "I'm Jesse" she said smiling as she returned the handshake. His hands were very soft for a boy she thought as she blushed slightly. "Anyway I have to go now, my ride is here." Brian pointed to the black Volvo that had just pulled up. "See ya next class."

"See ya" Jesse whispered. Lisa had just run down the stairs in time to hear the end of the conversation.

"Who the hell is that?" Lisa pinched Jesse.

"Brian" Jesse answered. "He is soooooooo cute," said Lisa. "Wow, he must like you. Ah mean he spoke to you on your first day at class."

"He seems real nice," said Jesse softly. The pair had only just come out of the courtyard to begin their walk towards City Gate when a deep voice asked "Are you all walking down to City Gate?" They turned to see the very attractive looking QRC student, who, with Brian, were their picks for the cutest guys in the class. Lisa and Jesse glanced at each other trying not to smile too much. "I don't mind the company. I was heading that way anyway. Plus it ain't too safe at this hour of the night," he said. Lisa and Jesse didn't feel scared but they didn't mind the company either. Besides he was going their way anyway. "We're alright thank you but since you're walking this way I guess it's Ok right Jess?" said Lisa looking across at Jesse. Jesse nodded. "What's your name again?" she asked. "Eddy, Eddy Torres."

Krishna was already on the Lady Young Road heading home. He had managed to take a few notes in Mr. Lee Wen's class and had made a friend, Ravi from St. Mary's College but he hadn't spoken to any girls. Both he and Ravi agreed that Cindy was hot. "But she look real stuck up if yuh ask me. I doh like gyuls who feel dey too hot," Ravi had said. Krishna thought that was just an excuse because Ravi knew he was way out of Cindy's league. Ravi was scraggly looking and very dark skinned. He didn't stand a chance with Cindy. At least so Krishna thought. That Spanish looking fella with the black hair from QRC looked real familiar to Krishna. He didn't know where he knew him from but the minute he saw him, something told him that they had met before under different circumstances. Either way Krishna felt satisfied that there was game at Mr. Lee Wen's class, he just had to come up with a good strategy and use some of his Rajkumar charm.

Tommy was just waking up and everything seemed blurry. He blinked his eyes several times but there was no improvement in his vision. He had a terrible headache. Sitting up slowly Tommy looked around. It was night time. He felt the dried patch of crusty blood at the back of his head and tried to remember what had happened. He remembered he had Bayrum but looking around he could see that there was neither Bayrum nor cardboard nor tin of coffee ends in sight. Not even his stick was there. The headache got worse when Tommy stood up. He was feeling hungry too. He walked toward Royal Castle and ripped open the first garbage bag he saw. Maybe if he ate the headache would go away. He was on his third garbage bag when he saw Bullerboy. All Tommy had managed to get so far was a little warm red sweet drink and some pastry crusts from a left over pie. He had made a considerable amount of mess on the road and was still very hungry.

"Aye boy. Yuh have anyting on you?" a desperate Tommy asked Bullerboy. "Boy I jus struggling like you. What de hell yuh tink it is at all. Look ah have a customer down so but it have a fella over so dat want a suck. Ah will give yuh dat one if yuh want but ah cyah do de two right now," said Bullerboy in a high pitched feminine voice that didn't quite suit him. Bullerboy was slim; thin almost. Although he looked a bit ragged, you couldn't really tell he was homeless until you looked down and saw that he wore a busted up pair of rubber slippers. "Steups. Yuh want de change or not. Ah have customers yuh know," said an impatient Bullerboy with a feminine fling of the wrist. Tommy nodded and followed his friend's effeminate swinging hips to an empty car park on South Quay.

Tommy had not done anything like this for money since he moved on to Tamarind Square but tonight he was desperate. They walked toward a little Nissan Sunny in the corner of the car park. "Dis fella go fix yuh up nice alright," Bullerboy said to the waiting gentleman and then he left. Tommy was surprised to see that his would be customer did not look more like himself. The man looked employed; after all he was driving a car. Before Tommy had time to think, the man had already pulled down his pants and exposed himself. "Hurry up nah boy," the man grunted. Tommy dropped to the ground on his knees. He closed his eyes tight and opened his mouth. It was almost midnight.

As Sally looked out the bedroom window she wondered where her husband was. What was he doing at this God forsaken hour? Who could he be with?

She thought of calling the office or his cell phone but she knew better than to do that. She just wished he would come home. She regretted her earlier outburst and reminisced on happier times in their marriage; those early days when he couldn't wait to get home to be with her; when they'd spend long afternoons together watching the sunset from the loft of the house in Cascade. They were so happy then. What had happened? Her thoughts were interrupted by the headlights turning down Columbus Drive. The dull grating of their electronic gate opening made her breathe a sigh of relief. She turned off the lights and crawled into bed under the cool polyester sheets. She didn't want him to see that she had been crying or know that she couldn't sleep. Soon enough Matt came to bed smelling of rum and coke and cigarette smoke from Smokey's and Bunty's. It was too much for Sally to hope that he would want to snuggle. He turned his back to her and in a few minutes began to snore.

In the Guevara household there was only one light on in the house. It was the kitchen light. Jesse didn't have a desk lamp of her own. She would study in the kitchen after everyone had eaten or sometimes she would sit in one of the living room chairs but the kitchen table was better for study. This way she could spread out all her books and really lose herself in whatever she was studying. Tonight she was going over her notes from Physics lessons and catching up on some Chemistry homework that she had for school. Jesse was tired but she knew that she had to push herself hard if she was going to win the scholarship she so desperately needed. She had hopes of studying medicine and she knew that the only way she would be able to grace the doors of the University of the West Indies would be with a full government scholarship. It was not beyond her grasp either. She just had to keep her focus and keep plugging away at her studies. She was so engrossed in her reading that she didn't hear her mother's bedroom door squeak open and was startled by the hand that rested gently on her shoulder. "Ah sorry darling. Ah didn't mean to frighten yuh," Ms. Janice apologized.

"How is it going?"

"It hard Ma. A lot of reading but ah trying," said Jesse with a smile. Ms. Janice wanted so desperately to help her daughter but she knew that she couldn't understand most of the words in Jesse's heavy textbooks anyway. She was so proud of her. She needed Jesse to get that scholarship so badly, not just for herself but for Mr. GG and Steve and all those behind her. Ms. Janice needed something really good to happen to the Guevara family soon. Something that would lift their spirits and make them know that Mr. GG was looking out for them somewhere up there in the big blue sky. "Leh meh make some hot chocolate fuh yuh so yuh could feed dem brains ah yours." Ms. Janice, lit the little gas stove, poured some water into the worn out silver kettle and placed it on the burner as gently as she could.

"Yuh tink I could get ah scholarship Ma?"

"Of course chile!" Ms. Janice almost rushed back to her seat next to Jesse at the kitchen table. "You listen to me chile. It ent have no difference between your brains and all dem scholarship winner brains. Ever since yuh is a baby everybody saying how bright yuh is. An yuh do everything firs and faster dan all de rest. Yuh walk before one year. Yuh start to talk by de time yuh was one and a half. An den dey skip yuh from first year infants to second year. Gyul it have nuttin standin between you and dat scholarship except God and you. Yuh mudder brains not so good but any extra lessons yuh need yuh will get you just say. Doh forget who chile yuh is. Yuh is Gregory Guevara chile and yuh born and grow up here in Santa Cruz. God smiling on yuh chile. He smiling on yuh."

She pinched her daughter's chin and looked her squarely in the eye. "Yuh will get it Jesse. Jus believe in yuhself an wok hard. God will give it to yuh." The whistle of the kettle interrupted Ms. Janice's little motivational speech. Jesse smiled to herself. She knew her mother was right and if her father was smiling down on her from heaven, she knew Pa would put in a good word for her to get the scholarship. That night before climbing into bed, she knelt and asked Pa to help her get a scholarship. She was sure he had heard.

Jesse was not the only one praying that night. Eddy was too. His afternoon was not going too well. When he got home, his mother had quarreled with him for not going to look for his uncle Tommy in Tamarind Square. "He ent looking good Eddy. If he die anytime now, yuh wouldn feel good dat yuh didn go an look for him. Dat is yuh flesh and blood. He love yuh like a son from ever since." She had pleaded with him. He had ignored her until she pulled out a cigarette to have a smoke. "Alright ah will go an look fuh him next week," Eddy had promised. He had hated to see his mother smoking. It was not something she did often but it was bad enough considering the house was already so small and poorly ventilated.

She left home around eleven o'clock that night and Eddy knew better than to ask where she was going or when she would be back. He was used to being home by himself and had become pretty self sufficient over the years. He reflected on his evening walk down to City Gate with Lisa and Jesse. They both seemed so down to earth and so simple. It had been a refreshing conversation that had left him filled with an excitement to see them again. But that excitement had been killed by his mother's laments about Uncle Tommy.

"Uncle Tommy had made his own bed," Eddy thought to himself. Why should he care or feel sorry for him? After all nobody was holding a gun to his head when he started using. It wasn't as if he didn't know that dealing with Cut Outta would have landed him eating out of garbage bags in Tamarind Square. Eddy was determined not to end up like the fellas inside the Beetham or worse like his uncle. He had a brain and he was going to use it to get himself out of the Beetham if it was the last thing he did for himself. He had hoped to study till midnight but his study had been interrupted by the intermittent sound of gun shots and occasionally a scurry of feet in the dirt road. It didn't help either that their tiny home of galvanize and wood was only a few yards away from the basketball court.

The fellas in the area mostly left him alone. "White boy" or "Whitey" is what they would call him. Sometimes they would pelt little stones at him but he mostly ignored them and they mostly left him alone. Once when he was fourteen a couple of young fellas his age had tried to beat him up. He managed to escape with some bruises and a black eye. He had fought them off like a wild bull and had put a few knocks in them. The next day his Uncle Tommy and some pardners 'put down a wok' on them and they left him alone after that.

His Uncle was well liked in the area before becoming a piper. He was friendly with the neighbors and the older folks in the community like Uncle Tremble. Now that Tommy was gone, there was no one to look out for him. As he curled up on the tiny mattress which lay on the ground in his room, he wondered to himself what his father was doing and where he was. Eddy wondered if his father had a family and if he had half brothers and sisters. Maybe one day he would find him. He wondered if his father even knew he had a son in Trinidad. As more shots rang out in the night. Eddy closed his eyes and dreamed that he was somewhere in America with his father in a big house with a bedroom of his own where shots never rang out at night.

Chapter Six

Those Damn Politicians

"Dese politicians and dem doh give a damn bout poor people like we. Dey only know bout we when is election time," said Uncle Tremble gesticulating with his already trembling hand to the audience of three. Uncle Tremble was in ripping form. He had about three shots of rum in him and his tongue was loose. "Well election time comin soon an ah waitin for dem." Grey uncombed heads and unbrushed teeth in smelly mouths nodded in agreement with Uncle Tremble. "We go vote dem out boy," another half drunk voice slightly stronger than Uncle Tremble's exclaimed. "Yes, dat's right" the other men agreed. "Dese fellas jus want a lil wok to do and de govunment not giving no jobs out here, dat is why de fellas getting involve in all kinda wrong tings. Is not dat dey want to do wrong tings but it have no wok."

His eyes still full of the morning yampee, Uncle Tremble continued his remonstration. "Black people sufferin out here and nobody ent care bout we. Only fellas like Cut Outta does make sure fellas like we ain't starve to death. Doh mind he doing wrong ting heself but ah mean how a man suppose to live on nine hundred dollars a month in dese times. Yuh eh see govunment want penshuners to dead out here!" Uncle Tremble remonstrated. "Dese young fellas go start a revolution watch an see. Is only so long black man go be sufferin so," said Uncle Louis who like Uncle Tremble was a fixture on the culvert. "When dat time come it go ha real bloodshed."

It was October and the Christmas and Carnival jingles had already begun. There was no longer a clear distinction between the two seasons anymore. Band launchings began from as early as September so that by the time November rolled around, Carnival was in the air and fully in swing. The creation of soca parang only helped to merge the two festivities even more, much to the dismay of many die hard paranderos and anti-Carnival Christians. It seemed almost vile to have a Soca Santa. But for the average Trinbagonian who embraced festivity, soca parang was very welcome. In this pre-Christmas, pre-Carnival atmosphere, there was great excitement and anticipation in the hearts of many but there was also a great deal of desperation. It was the kind of desperation that led men and women to engage in desperate acts often with dire consequences. Money was the key; the only key; and it was not the type of key that was coming down the chimney with Soca Santa.

Up in Trou Macacque some of Cut Outta's associates were busy planning a hit on the son of a wealthy businessman. These men were not your regular maxi taxi bandits; they had connections inside of the police force. The kind of connections that would give them some time and time was essential in this sort of business. The relationship that law enforcement officials had with the criminal element in certain parts of the country was like a twisted pumpkin vine, running unnoticed for yards except for the occasional and sudden appearance of a green monstrosity revealing the identity of the fast growing foliage. This alliance of law and lawbreaker allowed crime to flourish not only in Laventille but in Central, South and parts of the East West corridor. The murder rate for the year was steadily climbing and more and more citizens were becoming increasingly disturbed. But Christmas and Carnival were in the air and these two seasons had an intoxicating effect on the general population. The government of the day was hoping that this opium would keep the masses in sweet stupor until Ash Wednesday. At least that would give them some time to develop an adequate response.

Economically Trinidad was experiencing a second financial boom. Discoveries of oil and natural gas off the East coast and in the Gulf of Paria, coupled with the aggressive wooing of foreign investors by the government, was giving rise to the emersion of a new generation of consumers who were eager to spend.

Yes, there was money flowing through the land and the hands of many, but not everyone was experiencing that outpouring from the oil cornucopia. Exclusivity was the social screening methodology which seemed to work best in this Trinidad capitalist society. It was the kind of exclusivity which could only be accomplished by creating an environment that was prohibitive for the average working class family. Still, it was the kind of exclusivity that many craved.

Some journalists spoke of a neo-colonialism that was driven not by race but by money. They believed that if the disparity of wealth in the country was not addressed the crime situation would worsen and there would be trouble down the road. Some even spoke of a repeat of the 1990 coup lead instead by a different Imam with a Marxist agenda. But for those whose wallets were being filled with oil money, these doom and gloom prophets were like voices crying in the wilderness never to be heard. While the wisdom of the sages was dulled by the anxious humming of the engines of the BMWs and Mercedes Benzes on the highways, the seemingly noiseless stirrings of discontent and unrest grew louder in the hearts of the young people all over the land who felt that they deserved to have wallets to open too. For the men of the Beetham and Laventille, their cries for an equal share of the pie seemed to be going unheard. They believed that the time for action was drawing near. They had waited too long and had suffered enough. The dam of frustration was getting ready to burst and nobody, not even the folks on the Beetham, would be prepared for the flood.

"Yes ah expecting some money from a Nelson Williams."

"Do you have some ID?" the voice behind the glass window asked Vonetta. Vonetta began to dig in her handbag with one hand trying her best to prevent the sunglasses she was wearing from falling off her face. She slid her identification card under the glass with a tiny piece of paper bearing the address of Nelson Williams. After a few hurried clicks of the keyboard Vonetta would hear the disappointing news. "Sorry mam, we don't have any transaction for Nelson Williams. Do you know if Mr. Williams has changed his address? Maybe he has not put through the money as yet."

"No he usually very on time. As a matter a fack he one week late."

"I'm sorry I can't help you. Perhaps if you can you should contact Mr. Williams," the voice behind the glass advised.

Vonetta adjusted her sunglasses again, put her ID card away and walked away. She was perplexed. The middle aged woman of mixed heritage wondered what had become of her husband as she walked down the stairs of the Excellent City Store in her fluorescent green stiletto heels. "Pssst...douglas yuh look real nice baby," a peddler on Queen Street called out to her as she sauntered along. Her faded blue jeans which fit snuggly on her petite waist, together with the fluorescent green halter back top she was wearing accentuated the curves of her body and made heads turn. She had grown up hearing people calling her a douglas and it didn't bother

her in the least bit. She was half East Indian, half black and felt no shame about that.

As Vonetta made her way towards City Gate, she couldn't help but notice the multitude of sale signs in the display windows. There seemed to be a sale on everything - curtains, furniture, shoes. She needed money for some new curtains. Where the hell was Nelson? She had tried to call him but his phone had been disconnected. They were cracking down on illegal aliens in New York and she hoped with every fiber of her being that Nelson had managed to stay out of the police's net. He couldn't come back to Trinidad now to find her living the way she was. As she pushed the glass door to enter Bazzey's drug store, she was filled with a sense of dread. What would she do if the test was positive? What would Ted say?

Sally needed to talk to Marlene desperately about Matt's strange behavior. She had not slept much the night before and was reluctant to leave the house before speaking to Marlene. Marlene always knew exactly what to say to make her feel better and Sally really needed to feel better soon. Matt had left for work that morning without so much as uttering a word to her. Sally wished the ground would open and swallow her up. She had reached a new level of despair and desperation and was fresh out of ideas as far as communicating with Matt about their marriage was concerned. "Yes can I speak with Mrs. Mathias please? Tell her its her bestest friend Sally." Sally held the sleek looking black cordless phone close to her ear and waited with bated breath to hear Marlene's voice on the other end. "Hi my bestest friend. What's up?" Sally heaved a sigh of relief. "I need to speak with you right away Marlene." Marlene was concerned. "Is everything alright? Are you Ok?"

"Yes I'm fine. I just really need someone to talk to. Can you come over?" "Oh gosh its real busy now Sally...Hmm, let me see if I can get one of the supervisors to hold on for me. I'm not promising anything but give me an hour or so. I'll try to get away from this mad house Ok." Sally was grateful when an hour later the wheat beige Mercedes Benz pulled up in front her white wrought iron gate on Columbus drive. As she opened the solid oak door to let Marlene in, Sally wondered how she would have survived without a friend like Marlene.

"What's wrong Sal? You look like you haven't slept all night," said Marlene as she entered the living room and placed her hand bag on the black leather couch. Sally really looked a mess. Deathly pale, she was still in her night gown, hadn't combed her hair or brushed her teeth and Marlene was not used to seeing her friend like this. "It's Matt. I don't know what to do," she sobbed as she plunked herself down in the couch, eyes swollen and red. Marlene sat beside her and gently rubbed her friend's back.

"Calm down Sal. It's ok. It's ok. Tell me what happened."

"I think he is seeing someone. We haven't had sex in months and I think he doesn't want me anymore." Sally was hysterical and her face and hands were wet with tears. "Oh Sal" Marlene hugged the distraught woman. "Don't cry darling. It'll be alright. Just calm down and tell me what happened."

If the little Portuguese girl from Belmont with the cute dimples had achieved the life of wealth and prestige she had so desperately sought after, why was she crying all the time? Why was Marlene Mathias the only person Sally could call family, when she in fact had come from a large family herself. In her obsessive quest to become a Chow Fatt, Sally had ostracized herself from all her relatives. Ashamed of the poverty from which she had come, embarrassed by the simple aspirations of her siblings, and the illiteracy of her mother, Sally refused to let the ill fortune of being born into a family that was of no consequence prevent her from becoming a woman of importance in society. Shortly after her marriage to Matt, Sally began to shun all her siblings and extended family. "I just don't want them to expect that I will be giving them a lot of things now that I'm married," she had told Matt adamantly. But the truth was that the thought of her illiterate mother and uncultured siblings up and down her new home, attempting to hold intelligent conversation with her in-laws was not an endearing one. Having to endure them for the wedding was bad enough but that was the last time.

Sally considered herself lucky. She was the only one in her entire family who had the foresight and the ambition to elevate her social self far beyond what her sisters and brothers ever thought possible. It wasn't her fault that her sisters wanted to work as public servants, teachers and postal workers. They were doomed to a life of mediocrity as far as Sally was concerned. It was that mediocre living that marrying Matt Chow Fatt had helped her to escape. The difficulties she currently endured with Matt couldn't possibly compare to the horrors her sisters had to endure. One of her sisters was married to an electrician and the other to a plumber. Even though the fights with Matt were getting progressively worse, in Sally's mind being married to a plumber was an infinitely greater ignominy.

"Stopping here driver." Vonetta opened the taxi door and got out on Bushe Street in Curepe. She was anxious to know whether she was pregnant or not and walked as fast she could in those damn stiletto heels. Today was her day off and she was thankful for it. Working at Penny Savers cosmetics was never her idea of a dream career but it was better than nothing. It was a job and it helped to pay the bills. Her meager salary together with the change that Nelson would send for her by Western Union took care of Lisa's passage money every week, paid for extra lessons, paid the rent and electricity bills and supported Ted who would be working one Monday and unemployed by the following Friday.

Without Nelson's monthly contribution things could get a bit tight. Vonetta looked at her watch as she turned the key to open the door to the apartment she called home. Ted would not be home now. He was out looking for work and wouldn't be home till about six o'clock or midnight depending on whether he decided to make his favorite detour. She kicked off her heels and collapsed on the floral upholstered living room couch. The apartment wasn't that big, there were only two bedrooms a choked up dilapidated kitchen and a dingy looking living room. All the walls were painted a mild yellow and bore evidence to the fact that the apartment was old by the many cracks and dirt marks on them. The artificial floral arrangement on the termite ridden coffee table in the living room was dusty and stale looking. In fact all the furniture had an old, musty smell that air refresher could only temporarily mask. Vonetta had been living there with Nelson for five years before he went foreign. They had talked about going to America all the time. How she wished he had never left her.

Vonetta walked over to the mirror above the toilet sink and removed her sunglasses so she could see if the darkness around her eyes had begun to clear up. "Steups!" She inspected her left eye in the mirror and was disappointed to see that there had been no change. She would put some ice on it in a wash rag. That should help it some she thought. This wasn't the first time Ted had given her a black eye but she knew he didn't mean to. He was so sorry this morning when he woke up sober. The alcohol would make a demon out of him. She knew he was a good man and she truly did love him. If only he could stop the drinking they could have such a good life together. Maybe a baby would make the difference. Maybe it would help him to change. Suddenly being pregnant for Ted seemed like a blessing in disguise. She sat on the cold broken toilet seat and soon enough the white styrofoam cup she was holding underneath her began to fill up.

Sean Mathias, remote control in hand flipped through the channels one more time. He was sick with diarrhea but was ecstatic that he was allowed to miss a day of school. He would be better by tomorrow in time for choir practice. He had to be; after all he was the lead vocalist in the upcoming Christmas production *Wish Upon A Star*. Sean loved to sing and was blessed with his mother's beautiful singing voice. Sometimes Eddy would tease him about the school 'faggots' who were in the choir and warn him not to end up like them. But Sean didn't care whether they were really faggots or not, he loved the way he felt when he was singing. It was the only time he felt truly happy and alive. Brian and Eddy didn't really understand him anyway. Eddy was cool enough but Sean knew that he and Brian were only friends because their parents were. They had very little in common except for the fact that they had both been involved in some of the same extracurricular activities in the same places for the last four years or so.

As Sean flushed the toilet and looked at himself in the nearby wall mirror he wondered how much weight he was losing today with this miserable diarrhea. The last thing he needed was to lose weight, he was tall and skinny enough already. He lifted his arm and clenching his fist at right angles to his shoulder, tried to see if there was any definition in his biceps muscles. Alas it was a hopeless case. Sean hated his physical appearance ever since he turned fourteen. In the space of a few years he had lost all his baby fat, shot up like a bean stalk and developed his Adam's apple. No longer was he the cute chubby cheeked boy whose cheeks everyone wanted to pinch. He'd never had a girlfriend but had not really been attracted to girls; at least not the way Brian and Eddy were.

He had had a huge crush on Mr. Alfonso the Science and Biology teacher but had never told anyone about it. Mr. Alfonso really was everything Sean wanted to be. He was tall and dark skinned, muscular with a broad chest and firm looking buttocks. He was always well dressed and wore Joop for Men, a cologne Sean loved. But best of all Sean was mesmerized by Mr. Alfonso's voice. He had a deep husky voice and well formed lips. Sean often wondered what it would be like to be kissed by Mr. Alfonso. In fact he had dreamt about kissing him several times. When Mr. Alfonso was transferred by the Ministry of Education to work at a school in Fyzabad, Sean was devastated.

Sean had read somewhere when he was fifteen that it was not uncommon for teenagers his age to be attracted to persons of the same sex; so he had not been unduly distressed by his feelings for Mr. Alfonso. But he was almost eighteen now and he was beginning to have some serious concerns about his sexuality. He had never felt about any girl the way he felt about Mr. Alfonso and although Brian had tried to hook him up with a very attractive looking Convent girl when he was sixteen, Sean had found her very uninteresting. They had completely different interests and the hook up turned out to be a real disaster when the girl, Claudette, tried to make out with him one night in the car park at Movie Towne. Sean had been completely repulsed by the way she kissed him. It felt

73

like she was trying to choke him with her tongue. She was hoping for more but he declined and the date and the relationship ended disappointingly for Claudette who subsequently spread rumors that Sean was gay. Thankfully Brian and Eddy countered the rumors by saying that Claudette was desperate to be 'screwed' and was just unhappy that she had been rejected by Sean. Yes Brian and Eddy truly looked out for him but they didn't really understand him, at least not the way his choir buddies did.

"Hawl yuh mudder's ass. Yuh is a f—king liar!" Lystra was shouting at the top of her voice. "Mine yuh damn business!" Lystra flung her arms in the direction of her cantankerous neighbor and slammed shut the door of her half galvanize, half wooden home. This latest news about Tommy made her more determined than ever to pay another visit to her brother. She had not seen him in about a month and knew that she had not given him enough condoms to last that long. Her voice was hoarse from cursing out Ms. Fiona and she needed a drink to soothe her aching throat. She would rest a while before walking over to the rum shop. Her heart was racing and her blouse was soaked with sweat. She wiped the beads pouring down her face with her hand and dried the hand in her black short pants. This was not the way she had hoped her brother would end his days. She knew Ms. Fiona wasn't lying about Tommy but the truth was too much for her to take. Ms. Fiona's son had seen Tommy working on his knees on South Quay.

"What de hell yuh son was doing dere dat hour ah de night. Is your son who is de f—king homo!" was the response shot back at Ms. Fiona. Her brother had become a piper, a vagrant and now a prostitute all in the space of a few months. Her heart ached. All she had left was Eddy. She remembered the words of the healer who had rubbed her down with olive oil in Laventille and hoped that Eddy would be coming into some kind of money soon. If nothing else, she needed Eddy to stay in school and not end up like Tommy. Lystra had two other children, two daughters. She had heard one of them was living in Grenada now and that the other was married to a good fella and living down South. Neither of them kept in touch with her. She believed she had done her best for them as much as she could do as a mother. Her daughters thought otherwise.

For her effort she had received no gratitude at all. Someone told her that her daughter in South had become a born again Christian. Lystra had thought this daughter would be moved by Christian charity to visit her on the Beetham but she was wrong. Her hopes lay now on Eddy. She wanted to talk to him about his school work and about his plans for when he finished school but he rarely listened to her these days, and since she put Tommy out on the street, Eddy had grown very distant.

Lystra had a half brother named Harry living up St. Augustine; an Indian fella. He acknowledged her as his half sister even though she was an outside child. When Eddy was a baby, she used to visit him and his wife Sunita every once in a while. They had a baby born around the same time as Eddy. Harry and Sunita never looked down on her but one time while she was there, Sunita's family stopped by for a visit and had made Lystra feel kind of 'funny'. Since then Lystra never really went back to Harry's home although she would see him from time to time and would try to make a small black cake for him every year at Christmas time. She always made it small because she knew it would never make it into his house and there was no point on wasting good ingredients on a cake that was going to end up in the garbage.

For a brief moment, she mused with the idea of giving Harry a call to let him know what was going on with Tommy, but Tommy never cared for Harry anyway and used to scold Lystra for trying to have a relationship with him. "Dat Indian man is not yuh brudder. Yuh stupid ah wat. If he is yuh brudder, why de hell he doh help yuh eh? Carrying yuh chile to play wid he chile like dat go do something!" Tommy used to say angrily. She would give anything to hear Tommy scold her again; to hear his voice in the house once more. She didn't know the thing he had become but she hated that white powder that had rendered him so helpless that he didn't even have the sense to know when he needed to buss a piss.

"Toooooooooo dollars for one. Dry coconut here, tooooooo dollars for one." Port-of-Spain market was busy today. It was fortnight Friday and fortnightly workers had been paid early. Ma Thomas was busy hustling, selling, advertising and delivering change. Ms. Janice was busy too, her sun bronzed face was oily and she was a bit tired but she needed to make a couple hundred dollars to fix up her car for inspection. That car was how she made it to market everyday and she couldn't afford to pay any fines for not having it inspected. "Dat is tree fifty," said Ms. Janice as she put a few eddoes in a clear plastic bag and handed it over to a customer. "Yeeeeesssss get yuh grong provisions here fuh dat soup, eddoes, green fig, sweet potato. Yeeeeessss my frens, grong provisions here." Ms. Janice's sweet voice rang out among others in the assembly of stalls. "Ay-Ay...but look who here," said Ma Thomas with a smile. Ms. Janice turned to see a visibly thinner Papa Netty staggering towards her stall. "Well, Well, Well. I say yuh geh married an gone away." Ms. Janice said laughingly. "An I say yuh did dead and eh tell we nuttin." Ma Thomas added.

"Good morning ladies," said Papa Netty with a smile and almost bowing. He started a fit of coughing and his bare, bony chest seemed to rock up and down with each cough. "Allyuh lucky to see meh today. Ah almost dead yuh know. Ah geh one bad cole yuh hear," said Papa Netty when his coughing fit ceased. "But like yuh still have de cole boy," Ma Thomas responded. "It geh good now. If yuh did hear meh las week yuh wouda tell Saint Peter to open de gates fuh meh right away. Is only lime an honey ah had was to drink right thru to geh betta. An well yuh know ah like meh lil spirits an ting. Meh big son had to come down and take meh to emergency. Dey gimme me some tablet and ting. I ent really taking dem but ah feeling lil better nah so ah say leh meh come out an look fuh allyuh."

"Ah didn know yuh had a son Papa Netty," said Ms. Janice. It was the first time she had heard him make mention of any children and was happy to know that there was someone who was looking out for ole Papa Netty. "Yeah ah ha one son here livin South an a daughter in America but she doh spit on meh at all, only dis one ah ha here does check fuh meh now an again." Papa Netty explained rubbing his hairy little chest. "Well ah glad yuh feeling better although yuh look like yuh lose some weight," said Ma Thomas with a smile. "Yes well yuh know how it is when yuh sick an ting. But ah feelin much better tanks. Allyuh miss me nah," said Papa Netty with a mischievous looking smile. "Ah know allyuh miss me."

"Miss wha?" Ms. Janice steupsed. "I wanted some limes to cook some Cascadoo ah geh de udder day an ah say leh meh give Papa Netty a sale but yuh wasn here." Ms. Janice was lying. She just didn't want the old man to think she had noticed his absence that much.

"Why yuh ent tell meh yuh like Cascadoo. Ah could get some fuh yuh. Ah have a pardner dat does geh Cascadoo regular."

"I eh want no Cascadoo Papa," Ms. Janice quickly retorted.

"You doh frighten yuhself I will get some Cascadoo fuh my honey," said Papa Netty.

"Steups. Yuh betta go home an lie down yuh hear and stop drinking so damn much. Is all dat rum dat get yuh sick. An ah sure Pinto eh come an look fuh yuh wid all dat rum yuh does buy from he." Ma Thomas scolded.

Papa Netty gave Ma Thomas a couyah mouth. "Anyway ladies Papa Netty is a very busy man. Ah glad to see dat allyuh still lookin rosy as ever but ah ha to go to wok now. Ah will see allyuh lovely ladies tomorrow." And with that note of farewell, Papa Netty sauntered off in the direction of his favorite haunt, Pinto's rum shop.

Christmas time was the worst time of the year for Papa Netty. His son Joseph would visit him but he never brought Papa Netty's grandchildren to see him. Joseph would scold him about coming off the booze and they would argue about the way Papa Netty was living. He was always happy to see Joseph but he hated not seeing his grandchildren. He had seen pictures of them though but longed to hug them and touch them. Joseph wouldn't allow it, at least not until he kicked the habit. Papa Netty really wanted to stop drinking but he wasn't sure if he would be able to live with himself if he were sober. He didn't know who he was without his White Oak rum. His brandy, his scotch, these were his friends, more like his family and he was not yet ready to give them up, even though he desperately wanted to be a grandfather to his grandchildren.

Bellies had just come from a meeting with the fellas up in Trou Macacque and everything seemed set for next week Thursday. They were going to change vehicles at an abandoned house in Gonzales and head for Central where the hideout was located. Corporal Antoine in the anti-kidnapping squad was their liaison and they had enough artillery to form a small army. Cut Outta was pleased with the report he had heard.

He had been busy that day making arrangements with some Venezuelan associates for another shipment that was coming in via Cedros.

He had taken Jonathan also known as Top Shotta with him. Top Shotta was Cut Outta's left hand man whenever Bellies was attending to other equally important business. Top Shotta was tall and lean, not as muscular as Bellies but with a face that was equally as intimidating. "Yuh show dem de fella so dey doh geh mix up?" asked Cut Outta sternly. "Yeah, yeah, dey done spot de fella ahready. A chinee lookin boy. Dey spot de driver an everyting. Dey just ha to collec him before de driver reach. White boy is he fren," said Bellies. This was an interesting piece of news. "Yuh mean Tommy lil brudder, de fair one?" asked Cut Outta.

"Yeah dat one," Bellies confirmed.

"He eh see yuh doh?" Cut Outta asked concerned.

Bellies steupsed. "Yuh tink is yesterday I in dis business ah wat." Bellies was irritated by Cut Outta's last question but knew how to mask his irritation with the much shorter man who was his boss. "White boy feel he white eh, frennin wid de rich. Hmmn. Jus keep ah eye on whitey. Las ting we need is fuh some stupidness to mess up dis wok."

Chapter Seven

Those Who Eat The Cascadura

The draw of the cash register opened and closed as Sunita put away the hundred dollar bill she had just received and delivered the change and a plastic bag with some notepads and pens to the waiting customer. Harry Rajkumar was just turning fifty-five. He was of average height with a well rounded beer belly which had grown over the years from lack of exercise. He was the eldest of seven children and had been born and raised in Kelly Village. His father was a cane cutter at Caroni 1975 Limited and his mother stayed at home in their tiny wooden unpainted house on stilts, taking care of the babies that seemed to pelt out of her belly every nine months.

Every morning she got up early and made sada roti with ochro or potatoes or channa, wrapped it in a recycled piece of wax paper, and placed it in a brown paper bag. That was breakfast for Harry's father and eventually Harry who joined his father in the tall green cane fields when he turned fourteen. Harry never wanted a career as a laborer. It was only when his father died that he was able to get a start in life with some of the lump sum benefit money from Caroni that his mother gave him. He took a chance on himself at twenty-three and started a small business selling doubles with Sunita at Mohess junction. The rest was history. Their hard work paid off and Harry had managed to amass a fortune without the ostentatious display of wealth that some of his siblings in business had been prone to.

Being able to give his sons a better life filled him with a deep sense of fulfillment. His eldest son was studying law at the University of the West Indies and Krishna expressed interest in studying medicine. Kiran, the youngest, attended St.Augustine Presbyterian Primary School and was doing well in class consistently. Yes, Balo, Harry's father would have been proud of him. He had left a legacy of hard work and rum drinking to all his children but there was one child who would never know that legacy and that was Harry's half sister Lystra. Wine, women and song was Balo's addiction, or was it Fernandes Vat 19, women and song, Harry couldn't remember. Harry wished for his mother's sake that Balo could keep his zipper up, but he knew his father's weaknesses and Balo was most certainly the village ram.

Often Harry wondered if he had other half brothers and sisters in Kelly Village that he didn't know about and from time to time his mind would run on Lystra.

Why had she stopped coming by? It was not that he wanted her to be a frequent visitor but he liked to believe that he had transcended the fact that she was his half sister by a Negro woman; a thick, big breasted, big bottomed black woman, with a nose as big and as spread out as the whole of Kelly Village. He had tried his best to make Lystra and her son feel welcome. He remembered the soft haired child and wondered what kind of life Lystra could give him on the Beetham. But that was years ago and Harry hoped that his father's bastard child had met with good fortune.

Sunita had only tolerated Lystra's visits but was relieved when mother and child stopped coming around. How could she tell her family that Harry had a half sister who looked like Lystra and lived on the Beetham? "The less yuh have to do with dat woman de better," Sunita had pleaded. Lord Krishna had heard her prayers. However, it was too much for Sunita to hope that Trinidad would be big enough and the Beetham far enough to keep her son from meeting his first cousin. In fact their worlds were about to collide at meteoric speed.

Vonetta stared at the two purple parallel lines and they seemed to stare back at her. Almost as if they were saying "Yes, watch meh good. Is pregnant yuh pregnant." She sat fully clothed on the toilet seat staring in disbelief at the results of her pregnancy test. "Oh God oy!" She felt a sudden belly pain and weakness in her stomach that seemed to radiate down to her legs. Burying her head on her lap she held on to her belly. Crying turned to bawling, bawling to sobbing and sobbing to sniffles. By the time she was done, several crumpled blocks of toilet paper lay on the floor around the base of the toilet bowl, bearing witness to the pain this news had brought her. When she was strong enough to raise herself off the toilet seat, she headed to the kitchen. Vonetta didn't drink but she needed a beer. Thoughts fleeced through her brain like maxi taxis up and down the bus route. How could she keep this child? This should have been Nelson's child. How she wished it was. How could she bring another child into the world for this good for nothing rum-bud of a man that lived with her? How come she got pregnant while taking the pill? That was the question that baffled her the most. All this time and then bam; all of a sudden just like that.

She remembered being pregnant with Lisa. She was so sick for the whole nine months and then she was in labor for almost twenty-four hours before the doctors cut her open. Nelson was with her all the time. He was a good husband to her. Sometimes Vonetta thought he was too good. She felt a deep sense of guilt. There he was in America working hard doing construction, always looking over his shoulder for immigration police, sending money to Trinidad for her and Lisa, and there she was living with another man and a "waste ah time" man at that. She wondered if he knew about Ted. If he did then he didn't seem to care because he never stopped sending the money for her and Lisa. If she kept the child, the responsibility would be all hers, but maybe having a child would be good for Ted. Maybe it would cause him to finally be the kind of man that she knew he could be. The flood of thoughts was getting Vonetta tired, she dragged herself to the tiny bedroom she and Ted shared and collapsed on the bed.

"An dis govuhment doh care bout poor people. Watch wha dey doing to we eh. Crime gone up. Every morning when yuh read de newspaper is a shooting, is a killing, is kidnapping. But look how Trinidad geh bad eh. Dis govuhment wicked yuh hear. One setta tief. All a dem is tief. It eh matter which one in power, PNM, UNC, ONR, NAR all a dem is de same damn ting." It was midday and the University of Woodford Square was in full swing. Young and old men gathered around to hear the scathing attack by some never-to- be-a- politician politician. It was open floor and anybody could say anything about anything or anyone. There was no selection of topic for discussion; the commentary just flowed and flowed like the East Dry River, sometimes full of garbage and old junk, other times full of valuables that just passed for rubbish because of the attire and level of education of the person who was on his feet. Like the East Dry River all contents emptied into the sea of despair where there were no real solutions to the societal problems.

Regarding politics, the conclusions were always the same. The government was 'tiefing'. The country needed a new government but no one party was up for the task since all politicians were corrupt and those who were not yet politicians would soon become corrupt if they entered politics anyway. Men, and on the odd occasion a few women would assemble everyday at this university where wise man and fool, learned and unlearned, would meet for their daily 'education'. For many, these political and social diatribes and monologues were an opium necessary in order to deal with the stresses of their existence. However, there were many people like Tommy whose mental capacities had been so greatly altered by drugs, or the chemical changes of the brain, that it made no difference what the university 'professors' were saying.

Ever since his buss head Tommy had been hanging around Woodford Square in the daytime and only going to Tamarind Square at night. Stretched out on one of the benches in the Square, Tommy was sunbathing his dirt caked skin. He enjoyed the warmth of the sun on his body. As Christmas drew nearer and the nights became colder, Tommy looked forward to being baked in the midday heat. He had lost at least ten pounds since Lystra had last seen him and his body reeked of piss, feces, vomit, and other bodily excretions that had all dried and become one with his tattered clothes and his skin. He had developed a few open sores on his arms and legs that oozed a thick yellow pus but this had not significantly hindered his lifestyle. He and Bullerboy had grown closer in the last few weeks and although they were usually apart during their daily wanderings, at night, after business had been conducted, money made, drugs bought and sniffed, and higher levels of consciousness reached, Tommy found solace in Bullerboy's arms.

Bullerboy had taken a bit of a beating in the last few weeks both figuratively and literally. He had made some money but had spent it all on coke and hemp and some items bought from another piper who traded merchandise. Bullerboy wanted to keep himself smelling and looking presentable enough for his clients and he really had tried but ever since he began hanging out with Tommy, self maintenance had become very challenging. Bullerboy had begun to resemble Tommy in many aspects, sores and all, and was convinced that Tommy was 'bringing him down'. But he had a soft spot for Tommy. Tommy had come from somewhere; a family. He had a sister that came to bring him food even if it was only that one time and Bullerboy respected that about him.

A few yards away from Tommy's bench in Woodford Square, yellow and white tents gave shade to tables set with an array of Christmas items. Table cloths, table mats, coffee makers, figurines made in China, yellow haired dolls with blue eyes winking inside their plastic coffins, lay side by side with torchlights, batteries, and shiny toy cars and trucks. All day long, behind the tables, women hustled to sell their goods to the waxing and waning crowd. It was not until about one o'clock that day, that Jesse and Lisa passed through Woodford Square. They were not on their way home, although they had been given a half day of school. They both had extra lessons later with Mr. Lee Wen. The two were just window shopping as girls their age often do. As they wandered from store to store, touching each pair of low rider jeans, they imagined what life would be like if they really could afford to buy all the clothes and the shoes they wanted. The tents and the surrounding crowd drew them into Woodford Square. "I think

Becca will like this doll," said Jesse as she showed Lisa a black haired doll with big brown eyes. "Your eyes look just like that when yuh talking to Brian," Lisa teased.

"Very funny....Steups," Jesse responded with a smile and an upward roll of her eyes. "We are just friends Lisa, nothing more. Besides do you really think he would pick a girl like me from de country to be with when it have girls from school throwing themselves at him all the time?" Jesse had a huge crush on Brian. They had been talking after Mr. Lee Wen's class and over the phone but Jesse's heart was preparing for disappointment. There were times in their phone conversations when she felt so close to him, almost as if he understood her. It was weird for her. This very attractive, popular guy seemed to enjoy talking to her, the simple girl from Santa Cruz whose mother sold lettuce and yams in the Port-of-Spain market. It was the kind of attention that Jesse had not been accustomed to. She had had crushes on guys before but never one like Brian. She daydreamed of what it would be like to kiss him, to be held by him, to make love to him and yes even to be married to him.

Ms. Janice had not entirely approved of their friendship. Jesse's smiles and girly giggles over the phone only meant trouble. She had interrogated her daughter about this Chow Fatt boy in a loving motherly way. She knew that she couldn't shield her daughter from boys and men for the rest of her life the way Mr. GG would have wanted to but she didn't want Jesse to be hurt. How could she tell her beautiful, intelligent, caring child, that this boy she was so obviously developing feelings for, would never be able to have a future with her? How could she explain that his family would never allow their son to have a serious relationship with the offspring of farmers? How could she tell her beloved child who no man would ever be good enough for, that for Brian Chow Fatt she would never be good enough?

Ms. Janice knew that she had to do something soon, because although Brian didn't call Jesse every day, his telephone calls significantly altered Jesse's mood and usually made it almost impossible for her to concentrate on her school work. Ms. Janice had noticed the change in her daughter. Jesse had begun shaving her legs and her eyebrows, paying more attention to her hair and had even asked for money to perm it. Jesse was infatuated, in love even; and although Ms. Janice could remember only vaguely what those racing hormones and emotions felt like at Jesse's age, she had to stop this budding romance or whatever it was before it ruined her precious Jesse.

"Yes, this is Sally Chow Fatt. I'd like to get two tickets to Tobago please." Sally with cell phone in hand was heading along Wrightson Road on her way to her bankers in Maraval. "Oh let me call you right back. I'm getting another call." It was Marlene. "Hi darling. Long time no hear no see." It had been at least a week since she had spoken to Marlene and she missed her friend terribly. "What have you been up to?" the animated voice on the other end of the phone asked. "I'm planning a surprise trip to Tobago," Sally said bubbling with excitement. "I found this really exclusive, private set of cottages near to Pigeon Point. They opened recently and they are absolutely gorgeous. I'm planning to surprise Matt tomorrow. You know, something different instead of going to our beach house in Speyside." There was a long silence on the other end. A perplexed look came over Sally's face.

"What's the matter? You don't sound excited."

"Don't you think it is a little too much Sal?" Marlene asked. "I mean do you know if he has plans this weekend?" Marlene was genuinely concerned. Sally and Matt had been fighting like cat and dog for weeks. Sally had repeatedly accused Matt of being unfaithful and Matt in response had launched scathing attacks on Sally's greed and pretentiousness. Worst of all he had reminded her of the one thing she knew to be true about herself, the fact that if he were not a Chow Fatt, the son of a prestigious multimillionaire, she would never have married him.

It was this that had hurt Sally the most. It was true yes, but over the years she had grown to love Matt. She had looked past his scrawny frame, his poor social skills, even his initial clumsiness in the bedroom and had loved him. He had done for her the one thing her family could never have. He had given her a name. A name that could be respected in society. He had elevated her status in the eyes of French Creoles, Portuguese, Syrians, British and American expatriates and all people of class and importance in society and had made her a somebody. She was grateful for that and she loved him for that. But more than Matt, she loved the life he had been able to give her and she was not about to give it up.

"Well I don't know if he has plans but I really want to do something spontaneous. Something that will really knock him off his feet you know."

"Oh that is sure to knock him off his feet darling. I just hope he goes for it and you aren't disappointed," said Marlene.

"I really think we need this. Someone has to get this marriage back on track. We've been fighting so much and he's been working so hard since its Christmas time. I think if we could just get away from it all for a while it would make a huge difference." Sally was so optimistic and so excited that Marlene felt sorry she had injected the slightest doubt that Sally's plans would be anything other than perfect. "Well make sure and get a nice tan when you hit the beach," Marlene joked. Sally smiled revealing her recently whitened teeth. What would she do without Marlene? She had missed talking to her all week long. Marlene and her husband had been busy with work and functions and so had Sally and Matt. It would be that way right up to Christmas time. After fighting behind closed doors, the Chow Fatts' presented a strong, confident and harmonious front. No guest would ever guess that there was trouble in paradise. "Sal I have to run. I'll talk to you again lovie. Let's have lunch when you get back from Tobago ok."

"Yes let's. That would be nice," said Sally.

As Sally turned into the car park at Ellerslie Plaza in Maraval, she wondered who she might spot at the bank. There was always someone to exchange pleasantries with, whether it was the bank manager, one of Matt's friends, or someone who just wanted to be able to let everyone in the banking hall know that they knew Mr. and Mrs. Chow Fatt. This was what Sally lived for. She had already determined that Matt was having an affair. The late nights at work, the mood swings, the accusation that she had ensnared him together with the constant fights, were enough to raise her suspicions. Sally was bigger than that. Matt having an affair, as painful as it was for her, was still understandable. Matt getting a divorce and marrying another would be an unforgivable offence. But as long as the D word never came up she was going to do her best to re-kindle whatever left over cinders existed in their relationship. This trip was exactly what their marriage needed. At least that is what Sally thought.

"The virgin Mary had a baby boy."

"STOOOOPPPPP! What in heaven's name was that!" screamed Mr. Mc Master. The usually reserved choirmaster stared at the almost men standing at attention before him with a look of frustration written all over his face. It was four in the afternoon and the QRC boys' choir was preparing for their upcoming Christmas concert. Mr. Mc Master was exasperated. "Come on let's try again," he shouted, pushing his glasses up on his nose and wiping away the sweat on his forehead with his right thumb. Sean Mathias lifted his head with shoulders back and joined in singing the familiar Christmas carol which had been modified with a soca beat so that it sounded almost like a calypso. His Adam's apple rose and fell with each note and his eyebrows rose each time his mouth opened wide to form the notes he was singing. Standing next to him was Alex Thornhill who it was rumored was not only a 'faggot' but an open one as well.

Alex was the butt of many jokes but seemed to be immune to the comments and the ridicule. Sean couldn't understand why anyone would want to subject themselves to that kind of embarrassment. "Being gay must be hard enough," he thought; why would anyone want people to know in the first place? Sean neither liked nor disliked Alex he just didn't want to be bothered with his antics. *"And they said that his name was Je-sus"* Sean felt something moving gently up the side of his thigh or was that....no it couldn't be a hand. A strange feeling enveloped Sean. It was a mixture of shock and fear with a hint of some other emotion. He knew Mr. Mc Master would shout at him but he made a step to his right and continued singing. Still singing, he looked straight at Alex with a look of extreme disgust and disdain. "STOOOPPPP!" Mr. Mc Master yelled. "Ok, Mr. Mathias, would you like to tell me what is going on up in the corner there with you and Mr. Thornhill." The rest of the choir burst into laughter and giggles. "SHUUUTT UPP!" Mr. Mc Master screamed, his glasses almost falling off his greasy little pug nose. "I hope you all don't intend to behave like this on the night of our performance. This is not a joke. If any of you want to get out of this choir leave NOW!" There was absolute silence in the auditorium. You could almost hear a pin drop. "But if you want to stay, you have to stop this God damn fidgeting and fumbling. DO YOU HEAR ME! Sean, Alex, did you hear that."

"Yes sir," was all they could quietly muster. "Ok let's take it again from the top." Sean had turned red. His palms were sweaty, and his shirt was wet with perspiration from a sudden outpouring of fluid from his pores. Alex had tried to touch his butt and Sean wasn't sure whether he should expose him right then and there or deal with him after the practice. He began to feel sick to his stomach. Sweat ran like a sea of marathon runners off his flushed face and in the front and back of his shirt, huge wet spots were the only signs of his inner turmoil and shock. Sean continued to sing heartily. He would deal with Mr. Thornhill after choir practice. It would be over soon. Nothing like this had ever happened to Sean before.

Deep in the belly of the Beetham Estate, amid the hellish odors of the huge canal that snaked through the area and identified it to all motorists, men and women were at work trying to save lost souls. Reverend Miller of the Seventh Day Adventist Church was one of those soul savers. His flock though small was zealous for the Lord and eager to help all man and woman-kind to turn from their wicked and sinful ways. Door to door evangelization was essential for them. And since the wickedness according to Pastor Miller was "great in the land," the enthusiasm of the faithful needed to be even greater. The poor faithful who were mostly in their sixties could be seen on occasion proselytizing from door to door. Jehovah's Witnesses were busy too. Although they had no assembly hall in the area, they too marched in the midday sun, umbrella in hand and armed with copies of the Watchtower magazine. They endured the barks and sometimes the bite of dogs, ridicule and curses, feeble doors slammed shut in their faces because "ah have a pot on de fire" and occasionally the pelted stone. On this afternoon in particular, Lystra lay on the ground on a flattened foam mattress which was her bed and wept silently. Without a sound and lying as still as she could, the tear drops cut a pathway from the corner of her eyes to her ear lobes. They stopped there until in a little while a tiny pool of tears had collected.

Looking up through the rusty galvanize roof shot with holes, Lystra wondered why her life had to be so hard. If there was a God, he surely didn't like black people and even if he did, she wasn't one of them. Lystra didn't have a steady job, but she worked whenever she could doing whatever she could. Most of her work involved cleaning drains, painting stones and cutting grass with CEPEP. When there was no CEPEP work she did other 'work'. The government had set up a new version of the Unemployment Relief Program but the politics of securing a job were still unchanged. Sleeping with the foreman was still a sure fire way of moving from the bottom of the selection list to the top. It was the only way Lystra knew how. She had seen her mother do it and many other women too. As much as she hated it, it was the foreman who had put food on their little table when her mother couldn't make ends meet.

At fifty, she like her mother had become a slave to the foreman. He had a different face and a different name but in Lystra's mind it was the same man she had visited with her mother as a child on numerous occasions. After Ma Vero received her envelope she would always buy her daughter a Kiss cake and make some meager groceries. Now, even with the envelope Lystra got, she still had to beg for credit at the neighborhood parlor and owe the scavengers at the labasse. She was so very tired of it all; tired of herself, her life, her failures and the many men who kept disappointing her; tired of living like a dog in the shack she called a home. True it was something which was better than having nothing at all but why did life have to be so hard for her? Why couldn't she have been one of Balo Rajkumar's legitimate children?

Her life would have been much better then, she thought to herself. Sunita would never have turned up her nose at her then. She and Harry would be so much closer. He would have been able to help her with her troubles. She had never felt so alone in her entire life. All she had left in the world was Tommy and Eddy and now Tommy was almost gone. She had grown so detached from the many men who had thrust themselves inside her, that she felt like a tool; something inanimate and void of emotion, but functional, still functional. She had few friends if you could call them that. She had cursed away most of them or slept with their men and even in the Beetham was a much hated woman. It was Tommy's pleasant smile, and jovial personality that kept many who would do Lystra harm at bay.

Tommy brought light and laughter every where he went. He was a happy and kind hearted soul to all he met before the drugs. She missed his presence dearly. Seeing him roaming the streets of Port-of-Spain sometimes naked sometimes clothed, hearing reports about his nighttime conduct only added to her grief. She wished that wooden floor would open and swallow her up, mattress and all, or that somehow she would go to sleep and never awaken. "Good afternoon, anybody there?" A woman's voice called Lystra out of her abyss of despair. She turned over and wiped her wet cheeks dry, peeping through a hole in the galvanize wooden door she saw a pink floral skirt and hands holding what could only be a bible of some sort.

Ordinarily she would pretend not to be home but today was different. Even if she didn't plan on being saved, the company would be good. Plus she needed somebody to talk to. Whichever church it was, she just didn't want to be alone. She didn't have on a bra and her breasts hung long and loose in a red jersey that barely covered her massive behind but Lystra didn't care about what she was wearing. Nothing these people could say could make her feel worse than she was already feeling. Fumbling for her keys she opened the rust ridden lock which secured her few but valuable possessions and let the light shine into her dark windowless home.

"*Sugar bum sugar bum bum, sugar bum sugar bum bum.*" Papa Netty was singing at the top of his voice as he drew near to Ms. Janice's and Ma Thomas' stalls. "But ay-ay. Wha wrong to he dis evening boy!" Ma Thomas exclaimed arms akimbo. "Like he ketch a glad!" said Ms. Janice while she put some potatoes in a clear plastic bag for one of her customers. Things were slowing down and in a couple of hours it would be time to pack up. As the high spirited Papa Netty drew nearer, the smell of rum went before him in the vanguard. "*Janice whey yuh get dat sugar. Darling dere is nothing sweeter*" he crooned out the old Kitchener favorite and did a poor imitation of the grandmaster's on stage dancing. "Doh be calling my name loud here boy whappen to yuh," a visibly upset Ms. Janice scolded. The singing stopped. "Guess what ah bring fuh yuh darling," Papa Netty said with a sly smile on his face. "Trouble as always," Ms. Janice answered. Pulling a black plastic bag from behind his back, Papa Netty presented it with extended arm to Ms. Janice. "What de hell is dat yuh givin meh dere?"

"But ay-ay! So wha yuh trying to say. Ah cyah be bringin something…. Hiccup…. nice fuh my gyulfriend?" a sincere but drunk looking Papa Netty asked. "Boy gone from here wid yuh drunken self," Ma Thomas intervened. "Is Cascadoooo. De same Cascadoo ah promise to bring fuh yuh." Ms. Janice wasn't sure whether she should take it or not but she knew that if she didn't, Papa Netty would linger in front her stall and his arrival was always bad for business. Besides, he would probably be very hurt if she didn't take it. It looked like about four pounds of fish and Cascadura was an expensive fish if it was in fact Cascadura in the bag. She looked at a disapproving Ma Thomas and relieved Papa Netty with thanks of the bag of fish or whatever it was. She didn't really think it was fish anyway but even if it was she wasn't going to have any of it. "So nice to see dat beautiful smile," said Papa Netty with a twinkle in his eyes. Ms. Janice stopped smiling at once. She didn't even realize that she had been smiling.

"*Sugar bum sugar bum bum, sugar bum sugar bum bum…..* " Papa Netty's voice faded as he went on his way with his old dirt stained jeans falling off his tiny bottom. Ms. Janice lifted the plastic bag to her nose with a frown and then opened the tightly knotted bag. A host of the thumb sized slimy black looking fish greeted her. She smiled to herself. Ma Thomas was still amazed that Ms. Janice had accepted this gift from Papa Netty. "Hmmm. Ah hope yuh not going to cook dat. Suppose he put some kinda maljoe or spirits on it. Yuh doesn know sometimes yuh know," Ma Thomas warned. "Doh worry gyul. Ah have a neighbor who like dis kinda fish. Ah go give it to she," said Ms. Janice, putting her friend at ease right away.

"Ent dey have a ting dey does say about de Cascadura? Ah cyah remember what it is," Ma Thomas asked.

"Dose who eat the Cascadura will, something something something, wheresoever dey go will die in Trinidad and Tobago."

"Ah! Dat is de ting self." Ma Thomas said smiling.

"Well gyul if yuh want to end yuh days in Trinidad with Papa Netty yuh could eat some Cascadoo. Is tie he trying to tie yuh foot. Ah hope yuh know dat. Next ting he go sweat in some rice and bring it fuh yuh." The two laughed and fatty bellies heaved up and down as they guffawed at the thought of Papa Netty's attempts to woo. After the laughing had ceased a serious Ma Thomas warned, "In all seriousness though, ah hope yuh ent tinking bout eating dat fish."

"Yuh tink ah want to end my days ah what. Ah still young and strong yuh know. Ah have to see all meh chilren geh big," said Ms. Janice with arms akimbo. She hadn't laughed like that in a long time and it felt very very good.

Chapter Eight

Definitely Not A Laughing Matter

"Today we have two specially invited guests who are going to speak to us about the sanctity of marriage and the dangers of premarital sex," Sr. Monica declared. With back as straight and as stiff as an ironing board and head erect she surveyed the murmuring assembly from which some hardly audible giggles had just been heard. "This is not a laughing matter young ladies," she said sternly. Her nose turned red as the blood rushed to her face. There was complete silence in the auditorium as her beady brown eyes searched the gathering to see if anyone dared to laugh again. For a moment you could hear the breeze blowing through the auditorium door. Only the students from Forms Four through Six

101

had been scheduled to hear this talk by the Tildens'. A round of applause arose from the auditorium as the grey haired couple made their way to the podium.

"Oh my God. Imagine those two old fogies still having sex. Ugh that is so gross," whispered Cindy Sawh to the girl sitting next to her. "Couldn't Sr. Monica pick a better looking couple to come and give this talk?" Lisa asked under her breath. "I just don't understand why they have to be American. Yuh mean they couldn't find anybody in the whole of Trinidad? What do they know about being teenagers anyway? They probably aren't even strong enough to have sex." Jesse steupsed and Lisa giggled under her breath at that last comment.

Jesse loved history and was very well read for a girl of her age. She knew all about the failed attempt at federation in the Caribbean and had become especially disgusted with Trinidad politics more so after reading a recent article in the Trinidad Guardian on the legacy of colonialism. "We always need some foreigner to tell us what to do. As if we can't think for ourselves," she mumbled. Although Jesse had tried to get Lisa interested in politics, social thinking and history, Lisa preferred a lighter less complicated perspective on life in general. Unlike Jesse she was free-spirited, easy going and carefree. Being that way somehow helped Lisa to cope with the drama of Ted and Vonetta. At the end of the forty-five minute lecture, both girls were ready for lunch. The Tildens' were as boring as they had anticipated but their message had come through very clearly – 'Marital sex was the only safe sex'. Most of the students were just glad to be out of their hot classrooms for the last forty-five minutes and couldn't care less about what the Tildens' had to say.

Sr. Monica really didn't realize that about forty percent of the girls in her auditorium were already sexually active and another twenty five percent were working on becoming sexually active within a year or two. For the remaining thirty five percent the Tilden's message had found a welcome home. However the girls in Forms One to Three needed to hear the Tildens' lecture just as much as the older girls. To imagine that somehow they were all in a bubble of innocence at that age was to be unrealistic. As the girls, almost women filtered out of the auditorium under Sr. Monica's watchful eye, pleated blue skirts swaying on hips of every size and shape, Jesse wondered if she would have a boyfriend by the time her Sixth Form graduation party came around. Maybe she could go to her grad with Brian. He was so cute and in the last couple of weeks they had become friends. "Yeah right!" She thought to herself. Who was she kidding? Brian was the son of Matt Chow Fatt and that made him way out of her league.

It was not that Jesse couldn't have a boyfriend but her life just made it impossible. With four other siblings in the house, and a market vendor for a mother, it was hard to even find time for herself. If she wasn't helping Steve and Becca with their school work or ironing uniforms for school or getting them all to help out around the house, she was helping her mother in the kitchen or making tea or dinner or breakfast.

Her life revolved around her mother and her siblings and they depended heavily on Jesse to hold things together. It was as if they all knew that she would always be fine. She could never have a bad day, or a day when she was just too tired or too fed up with it all. Jesse was the invisible helper. In the family's hierarchy of needs, her needs didn't exist. The older she got the more invisible she became and the greater the demands placed on her time. Jesse never complained, she just wished that her mother believed in using birth control. Why would anyone want as many as five kids anyway? Jesse felt times were hard enough already and couldn't understand the logic behind her parents birth control or lack thereof.

"Poor Ma; always tired, always working hard and always worrying," she thought to herself. Jesse swore that when she got married she would be the one determining the size of her family. As far as premarital sex went, Jesse knew she could wait. She didn't think it would be that difficult. After all she hadn't had a boyfriend ever in life and she was almost eighteen. While some of her classmates had already crossed the threshold of intimacy with the opposite sex, Jesse had yet to discover what it felt like to be kissed by a guy. Although she and Brian Chow Fatt were friends and her chances never looked this good, Jesse was a realist. And reality determined that even though she really, really, really liked Brian a whole lot, she would have neither time, nor her mother's blessings if Brian indeed felt about her the way she felt about him.

It had been two days since the touching incident at choir practice and Sean Mathias was still in a daze. He had left immediately after practice that day embarrassed by the complete wetness of every square inch of his grey school shirt. Although his intention was to confront Alex Thornhill he didn't want to make a scene for the other fellas in choir to think that something was really going on between them. Alex enjoyed being dramatic and loud, challenging him after practice about the touch would have given him the opportunity for a 'Jerry Springer moment' and unless Sean was prepared for a fist fight which he was not, the outcome of such a shout out would only serve to feed the gossip machinery of the school. Sean had been agonizing since then about how to handle the situation. He really wanted to talk to Brian and Eddy about it but he knew they'd probably make a big joke out of it and tease him for weeks to come. This was not even the kind of conversation he could have with his father who was rarely seen at home.

Who could he talk to without being judged? Without being made to feel that he actually enjoyed the touch? "Did I really enjoy that?" Sean battled with the remote and frightening possibility that the answer to that question was yes. This bothered him infinitely more than the fact that an openly effeminate Alex had tried to fondle him. Am I really gay? If I am then how come I don't want to be with another guy? These questions began to turn like coo coo in the iron pot of his brain. Even if he was gay which he knew he was not, he still couldn't see himself with Alex. Since the touching it seemed that Alex was looking at his every move. He could feel Alex's eyes on him at the cafeteria, in the library, in the courtyard. Why was this man watching him so? He had to talk to somebody about it before he exploded. Nothing like this had ever happened to him before and in a pre-dominantly Christian society that viciously denounced homosexuality and the gay lifestyle, Sean had to be careful about who he spoke to and what he said.

At home that afternoon, Sean felt slightly depressed after going through his cell phone and realizing that there was no friend or cousin he could talk to that would truly understand his dilemma. He was still holding the cell phone in hand staring at it when it began to vibrate and ring making him jump. He didn't recognize the number but answered the call anyway. "Hello," there was no answer on the other end. "Hello" said Sean again impatiently. "I knew you liked it," the voice said. Sean froze. It was Alex. "How the hell did he get my number?" was Sean's first thought but his jaw was temporarily paralyzed and he could not speak. "Look, I'm sorry. I shouldn't have done it, not there anyway, thanks for not ratting me out in front of everybody." There was a long emotion filled silence. Sean didn't know what to say but then the words came. "No I didn't like it. I didn't like it. I didn't like it at all. You real lucky I didn't buss yuh face right there and then. I'm not like that. I'm not like you. I'm not a faggot. I'm not gay."

Sean was shouting into the phone which had become wet and slippery in his hands. Beads of perspiration ran down his face, back and neck, and Sean didn't realize it but his hands were shaking. "Look I'm sorry ok. I just thought we could be friends," said Alex. "Friends? Friends? Why would I want to be friends with a faggot like you!" Sean shouted back. Sean never really cursed but he felt sure that the occasion warranted a strong dose of foul language. "Just leave me the hell alone ok!" Sean hung up and collapsed on the soft peach carpet below his feet, which seemed to welcome his scrawny body. A twisted mass of confusion, Sean was shaking and sweating. He felt a surge of emotion move like a fist up his chest to his throat where it turned into a stifling knot. It was the kind of knot that swallowing or coughing could not remove; the kind that forced its way into expression. Unable to restrict it, Sean punched his fist several times into the carpet floor as he yielded to the turmoil within him.

Ever since those two purple lines had slapped her in the face with the truth about what was going on in her womb, Vonetta had not been able to sleep. She tried to continue her daily routine as if nothing was wrong but in reality she was scared. She wasn't as scared about Ted's response to the fact that she was pregnant as she was about how Lisa would respond. She didn't expect Ted's response to be that of an excited, expectant father. Even if he feigned jubilation, Vonetta would see it for what it really was, feigned. No, she wasn't expecting anything from Ted. How could she expect anything good from a man who had broken her arms, tried to strangle her with a rope, given her black eyes, black and blue legs, beat her with a garden shovel, rolling pin, pressure cooker, dustbin, piece of wood and anything else that could inflict the blows he had for her after a few strong drinks.

Ted was not her concern, in this matter, it was Lisa. She wondered whether Lisa would be disappointed in her; disappointed that she had got pregnant for a man other than Lisa's father. Although she had tried hard to be a good mother, Vonetta couldn't help but feel that she had failed her daughter and repeatedly so. This was not the life she and Nelson had planned when the eight pound four ounce baby was cut out of her after almost twenty-four long hours of labor. Nelson was so proud to be a daddy. He had named the girl Lisa after his grandmother and was determined that she would want for nothing. Nelson was a man with dreams, many dreams; but Trinidad was too small for his ambitions. The three hundred dollars a week he made as a carpenter in Smith's Carpentry Shop seemed a paltry compensation for the long hours, the bruised coarsened hands and the never ending back pains he endured.

His brother in Brooklyn made $600 US a week as a carpenter and had been encouraging him to get his visa and come up to Brooklyn, the refuge of many illegal immigrants from the Caribbean. Vonetta had begged him not to go, Lisa was only three, but Nelson had a fire in his eyes, a longing that no food or sex could satisfy. He wanted more for his life, for his family. When he got on the airplane in Piarco, Vonetta never envisioned that her relationship and her communication with her husband would eventually be reduced to a monthly trip to the Western Union office. All her little aspirations had disappeared with Nelson on that BWEE flight and were now lost somewhere in Brooklyn. Instead of going to America she was stuck with Ted and his Fernandes Vat 19 rum. She wasn't even sure why she was still with him. Perhaps it was just her need to have a man around her, but whatever it was, she could see that being with Ted had brought her no good at all. Vonetta was still uncertain about whether she would keep the child or not. What she was certain about though was that having a child that wasn't Nelson's meant abandoning any chance that her marriage could be salvaged.

Matt Chow Fatt stroked the long black hair of his mistress and ran his hand along her arm gently caressing her elbow. Her hair smelt like flowers and her warm soft body tasted sweet in his mouth. Priya was everything Sally was not; independent, vivacious, spontaneous, hard-working and honest. Lying next to her naked body, Matt had found an oasis of peace in her arms. Priya was his refuge from the demands of his stressful job but most of all she made him feel loved. Priya was real and her love felt real and new to Matt, like nothing he had ever felt before. In the last six months, Priya had become his drug. She made him feel young again. She had helped him to laugh again. But best of all she loved him, not his money or his name. She enjoyed doing the crossword puzzle with him, massaging his feet, she laughed at his corny jokes and his clumsiness.

Matt couldn't go a day without hearing Priya's voice and agonized on the nights they couldn't have their regular rendezvous. As he looked at the curve of her hips, he marveled at how beautiful she was. Her breasts were like soft feather pillows and her legs firm and supple. Matt had fallen in love and although he was not ready to leave Sally, he wasn't ready to give Priya up either. "What time do you have to get back to work?" asked Matt. "Now, right now. I shouldn't even have come home for lunch." Priya sat up in her bed and looked down at Matt lovingly with almond colored eyes. "I just had to see you," she said with a sigh. She tucked her hair behind her ears and slid from beneath her bed sheets. Standing erect she looked even more beautiful than she had the first time he saw her. After spending time with Priya it was hard to go home to Sally. Matt admired the fact that Priya worked and had become successful in a man's world where decisions were made not only in the boardroom but at the golf course and over cocktails.

At twenty-seven Priya had been with other men before Matt and women too. Some of them had even been her bosses. She had worked hard on her feet and on her back to be able to afford the mortgage for her home at The Mews in Cascade. Say what you may, Priya had raw, unbridled ambition that would stop at nothing to accomplish her goals. It was this shameless ambition that had hastened her meteoric ascent up the corporate ladder. Matt opened his eyes and stared up at the ceiling fan above. How he longed to just stay there around the smell of sandalwood and perfume. Priya's smell was so intoxicating, he just couldn't get enough. "Are you going to join me Jack Rabbit or are you going to just lie there all salty and sweaty. Don't you have to get back to work or something?" Priya shouted from the shower.

Matt sat up straight in bed dreading all the unfinished work he had left behind at the office. He had to return to work yes but that was not as painful as going home to feather-brain Sally who would prattle for hours about her daily gallivantings, oblivious to the stresses he had faced for the day. "You didn't think I'd let you shower alone now did you." Matt had quickly slipped into the shower beside Priya and was whispering sweet nothings in her ear. Priya laughed and her laughter was the sweetest music Matt had ever heard. As he allowed the warm cascading water to wash away the smell of sex, Matt couldn't help but feel an inner heaviness. Tomorrow was Friday and the weekend would bring with it a whole host of social events which he hated but could ill-afford to miss.

These events would have been so much more bearable if Priya was coming along with him. Matt knew his weekends would be like this for a while, at least until after Carnival. Then there would be a nice long pause and perhaps he could go on a real vacation. He was thinking of going to Bequia for a weekend with Priya. Then in August perhaps he could take the family to Miami. Sally loved Miami, especially for the shopping. Matt loved to go for the trade shows though. He prided himself on keeping en courant with the latest in technology, business and management ideas.

Until Bequia though he would have to settle for late nights, lunch time rendezvous' and the rare business lunch with Priya. He had it all figured out in his head. He never thought he could be so duplicitous but in his mind he felt justified. With a wife like Sally, cheating was sure to happen eventually. He had given her the happiness she wanted; the cars, the diamonds, the trips to France, Spain, Morocco, and everything that money could buy. Now it was his turn to be happy he thought. He had been way too miserable for much too long. With Priya he had known true love and he was never going to give it up as long as he could help it.

It was afternoon time and Jesse was desperately looking forward to classes with Mr. Lee Wen. It was the one time during the week when she had an opportunity to see Brian face to face and nothing was more pleasurable than that. She had never felt this way before. All her daydreams were of Brian. She'd wake up thinking about him in the morning, wondering what his morning routine was like and she'd go to bed at night imagining him sitting behind a desk in his bedroom studying. Seeing Brian once a week made Jesse feel like a stick of butter melting in the midday heat. After each encounter her feelings for him grew stronger and stronger. Although she kept trying to remind herself that nothing of significance would most likely come of her relationship with him, she couldn't help but pray and hope that perhaps she was wrong and that through some miraculous intervention she could end up spending the rest of her life with this boy.

"Hurry up Lisa!" Jesse always seemed to be having to hurry Lisa up. On a day like today when time was essential, Lisa was moving extraordinarily slow and Jesse was getting impatient. "I have to get that Hallmark card and some other things," said Jesse excitedly. During her phone conversations with Brian, Jesse had shared a great deal about herself and her ambitions. She had told Brian about Mr. GG, her mom, about her siblings and about how she always felt that she had to be responsible because she was the eldest. Brian in turn had told her about his parents, their apparently loveless marriage, his ex-girlfriend and how hard it had been to balance being the Head Prefect with his school work. Jesse identified with all his anxieties. Sharing her heartfelt thoughts with him, made her feel closer to him than she had ever felt to anyone outside of Mr. GG. Talking to Brian was like talking to her Pa except that Jesse was seriously attracted to Brian and wanted to do things with him that she would never consider doing with Pa.

She wanted to buy a card for Brian to let him know that she considered him a dear friend and that she would always be there for him. She knew it was kind of forward but after discussing it with Lisa she was certain that the card would be well received. She was right. Actually Brian was experiencing emotions similar to Jesse's. After each telephone conversation with her, he felt a calm and peace descending upon him that he had never felt before, not even with Amy. He wanted to let Jesse know how he felt about her. He wanted her to be his girlfriend. He was just waiting for the right opportunity to broach the subject.

As for Eddy, he had been smitten with desire for Lisa. The tall chocolate skinned girl with the flawless complexion had him mesmerized. Eddy had been able to keep a running conversation going with Lisa and Jesse every Thursday when he walked with them from Oxford Street to City Gate, but he had not yet mustered up the courage to ask Lisa for her phone number. Part of the reason he hadn't bothered to get her phone number yet was because there was no telephone at his home on the Beetham. There were payphones aplenty on the Brian Lara promenade that he could call Lisa from but what if she wanted to call him back. Calling her might be the beginning of something. Discovering that he had no phone at all might make her see him differently. So after much deliberation, Eddy decided that he needed a cell phone before he could ask Lisa for her phone number. He was devising a plan to get one as well; he just had to tap into the right resources.

At the "House of Pain" Krishna Rajkumar had somehow struck up a friendship with Eddy and was in hot pursuit of the lovely Cindy Sawh. Krishna, Eddy and Ravi had discussed Krishna's chances of getting with Cindy in many of the ten minute intervals between classes. Eddy and Ravi had both agreed that on a scale of one to ten, his chances were at the level of a minus five but Krishna was undaunted. He was much more attracted to Cindy than he was to Jesse. Jesse was easy on the eyes for him, but Cindy was just super hot. Her continued annoyance at his attempts to make conversation with her, coupled with her refusal to acknowledge his existence, only made her more attractive to him. Krishna had his grandfather's boldness and charm when it came to women. Despite Eddy and Ravi's perception of his chances, Krishna was confident that if he stayed in the trenches long enough he would eventually be able to wear Cindy down. Eddy liked Krishna as a friend. He found his approach to everything entertaining and funny. Krishna had a good sense of humor and Eddy enjoyed listening to his incessant babble.

Though the poverty of his life could have made him bitter, Eddy tried to focus instead on the many things in life that he had to be thankful for. Growing up on the Beetham had opened his eyes to many things. Watching the scavengers heading off to the dump every morning reminded him constantly of what he could become if he made just a few wrong choices. Then there was his uncle Tommy. He had not seen him on the streets of Port-of-Spain and hoped never to see him either. Eddy had heard the disappointing news that Tommy was now 'taking wood'. Although a part of him longed to see his uncle, he preferred to retain images of him heading off to work or shooting hoops on the basketball court.

From what his mother had told him, Tommy had become less than human and Eddy did not wish to remember his uncle that way. Although sometimes Eddy would become jealous of Brian and Sean and the things they were able to afford, he never hated them. He knew that the lifestyle they were able to enjoy was as a direct consequence of the intelligent choices their parents had made. Even if they had been born into the lap of luxury, Eddy knew that somebody had to put in the hard work at some point in order for his friends to have the kind of wealth they had. Perhaps if his mother had made better choices, he wouldn't have been growing up on the Beetham. Perhaps she was just a victim of unfortunate circumstances. Either way, Eddy sincerely believed that by surrounding himself with friends who had ambitions he could identify with, he would be constantly steered in the right direction and avoid becoming another Beetham statistic.

If there was one person determined to escape the Beetham life it was Eddy. He pushed himself to behave in a way that belied his external environment and daily he adopted mannerisms which would help him better fit in with Brian and Sean and other students of a similar ilk. He might not have been fortunate enough to have the kind of comforts Brian and Sean did, but he would be damned if any child of his had to suffer the stench of that rubbish filled drain and the shame of being from a place like the Beetham.

Down at Tamarind Square a much leaner Tommy sat on the feces caked grass and combed through a black garbage bag he had managed to remove from one of the city dustbins. KFC cups, plastic wrappers and tin cans flew to both left and right of Tommy as he emptied the bag's contents in search of food. Tommy was very hungry. He had not eaten for almost two days and although his stomach had become accustomed to its irregular portions of scraps and cold left overs, it was not yet used to two full days of nothing pies and wind chops. Although Tommy had been working hard and getting paid, it seemed that all his money was disappearing into the willing hands of Bullerboy who not only managed Tommy's clientele but supplied Tommy with drugs whenever he could. Tommy was not as clever as Bullerboy.

A few weeks ago, one of Tommy's clients had paid him five dollars short. Since then, Bullerboy had decided to do the cash collection for all Tommy's clients insisting that clients pay up front. Tommy had willingly 'signed' his soul and body over to Bullerboy who was now responsible for supplying Tommy with food, drugs and the occasional cardboard box. Not much more was needed on the streets of Port-of-Spain to survive. Tommy had become "beh-beh" and had undergone a series of mental and physical deteriorations far greater than anything Bullerboy had every experienced. Although Bullerboy's appearance was only a slight improvement by comparison to Tommy's, his mental faculties had not been too terribly dullened by the drugs. He still knew how to count money and he understood that without Tommy's cooperation his very survival was in danger. Tommy was too far gone to understand the dynamics of what was playing out with his friend Bullerboy. Somewhere between Jesus on the motorbike, the voices inside and outside his head and the smell of stinkness emanating from his body, Tommy had found a window of insanity where he could feel at home in himself. Through that window he could look down at himself on Tamarind Square without understanding, judgment, or shame. He was just Tommy trying to get by; trying to deal with the harsh realities that life had thrown his way, trying to get a fix from Bullerboy and most of all trying to stay alive.

Staying alive was no small feat for a man, woman or child living on the streets of Port-of-Spain. There were predators lurking everywhere in broad daylight and in the dark corners of every car park, street and Square. Tommy was a walking target, although he really didn't know it. Bullerboy could offer him no protection and had already been badly beaten and brutalized on more than one occasion. Tommy had been fortunate though. Outside of the one time buss head he had received for not sharing his Bayrum and the occasional spitting upon, he had managed to escape the hands of violent men.

It was around six o'clock now and a tired Ms. Janice was making her way through the back roads on her way to Santa Cruz. Since finding out that she needed to get Ole Jane inspected she had been careful to avoid all major roads on her way to and from the market. She reached in the dashboard for a little green wash rag and wiped the sweat from her tired face. She was contemplating what she would cook for those hungry mouths when she got home. Jesse had lessons today, so she knew that Becca and the gang led by Steve would probably be up to some mischief as usual. She had not made much money at the market for the day, just about one hundred dollars. That was not even enough to take care of Jesse's extra lessons, not to mention the electricity bill which had been due a few days ago. She had to take care of T & TEC first; Mr. Lee Wen would just have to wait for his fees. As for car inspection, she would definitely have to leave that for at least another month or two. A mechanic down in the Croiseé had told her that she would have to spend a minimum of a thousand dollars in order to get the car ready for inspection. Inspection alone cost about one hundred and sixty dollars. She needed a new rear light, a new windshield wiper and her back right indicator light was broken too.

Ms. Janice suspected that she was being overcharged for all this work on the car but what was she to do. A widow with no man by her side, she was ripe for being robbed by tradesmen who were always on the look out for women who fit her profile. "Screeeeech" the sound of her squeaking brakes jolted Ms. Janice in her seat and brought her car to a sudden halt. The car in front of her had stopped suddenly for no reason it seemed. In a few moments the reason became clear, as two burly looking men, clad in starch ironed grey shirts and dark pants approached the vehicle in front of her. She felt an instant pain in her gut as panic ensued. She had to do something quickly. She put her car in reverse, backed up a few inches and turned out of the lane in the hope that the police officers were so focused on the poor fellow in front of her who seemed to be digging everywhere for his insurance, that they would not see her. But as if they had read her thoughts, the female officer a few feet off, pointed straight at her and signaled for her to pull to the side. In a few moments she knew that she would hear the words she had been dreading for weeks. "Madam can I see your license and insurance please."

Chapter Nine

Stymied Plans

The solid oak door slammed shut as Matt came grunting through the doorway. He wasn't grunting for any particular reason. It was just his way of saying he was home and wasn't the least bit happy about it. In fact there hadn't been any "Honey I'm home" sounds coming from him in quite some time. The aroma of curried beef had engulfed the living room. Sally was in the kitchen making dinner, a rare occasion for a woman who enjoyed having other people do things for her. Rosita her live-out housekeeper had been sent home early for the afternoon so that she could lay her snare for Matt. The food smelt good enough to force Matt to make a detour from his beeline to the bathroom so he could get a taste. "Hi darling. I got in early and decided to fix you one of your favorites," said Sally who looked odd to Matt with apron on and cooking gloves in hand standing over the stove. She quickly grabbed a plate from the dish drainer and poured a spoonful of steamy hot curried beef on it. "Would you like to have some?" She turned to offer Matt a taste with the best homemaker smile she had. Matt was speechless and for a brief moment was overcome with a sense of guilt from the knowledge that he had just left Priya's apartment.

"That's lovely dear. I forgot how good a curry you could make. I'll have some as soon as I grab a shower," said Matt who gave Sally a gentle touch on her buttocks. Sally couldn't stop smiling. Everything was going according to plan and she felt even more encouraged by Matt's response. Over dinner she would surprise him with the tickets for Tobago. She had spent all afternoon rehearsing what she would say. Everything had to be just perfect. The curried beef she had purchased from the Hott Shoppe in St. James was well worth it. She had emptied the beef into an iron pot and carefully kept it simmering till she heard the sound of the electronic gate. When Matt came out of the shower, she would set the mood and maybe, just maybe, if she used the right words, they would be on a plane in the morning heading off to Tobago. Sally was so excited that her palms were sweating. She had spent a lot of money at Gina's making herself look fabulous today. Gina had convinced her to try a different hair color called Crimson Rose. If things went well tonight with Matt she was definitely going to give Gina an extra tip on her next visit.

If Sally hadn't so ostracized herself from her siblings, she would have had a sister's ear to turn to and advice from someone that really cared. Sally had not only burnt that bridge but had earned the hatred of her in-laws as well, who could only tolerate her reluctantly at formal gatherings. They had seen through her wiles and her lies and were determined to keep her at arms length. So they fed her pleasantries with a long handled golden spoon, never drawing her into the circle of trust and never allowing her to fully become a part of the Chow Fatt family. Sally knew it but she didn't care as long as she had Matt's love, affection, and money.

As she laid the table and brought out the rose scented dinner candles she had purchased for the occasion, she felt grateful that Brian had not spoilt the night by staying at home. He and Eddy were going to Movie Towne with some girls to catch a movie. She knew that one of them was a girl that Brian liked but she didn't think too much of it. If there was one thing Sally felt she had done right in her marriage it was having Brian. And it wasn't just giving birth to him but imparting to him all the values, grooming, culture and etiquette that would allow him to fit into the world she had not been born into. This girl, whoever she was, couldn't have had a greater hold on his heart than Amy had and Sally felt certain that after Amy, Brian had come to appreciate the fact that he was of royal stock and could not be offering long term hope of a relationship to commoners. Besides, Sally had bigger more pressing concerns and didn't have time to micromanage her son's relationships especially at a time when her marriage seemed to be falling apart.

Matt let the warm jet of water beat heavily down on his skin. As he closed his eyes and soaked in the watery massage of his body, he couldn't help but wonder what the hell Sally was up to. Did she know about Priya? She couldn't have. Trinidad society was small but unless Priya's neighbors knew Sally or someone she knew, Matt doubted that Sally would ever find out. Sally's only real friend was Marlene. All the rest were of the cocktail party kind and Sally didn't trust them any. What if someone who lived near to Priya told Marlene and Marlene told Sally? That was a vague possibility; and the more Matt began to reflect on that possibility the more anxious he became. Sally wouldn't believe it he thought; even if the information was coming from someone as trusted as Marlene. If she did believe it though, Matt wasn't quite sure he knew what his wife's response would be. Either way he was getting ready to face whatever version of Sally was awaiting him in the dining room. He knew what was troubling her; he just couldn't find it in him to make love to her anymore. He knew that if he did, it would help to calm her anxieties but it would do nothing to help his feelings for her. Maybe she was trying to get pregnant. It wouldn't have been the first time she had tried. By the time Matt emerged fully dressed from the bedroom he had decided that he was going to play it cool and see where Sally was going with this cooked meal.

The outing at Movie Towne had been long in the planning for Brian and Eddy. Brian had considered it a combination of fortune and fate that he and his best friend had the "hots" for two girls that were also best friends. As he waited outside the entrance with Eddy he was full of anticipation. It was almost six o'clock though and he was wondering if the girls had difficulty getting transportation. He had offered to pick them up but instead they opted to meet him and Eddy at Movie Towne and take a ride home since it would be night time by the time they left. Although Brian had his own car, a royal blue Honda CRV, he never used it on the days he had extra lessons which was twice a week. His mother was of the opinion that since those days were longer for him, he should have the benefit of being chauffeured. But it was more than that; Sally liked the notion of her son having a chauffer. If it weren't for Matt insisting that it was a "damn waste of money" there would have been work for three chauffeurs; one for each of the Chow Fatts. His mother had been rambling on before he left the house about Amy and about having class and some other things but Brian let it all fly over his head. Jesse was on his mind and a Movie Towne double date he thought would give all four friends a chance to hang out in a setting other than Mr. Lee Wen's classes where there seemed to never be enough time.

Movie Towne was the playground for children of the rich and elite. It was difficult not to notice that most of the people walking around were of a paler hue than Lisa. BMWs, Rovers, shiny Nissan Almeras, and glistening vehicles of the most expensive kind, drove through the car park and dropped off teens or collected them. For some Movie Towne was a family outing but there was no mistaking that the regular Movie Towne clientele had to have come from some financial muscle. Of course you had those who really couldn't afford the $30 tickets but were going anyway for various reasons. Whether it was to impress a date or just to be able to say "I went to Movie Towne," the American styled cineplex was abuzz with activity. One patron could spend as much as $50 in going to see one movie - $30 for the ticket, $10 on popcorn, $5 on a drink, and $5 on a hotdog if the popcorn ran out and hunger was still lingering at the doorway. It was not just the cineplex part of the Movie Towne mall that was prohibitive in its prices; most of the other stores had two or three and in some cases even four hundred percent markups on goods that could be bought on Charlotte Street for a quarter of the price.

"Look them over there," said Jesse excitedly as she smoothed her hair back. "Try not to look so nervous nah gyul. Just calm yuhself down and keep it together," Lisa muttered under her breath. Lisa was turning many heads in her tight fitting low rider jeans and halter back baby pink top, which revealed a taut washboard abdomen. She had let her hair out and had used a tremendous amount of gel in order to make it more manageable and less like the bushel she was used to taming into a bun. "Let go of my hand Jesse and just relax. They'll think we are gay," Lisa whispered. Lisa was strutting confidently with a more timid looking Jesse beside her.

Jesse had dressed much more conservatively than Lisa had. Ms. Janice wouldn't let her leave the house in anything that exposed any part of her body that might entice a man; so Jesse had to settle for a pair of almost tight blue jeans and a red short sleeved not so close fitting t-shirt. She would have liked to let her hair out but she didn't have enough gel to get a grip on it. Unaccustomed to manipulating her hair outside of a bun or a plait, Jesse had tried to style her hair differently. However, after mounds of water, gel and anti-frizz spray, she seemed unable to obtain the look she wanted and settled in the end for the tried and true plait.

It hadn't been that difficult for Lisa to get permission from Vonetta to go to the movies. After breaking the news of her pregnancy to Lisa and seeing the look on her face, Vonetta would have given that girl anything she wanted. It wasn't a look of disappointment or even shock but a combination of the two emotions mixed in with that of complete disgust. Vonetta knew it would be a while before Lisa would come around. She was almost relieved when Lisa said she wanted to go to the movies. "Yuh should lime some more gyul. When I was your age ah was in everything," said Vonetta in an effort to lighten the tension that had created a deafening silence between her and her only child. It was hard though. Lisa only had vague recollections of her father and always wondered whether he had left because of her or because of Vonetta. Did he beat up her mother the way Ted did? Or was somebody cheating? Her mother maybe? Her mother was cheating now and she was still collecting the money he was sending from America.

Lisa wondered what her father would think if he knew that the money he was sending for his long lost wife was supporting her unemployed abusive boyfriend. At the end of the day after Lisa had churned the fact and fiction around in her head, she came to the conclusion that Vonetta was the reason her dad had left and never come back. Now that Vonetta was pregnant there was no chance Ted would ever come back. Something died inside of Lisa when she heard the dreadful news of her mother's pregnancy. There was no chance she would ever have the kind of life she had dreamed of with two normal parents and a backyard. Instead she was stuck and now more permanently so. She knew that education was the only way she could escape the hell hole of her life in Curepe. It was a hell hole she was determined to escape from.

Lisa wanted to never have to depend on a man to provide anything for her. She had seen the way her mother had needed her Dad and Ted at the same time, not being able to survive without either of them. Lisa was going to be her own woman. If and when she got married she was going to do it for love, not for financial stability. "Aye, whaz de scene," said Eddy with a smile. "Hi. Were you all waiting long?" Lisa asked. "We just got here about five minutes ago," said Brian. Jesse couldn't believe how good Brian looked and smelt out of his uniform. "Like allyuh plan to wear the same colors ah what?" Lisa joked. Jesse and Brian were both wearing red t-shirts. "Well you know what they say about great minds thinking alike," Brian winked at Jesse who blushed unreservedly from underneath her light make-up. "You all look really nice. I now see why dere was dat traffic jam on Wrightson Road eh Bri," Eddy joked.

He was taking them in, especially Lisa. She looked real good to him and fortunately for him he had secured himself a cell phone just in time for the occasion. It had required some piper-money but luckily he knew just the right piper and was able to get a fairly new cell phone for only $30. He didn't need to know who the original owner was. More than likely it was stolen but Eddy didn't care. It was not often that he had to resort to the resourcefulness of a piper but desperate times called for desperate measures and Eddy was not about to let an opportunity to really connect with Lisa pass him by. He wasn't too sure where he was going to find the money to keep buying the prepaid phone cards but he figured he would cross that bridge when he got there.

Jesse had barely said a word. She had just smiled and laughed when Brian had mentioned about great minds thinking alike. It was so unlike her to be so quiet but she was nervous. Every time Brian looked at her she felt a sudden warmth inside. She couldn't believe she was actually on a double date with Brian. Thank God for Lisa, because she knew there was no way under the sunshine that her mom was going to let her go out alone with Brian. "Well let's get some popcorn and things to eat before the movie starts," suggested Brian. "No probs," Lisa replied. As the four headed toward the cafeteria, Lisa whispered into Jesse's ear "Cat got yuh tongue girl? Yuh better open yuh mouth and say something quick or else yuh going to ruin all of yuh chances."

"So tell me how was your day?" asked an eager Sally as she lay the hot curried beef and serving spoons in the centre of the table together with the paratha roti. "Oh fine" Matt mumbled. He was not a man of too many words and usually left his work at the job. It wasn't that he hadn't tried to discuss business matters with Sally in the past but they usually went over her head anyway. In the end Matt figured it would be better to leave the complexities of the office in the office. Besides, asking Sally how her day went would be a whole lot easier than answering the question himself. "Oh my day was very hectic. I went over to Gina's and she put in this lovely color and then I….." Matt zoned out as his wife continued talking.

While Sally babbled on about her day, he savored the curried beef and paratha with the same intensity that he had savored the taste of Priya. Most of what Sally was saying sounded like what he heard before except for the part about the tickets to Tobago! "What the hell were you thinking woman!" Matt was furious and Sally was clueless as to why he would be. "Didn't it occur to you that I might have plans?"

"Yes but it's been so long since we…."

"Since we what! Since we what!" shouted Matt

"Since we spent time together. Since you touched me."

Sally was almost crying. Matt didn't know what to say. He knew what she meant about spending time together and he knew she was speaking the truth but how could he tell her that he couldn't bring himself to make love to her anymore. How could he tell her, that even though he loved her, and he did, that she didn't make him feel the way Priya did. How could he say that after all these years he had finally realized that their marriage was nothing but a lie? Her tears did not move him in the least. He was used to all the tantrum throwing and the crying and the making him feel guilty and he was sick of it.

"Is that why you want us to go to Tobago. So that I can f—k you. We don't have to go to Tobago for me to do that." A shocked Sally stared back at him for a few seconds before turning her reddened face toward the sink and getting up from the dining table. "I don't understand you Sally. What do you want from me? What the hell do you want from me?"

Matt pushed his chair back, stood up, and slammed his napkin down. "Look I can't go to Tobago this weekend. I have functions and I have business to take care of. You've wasted money again on foolishness." Sally felt her hurt surging like a wave in her body. "Are you seeing somebody?" Sally's tone had changed. She was not going to roll over and play dead this time. Matt felt a sudden lump in his throat. "Answer me Goddamn it. You think I don't know! You think I'm a fool! What! You want me to believe your balls are turning blue all this time. Who is she! Tell me who she is. At least let me know who is ruining my marriage."

Matt stood silent head down with hands on his waist. "What is she prettier than me? Does she give you a rush? Don't just stand there. Say something. I deserve to know!" screamed Sally through tears. Her face was flushed and her brown eyes full. "Answer me! Why are you ruining our marriage?"

Matt looked right at the frail woman that stood before him. Her crimson red hair shone in the rays of the evening sunlight coming through the dining room window. "Our marriage was ruined a long time ago Sally. A long time ago." Matt walked slowly to the bedroom. It was still early but he needed a few shots of rum and coke and he knew one twenty-four hour rum shop in St. James that could meet that need. After Sally watched the BMW pull out of the driveway she collapsed like a crumpled napkin on the grey and white marble tiled kitchen floor. Matt was cheating on her for God knows how long. For a brief moment Sally dared to accept what she had feared for months; that her marriage was truly over. Now it was simply a matter of figuring out whether she and Matt were headed for divorce or ten more years of maintaining the charade of a happy family.

While her daughter socialized at Movie Town an anxious Ms. Janice prepared dinner. It wasn't anything fancy just some ochro and rice with pig tail. The children loved that. As the smell of the food wafted through the air, she couldn't help but wonder what Jesse was doing. She had reluctantly allowed her to go to Movie Towne with Lisa as a chaperone but she had no good feeling about Brian Chow Fatt. A few days ago she had spoken seriously to Jesse about all this telephone love that was going on. She had tried to explain to Jesse that at the end of the day she would always be that country girl from Santa Cruz. "Yuh doh understan how dese rich people does tink Jess. Yuh will never be good enough for dey son. Even if yuh geh a scholarship, yuh still wouldn be good enough, even if yuh make ah doctor or ah lawyer or something like dat, yuh will never be good enough, because yuh not in dey class." Ms. Janice had held Jesse's face in her hands while she was telling her this. "Brian is not like that Ma. He's different. And even so is not like we getting married or anything like that. We are just friends." Jesse had tried to convince her. Ms. Janice knew better. She had been young once. She knew what the look in Jesse's eye meant.

"One day when yuh graduate from university and find a career an mek yuh way in de world, ah hope yuh meet a nice fella, a good fella; one who go love yuh wit he whole heart de way Mr. GG love me, but Brian Chow Fatt is not de one fuh yuh an ah hope you will see dat sooner rather dan later." Jesse had begged to differ. Ms. Janice knew she was giving Jesse some leeway by letting her go to Movie Towne so close to end of term exams but since Mr. GG's death, Jesse hadn't really had much time to socialize with her friend Lisa and her mother knew that. Now all of a sudden this Brian person was becoming the centre of her universe and Ms. Janice was sure that there could be no happy ending to this love story.

After the pot of ochro and rice had been emptied she retreated to the hammock under the ole Julie mango tree. She liked to lie there sometimes and collect her thoughts. There was a lot on Ms. Janice's mind. For starters she had to pay a police ticket of five hundred dollars. No amount of begging had helped her the night when the police officer had stopped her. Her insurance and driver's permit were expired in addition to the fact that she was missing that all too critical inspection sticker. "Please officer ah have five children waitin on meh home. Ah cyah afford no ticket. Ah will get de inspection an everyting, jus gimme a chance nah please," she had begged. The iron faced officer was unmoved by her tears as his pen moved swiftly across his ticket book. "Madam yuh lucky. Ah shoulda be givin yuh three tickets instead ah one so yuh real lucky is me dat ketch yuh and not some udder police." Ms. Janice would have liked to have money to bribe the officer with but she figured that if she had money in the first place she wouldn't be moving around with all these expired documents.

Poverty was indeed a curse and it seemed to her that the less you had the more you suffered. Poor people were always suffering. It was not that she hated the rich but it just seemed that even those who had no regard for God Almighty led fairy tale lives of comfort. She on the other hand was left to figure out where she was getting the money to pay for her ticket, her car inspection, Jesse's extra lessons and the electricity bill. Not to mention the telephone bill which she knew might be a little higher than usual. She was sure Brian Chow Fatt's mother didn't have this kind of stress.

Ms. Janice wanted to explain all these things to Jesse. She wanted to tell her that the world would not bow at her feet now that she was the friend of someone who had been born with a silver spoon in his mouth, but she knew Jesse wouldn't understand. Swinging slowly in the hammock underneath the mango tree Ms. Janice could see the red and orange flames of a brilliant sunset as the sun bid farewell and marked the close of yet another day. She imagined Mr. GG somewhere in that sunset and happy. She needed his help and his advice now more than ever; especially with Jesse. She had great plans for her first born and was afraid that they would be stymied by this Brian Chow Fatt boy.

The movie had started and the four friends were enjoying the recliner seats, oversized popcorn and oversized drinks. As expected, Jesse sat next to Brian and Lisa sat next to Eddy. Brian had paid for all the food. It was pocket change for him. Somewhere in between the popcorn and the movie Brian reached for Jesse's hand and held it. In that instant Jesse felt a range of emotions she had never felt before. Brian Chow Fatt was holding her hand. That must mean something. Later when she and Lisa were analyzing and interpreting every word, smile and facial expression of the date, she would remember those feelings and know deep within that she was undoubtedly in love.

Outside of the cineplex in the Movie Towne car park some of Cut Outta's men had been discretely observing the whole interaction between the friends. They had planned to snatch Brian the following week after extra lessons. They had already determined he was most vulnerable after Mr. Lee Wen's classes but were doing some additional monitoring just to ensure they knew who his associates were. They didn't want any surprises on Thursday. Brian was to be snatched and taken to a secret location in Central. Nobody would be looking for him there. A hole had been dug in a remote cane field and covered with brown tarpaulin and burnt cane. He was to be held there until the three million dollar ransom money was paid.

Cut Outta was sure it would be paid too. He had seen the kind of care and attention Brian was receiving. They had scoped out his residence and knew the average hour that both his parents returned home. Their connection in the police service had confirmed that Matt Chow Fatt was indeed licensed to carry a firearm but unless he was coming to pick up Brian next Thursday which was hardly likely, he posed no threat. As long as Brian's friends didn't try to do anything stupid, the kidnapping was expected to be successful. In fact Cut Outta already had plans on how he was going to spend the one million he was going to make after everyone had been paid off. Some of it was going to be put back into the community; the rest would be reinvested in Cut Outta's 'business' ventures.

Although Cut Outta didn't think they needed a whole lot of firearms for the operation, Bellies had advised against being too lightly armed. The police were sure to be on the lookout for such a high profile kidnap victim but if things went smoothly, by Sunday the Chow Fatt's would have their son back. This was not Cut Outta's first kidnap attempt. In fact it was his second. The first had failed when one of the men keeping watch over the victim, a ten year old girl, felt sorry for her and let her go. The unfortunate man was a fella called Stingray from Sea lots whose decomposing body was found floating in the water near the Port Authority a few days later. This time Cut Outta knew it would be different. He had carefully chosen his men and was satisfied that they were not "mama men", "panty men" or boys. Cut Outta knew what it was like to be behind bars and he wasn't ready to refamiliarise himself with the luxuries of Golden Grove.

Down at Tamarind Square, Tommy had become so cachectic from lack of food that he was literally wasting away. Even though he looked so poorly, he was still receiving clients who handed over the money to Bullerboy and had their way with Tommy. It wouldn't be too long before Tommy crashed. Bullerboy could see it and was trying to suck the last bit of life out of him before he was no longer of use. He was also attempting to make recruits out of the newer entrants to Tamarind Square. There were always new entrants to Tamarind Square; some stayed a few days and moved up to Woodford Square or other haunts while others stayed on and tried to find their own pee soaked corner of grass. Each one of them had a story to tell, whether they were sane enough to relate it or not.

Being so close to the St. Vincent De Paul Society centre, meant that those Tamarind Square residents who wanted to be clean or have breakfast could get such luxuries for free. But for those who were not sane enough to know when it was time to bathe, or those who were hooked on the white rock, it made no difference. Tommy formed part of the latter group and was not sane enough to know it. It was highly likely that he was HIV positive. The rumor on the street was that he had HELP. His skin was covered with sores and eczemas and between them was a fine rash which caused him to itch uncontrollably. This itching helped only to worsen the condition of the sores so that Tommy smelt and looked like a piece of rotting meat which had been left for too long in a very hot place. It was the kind of smell that made people turn their heads, faces and noses to avoid it.

As hard as it was to imagine, there were still respectable men with jobs that got some excitement out of having an orgasm inside a man like Tommy. Tommy somehow sensed that his demise was forthcoming. Everything had become a huge blur to him. He would have liked to see Eddy though and Lystra too. Seeing them as painful as it would be, would help him to release his spirit. Then there was Eddy; how he had loved that boy. Eddy was like a brother and a son to him at the same time. Tommy knew he had let him down in so many ways but if he could see him one last time then maybe, just maybe, he could say something to ensure that he didn't end up taking a similar road - the road that Cut Outta and his men never warned about when they offered him his first 'pull' for free. Yes the road to hell had been paved with seemingly good intentions and a series of bad decisions. Tommy had arrived in his own hell and nobody was about to save him from it.

Chapter Ten

Fire On The Beetham

It was Monday morning and although Lisa and Jesse were standing sweaty backed in the late line, they couldn't stop whispering. Jesse had been kissed and neither she nor Lisa could get over it. Although Jesse had gone over every tiny detail a thousand times with Lisa, she couldn't stop talking about it. Brian had asked her to "go around" with him. In other words he wanted her to be his girlfriend. She didn't need to think about her response. It was like a dream come true. In fact she was more worried about her wardrobe or lack thereof than she was about whether being his girlfriend was a good idea or not. The drive home had been a long beautiful conversation about life, school, career plans, children, marriage and Jesse had enjoyed every sweet minute of it. Brian had never driven to

Santa Cruz before so Jesse pointed the way out to him and gave him a little information about the entire area and the lifestyle of the San Antoñio residents. She was a bit embarrassed when he pulled up in front the quaint looking one story wooden house she called home, but Brian didn't seem to mind.

"Were you expecting something bigger?" Jesse asked

"Not really. I can't say I was expecting any particular thing. I just wish it was further away so that we could keep talking."

Jesse melted. She didn't know what to say but she knew that somewhere behind the living room curtains beady eyes were peering through, trying to figure out what was going on behind the heavily tinted windows of the vehicle. If she lingered too long, she was sure she would see the porch light come on and eventually her mother would emerge. "I had a really nice time tonight Brian. I really liked liming with you guys. You all are really…." Jesse couldn't finish the statement because Brian's hand was gently touching her face. "I really want to kiss you. Can I?"

Jesse was speechless. Her head and heart had just exploded. She felt his lips wet on her hers and then his tongue in her mouth. Her heart was beating so fast, so hard and so loudly that she knew he must be hearing it. She couldn't believe she was being kissed. By the time it was over she was in a daze and giddy with bliss. "You should probably go inside now. I think your mom just put on the porch light," he said smiling. "Yeah" was the only word that could come out of Jesse's mouth even though a zillion thoughts were racing through her brain. Like an alcoholic in a drunken stupor, Jesse fumbled for her purse and alighted from the car. Brian put the automatic window down and said something about calling her, but Jesse was still in shock and temporarily deaf. The noise in her head was way too loud. Brian waited till she was on the porch and had opened the front door. He caught a glimpse of a round faced woman who he assumed to be Jesse's mother at the door. Jesse stood and watched the CRV turn and waved as the back lights of the car disappeared down the road. "Oh my God! I've just been kissed!" Jesse screamed silently in her head.

Jesse felt as though she would burst from the excitement welling up inside her. She wanted to tell somebody, anybody. She would have to wait till she next saw Lisa. "So how was it Jesse?" Ms. Janice inquired. "It was nice Ma. It was Ok. Movie Towne real expensive but I had a good time." Jesse did her best to give a tame account of the evening to her mother before going to her room. It was not that she didn't love her; she just knew that her mother could never fully understand what it was like to be a teenager in these times. Her mother could never comprehend fully the challenges of being a farmer's daughter in a school like St. Joseph's Convent. That night, Jesse wrote everything that happened down in her diary. It was the only way she felt she could prevent herself from screaming the news to the whole of San Antoñio. She was going to be Brian Chow Fatt's girlfriend and as far as Jesse was concerned life could not get any better than that.

Eddy's ride home with his friends had been short and eventful. He had told Brian to drop him off in Belmont since he was spending the night at an uncle of his. He had picked a random house that had no lights on and had stood outside the gate of a complete stranger to wave goodbye to Brian, Lisa and Jesse. It was fortunate for him too that the stranger put on a light and pulled their front curtains back two seconds after Brian had driven off and Eddy had put his hand on the small iron gate pretending to go inside. Before the stranger had a chance to raise an alarm or figure out what was going on, Eddy had bolted off into another street. Happy to have kept his secret safe yet again, Eddy began to walk briskly into town. Belmont wasn't too far from downtown Port-of-Spain. Although he had lied about where he was really from on numerous occasions, something about that night made it harder for him. The evening had been fun though. Lisa was definitely the kind of girl he could see himself with in the long term. She was funny and smart and so very sexy. Eddy had undressed her with his eyes in that outfit and she still looked good to him.

He really wanted to get to know her better. He just had to figure out how to keep the lines of communication open, because although he now had a cell phone, Lisa did not. She didn't even have a telephone at home which had surprised Eddy a great deal. Eddy was beginning to feel that his efforts to obtain a cell phone had been in vain. How was he going to connect with Lisa if he couldn't even call her? He should have made sure she had a telephone at home first he thought. As he walked past the lit showcases of shoes and clothes on Frederick Street, feeling like he could kick himself, the idea came to him suddenly. "I know I'll get her a cell phone," he blurted out loud. That would solve the problem. He just needed to get the money. He was feeling so ecstatic about his plan that he decided to walk home instead of taking a maxi. It was only ten o'clock and now he had even greater reason to save up his money.

The Christmas tree lights on every tree up and down the Brian Lara promenade were a colorful reminder that Christmas was in the air. For a brief moment Eddy reflected on how quickly time had flown. Last year Christmas had been one of his best Christmases yet. Tommy had taken his pay cheque and bought a ham, half a turkey, and a few pastelles which they had kept in their tiny refrigerator. He even got a little second hand Christmas tree and some lights from the labasse two days before Christmas. So even though all he could give Eddy as a gift on Christmas day was a second hand watch and a pair of socks, Eddy was grateful. Lystra got a pair of earrings too, it didn't matter that they were the cheap kind; it was the thought behind it. Everything seemed so hopeful then. Tommy had just started working again and Eddy and Lystra were beginning to feel that things would begin to look up for them.

Christmas day was the first time in a long time that they had all been together as a family. Eddy had been so proud of his uncle. Nobody had anticipated the horror that would follow in the months after Christmas when Tommy started using. The endless arguments, the never knowing what would be gone from the house when he returned from school, had been too much for Eddy to cope with. Lystra had had enough when one night she came home to find that there was nothing in the spot where the fridge used to stand. After that Tommy had to go. "Get out! Get the f—k out! What again yuh will take from meh. Oh God what again ah have fuh yuh to tief! Get out and doh come back here!" Lystra had screamed at him that fateful night around midnight when he had tried to come back in the house. Tommy was banging down on the already weak door for a long time before he got tired and realized that Lystra had finally put him out. Eddy wondered where Tommy was now. He knew Lystra had told him that Tommy was living on Tamarind Square; he contemplated walking past to see him. It was late enough. Almost fearful of what he might see but propelled by a sudden desire to see the uncle he loved so much, Eddy turned his feet in the direction of Tamarind Square and braced himself for whatever he might find there.

Lisa had thoroughly enjoyed Eddy's company that night. There was something about him that was different from Brian; something that made her feel at home with him. He was street wise, not stuck up and she had so much more in common with him than she had imagined. He wasn't the average 'town boy' who didn't know what happened past the light house. He asked her how close she lived to Curepe junction and whether she had ever seen the transvestites that used to hang out there. He wanted to know if the doubles people really worked twenty-four hours and he asked her if she had ever been up to Mount Saint Benedict and if "you could really see all of Trinidad from up there." He was "soooo" cute. She loved his smile and his big brown eyes. When he asked her for her phone number she was so embarrassed to say that she didn't have one.

"Doh dig ah horrors, we will have to find a solution to the problem," he had said wanting to make her feel at ease. Lisa was glad that his reaction to the fact that she was without what was for many a basic necessity of life was not extreme. They couldn't stop talking and although Lisa was just getting to know him, she felt that she could see a future with him. When she got home, Vonetta was there looking at some Lifetime movie on cable.

"So tell me how it went?"

"It was alright. I had a good time," an unexcited Lisa responded. She was still terribly upset about her mother's pregnancy and had wanted to punish her for what she felt was an obvious life blunder.

"Ted eh reach home yet?"

"No, ah think he gone by a pardner about a job."

"Steups!" Lisa scoffed before going into her bedroom.

It hurt her to hear her mother lie to her. They both knew that Ted was at some watering hole getting drunk and preparing to come home and disturb whatever little peace the night could offer. Lisa had not spoken to her father in at least three months. She wasn't usually at home when her mother spoke to him from her cell phone but when she did speak to him, the conversations were short and strange. Lisa wasn't even entirely sure what part of Brooklyn her father was working; all she knew was that he was doing some sort of construction work. He usually wanted to know how she was coming along in school, if she was taking good care of her mother and if she had everything she needed for school. Lisa suspected that he knew about Ted but her mother had made her swear she would never tell him. The truth was that Lisa didn't feel close enough to her father to discuss her life with him anyway. Their conversations usually lasted for five minutes. Sometimes she wondered why he even bothered to call. But she knew why. One day he would come back for them and then he would know that unlike her mother, she had always been waiting for his return.

As tempted as she was to tell her father about Ted, Lisa was afraid that that knowledge would discourage him from coming back for them…for her. Lisa dropped on her bunk bed and held her pillow close. With every passing day, the place she called home was becoming a place she hated to be. It was such an anticlimax after returning from such an interesting evening. She turned on her alarm clock radio and put the radio station on 96.1 WEFM. The music helped to soothe her nerves and block out all the negativity that surrounded her. She wouldn't be there forever she thought. One day she was going to be a bird, free to fly and soar as far as she wanted to. She felt as though she was waiting to exhale, waiting for her life to start.

Eddy couldn't believe how many bodies lay in the darkness of Tamarind Square. A malodorous unidentifiable smell wafted up from the earth and the bodies in the Square. Some bodies moved under flattened cardboard boxes and newspaper sheets; some lay still almost appearing lifeless. In the shadows made by the light coming from the nearby Wee Lee bakery store, Eddy could barely tell whether the bodies were those of men or women. Suddenly he was overcome by the apparent futility of his action. There was no way he would be able to find his uncle in that cesspool of bodies. Just as he was about to turn and walk away, a fit of loud coughing drew his attention to a flattened moving cardboard box.

As Eddy stepped closer with caution, the cardboard cover shifted revealing two bodies one beside the other. He was only a few feet away from them. The sight sent a chill up his spine. He couldn't see the men's faces but as if one of them had heard him, the coughing man turned his head to look at him. The headlights of a passing car illumined the man's face. Eddy gasped. Covering his mouth with his hand, he stood almost frozen in the spot. In that instant Eddy felt a pain in his stomach. His skin became cold and he began to cold sweat. His eyes made four with the coughing man and a surge of pain overwhelmed his heart and his body. The face stared at him blankly without recognizing him. Eddy's feet took charge. He turned and ran and ran and ran; past City Gate, past the light house, past Sea Lots, past Port-of- Spain Market. He ran till his chest hurt and he had to stop and catch his breath, taking in large gulps of air. The pain in his stomach had turned to a knot in his throat. A weakened Eddy collapsed in the grass at the side of the bus route in his good shoes and jeans and burst into tears. The image of Tommy's face in the Square would forever be etched in his memory. It was an image that would haunt him for the rest of his life but it was also an image that would save his life.

All in all the weekend had been eventful, leaving much food for thought on a Monday morning. Lystra had begun going to church regularly for the first time in a long time. She wasn't entirely sold on the idea of becoming a Seventh Day Adventist but giving her life to Jesus certainly had benefits. For starters, her newly found brothers and sisters in the Lord were working on trying to get her a job working as a domestic for one of the less impoverished church members. In the meantime she started receiving a bag of groceries every two weeks from the church. She was made aware of her need to be saved, baptized, and born again in the spirit. Members walked her home from church and picked her up to take her to rallies and other church events. And of course there was the Sabbath which started from Friday evening around six o'clock. Her Saturdays were now devoted to "the Lord" and rest.

Lystra was enjoying all the attention and the benefits of being a neophyte. She was genuinely impressed by the zeal of the church members even though she could hardly imagine herself being so zealous for the Lord. Belonging to the church gave her an opportunity to meet people with indomitable faith. Perhaps if she had that kind of faith and prayed hard enough, Tommy might be able to make a comeback. Either way, regardless of what her neighbors thought regarding the sincerity of her "conversion", Lystra was sticking with the church and all her benefactors at least until she could begin to "see her way" for herself again.

Monday morning on the Beetham was like any other day except Sunday. Those who had work in Port-of-Spain and environs could be seen up early walking out to the bus route or to Morvant junction to await transport. Scavengers were up early too, getting ready to dig for 'gold'. Bare backed and in ragged pants, eager with anticipation, they waited on the dump trucks from the regional corporations. Those scavengers who lived in the dump on a more permanent basis rose from their beds made of wooden pallets to prepare for the day's dig.

There had been a gathering at the basket ball court on the weekend and talk of a planned protest. It was not scheduled for Monday; actually the community elders wanted it to come off on Tuesday. All around the court and at Charlie's rum shop men and women were grumbling and there was a lot to grumble about. "All dem oil dollars eh. Beetham people cyah geh nuttin. People out here ent ha no jobs. Is not like we ent want to wok but wha it ha to do? Is only de dump a lotta dese young fellas have an is only de dump dey know." Uncle Tremble was centre stage as usual.

It was Monday morning and a group of agitated young men and a few women too had assembled around the basketball court ready for a protest. Some of the women were making placards from pieces of used cardboard boxes. A few yards off on the Beetham highway some young men could be seen dragging tires, wood and metal, toward a miniature barricade consisting of three old rusty barrels and some pieces of old wood. Within minutes, that clearing would turn to a pile of flaming rubbish and the gathering would be shouting a variety of slogans - "Beetham people is people too!", "We want jobs!", "We want justice!". The placards also conveyed the frustration of the residents. Although the spelling was not correct, the signs read "We ent crimenals. We jus wanna live!". " Beetham drain stinkin up. We chilren getin sick!", "We ent even getin a CEPEP!" and the most thought provoking of all, "Whey de oil dollars 4 Beetham people!"

As soon as the fire started the smoke from the blaze was carried by the wind in the direction of the dump. Because visibility was poor, cars began to slow down and it wasn't too long before traffic began to pile up on the Beetham highway. A very vocal Lystra was to the forefront of the protesting crowd. She was one of the first to be interviewed by the TV6 reporter who arrived on the scene with his camera man.

"So mam why are you out here protesting today?" the reporter asked.

"Ah here because govuhment eh realisin wha goin on out here. De young fellas out here ent have no wok. Every day dey going in de dump to look for ting to make a dollar. Dey works nowhere. Dese fellas eh want to be criminals but poor people ha to try and mek a livin some how. It real hard fuh we. So ah here today to say to de Prime minister, is Beetham people whey put yuh dere an we could get yuh out too." Shouts of approval rang out and sticks hit tin drums in support of what Lystra had just said. Uncle Tremble also spoke to the media echoing similar sentiments.

"Police only down inside here aressing de small man but it have big drug dealers out dere doing big business. Why dey ent going after dem fellas. Yuh know why? Is because de damn police too corrupt." More applause followed. Most of the rush hour motorists on their way to work were caught in a massive pile up on the Beetham Highway due to the protest. Although the protest was taking place on the east bound lane of the highway, there was traffic on the west bound lane as well, created by motorists slowing down to "maco" the events. There was a steady flow of scavengers running back and forth between the dump and the protest. They wanted to lend their support to the protesters but they were not about to lose out on their daily bread. Somewhere between the smoke coming from the protest, the dump, the traffic jam and before the police could arrive on the scene, an opportunity presented itself.

It happened in a flash. A woman screamed as her chain was snatched from off her neck, another man cursed and although tempted to come out of his car to retrieve the money he had just handed over, opted to release some expletives instead. The scavengers had descended on the driving populace stranded on the Beetham and were helping themselves to whatever they could. Red, blue, green and purple notes were being filched from wallets, purses and pockets, gold wristbands and other valuables were being passed through windows by frightened passengers. No guns or weapons were used in the attacks which were over in a matter of minutes. The wailing of police sirens would bring things to an abrupt end and send the scavengers and residents turned robbers back into their holes. The traffic jam would worsen before improving after the police arrived. Cars had to be pulled to the side so that those robbed could give their account of events; not to mention the TV6 reporters.

All in all it was a Monday of chaos on the Beetham. By midday, the pile of fiery debris was gone, the traffic flow was normal, the scavengers would be back at work, Uncle Tremble would be sitting outside the rum shop in his usual spot and all the residents of the Beetham would be "blessed" later that day with the earnings from the traffic jam siege. A subdued Eddy had witnessed all the happenings. He too was expecting to get some 'blessings' from his scavenger friends. He had been careful to avoid the lenses of the camera men and watched as his mother spoke out for Beetham people. It had been a while since he felt so proud of her. Maybe those in authority would hear and would listen.

Still Eddy remained quietly on the sidelines, not wanting to be seen, remembering that TV6 news was widely viewed by many people. Being seen on the news would ruin everything for him. Nobody from his class had ever seen his mother and he wanted to keep it that way. So although he was slightly uncomfortable about the cameraman who got a good close up of her in her ole red PNM t–shirt and a floral printed skirt she had got from her church friends, Eddy didn't mind. He was grateful that she wore a brassiere that morning too.

If nothing else her new found faith in the Lord was directly impacting on the way she dressed. Apart from the fact that her scanty wardrobe was expanding, she began to dress more conservatively, more skirts, less pants and fewer tight tops that accentuated her large breasts. Eddy was glad to see that his mother was trying to turn her life around. He hoped that through the church she would meet a real man, not like the kind she had been used to; someone who could be more than just a foreman for her. He was relieved too that she had not tried to force him to attend church with her or make him keep the Sabbath. Lystra was taking baby steps but Eddy wondered if it would not be long before she started referring to him as an unbeliever.

He had already started planning his future, after A-Levels. He was thinking about getting a job and renting a small place in Belmont; somewhere he and his mother could live and maybe even Lisa. He doubted that Lystra would ever leave the Beetham though. It had been her home for so long. The thought of living anywhere else would be scary for her. Once he had asked her if she would ever leave to live anywhere else. "Whey else it ha fuh me to go eh? Whey else in town we could squat? Sea Lots? Steups!" was Lystra's response.

Eddy would have liked Tommy to be in that picture too but he had abandoned all hopes for Tommy after Friday night. He had made no mention of seeing Tommy to his mother. He knew it would only bring her grief and he had no intention of introducing despair into the spiritual equation she was building. He had been emotionally numb since he saw his uncle and was deep in thought all weekend long. Even his scavenger friend Soldier, the one who had hooked him up with the piper for the cell phone had noticed a change in his mood. Eddy felt as though his uncle had died, except that he was still very much alive. A feeling of powerlessness had overcome him the night he saw Tommy, and every time he thought about Tommy after that, Eddy felt the same hollow feeling in the pit of his stomach.

Eddy never liked missing school; it was his escape from the smell of the Beetham. But when Soldier brought him the news about the possibility of a protest on Monday morning, Eddy opted to stick around for the excitement. He was sure to see or hear something that would improve his mood and he did. Between Uncle Tremble, the camera men and the look of frightened motorists being robbed, Eddy had witnessed enough bacchanal to fill his belly. He spent the rest of his day wandering aimlessly about on the Eastern Main Road. He stopped off at the tyre shop where Tommy used to work and enquired whether they had any weekend jobs. He was beginning to think that he should get a weekend job but not one that would put him in the eye of the public too much and certainly not one that could interfere with his social life.

However if he was going to get involved with Lisa, getting a job would be crucial. He couldn't always beg his mother for money and now that she was trying to become less dependent on men for her daily bread, things would be expected to be tighter financially before they got better. By six o'clock that evening when Eddy returned to the all too familiar smell of the Beetham he could hear the loud voices of the men on the basketball court as they argued about the day's proceedings. "Next time we ha to put de rubbish on both sides a de highway. Dat way we wouldn have to do no running like how we do it today," said one man. "Yeah but dey go say we only put de protest on de highway so we could rob people," another replied. "It doh matter wha dey say bout we. What again dey could say bout we dat dey ent say already." All but one agreed.

"Govuhment ha to listen to we. Is we whey put dem dere and we could take dem out again," said another. "Yeah but if dat eh work we go ha to go in town and light up tings."

"Yeah dey goin and tink bout we when dat happen. When Beetham people light up de whole ah town and shake up de whole ah town dey go know dey cyah treat we de way dey treatin we now."

Chapter Eleven

Mouth Open and Story Jump Out

"Ok so let's take it from the top again" said an oily faced Mr. Mc Master. The pianist struck up a few notes and the choir began once more.

"Crown Him"
"Crown Him"
"Crown Him the King of Kings"

The voices were fresh and sharp on each note. They had been practising for weeks in preparation for the production but Mr. Mc Master was not yet satisfied that the group would be ready for the big day. He was especially concerned about Sean who in the past weeks seemed much more distracted than usual. Ever since the touching incident with Alex, Sean had been experiencing a great deal of inner turmoil. What was worse, he felt that there was nobody in all the world that he could talk to about his feelings. He had been noticeably distant in his interactions with Brian and Eddy who had tried their best to figure out what had been troubling him so much. Sean had serious doubts about his sexuality and was consumed with the possibility that he might be more attracted to men than he was to women.

Deep inside him, Sean knew this to be true but to add insult to injury, he began having dreams about Mr. Alfonso, Alex and Brian. In every dream they were either touching him or smiling at him, hugging him or kissing him. The dreams were particularly disturbing and on occasion he found himself getting hard in his pajama pants. Not being able to talk to someone he felt would understand made it all the more painful. His parents were both busy with work and Christmas time was particularly hectic with shipments coming in for the Fabulous Fabric chain of stores.

Often he and his younger sister Sianne would come home from school to the housekeeper, who seemed to be the only one who was always consistently at home except for Sundays. The one person that seemed to want to befriend him during this whirlwind of confusion was the last person he wanted to communicate with. Alex had been watching Sean for some time. He had tried to keep his distance ever since the incident but he could tell that Sean was deeply troubled. He was very attracted to Sean; he just didn't know how to show it. What was worse, Alex felt that he had ruined all chances of them ever becoming friends. They had not spoken since Sean had cursed him out over the telephone, and although Alex wanted to call him, he was very much afraid. Sean struggled bitterly with his feelings, dreams and the gamut of thoughts that tormented him in the weeks after. He had busied himself with reading up about homosexuality. He wanted to learn about it so that he could confirm that he was everything but gay. On the internet he found a wealth of information and different perspectives on the subject.

He read about the debate of 'Nurture versus Nature', Christianity's denouncing of homosexuality, the fight to legalize gay marriages, hate crimes against homosexuals and a host of other things, which left him even more confused. If he was indeed gay which he was sure he wasn't, then he felt certain that it must be due to some genetic disorder or hormonal imbalance. Sean knew that nothing in his upbringing could be held culpable for his sexuality. After all his reading and much introspection, Sean came to the conclusion that he really wasn't gay at all. He was just going through a phase which was perfectly normal for someone his age. His attraction to persons of the same sex was fleeting and although he wasn't about to launch into a relationship with any girl, he certainly wasn't about to explore whatever homosexual inclinations he might have.

Alex was an oddity for Sean. He stood out like a sore thumb every where he went, had no real friends and was constantly teased, the butt of many faggot jokes. He couldn't understand why Alex even tolerated it. He almost felt sorry for him but at the same time was not about to extend a hand of friendship. "OK, next practice is on Friday at five o'clock. We still have a lot of work to do so be on time," said Mr. Mc Master as he wiped the sweat from his brow. The underarms of his short sleeved blue cotton shirt were soaked with perspiration.

Mr. Mc Master loved what he did. His love for his music and singing had cost him his marriage. Mrs. Mc Master had left him for another man after only three years of marriage. A shuffle of feet could be heard as the post-pubescent men stepped down from the wooden ramps of the stage to head home or to whatever their activities were. Sean grabbed his purple grey knapsack and flung it over his shoulder. Out of the corner of his eye he could spot Alex approaching. Sean immediately began to quicken his pace but in a flash Alex was right beside him. "Eh ah could talk to yuh for a minute" said Alex. Sean, not wanting too many people to see them speaking to each other, responded hastily. "About what!" Sean grunted back. Sean had not stopped walking, he just slowed his pace down a bit so that it wouldn't seem that he was running away even though inside that was what he really wanted to do.

Alex was silent for a while. "Well just call me ok. I don't have time now," said Sean almost vexed that he had entertained conversation. Sean hurried off to his waiting driver Norman, who never failed to become irritated when choir practice went over the stipulated time which was always. Sean jumped into the black Peugeot four door sedan without daring to look back to see whether Alex was still standing there looking in his direction. The whole interaction had made him feel uncomfortable but he felt sure that if he didn't wiggle his way out of the conversation quickly, enough fellas would have noticed to make it a source of picong the following day. If Alex did in fact call him, he was going to calmly make it clear that although he didn't condemn Alex, he was not in the least bit interested in being his friend. That should settle everything he presumed, all would be well.

"Ay-Ay but Harry ent dat is yuh half sister? Wha she name again? Is Lorna?" Sunita and her husband were looking at the TV6 news roundup at ten o'clock on Monday night.

"It looking like her," said Harry

"But like she put on weight boy. Ah wonder what de son doing now. He must be Krishna age by now eh?" A curious Sunita was taking in the protest on TV. She and Harry had just returned from making a night safe deposit at the bank. He never liked to go alone and some of his business associates had suggested that he leave that activity in the hands of a security firm because of the rising crime rate. But Harry was old fashioned. He enjoyed preparing his bank deposits with his wife and making the deposits himself. He had been doing it for years and was not about to change.

"Allyuh cyah come in quiet no time eh?" asked Krishna as he emerged from his bedroom barebacked and in his boxers. His hair was a mess and his eyes were red because he had just got up from sleep. "What is dat goin on on TV?" he asked. "It had a protest and robbing up in de Beetham today. Yuh father half sister was talking on de news," Sunita explained. "I didn know daddy had a half sister?" Krishna was alert now and full of questions. "Ay-Ay, look Eddy from lessons. But wha he doing on de Beetham?" Krishna wondered out loud.

The headline news report ended and it was Jacob Sant up with news of cricket. For a brief moment all that could be heard was the sound of the TV and the newscaster calling the names of the cricketers selected by the WICB for the next four day series in Grenada. Sunita and Harry had seen Eddy. They had recognized him well. "So how come I didn know yuh have a half sister pa? Yuh mean Grand-pa had a outside woman?"

"Son dat was a long time ago, and well yuh know how it was long time nah. We grow up in de cane where men drinking rum all de time. When man drunk he could make all kinda mistake."

"So how you know dat Eddy, he in school with you?" Sunita wanted to change the topic immediately. "No. Ah know him from Mr. Lee Wen classes. He's a real cool fella, real down to earth and thing. Ah just doh understand what he doing on de Beetham though. Ah mean it look like him but I thought he living up San Juan side," Krishna explained. Harry and Sunita knew that Krishna had met his cousin, except he didn't know that. "So tell me who was de outside woman Daddy?"

"Boy you better go back in yuh bed. Ent yuh have school tomorrow?" Sunita was sorry that she had spoken so quickly about Harry's half sister. "But I want to hear about Grand-pa and de outside woman," said Krishna. "Look boy just go in yuh bed," an irritated Harry snarled as he rose from his lazy boy chair in the living room. "Yuh could hear bout dat another time." It was not that Harry was ashamed of his half sister or the fact that his father had had this indiscretion in his youth, it was simply that he didn't plan on telling Krishna about it so soon or in the way that his wife had. Harry had always wanted to maintain a relationship with Lystra. He suspected that it was only because of his wife's behaviour that Lystra had not felt comfortable enough to keep visiting. Harry loved Sunita with all his heart but he hated the way her family turned their noses up at other people. That his father had made an outside child with a black woman like Ma Vero was a thing of great shame.

Harry's mother bore that shame with all the dignity that she could until the day she died, but in that little community of Kelly Village, Harry would never forget the taunts he received about his father's black child. It didn't help any that the child had inherited her mother's broad nose and tight spongy hair. Lystra and her mother too had many an insult to endure. Ma Vero had decided to keep no contact with Balo after Lystra's birth. She had loved Balo; it was not about money for her. When the child was born looking nothing like him, Balo vehemently denied that the child was his. "Dat eh my chile. De chile eh look nuttin like me at all, at all, at all. Which man yuh make dat chile for eh?"

Balo's accusations had hurt Ma Vero deeply. It was hard enough to be an unmarried black woman in a community like Kelly Village but to be called a jamète when all she was trying to do was live and take care of her children was too hard to bear. She moved to Laventille with her six children and eventually to the Beetham with her two youngest, Tommy and Lystra. Lystra never had an opportunity to meet her father before he died. She had wanted to so badly though. It was on Ma Vero's sick bed that Lystra heard her mother speak about her eldest half brother.

"Yuh must talk to he. He name Harry Rajkumar. Ah hear he does sell doubles by Mohess Junction now. He is de only nice chile ah see yuh fadder make. He come an look for me when he was a lil boy yuh know. Dat boy brave. Dat chile run way an come to see who I is and who is meh chile. If he sellin doubles he makin some good money. Yuh never know how life does turn." That was before the stroke when her mouth wasn't twisted and she could still speak clearly. Years of hard work and chronic hypertension had led to her early demise at forty-nine, leaving Lystra to raise her younger brother. Regardless of what society thought of her, Ma Vero died a proud woman. She had made lemonade with the bittersweet lemons that life had dealt her and she was looking forward to meeting her maker. Seeing his half sister on TV had caused a Pandora's Box of emotions to be opened in Harry. He would leave the bed he shared with Sunita later that night to sit out in his porch and reflect on the silent agonies his mother bore because of Balo's love for the bottle.

Unfortunately, the Rajkumars were not the only persons looking at TV6 news that night. The report had run earlier at seven o'clock and showed a close up of Eddy a few yards from the protest on the Beetham. Perhaps it was because his light skin and wavy hair made him stand out in the sea of bronze colored faces. Whatever it was, the camera man managed to get a good look at Eddy before turning his camera lenses back to the protest. At the end of the day when some residents gathered around the TV set in Charlie's rum shop to examine and discuss the news they had made that day, Eddy was there too.

When he saw his face looking back at him on the TV, something exploded in his brain. He couldn't appreciate the cheers of the patrons who were slapping him on the shoulder. "Aye boy yuh make TV boy!" A knot of pain grabbed his stomach and held it tightly in grip as he made his way slowly out of the rum shop. How could this happen? Eddy thought he had done his best to stay away from the camera. How did this camera man catch him and why had he taken such a close up of his face?

There was not even a chance that he could not be recognized. His world was collapsing before his very eyes. Had his friends seen him? That would be the end of everything. They would know that he had lied all this time. What would Lisa think? What would Brian think? And Sean, what about him? He felt a swishing sound in his ears, almost as if water had got in them. His breath became short and shallow as his hands became cold and clammy. His secret was out. Everything he had worked so hard to hide had been exposed under the lens of an evil camera man. Brian and Sean would never forgive him and neither would Lisa. Perhaps they hadn't seen the news. Maybe they didn't know. Perhaps all was not lost. When he collapsed on his flattened foam mattress that night, Eddy prayed that if there was indeed a God, he would be able to fix this awful situation and make everything right when next he went out to school.

Ms. Janice sensed that a lot more was going on between Jesse and Brian than Jesse was letting on. "Come an help me cook this Cascadoo nah Jesse." Although she had intended to give the Cascadura away, Ms. Janice interpreted her discovery of it in the 'deep-freeze' that Sunday morning after church as a sign that she should cook it. She loved fish and she hadn't had fish for a long time; besides Cascadura was expensive and four pounds of Cascadura would have been a lot of money to give away.

"So yuh didn tell me what you and Brian was talking about in de car so long Jess."

"Nothing much Ma. Well he like me yuh know."

"Ah know. An ah know yuh like him back too," said Ms. Janice. Jesse blushed and looked down at the lime she was cutting up to clean the fish with. "Nuttin wrong wit dat yuh know baby. When I was your age ah did like boys too. Yuh suppose to like boys at your age." Jesse felt awkward having this kind of conversation with her mother. She had a great deal of difficulty envisioning her mother as a teenager, far less a teenager in love. "Yes it nice to have boyfren an all dat but remember ah tell yuh dat Brian family not like us baby. Dese people have a lotta money and dey probably have a wife plan out fuh Brian ahreday, and ah sure is not you." Ms. Janice was trying to be as gentle as she could be.

"Why yuh have to say dat Ma? Brian is a good person, he might be rich but he not stuck up or anything. He doh care dat I live in Santa Cruz. He really likes me Ma. Why yuh can't just believe dat." Jesse's eyes were full as she looked piercingly at her mother, kitchen knife in one hand and lime in the other. "Doh geh vex with yuh mudder baby. Ah just want de best fuh yuh. Yuh is meh precious precious chile. Yuh tink ah want to see yuh geh hurt or disappoint?"

"Why yuh feel I will get hurt Ma?" Jesse swung back.

"Baby I ent born yesterday yuh know. Ah hear bout a lotta girls in my mudder day get fool when dem American soldiers come down here. Up in Chaguaramas dem Yankees was making mas, tiefing de hearts of people gyul children; good gyuls, decent gyuls, de kinda gyuls dat man does marry. Next ting yuh know, soldier gone and gyul belly start to rise and parents shedding tears. Half breed chile born an nobody know whey de fadder gone. Now ah not saying dat will happen to you but ah saying dat sometimes when woman feeling strong bout man, dey does end up doing tings dey wouldn do ordinary." Ms. Janice looked across at her daughter's face still red. "Love is like dat baby. Trus me. I know. Love is like dat." Jesse couldn't imagine that her mother had any clue about love. She wanted to tell her that she had only kissed Brian but she was afraid; and it was obvious to her that her mother was priming up for the birds and the bees talk which she had never received formally but had heard second hand through friends when she was only twelve years old in Form One.

"Woman doh plan to geh pregnant all de time yuh know. It does happen fas fas fas in de heat ah de moment." Jesse was wondering if that was how it had been with her mother and Mr. GG for all the pregnancies. "Dey ever tell yuh bout sex and dem tings in school Jesse?" Her mother had spoken the S word for the first time. Jesse was in shock. "Yeah as a matter of fact some weeks ago a couple came and spoke to us about waiting to have sex when you are married and things like that. Plus we did all the biology of it in biology class already," said Jesse.

Ms. Janice was surprised at the ease with which the word sex rolled off of Jesse's tongue that Sunday morning. In a way though, Ms. Janice was relieved that she didn't have to explain sex to her daughter. It was an uncomfortable topic for her, to discuss. Her mother had only told her about sex the day before she got married to Mr. GG. Girls that were well brought up didn't have sex until they got married but Ms. Janice was no fool. She knew that times were changing. In her day, she could never go out on a date without a chaperone. The suitor in question had to write a letter addressed to her father stating his intentions and put a stamp on it, before he could even get an audience with her parents. Those were the days when men wore hats, women always wore dresses or skirts and to get married at the age of eighteen or even sixteen was not an uncommon thing. A woman's family needed to know the family of her suitor prior to courtship. If the families did not see eye to eye on the suitability of the match up, then neither marriage nor courtship could take place.

Ms. Janice wanted her daughter to see that she could never have a real future with Brian; even if he really did love Jesse. Ms. Janice wanted Jesse to see that his family would never accept the daughter of a lowly farmer to join their ranks. The Chow Fatts were a well respected name in Trinidad society. Not only were they well respected but wealthy to a fault. Both old and new money jingled in their coiffeurs. Ms. Janice knew that Jesse was too naïve to grasp what she was about to tell her but she said it anyway.

"Baby, Brian seem like a nice fella. Ah mean when ah talk to he on de phone he respectful an polite an ah know yuh like him plenty but jus remember dat yuh young still. Dey have plenty nice boys out dere just right fuh yuh. Brian family might like yuh now but dat is because dey mus be know dat when Brian finish exams dey sendin he away to study. Just try to focus on school fuh now. Yuh have to remember what is most important right now and yuh mudder doh ha money to send yuh to UWI so it have plenty time for boyfren. Now is time to study yuh book OK." Jesse was quiet and sullen-faced. Ms. Janice pinched her daughter's cheeks and managed to squeeze a smile out of her. "Now dat is how ah like to see meh chile smiling. Come it getting late, leh we fry up dis Cascadoo because ah know Steve an Becca go be coming round jus now lookin fuh someting to eat," said Ms. Janice. She lit up the stove and put an iron pot on it, poured some oil into it and got ready to cook the Cascadura.

It was around seven o'clock on Monday night when Sean's cell phone rang. It was Alex.

"Hello"

"Hello Sean. Before you hang up I just want to talk to you." Alex had rattled the words off with speed, afraid that Sean would really hang up.

"What about?" Sean grunted.

"I just wanted to say sorry about the other day," said Alex in a low voice. "Yeah OK. How many times you going to apologize. I forget about that already," Sean lied. He hadn't forgotten about it, not in the least but he didn't want Alex to keep feeling guilty about it and he didn't want to give him the impression that he was still upset. He also didn't want Alex to have an excuse to call him again.

"So how is everything?" Alex asked

"Everything good," Sean answered. There was an awkward silence.

"Listen did you understand what we did today in Math class. The integration of quadratics part?"

"Yeah" Sean was keeping his answers short.

"Can you explain it to me real quick if yuh have the time? I really don't understand it," said Alex. For a moment Sean hesitated. He could tell that Alex was genuinely sorry about what happened and wanted to reach out to him but Sean still wasn't sure whether he wanted to allow this guy that everybody teased about being a faggot to be his friend. Just because Alex was a faggot didn't mean that he had to treat him like someone with chicken pox Sean thought. He sighed into the telephone. "Ok what part you don't understand?" asked Sean. He could hear Alex smiling through the phone. For the first time in a long time, Alex felt that someone was actually listening to him, not calling him names or teasing him but treating him like a normal human being and it made him feel warm inside.

Chapter Twelve

When All Is Taken Away

"*J* am so sorry to hear that darling. Do you think he wants a divorce?" Marlene asked. "I don't even know what he wants," an exasperated Sally replied. Ever since her fight with Matt, the house had become hauntingly silent. He would come home from work and wouldn't eat the food she had prepared. They would both lie in bed without touching and without saying a word to each other. Sally had reached the end of her rope. She had cried many nights and was simply at her wits end even though she was not yet prepared to accept defeat. She was so depressed that not even her daily jaunts could get her out of the house. It was only Marlene's insistence that they meet for lunch that had forced Sally to get out of bed and leave the house.

"I know someone that you can see Sal," said Marlene as she put a forkful of broccoli in her mouth.

"A counselor?" asked Sally. "No, not exactly. She is from Venezuela and she is very good. She is kind of like an obeah woman but from Venezuela," Marlene explained. "I've been to her a few times about the business and I know some of the women who have been to her. She can help you. I promise." Marlene squeezed Sal's hand across the table. "Oh God I can't believe my marriage has come to this. Matt's not even speaking to me and now you are telling me to go see an obeah woman! When did things get so bad?"

"Sal what matters is that it can be fixed. Trust me. This is her card. You need to call her or I can call her for you if you like." Marlene wasn't sure whether Sally approved of the idea of going to Senora Velasquez but from what Sally had described to her, things had become very desperate. "Look it can't hurt Sal. Do you want me to call her for you?"

"No, no. I'll call." Sally wiped her eyes with her napkin. She had hardly touched her food, but seeing Marlene was some small comfort to her. "You should go see her today love. I know she works till late during the week. Go today and talk to her. She will tell you what to do. Do you want me to come with you Sal, because I can take the time off from work and go with you?" It had suddenly occurred to Marlene that perhaps Sally might want some moral support for her trip to Senora Velasquez. "No, it's alright. I know you're busy. I'd rather go alone anyway," a downcast looking Sally replied.

"Keep your chin up love. Nobody has a perfect marriage. If you can get through infidelity you can get through anything. You just have to keep looking good as always and don't miss any engagements or anything like that. You don't want people to suspect that things are going wrong with you and Matt. They must never see you down. Because I'm sure this Priya person is talking about the fact that she is with your husband but that is all she can do, talk. Matt will never leave you for her. I promise you that." Marlene was a strong voice of reassurance in the sea of mental chaos that Sally was experiencing. She had heard Matt speaking over the telephone in hushed tones with someone named Priya and was convinced that Priya was indeed the outside woman.

Going to see this Senora Velasquez couldn't hurt more than what she was currently experiencing in the house with Matt. Sally had lost a few pounds from her already tiny frame, there were bags under her eyes and her hair was breaking badly. "You should go to Gina's today too Sal. Your hair looks a mess. That is so not like you," Marlene added. "I think I will. I really need a lift. I haven't gone out of the house for a while and you are right, the last thing I need is for people to be suspecting that Matt and I have problems." Marlene had just finished her plate of food and Sally knew that she would be leaving soon.

"Thanks so much Marlene. What would I do without you," said a grateful Sally. "I'm not too sure what you would do," Marlene joked and managed to get a smile out of the weary looking Sally. "I hate to eat and run lovie but you know how it gets at the store and whenever I leave that is when all the bacchanal starts." Marlene found a great sense of fulfillment in her job and it was something Sally envied greatly. "This one is on me Sal; I know how you hate to support the competition." Marlene took her credit card out of her brown leather hand bag and slid effortlessly off her seat. "Call me later and let me know what Senora Velasquez had to say Ok." Marlene leaned in and kissed Sally on the cheek. "Get your hair done today," she whispered into Sally's ear drawing forth a genuine smile.

With that Marlene was gone. Sally watched as Marlene gracefully made her exit, her curly black hair swaying with each step. She wore a soft black pants and red raw silk blouse which complemented her pale complexion. Sally sat back in her soft arm chair and contemplated all that Marlene had just said. Marlene was usually always right thought Sally. If nothing else, she shouldn't let Matt see her looking so beleaguered. Sally decided that she was going to take charge of the situation. She was going to get her hair done then go see Senora Velasquez. Whatever Senora Velasquez asked of her she would do, no matter how silly it was. It was not Sally's cup of tea but she was desperate and her situation with Matt required serious action before it was too late. She quickly finished the glass of red wine she had been drinking and made her way to the ladies room to apply her make up before facing the world again.

The day after the Beetham protests, an anxious Eddy kept a low profile. He had received a few stares at school. "Aye I see a man looking just like you on TV the other night. Yeah up on the Beetham. You living up on that side?" the Third Form QRC student who Eddy spoke to occasionally had asked. "Beetham? Nah boy you mixing me up with somebody else. I living up San Juan side," Eddy replied as calmly as he could. He was prepared to deny every reference to the news report and had hoped that if he played it cool and repeatedly denied that the person on TV was in fact him, everything would blow over and be forgotten.

He was relieved when Brian greeted him as he normally did that morning with a friendly punch. At least he knew that Brian had not seen the report. Sean also allayed his fears by inquiring why he missed school the previous day and bringing him up to date about what he missed in the various classes. If he could just make it through the day without anyone noticing him, Eddy felt that he would be alright. It was at lunch time though when the principal asked to speak with him that Eddy became concerned.

"Please have a seat Eddy," said Mr. Harris as he closed the door behind him. "I have the letter from my mother explaining why I missed school yesterday sir," a nervous Eddy replied.

"Relax son, it is not about that."

"Am I in trouble?" asked Eddy as he sat down.

"No, well not really"

There was a long pause as Mr. Harris examined Eddy's face. Mr. Harris was tall and broad shouldered and in his long sleeved white shirt and blue pin striped tie, he was quite an intimidating site from behind the heavy mahogany desk. "I saw you on the news the other night son." Eddy froze. It was all over. If Mr.

Harris knew he lived on the Beetham it would only be a matter of time before the entire school knew. It was not that the entire school even cared where Eddy lived but Eddy had tried so hard to retain his secret all these years and had been so conscious about the stigma attached to the Beetham that he envisioned himself in that instant as being the laughing stock of all of QRC. "Our records show your address as being in San Juan so if you really do live in San Juan what were you doing on the Beetham on Monday morning?"

Eddy was uncertain how to respond. He could try to pretend that the person Mr. Harris saw was not him but he knew that would be pointless. He could lie and say he was visiting a sick relative but that would mean that his excuse for missing school was a lie. If he said he was visiting a sick relative like an aunt or uncle who had no children, that would explain the shabby attire that he appeared in on TV. And although it would confirm that he was not sick, he couldn't think of any other explanation fast enough or clever enough that would be acceptable to Mr. Harris. "I have a sick uncle who lives on the Beetham," said Eddy as his voice lowered and his head dropped. "He doesn't have any children to take care of him and he's dying from cancer. So every once in a while my mother sends me to look for him and to make groceries for him and things like that," said Eddy. "Oh that is a very generous thing you are doing son. How is your mother by the way?" Mr. Harris inquired.

"Oh she is fine, still working in that drugstore in Champs Fleurs." Eddy was not a very good liar. His palms were sweating and he was afraid that Mr. Harris was seeing right through him.

"So how long has your uncle been sick?"

"Oh about six months now."

"What type of cancer does he have?"

"Hmmn, well it's a kind of stomach cancer."

"That must be rough. And he has no kids?"

"Nope, none at all."

"Is that your mother's brother or your father's brother?"

"Father's" said Eddy; and as soon as he said it he realized that he had answered wrongly.

His father was reported as deceased on all Eddy's administrative forms. It was highly unlikely that a man living on the Beetham would have no children or that Eddy's mother who was never in school for a PTA meeting or anything concerning her child would be that concerned about the brother of Eddy's father. Eddy hoped that perhaps Mr. Harris would cease his line of questioning and was not connecting the dots in his head. "Well don't let me keep you. I know you must be hungry," said Mr. Harris as he rose from his chair.

"Is that all sir?"

"Yes that's all."

Eddy got up slowly and showed himself to the door. "Whew! That was a close one," he thought. Circles of wetness on his shirt, under his armpits and his back, gave testimony to the anxiety he was feeling inside a few minutes ago. He had managed to throw Mr. Harris off his trail; the day was not turning out as badly as he anticipated after all. The only other person he was worried about now was Lisa. If he was lucky she too had not seen Monday night news and life would return to normal. "Like you in trouble ah what?" asked Brian as Eddy entered the classroom. "Nah, ole man just wanted to ask me why I was absent yesterday." Mr. Harris was only fifty-two but every secondary school principal had a nick name and Mr. Harris' was 'ole man' or sometimes 'viper'.

"You showed him your excuse though." asked Sean. "Yeah, yeah, no worries man. Ole man just wanted something to do. He was just checking up on me I guess." Brian steupsed. "I doh understand that man boy," he said biting into a hamburger he had just bought. Eddy reached into his knapsack and unwrapped the wax paper around his stew chicken sandwiches. "I good. As long as I not in any trouble with Harris, I good," said Eddy just before biting into the soft hops bread.

On the other side of town, Sally was getting her hair done at Gina's. She looked quite a sight with strands of her hair wrapped in tiny pieces of foil and a black protective nape in front of her. A few other clients that Sally knew only as acquaintances were being attended to by Gina's assistants. "Are you Ok Sal? You are awful quiet today," said Gina as she carefully removed the pieces of silver foil from Sally's hair. Gina had never seen Sally looking so dejected and was genuinely worried. "I'm alright, just a bit tired. I haven't been sleeping too well. I think I might be coming down with the flu," Sally replied. It was a conservative enough answer which she figured would be able to throw Gina off what was really on her mind. Sally enjoyed chatting with Gina but she didn't feel comfortable enough to discuss matters as delicate as Matt's infidelity with her.

"How is that handsome son of yours?" Gina inquired. "Oh he is fine. Good head on his shoulders that boy. There's some girl he likes now. Her name is Jesse but I don't think it will amount to much."

"Why do you say that?"

"Well she lives all the way in Santa Cruz for starters, her mother is a market vendor, her father is dead and well I just can't see Brian going that route again after all we went through with Amy. Plus she lives so far out in the bushes. I don't see him driving all the way there every time he has to see her. I just think it is another one of those phases that he is going through," Sally replied. Talking about her son briefly helped her to take her mind off her marital woes if only for a moment. "I keep joking with Marlene that it would be so good if Brian hooks up with Sianne when she gets older. That would make life so simple for both of us and that way we would really be related." Gina and Sally laughed at the thought because Sianne was only twelve years old.

"I wouldn't worry about Brian. He'll probably do just like his father and marry someone very special and for all the right reasons," Gina added. She could tell Sally needed some buttering up. Sally on the other hand wondered about Gina's last comment. Did Gina know about Matt's outside woman perhaps? If only she knew the real reasons Matt had married her. She wanted to think it was because he loved her but what if there were other more disturbing reasons?

His family had not been in approval of the relationship from the outset, especially when things began to get serious. But Matt was already in his thirties and not a very sociable character. So even though the Chow Fatts were not fond of his choice of bride, they could tell that Matthew was sincerely happy and deeply in love. That and the fear that if he didn't marry soon there would be questions about his sexual orientation, led them to accept Sally with open arms. But that was at a superficial level only. Those arms continued to remain open and stiff like the arms of a plastic doll. Even when Sally tried to reach out to Matt's sisters by inviting them over to dinner there were always excuses. In the end Sally accepted the fact that her in-laws would always be distant and tried to avoid them as much as possible except for Christmas and Easter time when they would usually have huge family gatherings.

Before Sally could probe Gina about the latest gossip to find out if she had heard anything about Matt from anyone, Gina had turned on the hair dryer. "Ok Sal, just a few minutes under there and Matt won't take his eyes off you tonight," said Gina. Sally looked at her watch as she sat down and felt the warm air from the dryer blowing on to her ears. It was almost three o'clock and she was anxious about seeing Senora Velasquez, especially since she didn't have a firm appointment. Her probing of Gina would have to wait for another day. Hopefully it wouldn't even be necessary because she and Matt would reconcile things. As bad as their relationship seemed, Sally couldn't imagine her life without Matt or being anyone else but Mrs. Sally Chow Fatt.

Down at the Port-of-Spain market things were busy. Sorrel was in season and a desirable commodity at this time of year. It was as if Christmas signaled the beginning of cooking season and more cooking meant more selling of produce. At Ms. Janice's stall, experienced market shoppers were breaking off the ends of ochroes, squeezing tomatoes and red apples and heaping mounds of sorrel into the plastic bags that Ms. Janice was handing out to would be buyers. "Two pongs dat is five dollars," said Ms. Janice to a customer as she tied a knot at the end of a plastic bag of tomatoes and handed the bag back to one customer. "Yes get yuh grapes here fiiiive dollars a pong, fiiiiive dollars!" Ma Thomas belted out. Her voice was not as sweet as Ms. Janice's but that didn't stop her from advertising her goods. Her grapes and apples were selling fast and she was glad that she had diversified her market offerings even though she didn't know that was the term used to describe what she had done.

There was a steady flow of customers into Port-of-Spain market and many other voices of men and women, boys and girls of many ages singing their song of "Pigeon peeeees, get yuh fresh pigeon peeees here!" or "Chive and celery folks. Yeeeees get your chive and celery to season de chicken!" or "Smoke herring an saltfish, smoke herring an saltfish!" Even Papa Netty as drunk as he was, could be seen selling his few limes. In a high pitched playful voice he screamed out "LIIIMES!" Then in a low serious tone he added "Fuh de fish and chicken." Some of the consumers found his call to buy entertaining and turned in his direction to see the man behind the voice. Papa Netty was sitting on a stool with an overturned white plastic bucket between his legs and a scattering of limes on top the bucket.

"Well, well Papa Netty really takin de wok serious today," Ma Thomas remarked to Ms. Janice when there was a lull in the crowd. "Yeah boy, he ent making joke," Ms. Janice responded. "Yuh know ah cook dat Cascadoo he give meh on Sunday," said Ms. Janice. "What!" Ma Thomas could not believe that after all her good advice, Ms. Janice had actually eaten the Cascadura. "It taste good too." Ma Thomas shook her head several times in disapproval. "Ah doh know what to tell yuh again yes," she said in a disappointed tone of voice.

Just at that moment, Papa Netty having sold all his limes was making his way towards the stalls of his two favorite women with his bucket in hand. "Speak of the devil." Ma Thomas muttered under her breath. "How are my ladies doing today?" asked a half drunk Papa Netty. "Ah hope yuh ent spending all dat money out in de rum shop," said Ma Thomas. Papa Netty steupsed. "Why yuh doh leave people alone eh. Is my money to spend. But ay-ay!" Focusing his attention on Ms. Janice he asked "And how is de lovely lady today?"

"You doh worry bout me. I very good," said a smiling Ms. Janice. She had grown used to Papa Netty's ways and found him incorrigible. "What a pong for yuh tomatoes?" A would be customer interrupted Papa Netty's conversation with Ms. Janice much to his dismay. "Anyway ladies I gone," Papa Netty said with a wave of his hand. "Right oh," said Ms. Janice. Ma Thomas was silent. She just sprinkled some sell water over the goods in her stand. She didn't want Papa Netty's blight to affect her business.

It was almost five o'clock when Sally found the address of Senora Velasquez in Cascade. She was a bit uncertain whether she was in the right place so she called on her cell phone and asked the Senora to look outside. In the porch of a dainty yellow colored flat house with a brown wrought iron gate, a grey haired lady with large hoop earrings and a colorful head tie around her head opened the door and waved in the direction of Sally's black Volvo. Sally expected to see a host of cars outside the gate of this well known seer woman but was grateful that there was no one there; even though she began to wonder whether Senora actually had a clientele. She was wearing her darkest shades and quickly glanced in the direction of the nearby houses. She most certainly didn't want anyone to see her visiting the Senora.

"Come in mi hija," said the Senora with her heavy Venezuelan accent. "I've been expecting you," she said as she opened the tiny gate to let Sally in. Senora had on a little too much make up. Her cheeks were as red as her lips and her long red satin skirt matched her lipstick and blush but did nothing to complement her figure. Two brown and white Pompeks appeared out of nowhere and ran up to Sally's feet excitedly with tails wagging. "Don't mind them. They don't bite. They are my little angels." As she walked through the front door, Sally could sense that she was in the presence of some sort of force. Senora offered her a seat and smiled back at her gently through grey eyes. Sally removed her shades and sat down on the wooden chair across a round wooden table from the Senora.

There were not too many furnishings in the house. A lemon green floral patterned living room set, worn out and discolored, was the most outstanding piece of furniture in the living room. A beaded curtain separated the kitchen from the dining area and it made a gentle musical sound as it swung in the breeze. The floor was wooden and creaked as Sally pulled in her chair closer to the table. Sally focused her eye on a clear looking crystal ball that lay in the centre of the table along side a pack of oversized cards that looked like tarot cards.

"So tell me Sally, what is troubling you today?" Senora asked. Her hands were wrinkly and soft looking. She stretched across the table and gently held Sally's hands in hers. Sally wondered how the woman knew her name but then she reminded herself that she was Sally Chow Fatt and didn't really need an introduction. "Did Marlene call you about me?" Sally asked. "Oh no mi hija but my spirits told me to expect you today," Senora replied. Sally was not sure the woman before her was genuine or could even make a difference in her situation but she figured that nothing could make her marriage situation any worse. Sitting upright, Sally tossed her hair back and began. "It isn't anything too serious really. It's just that…"

"Darling you are here are you not?" Senora interrupted her while squeezing gently down on her hands. "If you are here then there is problem. If there was no problem you not here Si?" Senora bent her head and peered at Sally as if waiting for a response. Sally nodded. She knew why she was there, she just hated the fact that she was. She looked down at Senora's soft hands holding hers and thought about all that she had been through with Matt in the last few months. "Ok so we try again, no? Tell Senora what is troubling you my child" said the moon faced lady. "Let Senora help you."

Brian had been waiting at the QRC entrance for at least half an hour for his driver before he decided to walk over to Oxford Street for classes with Mr. Lee Wen. He had thought about calling his mother to let her know that the driver had not shown up but he was actually looking forward to walking somewhere for a change. It seemed that he never walked anywhere outside of the school gates. He was always either driving or being chauffeured from one place to the other. Something had probably come up, because Alfred was usually always on time. Brian and Eddy had been discussing their girl issues for at least half an hour. Eddy was grateful that Brian had not only missed seeing him on television but had completely ignored the suggestion by other students that the person they had seen was Eddy.

"I'll walk with you if yuh walking," said Eddy. "Are you sure? I mean it's Ok if you have to study and things like that," Brian replied. "Nah, no worries." The two set out crossing the Savannah first to stop and buy some phoulourie from the Creole lady that sold phoulourie there. The tamarind sauce dripped down the sides of their hands as they relished each phoulourie ball. As he walked around the savannah, Brian couldn't help but be thankful for a friend like Eddy. The breeze against their skin, the runners and walkers all trying to get fit in time for the Carnival season, the speeding cars passing by, even the exhaust fumes emanating from some of them, made Brian wish that he could walk more often to experience Port-of-Spain like that. There was a certain peace about the evening as the friends walked and talked about Lisa and Jesse, school and other students, teachers and of course Mr. Harris.

Brian felt that he could trust Eddy with anything and know that Eddy would not betray his trust. He didn't trust Sean as much as he trusted Eddy. Actually it was beginning to feel as if he just tolerated Sean because his mother and Sean's mother were friends. But Eddy was his real 'riding pardner' and he couldn't imagine how he could make it through Upper Six without him. They had just arrived outside Mr. Lee Wen's 'House of Pain' on Oxford Street. "Alright then bro, I'll see you tomorrow," said Eddy as he turned to make his way home. "Ok then, later."

The words barely had the chance to come out of Brian's mouth when he heard the screeching brakes of a car stop in the middle of the road. Eddy turned to see three doors of a B14 Sentra motor car open. Brian had stopped too. He couldn't imagine why the car would stop in the middle of the road. Men wearing jeans and black t-shirts with masks covering their faces jumped out of the car and grabbed Brian by the arms and legs. "Aye! Aye! What allyuh doing!" Eddy had already dropped his knapsack and almost instinctively was rushing in to fight off the men. Brian only had a chance to let out a shocked yelp for help before collapsing in their arms under the powerful force of chloroform. Eddy ran into a swift punch which landed on the left side of his face rocketing his jaw. He stumbled back and his head hit the concrete with a loud thud. Eddy's head was throbbing with pain as he struggled to get up.

"Stay down if yuh know what f---king good fuh yuh white boy." A husky voice from behind the dark stockings boomed at Eddy and he could see the gun in the man's hand pointing directly downward at him. "Oh God!" a passerby screamed when she saw what had just happened. The driver in the car behind the B14 sat speechless and stunned in his car. Two of the men stood guard at the open doors with semi-automatic rifles and dark stockings covering their faces. When Brian was securely in the vehicle, they surveyed the onlookers jumped in and with a loud screech the car sped off.

Eddy's heart was beating fast. In the smoking fumes the car left behind he was able to see that there was no license plate number on the rear of the vehicle. A woman crossed the street and stooped beside Eddy who was still trying to get up. "You alright boy?" she asked as she gripped his arm and helped him to his feet. Eddy had a massive headache that radiated all the way to his eyeballs. He touched the back of his head and felt wetness in the area where he had taken the fall.

He looked down at his hand and saw the bright red fluid on his fingertips. "Oh gosh. Yuh better go to the hospital. He buss yuh head. Somebody call de police and emergency."

Everything happened in the blink of an eye but by the time it was over, onlookers and students had gathered around the gate that marked the entrance to Mr. Lee Wen's building. Mr. Lee Wen and his wife came scurrying down the stairs as a crowd began to gather around Eddy to speak about what they had seen. Some girls that had seen Brian being bundled into the car began crying. Some who had seen nothing at all were also crying by the time they had heard what had happened.

"Yuh alright Eddy?" Mr. Lee Wen asked.

"Yeah I alright."

"He needs to go to the hospital" the woman who had helped him insisted.

"What happened?"

"Sir I was walking away and then next thing ah turn around and ah see dese men struggling to get Brian and by de time I rush in one of de fellas just cuff me outta no where." All eyes were on Eddy as he related what he had seen to the worried crowd. "Somebody needs to call that boy's parents. Oh Lord what Trinidad coming to," another Good Samaritan interjected.

"We need to call the police right away and Brian's parents," Mr. Lee Wen told his wife who quickly left the crowd and ran up the stairs to do the needful. Motorists parked their vehicles at the side of the road and came out to see if they could be of assistance. Before Eddy knew what was going on, he was in a car being taken to the Port-of-Spain General Hospital. Still in a daze from the whole event and with a very bad headache, Eddy felt that he was watching a movie play out before him. As the stranger whose car he was in pulled up at the entrance to the Accident and Emergency room of the Port-of-Spain General hospital, all Eddy could think about was Brian and what had just occurred. He wondered about the men that had just taken Brian. Why did they take him? What did they want? Where were they from? But most of all was he ever going to see Brian alive again?

Chapter Thirteen

We Turn to God and Other Things

*A*s Sally looked into her rear view mirror and touched up her make-up, she wondered how Senora Velasquez had been able to get her to talk so much. She felt ten pounds lighter, as though a huge load had been lifted off her shoulders. She looked again into her black leather handbag at the tiny cloth bag that Senora Velasquez had given her. "If this doesn't work nothing will" she thought to herself. She had just started the key in the ignition when she heard her cell phone ring.

"Hello"

"Yes this is she." Sally could not believe what she was hearing.

"What. Oh my God! Where is he now? What!"

"Ok, I'll be right there."

Her heart was pounding in her chest as she put the gear in reverse. A plethora of questions ran through her mind. Why would anybody want to take Brian? Did they plan on killing him? Was he hurt? Where were they taking him? Who would do something like this? Enemies of Matt? What did they want with her child? Sally felt ill as she thought of her child, her one boy child that God had blessed her with, taken at the hands of strangers. She didn't know how she would be able to live if anything happened to him. Losing Matt was one thing but Brian was hers and nobody, not even Matt could take him away from her. She anxiously picked up her cell phone with her free hand and called Matt. "Matt I just got a call about Brian," her voice was trembling and her face had gone a deathly pale. "Yes I know. I'm down on Oxford Street now with the police. Where are you?" Sally couldn't believe how calm and steady Matt's voice was.

"I'm coming around the Savannah"

"Ok, well I'll see you in a few minutes" and before Sally had a chance to say more, Matt had already hung up.

Hearing Matt's voice on the phone reminded Sally of why she had been at Senora Velasquez's instead of …..then it suddenly hit Sally. She had given Alfred their driver the day off on a day when Brian had extra lessons. Brian must have walked to Mr. Lee Wen's. "Why didn't he call me?" she thought. She had been so busy with trying to salvage her marriage that she had not been paying attention to her son's weekly schedule.

The thought that her negligence could have created an opportunity for someone to harm her child weighed heavy on her brain.

Brian's whole life flashed before her in that instant. She remembered how she had endured a long ten hour labor at the St. Clair nursing home which was eventually ended when the doctors decided to do a Cesarean section; Brian's first birthday party when he was one year old; his first pet, Fluffy, a loving Pompek who had to be put down because she was dying of cancer and more recently she remembered how upset he had been when he realized that Amy was really going away. Sally knew that her child would never be able to survive a beating or whatever these people, whoever they were planned to do to him. Did Brian have enemies perhaps? Surely not she thought. He was the most well liked, well loved boy in his school. He was the Head Prefect. True there may have been jealous classmates but not enough to harm him. If these were men that had taken Brian, they must be men who were Matt's enemies; men who wanted money.

It didn't take Sally long to get from Cascade to Oxford Street but by the time she arrived, she could see that a crowd had gathered. Matt was on his cell phone and there were about seven police officers in uniform and bullet proof vests standing around. Mr. Lee Wen and his wife were in that circle too and Sally could see Mr. Lee Wen gesticulating in the direction that the car had probably driven off in. Sally pushed her shades up on her forehead and ran out of her car in a daze toward Matt. She ran straight into his arms almost instinctively and he gently held her close. "Mr. and Mrs. Chow Fatt, we will need for you all to come down to the station to answer a few questions. The anti-kidnapping squad will want to speak with you also," said a burly looking Corporal Stewart.

"Of course" Matt seemed almost emotionless but Sally had grown used to him after all these years. She wasn't sure if it was genetic or simply a result of Matt's upbringing. All she knew was that when she really needed him to cry or to laugh or to show some sign that there was really a human heart inside of the stone-faced exterior that he was presenting he would disappoint her miserably. "I'll follow you down to the station," said Matt to the police officer. "Alright then" Corporal Stewart and his fellow officers began walking towards their vehicles. "I'll take you down with me in the Volvo," said Matt as he placed his hand on Sally's back and guided her to the car. Sally had a million questions to ask but none of them formed on her lips. It was if all of a sudden she had become confused and beh-beh. Her entire body seemed to become weak and her head was spinning. The weakness seemed to envelope her head like a shroud and a mist of darkness was slowly hovering above her eyelids. She could feel herself falling, and then suddenly everything went black.

Earlier that day Lystra had embarked on a mission to carry food for her brother and to see what his condition was. She had been the source of ridicule for her neighbors even before Tommy went on the streets but now that she had decided to give her life over to

Jesus, it seemed that the attacks on her character had become more scathing. "What dat ole ho playin at all eh? All de time she takin she man now all on a sudden she goin to church. Look like anybody could become a Christian yes gyul." It was comments like this that would hurt Lystra to the core. She knew she had done a lot of things with a lot of men but she had a child to feed and it was because of her he was able to go to school and do so well. She was damn proud of that and although she knew in her past life she was not the pinnacle of virtue, as far as she was concerned she was doing her very best to change, which was a lot more than she could say for the rest of her neighbors.

"Allyuh see a fella name Tommy here recently?" Lystra was standing arms akimbo in the heat of the midday sun at Tamarind Square. None of the residents of Tamarind Square responded to her question. They were all very busy. In one corner a young man no more than thirty years old sat emptying the contents of a garbage bag he had just pilfered from one of the city litter bins. Another barebacked young man in tattered green short pants lay outstretched and stiff as the cardboard he lay on. One grey haired man was squatting and relieving his bowels on the grass. A few others were mumbling to themselves or cursing out loud. Lystra stood close enough to the man who was searching the garbage bag for food or whatever he was looking for.

"Yuh see a fella name Tommy out here today?" The man looked straight at her, with his dirty beard and uncombed tuft of hair. Lystra had to describe Tommy to the elderly man before she could get a response. "Go by Woodford Square nah. He real sick. Dey run he from here de udder night." With that, he was at it again pitching bottles and every type of rubbish out to left and right of him. Lystra was deeply disturbed by the words of this garbage hunter; she turned and made her way hastily toward Frederick Street. She didn't hear the angry horns of the cars stuck in the congestion of Independence Square or the sights of stalls with bunches of grapes hanging down and arrays of red, yellow and gala apples. The Christmas music emanating from the boom boxes of the hustlers as they pushed their battery operated carts on wheels flew over her head. She could not appreciate the Christmas tree decorations and lights in the showcases of the stores she passed by either. Tommy was the only person on her mind. What had become of him? The moment she had heard the words 'real sick' she knew that it could only mean one thing. Tommy had AIDS. What else could it be she thought? If he was "bulling" that was the only logical interpretation of the words 'real sick'.

The pavement was crowded with Christmas shoppers on Frederick Street. Everyone was buying something; whether it was Christmas curtains, kitchen towels, ornaments, shoes or children's toys. It was a very good day for commerce. Lystra had to push her way through but eventually she arrived at the St. Ann's taxi stand and could see Woodford Square across the street from her. The Square was busy too. Tents had been set up to catch the business of pedestrians passing through on their way to work or home. Lystra entered the Square. Her eyes were not on the displays of household items and toys on sale but on the benches and the Square corners. If Tommy was sick he would most likely be lying down somewhere.

Her heart was pounding in her chest as she looked for any sign of Tommy on the faded green benches. One dark skinned man lay sunbathing in tattered red khaki pants with his head turned aside and for a moment her hopes went up. He didn't look too badly she thought but as she approached the bench and looked at his face she realized the man was not Tommy. She moved away quietly not wanting the man to be awakened by her presence. She passed the University of Woodford Square which was in progress and looked around for Tommy but he was not there.

"Oh God poor Tommy!" Lystra could not hold back the tears as the thought of him in some corner sick and dying flashed through her head. If only she could find him. In her hand was a plastic bag containing Tommy's favorite in a styrofoam container; rice with pigeon peas and a stewed chicken leg. It was still warm and she wanted to find him before it began to get cold. Where the hell was Tommy? Where could he be? She walked out of Woodford Square and contemplated whether she should look for him on Duke Street or return to Tamarind Square and try again. Instead, she turned and began making her way back to Independence Square; perhaps he was there at least closer to the Wrightson Road side. There were vagrants on Independence Square; perhaps he was on a bench there. Lystra was determined to locate her brother. She was going to do something to help him this time, not like the other times when she had just left him there. If he was dying, at least he should die in the comfort of a hospital bed and not out on the street like some dog.

When Sally came to, she was sitting in the passenger seat of her car with no shoes on and her head between her knees. She raised her head up knowing that it was probably looking a bedeviled mess anyway. In front of her stood Matt's sister, Lue-Ann with a Chinese styled hand fan she was waving vigorously in Sally's face. "Where's Matt?" Sally asked. "How do you feel?" Lue-Ann asked without answering Sally's question.

"I'm Ok. Where's Matt?"

"He went to the police station."

"I'll take you home Sally" said Lue-Ann in a low authoritative voice.

Lue-Ann was Matt's eldest sister. She had no children and had never married. She instead had become a covenant member of the Water of Life Catholic Community on Frederick Street where she lived. She wore a long jeans skirt and a white cotton blouse with an oversized crucifix around her neck which in Sally's mind was only one adjective away from gaudy. With her low hair cut she could easily pass for a nun if it were not for the tiny gold earrings that peeked out from her ear lobes. She helped Sally put her legs in the car, slammed the door shut, walked around to the driver's side of the car and hopped in. Sally lay back in the passenger's seat which had been adjusted so that she could almost lie down in it. She still felt a bit weak but was furious that Matt had left her with the sister he knew she liked the least and had gone to the police station without her.

"Can't we go to the police station?" Sally asked as nicely as she could. "No. Matt said it would be best if I took you home" Lue-Ann replied, in a tone that made it clear to Sally that it was not a subject for debate. Sally hated feeling like second place to Matt's sisters but she knew that she was. The two drove home in silence and at a time when there was so much to be said not a word was spoken between them. Sally kept trying to reach Matt on his cell phone but he would not pick up. "Matt said Rosita is waiting for you at home," said Lue-Ann with a stiffened upper lip reminding Sally of all the reasons why she disliked Matt's sisters. When the car pulled up in the driveway Rosita came running as fast as her knobby legs would carry her. Lue-Ann quickly greeted Rosita, said a few words to her, gave her the car keys and left in another vehicle that had followed them there.

"Mrs. Chow Fatt, I heard what happened. It's terrible," said Rosita as she opened the car door and tried to help Sally out of her seat. Rosita was speaking at a mile a minute but all of it was going over Sally's head. She couldn't understand why Matt had been so insensitive toward her at a time like this. She had not managed to get any information from him, the police or Mr. Lee Wen before collapsing and now Matt was at the police station while she had been tucked away at home and sidelined. "Brian is my child, more mine than his," she thought to herself. As she hobbled through the door way with one arm over Rosita's neck she wondered whether Matt would have waited for Priya if she had fainted. And as silly and as inappropriate as the thought may have been, she began to question whether Matt's liaison with Priya had something to do with Brian's snatching.

By three o'clock Lystra was so hungry that she had bought a potato pie from a pie man on Brian Lara Promenade just to kill the gas bubbling in her stomach. After walking the length and breadth of the promenade, she returned to Tamarind Square asking around for Tommy again and was directed by an old half naked lady to South Quay past the old police traffic branch building. "Dat man is a nasty man" the woman had said. She wore no underwear beneath the long tee-shirt she had on. She was certainly not in a condition to comment on hygiene but Lystra knew that that was not what she meant when she had called Tommy a 'nasty man'. "Gimme a dollar nah lady" she shouted behind Lystra as she walked away. When she realized that for her help no money would be forth coming, she hurled a heap of curses behind Lystra leaving passers by to wonder what had transpired between the two women to cause the unleashing of such a venomous attack of foul language.

Not at all perturbed by the woman, Lystra continued her search. Behind the wall of an old abandoned building down on South Quay was where she eventually found her brother. The smell of a dead dog in the area forced her to cover her nose and mouth with her free hand. Tommy couldn't be here in this abandoned place she thought. There was rubbish everywhere; old drums, emptied garbage bags and old appliances piled up high. Lystra steupsed feeling like a fool for believing that a half naked crazy woman could actually be giving her accurate information. Just as she was about to consider her time wasted, she heard a groan. She stood still for a moment waiting to see if she would hear it again. She did. It seemed to be coming from behind one of the mounds of rubbish. Lystra was a bit apprehensive but holding her skirt gingerly, she stepped over the debris determined to find the groaning being whether it be man woman or child.

A swarm of green horse flies were buzzing around something that smelt like a dead animal. Lystra gasped when her eyes beheld the man she once knew as a brother. "Oh God!" the bag of food she was carrying fell from her hands. There amidst the old bricks and garbage, twisted into a bony fleshless mass, Tommy lay with his mouth open, flies buzzing all around his naked body. His eyes were bulging out of his head and she could count every rib. His face, indeed his entire body was covered in large sores that oozed pus. The stench was unbearable but Lystra stood there with both hands over her mouth as she watched her brother labor to take each breath.

His eyes seemed lifeless and he was gazing upwards as if looking at something; he had not seen her and even if he did would probably not be able to recognize her. The tears flowed free and fast down Lystra's cheeks. "Tommy! Oh God Tommy! Oh God! Sweet Jesus!" Lystra screamed. "Jesus, Jesus, Jesus!" She put one hand over her stomach. She could feel it churning as if a sudden gripe was coming on. Her hands and forehead became cold and clammy. She looked into his yellow eyes and knew he could not see her. She could not bear to see him. "Oh God meh brudder. Jeeeeeesuuuus!" she screamed to the sky as she beat her chest. "Jeeeeeesussss what yuh do to meh brudder!"

Lystra was like a woman gone crazy she turned away from Tommy and leaving the food right where it fell from her hand ran bawling and screaming from behind the shell of the building behind which Tommy lay. A few passers by wondered what had happened to her but nobody stopped to ask her anything. She walked back to City Gate and boarded a bus route maxi taxi, clutching her chest, shaking her head and crying; all the while attracting the stares of many commuters. She would be sick in bed for a few days before finding the strength to go outside. Her sorrow was so great that no scripture verse from the bible or prayers said over her by her Christian brothers and sisters would console her or make her body strong enough to get up and walk.

By 6.00 p.m. that afternoon the news had hit the radio stations. "The son of Port-of-Spain businessman Matthew Chow Fatt has been kidnapped. Witnesses say around 5.00 p.m. as Brian Chow Fatt was about to enter a building on Oxford Street, he was attacked by armed gunmen wearing masks, who dragged him into a waiting Sentra motor car. No ransom demands have been made by the kidnappers and in a statement to police business magnate Matthew Chow Fatt says he has no enemies and does not know why anyone would want to hurt his family. He is asking the kidnappers to spare the life of his only child and is offering a one hundred thousand dollar reward to anyone who can provide information that will lead to the recovery of his son. His wife Sally Chow Fatt is reported to have collapsed shortly after she arrived on the scene. Port-of-Spain CID and the anti- kidnapping squad are investigating."

Priya picked up the handset on her desk phone and made one last attempt to call Matt. If she didn't get through to him she was going to the police station. She wasn't thinking clearly. She had heard the news on the radio half an hour ago and had been feverishly dialing and redialing trying to get in touch with Matt. Now more than ever he would need her and she was going to be there for him. If ever there was a time when her chances for becoming the next Mrs. Chow Fatt looked good it was now but only if she played her cards right. The phone rang twice before she heard Matt answer.

"Hello"

"Matt I just heard. How are you? Where are you?"

"I'm at the police station right now and now is a bad time. Look I'll call you tomorrow Ok."

"Do you need me there?"

"That is the worst thing you could do right now. Ok. Look I'll call you Ok." Matt was sounding impatient and irritated.

"Ok. I love you Matt." Priya was waiting to hear Matt say it back or at least respond in a way that made her know that he had heard her. Instead she heard him hang up. Maybe he hadn't heard her she thought. After all he was in a police station and there was probably a lot of noise around. She was a bit disappointed that he didn't want her to be there with him but then she reminded herself that Sally was probably there and her presence would probably be inappropriate even though she felt sure Sally didn't know who she was. There would be plenty of time for being there though. Matt needed her and she was the only woman who could make him feel the way he did when he was with her or so she thought.

Unlike Sally, Priya had underestimated the power of family and society to influence the behavior of men like Matthew Chow Fatt; men society had created; men who knew that logic and practicality always came before feelings and emotions; men who could distinguish between the yearnings of the groin and the yearnings of the heart; and men who knew that power, prestige and money should never be sacrificed for the love of a beautiful woman because beautiful women abounded everywhere on the island.

Even before the news had come over the radio the telephone at the Chow Fatt's residence had been ringing off the hook. Matt's relatives and friends began arriving in droves at the house together with camera men and reporters from the leading news houses and television stations. Poor Rosita had to assume the role of informant, receptionist, and hostess all in one. "Mrs. Chow Fatt lying down sleeping right now, yuh know. She very upset bout the whole thing. She had to get some medication in order to calm her down." Not the kind of news those visiting wanted to hear but there was very little that could be done about it. Instead they busied themselves on their cell phones making phone calls and consoling Matt's relatives. Some of Brian's cousins appeared inconsolable, crying uncontrollably even though most of them were not very close to him. The men who were mostly outside in the front porch were either smoking, drinking or having important conversations on their cell phones.

Outside the front gate of the Chow Fatt residence, TV cameras and news reporters were camped outside trying to get a word of comment from those entering the premises without success. Like celebrities being stalked by the paparazzi, family members and friends whisked past the camera men taking a seemingly perverse pleasure in uttering the words 'No comment'. Inside, the women seemed to all group together around Matt's eldest sister Lue-Ann, who had returned with some women from the Water of Life Community and the well loved and respected Irish priest Fr. Fairtree. Lue-Ann was the only member of the Chow Fatt family who addressed the media upon arrival.

"This is an extremely traumatic time for the Chow Fatt family. We are truly shocked by the events of today. The Chow Fatt family is a law abiding family that has made a valuable contribution to this country. That this should happen to one of our own is simply terrible. I would just like to say to the men who did this, please reconsider your actions, it is not too late. Please let Brian go unharmed because we can assure you that if he is hurt in any way the Chow Fatt family will ensure that you are punished to the fullest extent of the law. We are also offering a one hundred thousand dollar reward for any information that will lead us to finding Brian unharmed. Brian is his parent's only son. Please think about what you are doing. That is all we have to say at this time." Lue-Ann Chow Fatt had spoken on behalf of the family as they expected she would. Although the reporters pressed her with questions, there was no more speaking to be done until she had consulted with Matt again.

Lue-Ann was the matriarch of the family. Ever since their parents had died, she had made it her business to be involved in every aspect of the lives of her brothers and siblings. If a decision did not have her blessing it was considered a bad decision destined for failure. From their choice of spouse to what kindergarten their children should attend, all the Chow Fatt siblings looked to Lue-Ann for approval. Her guidance was considered not just practical but spiritual as well. It was only when it was determined that more than prayer was needed in a situation, that a seer woman would be sought after but for most of the minor problems that arose Sister Lue-Ann as she was fondly called was able.

It was about 10.00 p.m. when a tired looking Matt returned home escorted by the police. By this time only a few family members and close friends had remained in prayerful waiting for some news. Sally had awakened too and had tried to join the group of devout Catholics in her living room who were reciting the rosary, singing hymns and calling on Saints Jude, Michael and Anthony; the last of which she knew to be the patron saint of lost items. Sally was too groggy and tearful to participate fully. How she wished Marlene was there. She had spoken to her on the telephone and she had promised to stop by but hadn't shown up. In a room without Marlene full of Matt's relatives and friends, the only person Sally trusted was Rosita. Rosita knew it too and had informed Sally as soon as she awoke of all she had heard and seen thus far on the radio and the TV. The police say the motive is money; the telephone line is to be left free in the event that the kidnappers call; Fr. Fairtree is conducting prayers in the living room with the family. That was Rosita's report.

"Matt, did you hear anything?" asked Sally who rose to her feet as soon as Matt had walked through the door. She was as helpless as a newborn baby. For a brief instant all prayers came to a halt, as Matt spoke. Very slowly and deliberately he spoke of his interrogation down at the police station, what the suspicions of the police were and what they hoped would happen. A few questions were asked and some answered and then as if Matt was oblivious to all the people who had been waiting anxiously for him, he disappeared into his bedroom. Sally followed him into the bedroom. She was pissed too that in a crowd of family and friends, Matt had not given her the individual attention that she felt she deserved as his wife. She had some questions of her own that needed answering and she wasn't about to be blown off.

"What did they tell you?"
"I told you what they just told me."
"So you were in the police station all this time"
"Yes"

"Did they say who they thought might do something like this?"

"I just told you everything I know Sally" said an annoyed Matt as he sat on the bed removing his shoes.

"Oh Matt, what are we going to do? What if we never see him again?" Sally started crying again. Matt put his arm around her and kissed her on her forehead. "It'll be alright. He'll be OK. We raised an intelligent child. These people just want money. As soon as they ask for the money we'll give it to them and we'll get Brian back. I promise." Matt was just as worried and as scared as Sally was. He was just not used to showing his emotions. The vigil for Brian came to an abrupt end after Matt had dispensed the information he had. Matt walked Lue-Ann and the other community members to the gate and exchanged a few words briefly with her before she left.

After everyone had gone, Matt opened his liquor cabinet and poured himself a drink. He needed a few drinks well in order to calm his nerves. He was overwhelmed with guilt. What if this was his fault? Was it someone from his past? Matt was clueless and worried sick. With glass in hand, he sat next to the telephone in the living room, staring at it; almost as if that would make it ring faster. But by midnight the alcohol was taking effect and he felt himself drifting off. He had just begun to doze off in the couch when Sally who couldn't sleep either came out into the kitchen. Then at 12: 35 a.m. the phone rang.

Chapter Fourteen

Not My Chile!

Jesse had heard the news about Brian's kidnapping over the radio station and in her distraught state, had called Eddy who told her what had transpired. She and Lisa had missed classes that evening because they were working on a class project and had to leave school at midday in order to go to Lopinot. Eddy in fact did not leave Port-of-Spain General Hospital until around 7.00 p.m. after receiving a few stitches to his head and being questioned by police. Lying about his address at a time like that was not a very good idea, but Eddy lied anyway. He didn't think anything would come of it. The officers had asked him questions which he thought made no sense at all. Did he know the men involved in the kidnapping? Of course he didn't. How could he? Eddy felt that he was being interrogated about the kidnapping, almost as if he had orchestrated it himself.

They obviously didn't know how close he was to Brian; that Brian was his "horse" from the beginning of Form One and that he was deathly afraid of not seeing his best friend again.

After an almost two hour wait in the emergency room during which time he answered the questions of the police constable, Eddy was finally seen by a doctor for his injuries. He received four stitches to his head and after examination, the shaking teeth in his mouth were left alone. The Good Samaritan woman who had helped him on Oxford Street remained with him right to the end. She was an elderly woman probably in her late sixties with a full head of grey hair and short in stature. She sat in the emergency room and waited patiently on Eddy, almost as if he were her very own child. When the police and doctors were done with him, he came outside to find her still waiting.

"Leh meh give yuh a ride home. Which part yuh going?" Eddy wasn't too sure whether he should say Belmont or San Juan, instead he said Curepe in the hope that she would not be from the East and at least offer to take him to City Gate but she offered no objection when he said he was going to Curepe so Eddy hopped in her car and figured that he would somehow find a way to see Lisa that night, even though he had never visited her before.

He had called Lisa earlier on the cell phone he had bought for her and had told her what had happened. Her deep concern for him made him even more certain that he wanted to be with her. She had all the qualities he thought he would want in a girlfriend. She was compassionate, down to earth, smart and confident and best of all she had an extremely attractive body. He desperately wanted to get close to Lisa physically and tonight was as good a night as any. Even if nothing happened he at least wanted to see her face and look into the deep pools of her lovely brown eyes. "Thanks so much." said Eddy as he bid farewell to his Good Samaritan.

"Will you be OK to get home from here?"

"Sure. Thanks again."

The Curepe junction intersection was a busy one, twenty-four hours a day.

"San'do by two, San'do by two"

"One for Chaguanas here"

Taxi drivers were hustling for passengers, maxi drivers were stopping to let off and pick up passengers on the bus route, fruit vendors were selling their fruit and doubles men were wrapping doubles at humming bird speed.

Eddy dialed Lisa's number while crossing the Chaguanas and San Fernando taxi stand. "Lisa, I'm in Curepe. Ah wanted to pass an check yuh but ah doh know where yuh livin."

"Yuh lie. Yuh at Curepe junction now?"

"Yeah, right outside Royal Castle."

"Why yuh didn tell me you were coming?" As excited as Lisa was that she would see Eddy that afternoon, she was completely unprepared for his visit.

"I'm on Bushe Street. Just stay there, I'll walk out to meet you."

"Ok" said Eddy smiling.

He really liked Lisa but it was more than that. She was not like some of the "force ripe" girls who used to flirt with him on Main Street Beetham. She had class and style but best of all she was always optimistic and up beat. She had shared only in brief though about her mother's boyfriend being an alcoholic and her father living abroad. Eddy admired the fact that in spite of the challenges she faced she had managed not to become jaded. She saw the beauty in life and in people, something that he somehow could not grasp at times. In a few minutes he saw her walking toward him. She had a distinct gait, almost like that of a model and an incredibly infectious smile.

"Hi, Eddy" she said as she gave him a gentle hug. "Are you Ok? Where did you get the stitches?" Her concern for him was addictive and made him want to lose himself in her love. She saw the stitches and almost instinctively touched them with her index finger. "Ouch" Eddy winced.

"I'm sorry. Oh gosh. I'm so sorry."

"It's Ok. It only hurts a little."

Lisa still couldn't believe that Eddy was standing before her.

"Come let me show you where I live," she said excitedly. If things went his way, Eddy hoped he might be able to have his first intimate moment with Lisa. She really liked him a lot, sometimes she felt that he was the brother she never had while other times the feelings were not so brotherly. Vonetta not being home was not worrying to Lisa. Her mother trusted her and had given her a great deal of independence

from an early age, so there was no question of Vonetta
disapproving of her having Eddy over. Besides, she had
had boyfriends visit her at home before.

A few rum shops away, in his favorite watering
hole, Ted was doing what he knew how to do best;
get drunk. He wouldn't be home till around midnight
when he would stir the entire household with his
cussing and carrying on. Vonetta meanwhile was
visiting with Nelson's youngest sister Carol down in
Tunapuna. Carol was the only one of his siblings that
still befriended her after Ted left. She understood why
Vonetta had taken up with another man. For women
like Vonetta and Carol, having a man was essential
for their existence in society. Vonetta had decided to
visit her sister-in-law because she had not heard from
Nelson in more than two months and she was worried.
She had called Carol who invited her over insisting that
she had some news for her. "So what yuh hear gyul?"
An anxious Vonetta had asked as she sat on Carol's bed
and placed her handbag down beside her.

"Vonnie gyul ah doh know how to tell yuh dis ting
gyul."

"Well just tell meh"

"Gyul ah hear like meh brudder marrid a white
woman up in Brooklyn."

"What! Who tell yuh dat" Vonetta was genuinely
shocked. Even though it had been more than ten years
since she laid eyes on her husband, she knew that
Nelson still loved her. She didn't expect that he would
be up in the US all this time and not have a woman
but remarrying was something she could not mentally

conceive. "Who tell yuh dat Carol?" Vonetta asked. "Dat is de talk Vonnie gyul. He only do it to get he green card ah hear. Ah even have a picture he sen for Mike."

Carol could see that Vonetta was genuinely shocked and had done her best to deliver the blow as gently as she could. She opened a shoe box and fumbled through it before putting her hand on the picture. "Gyul yuh know how it does be hard when yuh have to be looking over yuh shoulder all de time for police. Maybe he just get tired." The truth was that what had begun as a friendship between Nelson and the woman had blossomed into a full blown romance. When she discovered that he did not have his papers, she offered to marry him in order for him to be 'legal' and he accepted; neglecting to mention that he was already legally married and not divorced from his wife in Trinidad.

It was not uncommon in Brooklyn. Many West Indians married in order to become 'legal'. Some even married their cousins so that they could chase the American dream. In a few of the cases there was genuine love but for most it was simply a matter of convenience. Either way marriages of that nature usually served their purpose and came at a high price for the "papers seeking" partner. Vonetta's right hand was trembling as she clutched the picture Carol had just handed her. There was no denying it. There was her Nelson and a blonde haired white woman with her arms around him. They were both smiling like young lovers. He looked happy too. Vonetta couldn't stop looking at the picture. She placed a hand on her throat almost as if she needed to prevent something from coming out of it.

"Ah did try to call him but I eh get thru. Ah tink he change de cell phone he had or something," said Carol. "Vonnie gyul ah doh know what to tell yuh yes. Ah mean ah figure he woulda have a woman up dere but ah always thought he was coming back to Trinidad. But like he want to live an dead in America it look like." Carol could see that Vonetta was more upset than she anticipated she would be and was uncertain about what she should do or say to remove the heaviness that seemed to have descended quietly into the room. "I cyah believe Nelson woulda do me dat" said Vonetta in a shaky voice as she returned the picture to Carol. "Me too gyul I always thought he was coming back home. Well ah guess once he get regularize he go come back to visit an ting" said Carol as she placed the picture back in her shoebox of valuables.

"Yuh doh have a number fuh him eh?" Vonetta asked softly.

"No. Just de ole number. But ah tink ah could try to get his number from Mike if yuh want it."

Carol was beginning to feel badly about having broken the news to Vonetta. She honestly didn't think that it would be a big deal for Vonetta. What she didn't know was that Vonetta had never given up hope that Nelson would return to her. She had convinced herself that her life with Ted was only temporary. Nelson would return with heavy pockets from America and they would be able to buy a house and be a family again. She wouldn't have to keep that miserable job at Penny Savers and worry about paying bills. The hope of Nelson's return had kept her going from day to day. It had kept her warm on the nights when she lay beside the man who had beat her before holding her down and forcing himself on her. When Nelson came back there would be no more Ted, no more beatings, no more fighting. But Nelson wasn't coming back from the looks of things and Vonetta was having great difficulty accepting that.

"Ah have to go to de grocery before it close yes gyul." Vonetta rose to her feet and reached for her handbag. She didn't really have to go to the grocery but she needed a good reason to bring her visit to an end without it seeming rude. "Oh gosh, yuh going already?" Carol was looking forward to a much longer visit. There was so much family gossip that she needed to discuss with Vonetta. "Doh worry gyul. Next time ah will stay a little longer," Vonetta said with a smile.

"Yuh will be alright Vonnie?"

"Yeah, yeah, doh worry bout me. I good. Ah going home an make a pelau fuh Lisa an dat miserable man ah have dere."

"Alright chick" said Carol. They bid their farewells and Vonetta made her way to the Eastern Main Road so that she could get a maxi taxi.

She could not go home straight away. She needed a strong drink and something to take her mind off of what she had just heard. A cool breeze blew and gently caressed her face as she walked. The picture of Nelson and his new wife kept flashing through her mind.

Nelson had a new wife and a new life. The country boy from Marabella was going to become an American. Vonetta remembered those early days when Nelson was courting her. He didn't have much money or education but he was a hard worker and honest, not like the town men she was used to meeting. He talked his way into her heart with his broke self and had done his best to provide for her. Now he had a new wife and Vonetta couldn't help but feel that her only door of escape had been viciously and suddenly slammed shut.

Eddy had taken his shoes off and sat on the dingy living room couch as if he was at home. He had just eaten some sada roti and ochro that Lisa had prepared and was feeling very satisfied. They had spoken at length about Brian and had come up with possible motives for the kidnapping. Eddy had been very worried about his friend. It had all happened so fast that he didn't have a chance to process what had happened. "Sit down for a minute nah. I don't bite yuh know" Eddy pleaded, Lisa had been talking and washing dishes the whole time and Eddy was beginning to think that she was a bit nervous. Lisa obliged. As soon as she sat Eddy leaned over, kissed her on the cheek and said "Thank you." Lisa blushed a bit. "Small ting" she replied. There was a brief moment of silence. "Actually I just needed an excuse to kiss you and you've given it to me," Eddy said with a chuckle. Lisa slapped him across the arm playfully. "You don't need an excuse to kiss me you idiot," said Lisa smiling. Her eyes were like magnetic pools of warmth drawing Eddy in closer. She was so beautiful. He placed his hand on her soft cheeks and she closed her eyes almost instinctively. He leaned in and pressed his lips on hers gently. Eddy could feel himself getting aroused, her lips tasted so good. He opened his mouth to taste more of her and she yielded willingly. His hands moved gently from her face to her breast then under her blouse so he could feel her warm skin. Lisa had been waiting for Eddy to kiss her. She had played the scene over and over in her mind, except that now the scene was real and was moving forward rapidly at a scaringly pleasurable pace.

Her head was spinning and her body responding positively to each movement of Eddy's hand. She could feel him unbuttoning her blouse as he held her lips captive. Then her bra loosened and before she knew it, she felt his mouth kissing her breasts. "Lisa what the hell are you doing!" a voice in her head screamed. Lisa knew that she wanted to wait until she got married to have sex and as much as she cared for Eddy, she was not ready for all that was taking place on her mother's couch. She had to stop but it felt so good, so very good. Her heart was beating faster than she could think. She had to get a grip on the situation fast. Eddy had begun to unzip her pants.

"Wait" she pulled his head up from her breasts and looked straight at him. "We can't do this now," said Lisa softly. She pushed Eddy gently off her. "What's wrong?" asked a confused Eddy. He thought she was giving him all the signals to go ahead. Lisa was putting her blouse back on and Eddy began to wonder where he had gone wrong. "I really like you Eddy. I mean I care about you a lot but I'm just not ready to have sex right now," said Lisa head bowed. "Whoa! Who said anything about sex? Do you think I was about to…….. Oh boy!" Eddy shook his head in disbelief. He was pretending. He was hard in his pants and very ready to have sex with Lisa right there on the couch but he could sense that he had moved too swiftly and had to rectify the situation immediately.

"I'm sorry Lisa. I guess I just got carried away. I wasn't planning on us doing it right here and now. I just wanted to make you feel good that's all. I would never do anything you didn't want to." Eddy was genuinely sorry. He didn't want to push Lisa too soon and he realized that he had. Lisa was confused by Eddy's response but grateful that he had mashed the brakes without complaint. "I'm sorry too Eddy. I care about you a lot I just want to do this when the time is right. I don't want to have sex before I get married," said Lisa almost ashamedly. She knew that she was probably going to see the last of Eddy because of what she had just said. Eddy felt a knot in his throat. "What! What de hell is dat about! Boy you ha to dump dis one fas dread!" a voice in Eddy's head said. Lisa's declaration had shocked him. It was not what he had expected either. A fine looking woman like Lisa, he just had assumed had some experience with men. Eddy had more sexual experience than most boys his age and was not at all looking for a virgin. "I understand," he blurted out, although the truth was he really didn't. Eddy just figured that he had to say something kind. Lisa was fully dressed by now. "Well that doesn't mean that you have to go. We can still talk." She was feeling badly and was sure that Eddy was only being nice to her when he said he understood. Few men understood her position on the matter and she was beginning to wonder whether it even made sense. "I wasn't going," said Eddy. "Unless you were planning on throwing me out," he joked. Lisa slapped his arm in that playful way again.

She liked Eddy's sense of humor and his playfulness. That night they talked about school and their plans. Lisa spoke of her father and the man her mother lived with, how he drank and how she wished her mother would just kick him out. Eddy told Lisa about his uncle Tommy and how he was living in Tamarind Square. He felt so at home with her, like he could tell her anything, even about him being from the Beetham. "Tell me the truth Lisa. If I told you I was living on the Beetham would you treat me different?" Eddy asked. "No. Of course not. Why should I? That wouldn't make you any different to the person I know. That is a very silly question." Lisa steupsed. "So if I told you now that I live in the Beetham you wouldn't feel less about me." Lisa was getting irritated. "Please. Look at where I live; it couldn't be that much worse."

"Well it is yuh know and I do."

"What do you mean?"

Eddy was feeling naked as he spoke about the thing he had never spoken about before to any of his friends. "I live on the Beetham. I was born there and I live there now." Eddy was looking for some kind of reaction from Lisa – shock, disgust, anything that would make him know that he had been right to hide his secret all these years. What Lisa did next made him know then that he could never let her go, even if she wanted to wait until she was married to have sex with him. She leaned over and held his face in her hands. Her eyes held his for a moment and then she hugged him. In that brief moment Eddy felt weightless and light as if someone had gently lifted a load off his shoulders. It was a feeling he would seek over and over again.

Brian was just waking up and coming to. His throat was parched and dry and he smelt an unfamiliar sweet but sickly smell. There was darkness all around and he could feel something over his eyes. His hands were bound in front of him. He wiggled his fingers and his toes. His feet were cold, and he realized that he had on no shoes. His head was pounding and he could hear the voices of men nearby but what they were saying was inaudible. He tried to open his eyes underneath his blindfold but it was too tight. He felt as though he was lying down sideways. He tucked his feet under him and tried to sit up. It took some effort but eventually he was upright. Brian tried to touch the ground beneath his feet with his hands. It felt and smelt like dirt. He bent his head backward and tried again to see something from behind the blindfold but it was pointless, there was only darkness. He moved his shoulders from side to side and found that he didn't have to move far to hit what felt like a dirt wall. He tucked his feet under him tightly again and tried to stand up but his head hit something stiff that moved. He lifted his tightly bound hands above his head and tried to touch it. The material felt like a tarpaulin.

What had happened? Brian began to recollect the events that had brought him to this hole in the ground which was what he assumed he was in. He remembered, the struggle with the men and he remembered Eddy raising an alarm but after that everything was blank. "Where the hell am I?" he wondered. Brian knew his parents would be going crazy with worry looking for him. He wondered what time it was and remembered that his watch had a watch light in it. He tried to wriggle his fingers to touch it in the hope that he would be able to see the watch through his blindfold but his hands were too tightly bound. Brian was deathly afraid of what his abductors might do to him. They hadn't killed him yet and except for a cramp that was developing in his calf and some tenderness around his arms, he felt ok. Was this one of his father's business deals gone sour? Who would want to hurt him? How did they even know he would be there?

Brian had so many questions in his head but the ring of a cell phone forced him to divert his attention to whatever was taking place above him. He strained to listen but it sounded as though the men were walking away. Fear like a shadow was smothering him, and he began to feel the air getting thick and heavy. He opened his mouth and took in deep gulps of air but it seemed that the more air he took in the less air he had. "I'm not ready to die. I'm not ready to die," he whispered between breaths. Brian thought about his parents, Eddy and Sean, his other friends at school and Jesse. "I can't die now," he thought. "I'm too young. I have so many things I still have to do."

He groped around his prison with his hands in the hope that he would find something sharp. Nothing. Fear of death turned into determination to live. He didn't know what his captors wanted but Brian figured that perhaps he could reason with them. There must be something that could appease them besides his bloody corpse. First he had to get their attention. Straightening up on his knees and forcing his head against the canvas like material above his head Brian took a deep breath in and began shouting at the top of his lungs.

There was no police officer present when the phone rang in the wee hours of the morning at the Chow Fatt residence.

"Hello" a tired Matt answered

"We ha de boy. Nuttin goin an happen to him. All we want is tree mil"

"Is he alright?"

"You doh study dat. If we geh de money he go be alright."

"You'll get the money, just please don't hurt...."

"Dis could go dong real smooth or real f—king nasty. No police. Bring de money in a black garbage bag bout eleven o'clock tomorrow night by de Charlieville flyover. Somebody go meet yuh dere"

"Ok. Can I speak to him?"

"And remember no police if yuh want to see de boy breeding again"

"But, can I..."

"Click"

From the moment Sally realized who her husband was speaking to she had picked up the other phone line and had heard every word. With her hand clenched against her chest she approached Matt tearfully. He looked at her almost as if the entire kidnapping had been her fault.

"We should call the police right away," he said as he picked up the handset to make the call.

"What are you crazy?" Sally snatched the phone right out of his hand.

"Did you hear what they said? Didn't you hear them? They are going to kill our son if we don't give them this money and you want to call the police! I don't believe you Matt! We can't do that! We have to do as they say!"

"Yes but they could kill Brian anyway. If the police are involved at least there's a chance they'll be able to catch these no good criminals and bring them to justice."

"Justice!" Sally's eyes opened in disbelief. It was bad enough that Matt had been sleeping with another woman, now he was getting ready to get their son killed.

"Justice! You want justice! I don't give a damn about justice! If they want money we can give them that. We are going to do exactly as they say. Our son is out there somewhere and who knows what they've done to him. You are not going to take my child away from me. No. No. No. Matt No!" Sally was shaking her head and getting hysterical. With tears in her eyes she looked defiantly at him. More upsetting to her than the thought that Matt would even consider going to the police was the thought of what the vicious sounding men on the phone may have already done to Brian.

Matt knew it would be pointless to argue with her in that state and as angry as he was that some strangers had the power to manipulate him, he was just as afraid that they might use that power to harm Brian in order to get what they wanted. " Ok, ok," said Matt scratching his forehead as he thought about how he was going to get all that money in cash by tomorrow night. Sally's face softened a bit, though the tears were still rolling down her face. Just thinking about what condition Brian could be in was painful enough for her. Matt could have his woman. He could take away the last echelon of sanctity that was left of their marriage but not her child. Not her baby. Brian was the one perfect thing she had done in her life and she was not about to lose him at the hand of savages.

By the time Vonetta had come home Eddy had already gone. Lisa had the good sense to know that her mother would not be pleased to return home and find her entertaining a young man after eleven o'clock; plus she had school the next day and homework to do. Vonetta had taken a detour and had had a few beers by a pub on the Eastern Main Road. She was not a big drinker but the news she had heard from Carol required some lightening of the head. She went straight to bed, having thought long and hard about the harsh realities of her situation as she gazed into the foamy pleasurable abyss of one Carib too many. She knew she was not supposed to drink because she was pregnant but she didn't care. Suddenly having Ted's child made no sense at all. With thoughts like these she fell fast asleep on the King size bed. Her sleep was cut short though when around 1.00 a.m. her bedroom door burst open and the light switch came on.

It was Ted. He was drunk. "Wha de f—k yuh doin sleepin eh." He dragged off the sheets and began pulling her by the feet. "Get up!" he screamed. Vonetta tried to get her feet away but his grip was strong. "Oh gosh Ted behave nah man. Oh God!" She fell with a thump straight off the bed unto the cold concrete floor. As she scrambled to get up, she felt the first painful blow; a kick to the stomach. She screamed in pain as she held on to her stomach. It was swiftly followed by another and another and another. "Ted stop it! Yuh killing meh! Oh God!" Vonetta was doubled over in pain and tried to escape but each blow was more forceful and more painful. Ted was waiting in every direction she crawled toward to lift his steel tipped boots. Lisa who had heard the screams shook her mother's bedroom door violently. "Stop it! Stop it! Mommy! Open the door!" She was crying. This was not the usual beating. "Shut yuh f—king mouth chile. I am the man here." When Ted felt she had had enough, he opened the bedroom door and swaggered out allowing Lisa to rush past him. "Dat woman too blasted stupid!" he shouted as he tottered towards the front door and disappeared into the night.

Vonetta's bedroom was in absolute chaos and she lay bleeding on the ground from her mouth and between her legs. The blood seemed to be pouring out as her night gown soaked it all up. "Mommy? Mommy!

Oh God Mommy!" Lisa was scared and confused as she struggled to lift her mother up from the pool of blood she was creating on the floor. Vonetta's eyes were beginning to turn up in her head. "Oh God!" Lisa screamed as she felt her mother's body getting cold. She rushed to her cell phone and taking the emergency numbers off the refrigerator dialed the number for Mount Hope Accident and Emergency. "Yes 24 Bushe Street." Lisa was shouting into the phone. "She bleeding heavy. Come quick!" After she hung up Lisa would find more rags to soak up the blood. Her mother was hemorrhaging badly and if the ambulance didn't come soon Lisa was afraid she might not make it.

Chapter Fifteen

Life and Death in the Balance

It was seven o'clock and rays of sunlight peeked through the holes in the galvanize roof of Lystra's home. In somebody's yard, a cock with a skewed sense of time was crowing and giving his morning wake up call. Eddy turned on his bed on the floor, not wanting to get up. If he stayed in bed one minute more, he knew he would be late for school but the thought of being attacked by a flurry of questions made him pull the covers over his head. He had not bothered his mother with the events of the evening when he opened the galvanize door that night and found her groaning in pain. Eddy knew she had gone to look for Tommy. When he enquired as to what was wrong, Lystra could only whisper Tommy's name through parched lips. Then she commenced a fit of crying.

Eddy had sapped her forehead with a wash rag soaked in Alcolado Glacial and Bayrum. It was the one thing that helped to make her feel better even though it made her smell like a hospital patient. Her night had been long and restless. Eddy was exhausted although he had not slept much that night. For a long time he lay in bed thinking about Brian and what had happened to him and about Lisa. The cock crew again and Eddy steupsed. "Somebody ought to cook that bird," he thought. He turned and looked up to see how his mother was doing. She was fast asleep.

Ever since she had given her life over to Jesus, things had begun to improve around the house. The church members had got a second hand single bed with a mattress for her, which meant Eddy could sell his mattress to a piper and get Lystra's old mattress. There were groceries on a more consistent basis and Eddy would find that whenever he got home, Lystra was almost always there listening to some gospel music on the Christian radio station instead of out doing whatever she usually did when she was out.

Eddy yawned and rubbed the yampee out of his eyes as he sat up. He could hear the horns of cars speeding past each other on the highway. Somebody, most likely Bobot, one of the pipers in the area, was blasting music on his 'new' radio a few houses down. But there was definitely something going on. Eddy could hear voices and people making a commotion about something. He dragged on his rubber slippers and short pants and opened the front door. The light of the sun on his eyes caused him to squint. He saw one of his neighbors knick-named "Spranger" running past. "Eh Sprang wha goin on?" he asked. "Boy ah hear Soldier dead in de labasse. Ah now goin an see wha happen." Eddy didn't think twice. In a flash he shut the door behind him and was sprinting after Spranger to the dump.

There a crowd of men and a few women had already gathered. Most of the men were scavengers in the dump. Barebacked and in short pants they stood around, and watched helplessly as Soldier's lifeless body lay in a clearing on the ground. Eddy was an oddity among the sea of dark colored bodies and clothing. He pushed his way through the crowd to see if it was really Soldier. It was. There he lay eyes closed, legs spread-eagled in a short pants. His brown skin was bruised and dirty and his dreadlocks lay all about his head. There was blood on the side of his face and arms. Eddy could hear the people talking. "If ah had know he was sleepin dere ah woulda wake he up dis morning," one scavenger said. Men shook their heads; women held their clothes to their faces and barefooted half naked children looked on in awe.

"So long we waiting on de ambulance to come here. What happen, ambulance doh come on dis side again ah what" a man steupsed. There was no one bawling or wailing over Soldier. He had no real family on the Beetham, except for the few scavenger friends he had made. Soldier was only twenty-five years old. The newspapers would read this way the following day. "A twenty-three year old man died suddenly at the Beetham dump yesterday when a garbage truck

229

emptied its contents on him, while he lay sleeping. Moses Sherwood was sleeping in the dump when around 5.00 a.m. a dump truck was emptied on him. The driver of the dump truck said he had no idea that Sherwood was sleeping there and insists that if he had seen him, he would have alerted him. Sherwood who had no next of kin in Trinidad is believed to have come to Trinidad illegally from Guyana. Besson Street police are investigating the incident."

"Moses Sherwood? Ah never know dat was he name." Eddy told Spranger the following day when they heard the news on the radio in Charlie's rum shop.

"Yeah me neither. I always know him as Soldier"

"Me too"

Soldier's death was yet another blow in a series of difficult blows for Eddy. Seeing Tommy in Tamarind Square had been depressing enough and Brian's kidnapping had been extremely difficult for him but Soldier's death was like the 'straw that broke the camel's back'. "Well at least he in a better place now. But ah wonder who goin an bury he?" Spranger asked. This question pulled Eddy away from the sea of despairing thoughts which was beginning to engulf him. "Ah think dey does stay in the morgue an den if nobody claim he dey go burn de body."

"Hmm.Poor Soldier."

"Charlie leh we take one more for Soldier" said Spranger. "May he res in peace. Amen."

"Mrs. Williams will be alright. She suffered a few injuries to the pelvic area and well unfortunately she lost the baby but she is going to live." A young Indian doctor who looked like he was only nineteen adjusted his spectacles as he brought them the news. "You should make a report to the police though. Whoever did this to her could have killed her." Lisa shook her head in agreement. "Ok take care." With those last words, the doctor was off white coating swinging as he walked. Carol and Lisa breathed a sigh of relief. A swarthy looking nurse who had been listening smiled at them. "Doh worry, she will be ok. Go home and rest now. She sleeping anyway so yuh could probably come back later during visiting hours," said the nurse.

"Can we see her?" Lisa just wanted to know that her mother was still breathing.

The nurse looked right and left almost as if she was about to commit some crime. "Well we not supposed to really but go quick. Five minutes," she warned softly as she showed the two to Vonetta's bedside on the gynecology ward. When Lisa saw her mother's petite frame lying under white sheets and looking almost lifeless, a sense of anger welled up inside her. Vonetta's face was swollen and there was a breathing tube around her nose hooked up to an oxygen tank. One of her eyelids seemed to have ballooned up to three times its size and drooped down almost as if it wanted to touch her nose. Each breath seemed labored and heavy. Lisa smoothed back her mother's hair and kissed her forehead lightly.

"Come chile, let's go. We'll come back later," said Carol as she gently pulled Lisa away from the bed. Lisa's eyes were full. She had never seen her mother like this before and she did not want to leave her side. Of all the savage things that Ted had ever done to Vonetta, Lisa was convinced that this was his most savage attack yet and was confused as to what could have prompted it. In a zombie like state, she walked out of the ward and through many hospital doors as she and Carol made their way to the bus route. Carol was talking a mile a minute, going on about how terrible Ted was and how Lisa's father would never have treated her mother like that and how Vonetta didn't deserve that. It all blew past Lisa's ears like the cool night breeze.

Now more than ever, Lisa was determined to find a way to get Ted out of their lives. If her mother was prepared to be a punching bag for him, Lisa was not about to standby and watch. Her mother would have to chose, between her and Ted. Whatever the choice, Lisa knew she could never have another night at Mount Hope Accident and Emergency like the one she had just endured.

By midday, the day after Brian's kidnapping, the Chow Fatt's had heard words of consolation and support from almost the entire business community. The kidnapping had made front page news the following day and sound bites were being replayed on every radio and television station in the land. Rosita had been busy fielding calls and taking messages while some of Matt's family, namely Lue-Ann and one of his older aunts who was not in the pink of health herself continued to pray in the house. Sally could not be rousted from her bed of pain. She had not been able to eat anything since she had heard the news. Although she knew there was a chance that he might be recovered that day, her stomach gurgled with anxiety. She was weak from crying and lay on her bed dehydrated, pale and exhausted from worrying.

Matt had been able to obtain three million TT dollars in one hundred dollar bills by two o'clock that afternoon. Later that night he transferred the money to two large black garbage bags as instructed. Matt was licensed to carry a firearm and had a pistol which never left the house. It was kept along with some other valuables in a safe in his bedroom. Against his better judgment, Matt took the firearm with him that night. It was difficult to leave the house with all the back and forth traffic of friends, family and well wishers but somewhere between answering the telephone and speaking with well wishers, Matt was able to slip away unnoticed.

As he drove down the highway that night, all he could think about was Brian. He was determined to get him back alive and in one piece even if God forbid he had to kill somebody. He nervously glanced into his rearview mirror wondering if anyone was following him. As he approached the Charlieville flyover he wondered how the kidnappers would recognize him. He drove up to the fly over and turning left veered his car off the main road and stopped. There, alone and afraid for his life, Matt waited. Someone must be looking out for him. He wondered whether he should put his window down so that the kidnappers could see his face, then he thought against it.

After a few seemingly never ending minutes he saw two men approaching the car and assumed that they must be the men he had to deal with. As they drew closer, Matt unlocked the doors. The two strangers entered his car; one in the passenger seat in the front and one at the back. It was almost as if they had expected the doors to be open. Their faces were not covered but Matt did not want to look at them too closely. He was afraid. They smelt of sweat, machine oil and bagasse. One of the men stuck a gun in his waist and ordered Matt into the rear of the car where he was blindfolded. The man in the back seat dug through his pants pockets and removed his wallet and cell phone. The man with the gun in the front seat took the wheel and proceeded South.

Matt didn't know what direction they were heading in. He didn't really care. He just wanted to see Brian alive at the end of it all. In a cane field in Chaguanas the driver turned off onto a narrow dirt road. The car bumped up and down creating a dusty haze in the darkness as he went. The men it seemed were anxious to finish business. When the car came to a stone grinding halt, Matt's blind fold was removed and he followed the instructions he received to place his hands above his head as he exited the car. A man who smelt stink of perspiration, patted him down to ensure that he had no weapons with him while three other men in masks which covered their faces armed with semi-automatic rifles looked on. Matt was glad that they had not discovered his firearm under the driver's seat in his car.

The men wore dark clothes and although it was nighttime, the headlights of the Volvo and the headlights of another vehicle facing them nearby made things fairly visible. Matt was made to face the car door with his back to the men. He felt the cold poking of a gun behind his back as another man from behind stepped forward. The car trunk was opened and the man who had patted him down quickly inspected the packs of bound blue notes there. "Better doh have no markers in here yuh know. Or else we go ha to finish de wok."

Salty beads of sweat poured down Matt's face and his heart was racing as he realized at that instant, in the murky darkness of a cane field, that for all his money, power and influence, his life and the life of his son lay in the hands of a few hardened criminals, probably thieves, murderers maybe. Everything he did, didn't do, said or didn't say would determine whether or not he and Brian walked out of that cane field alive. It was a humbling experience for a man as proud as Matthew Chow Fatt. He had never felt so defenseless and so vulnerable in his entire life. Matt heard the men discussing something and then, the engine of the other vehicle came on.

Matt was trying to see if he could make out the license plate number but he couldn't see one. He had been observing everything that his range of vision would allow him too and as scared as he was, was making mental notes in his head about everything going on around him. He had guessed the number of men present and had tried to get a good look at their sneakers, since they all wore black pants and t-shirts with no distinguishing feature. They all seemed to be around the same height and Matt would have liked to turn his head around to see what was going on behind him but he didn't want to cross the men.

The other vehicle screeched as it reversed and came to a halt right alongside the trunk of the Volvo. Matt could hear the men's feet in the dirt as they slammed his trunk shut and jumped up into the other vehicle. Matt gathered that it must be some sort of van they were using. All the while the man with the gun in his back stood vigilant so Matt could not see what was going on behind him but he gathered from all the movement that the money had been taken. If the money was in their possession then he should be seeing Brian by now. "They couldn't be taking all the money and not showing him his son," Matt thought. Even from what he was used to seeing in the movies, he knew that if he didn't make some demand to see his child breathing, these crooked men could drive away leaving him without money or Brian.

"I want to see him." All of a sudden Matt felt constriction around his throat as if someone had him in a tight grip. In fact he had spoken so softly that nobody had really heard him. Even the man who had him at attention had not heard him, because although his gun was sticking into Matt's ribs, he was closely observing the activity behind him. "I want to see him!" said Matt a little louder. His voice was trembling as he spoke. This time Matt knew he was heard because he received a quick painful jab with the gun that moved him forward.

"Wha yuh say dere boss man?" the voice boomed in his ear spraying a mist of spittle upon the side of Matt's face. For a moment there was silence as Matt attempted to speak up. "You have the money now where is my son!" he shouted. Matt doubled over in pain from the blow that followed to the side of his abdomen. "Who de f—k yuh feel yuh talking to so. Yuh is nuttin out here to we yuh know!" Matt's guard had become immediately incensed. A few more blows followed to his back, body and head, bringing him to the ground in pain and curled up in a ball. Matt tasted the blood in his mouth. "Alright alright, dread. We ent killing nobody here tonight," said one of the men. Those words were some consolation to Matt as he received a final "take that" kick to the stomach from his guard. "Come leh we go. De boy in a hole under yuh car Chinee. Just rev up and pull him out." Matt's guard jumped up into the back of what Matt perceived to be a minivan and in a whirl of dust and sand Brian's kidnappers sped off into the darkness, leaving Matt in pain on the ground, bleeding at the nose and mouth.

Slowly he dragged himself to the open car door, got in started the engine and reversed. A flat piece of wood about ten feet across lay on the ground. With every fiber of his being he needed to see Brian alive under that piece of wood. A sudden energy came over him and he pulled the board back, next was a tarpaulin which he dragged back hastily. There in the darkness, hair disheveled, he saw the eyes of his only son squinting upward because of the light that had suddenly been let into his prison. His hands were bound behind his back and his mouth was gagged but he was alive. Brian was alive and Matt was so overwhelmed with emotion that all he could do was jump into that hole where his son lay, hold on to him and cry.

The local newspapers would have a field day the following day. "BUSINESSMAN'S SON RECOVERED IN CHAGUANAS CANE FIELD" "FATHER PAYS ONE MIL RANSOM IN DARING RESCUE" the headlines would read. And although Matt Chow Fatt would have no comment for the media, his actions that night would be described by the business community and society at large as heroic, brave and demonstrative of the deep love of a father for his only son.

Chapter Sixteen

The Truth Be Told

"Again Jesse? Why yuh want to go dere so much Jesse? Eh. Yuh ent feel dat yuh should give de boy some space?" It was Friday night and Ms. Janice was not happy. "Ma is not like ah asking to go dere yuh know. He wants me dere and his mother too. She even told me so last weekend," Jesse replied defiantly. "She say dat yes but yuh know wha she saying bout yuh behind yuh back. Ah tired tell yuh all skin teeth is not grin yuh know." Ms. Janice steupsed and turned down the heat on her stove. She was making fry bakes and saltfish buljol for dinner. "And why ah only hearing bout dis now at dis hour ah de night? And how come arrangements being made wit you now as if you doh have a mudder. Ah doh like this ting at all, at all, at all. Since when you get so bazodee about dis boy dat yuh cyah even listen to what yuh mudder trying to tell yuh eh chile."

"Ma, yuh not understanding. Do you know what it is like to be kidnapped and tied up in a hole in the dark? Do you know what it is like to not know whether yuh going to live or die, or whether yuh will see yuh friends and family again?" Jesse's face was turning red. She was infuriated that her mother could not understand how essential she was to Brian's emotional well being and just how much he needed her right now. "An ah suppose you know. De way yuh talking like yuh was dere in the hole wid him too. Look at how yuh changing Jesse. Yuh never used to answer me back so and talk the way yuh talking to meh now. All of a sudden since yuh meet dis boy, yuh behaving in a kinda way ah doh like. Yuh want to dress in short clothes and shave legs and shave eyebrows. Yuh not behaving like Mr. GG daughter at all."

"Ma, that is not true. I just want to…"

"Wait." Ms. Janice interrupted. "Ah not finish yet," she said wiping her doughy hands in her apron and turning away from the pot to face Jesse fully. "When dis ting start up, eh, ah talk to yuh, ah warn yuh how dese rich people and dem does think. Ah could ah stop it in de beginning but ah say no, ah will give you ah chance. Ah tell mehself, yuh turning eighteen jus now and ah cyah hold on to yuh too tight fuh too much longer. Ah tell mehself dat I and yuh fadder raise a chile wid good sense, common sense. Ah thought yuh had understand what ah tell yuh about dese people an dem. But now yuh taking it to de extreme. Firs it was telephone love. Yuh run up meh phone bill till ah had to put it on one way with TSTT. Dat was number one. But ah tell mehself, ah shouldn be too hard on yuh, dat is just one ting. Den, ah leh yuh go out wid Lisa an him a few times. Ah say alright dat going good. Now ever since de boy geh kidnap an come back yuh want to spend de whole Saturday wid him. One Saturday ah say alright. Ah talk to de mudder on de phone and she explain and ah say alright, he mudder go be around. Second time ah say ok, but now dis ting gone clear. Dese people doh know yuh fadder dead and yuh have four udder brudders and sistas ah what! Saturday is de biggest day ah de week fuh me. Ah have to go in de market Saturday morning and wok while dey waking up late and drinking tea and ha yuh like a fool feeling like you is one ah dem. Ah sorry Jesse but ah cyannot allow dat. Dis ting have to stop." Ms. Janice turned towards her pot so that her fry bakes would not burn. "Ah letting yuh go dis time but dis is the last Saturday. Doh say ah didn tell yuh. De next time dey ask, yuh will have to tell dem no."

"But Ma. That isn't fair," Jesse protested. "Do you have any idea how hard it is fuh him?"

"Ah don't care how hard it is fuh him, dat is not my problem. You are my problem. His mudder care how hard it is fuh you? Eh Jesse?"

"Ma, his mother likes me a lot, she treats me very nice. Aunty Sally is…"

"Aunty Sally! Aunty Sally!" Ms. Janice was enraged. "Ah want to know if yuh Aunty Sally will pay fuh yuh to go to university when de time come. Little girl yuh doh understand it now but yuh will understand it later," said Ms. Janice as she placed the crispy golden brown bakes on a half of a brown paper bag resting on a plate.

"Ma. We not doing nothing wrong. His security guard with us all de time. All we do is talk and go to the malls and sometimes watch a movie."

"Well ah glad yuh had a nice time an ah glad yuh didn do nuttin wrong because it going to stop before yuh get a chance to do something wrong."

"But Ma…"

"Doh answer me back yuh hear." Ms. Janice cut her short. "Yuh not too ole fuh a backhand slap. Tomorrow is yuh last Saturday going dere and dat is final. Yuh lucky ah even letting you go."

Jesse was furious and hurt. Her eyes were bloodshot and she was grinding her teeth. "Yuh know what yuh problem is Jesse," said Ms. Janice as she turned her head away from the raw saltfish that she was pulling apart with her hands. "Yuh have things too nice. Dat is de problem. Yuh doh know what it is to stand up in de hot sun all day in Port-of-Spain market and barely make a sale. Yuh doh know what is like to go out and work in de fields like yuh fadder. Yuh have shoes on yuh foot, clothes on yuh back an a hot plate ah food to eat when de night come. Yuh know how hard yuh mudder ha to wok to get dat? How many nights ah ha to lie down in meh bed worryin bout whey ah going to find de money fuh Mr. Lee Wen lessons from or how ah going to pay de electricity bill? Yuh know how hard ah had was to wok to geh dat money fuh yuh lessons. Steups."

"Look at meh nails Jesse." Ms. Janice removed her wet fishy smelling hands from the water filled bowl and wiped them on her apron. She held her hands out for Jesse to see. "Come closer an watch dem good Jesse. Jesse came closer and looked down at her mother's blue green nails, warped and curling back and forward, almost as if they were rotting and confused as to whether they should rot forward or backward. "Ah want when yuh go by Chow Fatt tomorrow to watch yuh Aunty Sally nails. Watch she nails good an tell meh if dey looking anything like dat. Yuh see dese hands, dese are de kinda hands me and yuh fadder get from digging up in de dirt too much and woking too hard. Woking fuh you Jesse. Working fuh you so dat yuh wouldn have to have hands so. So yuh could make a betta life for yuhself and Becca and Steve and de rest ah dem coming up. Now yuh telling me dis nonsense. Exams is jus now yuh know, an de amount a time ah see yuh wasting on dat boy, ah ent tink yuh going an get de scholarship de teachers tell meh yuh could get."

Ms. Janice steupsed and with head shaking in disappointment returned to the saltfish buljol she had been shredding. Jesse stood there tears rolling down her flushed cheeks. "Just because you doh like rich people, doh mean I doh have to like them too Ma." With those words, Jesse stormed off into the bedroom she and Becca shared. Ms. Janice turned and watched her go. It had hurt that she had to put her foot down with Jesse in this way but Jesse had left her no choice. Ms. Janice couldn't help but feel that Brian had manipulated his circumstances in such a way that his mother could not refuse any request of his during his post kidnapping recovery period. Having Jesse spend the day with him, he had told his mother was helping him to recover and to cope. His mother had conceded to his request and had been superficially friendly over the telephone when speaking to Ms. Janice but Ms. Janice knew that it would only be a matter of time before the frequency of Jesse's presence would begin to cause Brian's mother concern and force her to bring the blossoming romance to a halt.

As far as Ms. Janice was concerned, she was only protecting her daughter from eventual hurt and heartache and pre-empting the inevitable. She knew Jesse was hurting but she was certain that in the years to come, after Jesse had got her scholarship and graduated from university, that her daughter would thank her. It was at times like this that Ms. Janice missed her husband most. She was certain that if Mr.GG had said the same thing to Jesse in his own words, there would be much less resistance to the idea. How she wished that 'old goat' was still alive. She was certain that he would have handled the situation infinitely better than she had. Who knows, with him around there might not be a situation at all?

Next morning around nine o'clock, a white Mitsubishi Lancer with heavily tinted glasses would pull up in front the Guevara house to collect Jesse and take her to the Chow Fatt residence. Jesse had enjoyed being picked up in this way. It was almost as if she had her own chauffeur. She especially liked the attention this drew from the neighbors who peeped through windows from behind curtains to see the vendor's daughter who had suddenly got airs. Already she had begun to fall in love with the trappings of wealth and imagined what her life would be if she were married to Brian. Jesse Chow Fatt. It had a sophisticated ring to it. Jesse liked the way the name sounded and had even practised signing the name in the back of one of her notebooks. Now her mother was about to ruin everything.

"My mother doesn't realize that if Brian and I stay together and let's say get married, I will have all the things she wants for me and more. But if she breaks us up then not only will I never be able to be with the man of my dreams but I'll probably be so sick I won't be able to get the scholarship," Jesse had explained to Lisa. Thankfully Lisa was the only person other than Brian who seemed to understand what she was going through. However Lisa had been going through her own turmoil as well, both at home and in her relationship with Eddy. She had been staying with her Aunt Carol while her mother had been in hospital. After her mother had been discharged from Mount Hope, Lisa had missed a week from school, nursing her back to full strength. In that week Vonetta had shared with her daughter about Nelson's marriage and had begged Lisa not to hate him or be too disappointed but for Lisa it was too late. She loved her father but news of his marriage only meant the end of a dream for Lisa. He had officially abandoned them and that meant she had to create a new plan that did not involve her father or his money.

With endless apologies and promises that it would never happen again, Ted had tried to be attentive to Vonetta's every need; and when he was at home, had waited on her hand and foot. But it was too late for Ted too. Somewhere between the many kicks to her head and her life saving ride to the emergency room at the hospital, Vonetta got sense. While she was in hospital Carol had convinced her to make a report to the police and to get a restraining order for Ted once she was discharged. Carol was particularly worried about Lisa. The whole event must have been affecting her school work Carol thought. She knew that Vonetta would not feel safe to put Ted out on her own. A man so violent was sure to not go quietly. Carol decided to talk to Mike.

Mike was Nelson's brother and he was not very fond of Vonetta but he was very fond of his niece and Carol was very persuasive. "Do it fuh Lisa nah. If yuh see how de chile sufferin. It doh have nobody to help she. If I wasn dere wit she dat night she wouldna have nobody in de hospital. A young gyul like dat musn be going thru ting like dat. Yuh know Nelson wouldna like dat," Carol had pleaded with her brother. Mike knew his sister was right. He had visited Vonetta in the hospital and had seen how distraught his niece was. "Alright, alright. But if she take back dat man after all whey he do she, doh expec meh to help she again," said Mike reluctantly.

When Lisa learnt of the plan to put Ted out she had welcomed the idea. Uncle Mike would have to stay a few days with Vonetta and Lisa to ensure there was not any trouble. In the wee hours one Saturday morning when Ted came home, he found new locks on the doors and a few garbage bags with his clothes in it on the front steps. He banged and cursed but because of the burglar bars, there was no way he could enter the house unless he jumped on the roof and ripped off several pieces of galvanise. Then when Uncle Mike emerged with a cutlass in hand which he seemed prepared to use, Ted backed down.

It had been a hard but necessary move for Vonetta but she was determined that Lisa should never have to endure what she did that night again. In fact Vonetta was convinced that losing the baby was a blessing in disguise and a sign from God that she was not to stay with the likes of Ted. Ted needed a place to stay and he was not going to give up so easily. He visited Vonetta at work and pleaded with her. When that did not work, he kept calling her and begging. After a while though the begging turned to threats of death and disfigurement. However, by the time Vonetta got the restraining order and after a couple of Uncle Mike's partners put a good 'cut arse' on Ted, he began to realize that she was really not going to take him back. He thought he loved Vonetta but he loved the bottle more and so Vat 19 became his sole raison d'être.

Lisa was glad to see Ted go. It had been enough years of watching her mother suffer. But as glad as she was to see him go, she was not at all happy about the condition that he had left her mother in; poorer than she was when she first met him and badly bruised and beaten up. She had tried to talk to Eddy about her feelings but he seemed to be in his own little world, where only Brian's opinion of him mattered. Eddy was in fact very depressed about all that had happened in the weeks that followed Brian's kidnapping. Police received a tip off a few days after Brian had been recovered and arrested seven men from Beetham Estate in connection with the kidnapping. Matt was only able to clearly identify one of the men. Even after the media hype had died down, the Downtown Merchants Association had not let the crime issue rest since Brian's kidnapping had been followed by the kidnapping of the fifteen year old daughter of a another wealthy businessman. DOMA members met with the Prime Minister at his White Hall office on the state of crime in the country and all around the nation as the crime rate mushroomed, community groups were agitating and preparing for marches against crime, walks against crime and even marathons against crime.

Eddy was taken down to the Besson Police Station when the police had made their raid together with a lot of other men. They recognized him as the boy who had been with Brian on the day of the kidnapping. They told him that he was not under arrest and had just been brought in for questioning but Eddy's face had appeared on the front page of all the local newspapers, together with pictures of Cut Outta, Bellies and some of their Laventille cohorts who were involved in the kidnapping. Although Eddy was released the following day, this fact seemed to go unnoticed by the reporters and was only a one-liner in a few newspaper reports. That he lived on the Beetham and was from there was now common knowledge to everyone. All his friends in Mr. Lee Wen's lessons knew it, his friends at school knew it, his teachers knew it, but worst of all Brian and Sean knew it.

Although Eddy was elated when Brian was rescued and had traveled with Lisa and Jesse days after his rescue to see him, that he was later taken into police custody in connection with the kidnapping raised a lot of questions in the mind of Brian and his parents. The next conversation he would have with Brian over the phone would be awkward and strange. "Whey boy. I dunno what to say about the police. Dey real confused boy. This thing have me real real upset," Eddy had said to start off the conversation. There was silence on the other end of the phone.

"You doh think I had anything to do with it right horse? I know you wouldn't be thinking that."

"Why didn't you tell me that you live on the Beetham?" was all that Brian could ask.

"All this time and you never told me. All this time you said you were living in San Juan and staying by an aunt in Belmont and you were really living on the Beetham all this time. Why did you lie to me Ed?" Brian's words cut Eddy deep and hurt more than Brian could ever imagine. "I really thought I knew you. I really thought we were pardners for life. I guess I really didn't know you as well as I thought." Brian's voice was full of hurt and disappointment. Eddy was clueless about how to respond. Saying that he lied because he knew that Brian would look down on him if he found out he was from the Beetham, suddenly seemed like an inappropriate answer. Although at the time when he began the lie his actions had made perfect sense, he realized that perhaps it was not the wisest decision he had made. The Brian that he had come to know and love like a brother would not have denied him friendship whether he was from the Beetham or from Westmoorings.

"I'm sorry Brian. I was going to tell you eventually. I just didn't know how," was the best Eddy could manage to say. "Well I guess you don't have to worry about that now eh Ed. Anyway I have to go now. I'll catch up with you in school ok."

"Yeah we'll pick up in school" said Eddy.

The truth was they would never pick up again, not in school or anywhere else or ever again in life. The friendship had been shaken at its foundation and could not be repaired. In years to come Brian would remember the friendship he and Eddy shared all through school and the fun times they had together but at the end of the memory the dubious connection between Eddy and his kidnappers would always leave a sour taste in his mouth. Brian would always wonder whether it was Eddy who had told the men where he would be that afternoon and the possibility that a friend as close and as trusted as Eddy would do that to him left Brian with a deep sense of mistrust that would follow him the rest of his life.

In the midst of his pain over the loss of his friendship with Eddy, Brian turned to Jesse. She had been so supportive ever since he had been recovered. He would call her every night and talk for hours until he fell asleep and on his and Sally's request she would spend Saturday's with them. Brian was delighted that his mother liked Jesse. She didn't like Amy half as much as she liked Jesse. He was grateful too that Mrs. Guevara had allowed Jesse to spend a few Saturdays with him.

A great deal had changed for Brian ever since his return from his prison in the cane field. His old chauffeur had been fired and a new chauffeur and two full time bodyguards had been assigned to him. They were with him everywhere, except in the classroom during the day time. His every move was monitored constantly but apart from that he received many special considerations from teachers. If his homework was not done, it was because of the post-kidnapping trauma and the principal even offered to relieve him of his duties as Head Prefect. Brian declined that last gesture of kindness but it was clear to all his friends at school that something had changed.

Brian had lost that spark in his eye. Losing Eddy's friendship had left him jaded and confused. What was worse, Sean Mathias had overnight it seemed, a new clique of friends that all seemed queer. Although Sean was glad that Brian was recovering from his ordeal and realized that there was an irreparable rift between Eddy and Brian, he was not about to take Eddy's place as Brian's right hand man. Sean was creating a whole new identity for himself and one that did not revolve around the traditional masculine stereotypes that were the foundation of men in West Indian society. Brian's kidnapping and Eddy's subsequent arrest had changed all their lives. For Brian and Eddy in particular the rose colored glasses had come off. Now they were seeing the world through different eyes.

"Hi Brian", Jesse had just walked through the door of the Chow Fatt residence in a pair of jeans and a t-shirt. She set the knapsack that she was carrying down and the two embraced. Her hair was damp and smelt sweet like vanilla. Brian held her close and felt her soft breasts pressing against his chest. He had been waiting for her. He kissed her mouth and tasted her for a while. He enjoyed kissing her, holding her, smelling her and just being around her. When the kiss was over she sat him down on the living room sofa.

"Where is your mom today?" she asked. Sally would usually be the first to greet her and exchange pleasantries. "Oh she had some errands to run. She said she'd be back by three this afternoon but she said to tell you to make yourself at home." Brian smiled gently as he put a few strands of Jesse's hair back in place. "How is your mom?" Brian asked. He could tell that something was bothering Jesse. "Not happy" she replied. "She said that this is my last Saturday here," said Jesse with a frown.

"Why?" Brian was visibly upset now. The thought of not being able to see Jesse on Saturdays was deeply distressing to him.

"She just doesn't understand. I tried so hard to explain it to her but she just doesn't get it."

"So she doesn't want us seeing each other at all?" Jesse nodded. "She thinks that your parents don't care about me. She says that because your family is rich it is just a matter of time before they don't want me around and that even if you wanted to they'd never let you marry me." Jesse had delivered a mouthful but the situation was urgent and she knew that they didn't have much time. "Why does she think that? I mean there must be something we can do," said Brian.

"Maybe your mom could talk to her," said Jesse. "If your mom talks to her she might listen. Or maybe even your dad."

"That might work. Or maybe I could talk to her."

"I'm not sure that would help things Bri," said Jesse as she rested her hand on his shoulder.

"I could talk to her. I could tell her that I would never do anything to hurt you. I could tell her that if it weren't for you I don't know how I would have survived these last six weeks. I could tell her that….." Brian looked off.

"What is it?" Jesse asked. "I could tell her that I love you." Brian was looking straight at her, straight into those beautiful eyes. Jesse was melting inside. "I love you too Brian. I do. I love you so much." She leaned in and kissed him. She could see the pain in his eyes at the prospect of them having to spend their Saturday's apart. "Let's not worry about that right now Ok. If we do we'll spoil our day," said Jesse trying to be upbeat about the whole thing. "It's just that I couldn't bear the thought…" Brian couldn't finish the sentence as he struggled to hold back the tears. "It'll be Ok" said Jesse. She pulled him close and he rested his head on her breasts. Her skin was so soft and smooth like velvet. Brian wanted to stay there, safe and loved. He wanted her so badly. "Come I have something to show you." He took her by the hand and led her to his bedroom. "It isn't much but it's my way of saying thanks for being here for me."

Jesse didn't know what to say as she opened the tiny box he had presented her with to find a pair of gold earrings in the shape of hearts. "Oh they are so cute. I love them." She hugged him again. "I love you Jesse and I want to always be with you." Brian was serious as he spoke. Then he kissed her and like a fly drowning in a glass of water, Jesse lost herself in his kiss. She could feel his hand on her warm skin as he gently slid it up her back and unhooked her bra. Her heart was racing. The sensations of her body were confusing her thought processes. She wanted him so badly. Her bra slipped off and fell to the ground and she could feel Brian moving her body towards the bed as he kissed her. "I love you so much Jesse," he whispered softly in her ear. The thought of stopping him didn't even cross her mind. She wanted him as much as he wanted her and her body was enjoying every touch and clumsy caress.

As he lay her down on the bed, Jesse thought about how harsh her mother had been with her the night before. For all her years of being the best child she could be, of taking care of her miserable brothers and sisters, she had never made any demands. Silently she had wiped the noses, changed the diapers and cooked the food for the brats. Wasn't that a mother's job? Now her mother wanted to take away the little bit of happiness she had. Jesse would not have it. Naked, scared and excited at the same time, she wanted more than anything to give herself completely to Brian. As the warmth of his naked body enveloped her skin, Jesse closed her eyes and yielded to the desires of her heart.

It was just after lunch when Lystra heard the news. She was walking on Main Street having just come from church. In a straw hat and a black and white cotton dress, Lystra was almost unrecognizable to her neighbors and looked quite the lady. Two other women from the area accompanied her on her way. Although it was hot and sweat poured down their necks and underneath their sheer stockings, they walked without haste as if there was no special place they needed to hurry off to on the Lord's Sabbath. Esmeralda, the neighborhood Jezebel and Lystra's closest neighbor prior to her conversion came running out as she saw the threesome. "Good afternoon ladies. Lystra girl accept my sympathies. Ah only hear de news jus now," said an out of breath Esmeralda.

"What yuh talking about Ralda? Who dead?" said Lystra with a confused expression on her face. Esmeralda gasped. "Oh gosh, nobody ent tell you. Ah sorry. Ah so sorry. Is Tommy. Dey find he body dis morning behind a building on South Quay." Lystra's knees buckled and her head began to spin. It was not that the news was unexpected, it was just that it had been almost six weeks since she had last seen her brother. He had looked so near death then that if he didn't die that week, Lystra feared he would rally a bit longer and his suffering would increase. He had in fact rallied for quite some time in the cesspool of bodily excrement that had become his bed. With flies, rats, roaches and dogs for bedfellows, his condition was bound to deteriorate. One day while he was looking at Jesus on the motorbike, Jesus got off and invited him for a ride. He stretched out his arms and got on. He couldn't believe that he was actually riding the motorbike he had seen so many times before in the sky. He wrapped his arms around Jesus waist' and held on tight. He wished the ride would never end. Tommy's wish was granted.

Chapter Seventeen

The Feeling of Christmas

"*Jingle bells, Jingle bells. It's Christmas time in the city.*

Ding-a-ling, here them ring. Soon it will be Christmas day"

The words of the old Christmas tune rang out from a record store in Town Centre Mall. The signs of Christmas were everywhere; from the shoppers purchasing last minute Christmas presents to the store fronts decorated with Christmas trees, Christmas wreaths and bright red bows. Mannequins dressed up in Santa hats and Christmas and "X-Mas" sale signs were ubiquitous. Christmas was the second time of the year when Trinbagonians put aside race, creed, class and religion to celebrate. Not everyone celebrated Jesus' birth. For some, Christmas was only about having that perfect ham, that special fruit cake or punch-a-crème, new curtains and of course the pastelles.

'Putting away' one's house was a must at this time of year. Whether the putting away was being done two months in advance or at the ninety-ninth hour on Christmas Eve, it was a tradition to have one's house ready to receive early morning paranderos or visiting relatives and friends on Christmas day. That didn't only mean having a clean house, it also meant having enough of ham, turkey, pastelle, sorrel, ginger beer, pork, fruitcake, punch-a-crème and other delicacies for the offering.

The Chow Fatt businesses were doing exceptionally well. The marketing manager for Chow Fatt enterprises had an entire Christmas Eve and Old Year's Night Party promotion going for the Sans Souci restaurant which allowed patrons to overnight in a deluxe suite of the Hibiscus hotel. Matt had been working many late nights, only this time he really was working. Although his managers were reliable and hardworking, Matt always felt the need to keep them in check and remind them that he was always on the job and aware of every aspect of the business.

His rendezvous' with Priya had been reduced to lunch dates and she was not at all happy. Matt simply didn't have the time, but it wasn't only that. He had been filled with a deep sense of guilt over the kidnapping. While he had been cavorting with a woman more than twenty years his junior, he had neglected his family. That was not how his parents had raised him. Ming-Ho and Lue Chow Fatt would not have approved of that behavior if they were still alive to see it. Matt couldn't remember the last father-son talk he had had with his son or even when they had done something together as a family, so lost had he been in Priya's seductive allure. Now, more than a month after Brian's kidnapping, he had not had a single moment of intimacy with her.

Although he missed the sex, Matt had basically decided that he was going to try to cool things down in the relationship; at least until after Christmas. Priya could not understand Matt's strange behavior. She loved him. What they had was more than physical in her mind. She missed the warmth of him beside her in her bed. She longed to hear his laughter and see him smile again. He had not returned many of her calls and they had only managed to have lunch a few times at the Sans Souci. Even then, he seemed distracted, avoiding her direct gaze. At a time when she had hoped they would be growing closer they seemed to be drifting further apart and Priya couldn't figure out what had gone wrong.

"Is there any chance that I'll see you later?" Priya's voice was hopeful on the other end of the telephone. Matt coughed. "I doubt it. It is crazy over here and I have so much work to do."

Priya was getting tired of the excuses. "How long are you going to keep this up?" Matt could sense the irritation in her voice.

"What are you talking about?" he answered.

"You've been avoiding me. I know you."

"Priya, now really isn't a good time."

"When then Matt? When is a good time?"

"Everything's changed since this kidnapping thing."

"So where does that leave us?" she asked.

Matt didn't know what to say. He couldn't make any promises to Priya. What did she want from him anyway? Did she think he was going to give up his life for her? This was not the understanding they had when their relationship started. Why did she seem to want to get so attached to him?

"Look I can't talk now. I'll call you later," was all Matt could say.

"Like the way you called me yesterday?" said Priya in a sarcastic tone. Priya could have any man she wanted. She knew it and Matt knew it. "It's just for a while Priya. Until things settle down."

"That's what you said two weeks ago Matt," she sighed. "I'm not going to wait on you forever." Matt was silent.

"Look I'll talk to you later Ok. I have to go."

Matt tried to sound as convincingly as he could but it was too late. If there was one thing Priya hated it was to be ignored. She was used to being pursued by men. This new role as pursuer did not become her, neither did she enjoy it. She knew when to let go; when she had got the most she could out of a man. She had hoped to be able to get more out of him but for now it seemed like she was beating a dead horse. So that night, when Matt didn't call, Priya closed the door on their relationship and a new beau she had been holding at bay for weeks, entered her apartment and her bed. Just like Matt, Priya knew the heart was deceptive and her number one rule was that the stirrings of her heart should always be in third place after the logics of the brain and the excitement of the loins.

"What time will you be home dear," Sally asked.

"Oh maybe around eight thirty," Matt replied

"Would you like me to get you anything on the way in?"

"Ah no. Oh maybe some whole-wheat bread, we are all out," Sally remembered.

"No problem. I'll see you later then."

"Bye love."

Sally smiled as she put the sleek black cordless phone on its base. Senora Velasquez was definitely worth every penny. Sally was satisfied that she was seeing a change in Matt's behavior and attributed the change to the fact that she had followed the Senora's instructions to the letter. Obtaining a hair from Matt's underwear had been easy. Getting him to take the potion Senora Velasquez had prepared was the difficult part. Matt never sat and ate breakfast at home. He was out of the house by 6.30 a.m. and even then usually only had a cup of coffee. Eventually with Senora Velasquez permission and because it had the consistency and appearance of peanut butter, Matt had consumed the mixture unbeknown to him in a peanut butter and jelly sandwich that Sally had prepared for him one night when he returned home from work.

Sally was convinced that whatever the goodly Senora had done with Matt's pubic hair or whatever the potion contained, something had changed about Matt. He seemed more attentive to her needs and was more concerned about what was going on with Brian in school and out. There was no doubt about it, Matt was a changed man. Although the kidnapping had been truly traumatic for all of them, she could sense that her family was growing closer and that best of all Matt was genuinely trying to be the husband and father she had known him to be. There was just one problem though, one that Sally was anxious to resolve. Things had still not heated up in the bedroom. She didn't want to initiate intimacy but she was starting to wonder whether she would need to fetch a few more hairs from down below for Senora Velasquez.

Her best friend Marlene had been delighted for Sally and was happy to see yet another of Senora Velasquez's satisfied customers. "Give him some more time Sal. Remember the kidnapping was rough on him too. Senora always delivers," Marlene had advised. It was not that Sally was dissatisfied with Senora's work; in fact it was quite the opposite. It was just that she was yearning for her husband's touch. It had been more than six months. About nine o'clock when Matt walked through the door with a loaf of bread in his hand he would find Sally up looking at HGTV on cable. With her feet folded under her in her red silk pajamas, Sally for a moment looked almost like a teenager. "Hi honey" Matt greeted her with a kiss on her cheek as he passed behind the sofa she was sitting on. "Can I get you anything to eat?" Sally asked. "Nah. I had something from the restaurant." Matt replied.

As he got into the shower and allowed his tired body to be beaten by the spray of warm water shooting out, he reflected on his conversation with Priya earlier. He knew he couldn't hold her off for much longer but he had already decided that perhaps it might be best if things just died a natural death. It wasn't as if he was going to divorce Sally and marry her anyway. The trauma of the kidnapping had helped him to realize that he really loved Brian. He loved Sally too but not in the way he had twenty years ago.

Sally was like an old shoe; one he couldn't wear anymore, but which he had grown used to and was not ready to get rid of. Somewhere along the way, he had seen beneath the layers of her make-up and camouflage and what he saw had made him cringe in disgust. Unlike some of his business associates who worried about their wives having extra marital affairs Matt never worried about Sally being unfaithful. He knew that his wife was so obsessed with herself and her life as his wife and the mother of his child that it would be hard for her to care about another man in that way. Still, she was an evil constant in his life; unchanging and predictable. Markets could rise and fall but Sally would still be Sally and in some strange way that knowledge was comforting to him.

By the time Matt emerged from the shower, Sally was already in bed with an Oprah magazine. Matt toweled off, put on his pajamas and settled down to his crossword puzzle as he slipped under the covers. "You smell very nice dear. What do you have on?" Matt asked.

"It's a lotion I picked up at the store." Sally was glad that he had noticed.

"It makes you smell like cherries."

"Well I'm glad you like it."

"How did things go with Brian today?"

"Very well. I think he has finally accepted the fact that his guards are going to always be around him now. I know he doesn't like it that much but I think he understands how necessary they are."

"Hmm. Well that's a relief. How are things with him and Jesse? I haven't seen her for a few Saturdays."

"Well I'm not sure to be honest. A few weeks ago he asked me to speak to her mom about her coming here on Saturdays and I did but it sounds like her mom doesn't like the idea of her spending the day here. Even though I told her that I am always around. So I think they've come to some sort of pause I guess, because I mean, I can't force the girl's mother to send her over. I don't mind though, I was afraid Brian was getting too attached and I really didn't want another repeat of the Amy drama."

"Hmm. She seems like a well raised girl though. Very pleasant."

"She's nice alright but her mother is a market vendor and not exactly what I would consider cultured from the conversations I had with her. Besides, its not like our son is going to have a future with this girl anyway. I was just trying to be as supportive as I could be ever since….. well you know. It had to come to an end at some point. I'm just grateful that I'm not coming out looking like the bad guy."

"Hmmm" was all Matt dared to offer. He knew Sally's perspective on these matters and he didn't want to get into a fight with her.

"He thinks he's in love but he's really just traumatized and needy since this whole mess."

"That's understandable though," said Matt.

"Of course. For God's sake I thought I was going to die from sheer worry. I don't know what I would have done if anything had happened to him or you," Sally looked over at Matt with soft eyes.

Aware that she was looking at him, Matt stopped for a moment and looked straight at her. For a few seconds they held each other's gaze, wanting to say so much yet not knowing what to say or where to start. Matt set the paper down and removed his spectacles. He turned to her and passed his hand along the side of her face. Then he kissed her. Sally closed her eyes. He had not done that in a long time. That night Matt made love to his wife and Sally thanked the Gods and Senora Velasquez for bringing her husband back to her.

A week later when Matt would hear the news from one of his buddies that Priya was seeing someone else he would be deeply hurt. Not so much because he had had any noble intentions for their relationship but because of the ease with which her love for him had grown cold. He wondered to himself whether it really was love at all. "If she loved me she would have waited for me," is what Matt thought to himself. Then a little voice in his head replied "Waited for what?"

Lystra did not have any money for a funeral, not a decent one anyway. Tommy had died like a dog in the road; less than human and even in death he had been treated like an animal. It had only been after the complaints of a nearby business place that a hospital ambulance had come to collect the rotting corpse and had taken it to the morgue. His body had been decomposing for three days. Lystra was beside herself with grief. The last two months had dealt her some wicked blows. First it was Eddy's arrest now her Tommy was gone. In reality, he had been gone a long time ago but it was the finality of his passing and the way in which he died that left Lystra riddled with guilt.

How she wished she had had the strength to take care of him in the end. How she wished she was not so afraid of the AIDS that he had. Ma Vero must be turning in her grave she thought. No matter what, Tommy was her brother. He didn't deserve to die like a dog in the streets. She arranged for his body to be taken to Brown's funeral home on the Eastern Main Road in Barataria. It was the funeral home where most of the poor in Laventille and environs took their dead. The funeral home had a fifteen percent down and monthly payment plan for those who could not afford the cost of a casket. So for about four thousand dollars, a mother or father, brother or sister could be laid to rest with some measure of dignity. Lystra knew it was time for her to make a trip up East and she did so the day after Tommy's body was taken to the funeral home.

At the top of Mount St. Benedict overlooking the whole of Trinidad she waited for the familiar green Honda motorcar. The sun was hiding behind the mountaintops and the breeze blew gently, caressing the huge trees behind her. She enjoyed going up to the Mount. It was quiet there. For the last four years since Eddy went into Form Three she would go there once every two months or thereabouts to wait for the driver of that green motorcar. In a few minutes she saw the car coming up the road. The driver pulled up near to where she was standing in the car park and parked the car.

"Accept my sympathy," were his first words of greeting as he gave her an embrace. A tired looking Lystra thanked him. "How is Eddy doing since dey let him out?" he asked. "Not too bad. Eddy is a good boy. Dese police does make mistake yuh hear. Steups. Dey nearly kill meh dat day when dey take him dong in de station. But he alright, jus vex cause dey put he picture on de papers so now people watchin he like he is a criminal. But otherwise he alright."

"Yeah. Well ah glad to hear that," the man said. "Anyway ah doh have much time cause ah have to get back to de store. Yuh know how it is dis time a year. So dis in here is for de lessons an a little extra for de funeral. Ah probably wouldn be able to make it but ah will send some flowers." The man placed a sealed white envelope in Lystra's hand. "Thanks Harry. Ah real glad for dis right now. Tings real tight wit me."

"Alright then I gone wid dat alright. We will be in touch." Harry Rajkumar jumped back in his car and with a wave and a smile disappeared down the winding St. John's road. Her half brother had come through for her yet again without her even asking. It was ironic though that Harry would be helping her with Tommy's funeral especially when she considered what little regard Tommy had had for him. As Lystra boarded the monastery run shuttle bus to take her down St. John's road, she wondered if Ma Vero had seen into the future when she spoke the words she did on her death bed. Whether she did or didn't, Lystra was glad that she had not ignored Ma Vero's advice.

"Oh Lord, My God, when I in awesome wonder
Consider all the works thy hands have made
I see the stars, I hear the rolling thunder
Thy power throughout, the universe displayed
Then sings my soul
My savior God to thee
How great thou art
How great thou art
Then sings my soul my savior God to thee
How great thou art,
How great thou art"

Four days after Lystra received the money from Harry, Tommy's funeral service took place. There was no wake. Lystra knew better than to waste money on food and drinks to feed the men and women in the area. A wake was an opportunity in the community for men, women and children to get supper at night. She made it clear from early o'clock that no wake would be held. "Steups. How yuh mean she ain't havin no wake? No prayers at all fuh she own brudder," an upset

Esmeralda would say. When the comments reached Lystra, she knew the upset was more about meals denied than about prayers for Tommy and remained firm in her stance. Some "sisters" from the church came every night to pray with Lystra and Eddy. A few well wishers in the area came by too in the hope of a meal.

Lystra would apologise for not having any food to give and offered everyone water in styrofoam cups, even though she did not have enough to go around. But that was all. The morning of the funeral, the poorly ventilated chapel of Brown's funeral home was crowded. Some of Tommy's friends from the basketball court, a few of his former co-workers from the garage and some of Lystra's neighbors from Main Street gathered in the hot chapel to bid their farewells. Uncle Tremble and Spranger came and Lisa came too. It was a closed casket funeral. An old picture of Tommy as a teenager which Lystra had been keeping in her bible lay on the cheap looking wooden box which held his remains. Tommy was all dressed up in a black suit with long sleeve shirt and tie that Lystra had bought for him but no one saw it. Lystra had bought a new black dress for the occasion because she really did not have anything appropriate to wear.

In the past she would go to funerals of neighbors and friends in one of her favorite red dresses which made her look like a circus horse. Her SDA friends had shown her the folly of many of her ways. Between Esmeralda and one of those SDA sisters Lystra sat with arms outstretched as if nailed to the cross bawling. Throughout the entire service she bawled, even while the pastor preached to the congregation, Lystra was bawling. Before, during and after the eulogy, which Eddy read, she bawled and cried and shook as if she was 'ketching power'. Lystra bawled till she fainted and when she came too, she started up all over again. "She really did love dat brudder boy," was all onlookers could say.

The women beside her held her up and patted her forehead dry every two seconds as if they had been commissioned to do so. Another woman who nobody knew as being related to the deceased or his family kept wailing at the back of the chapel. Eddy did not know who she was but assumed she was one of those people who go to funerals to bawl because she did not go to the cemetery with them. By the time the service was over, more mourners had filled the small cramped chapel. Most of them were strangers to Eddy, Lystra and Tommy but once there was a funeral there was always food after and once there was food there would always be people to grieve so they could partake of the food afterward.

Eddy didn't know where Lystra had got the money from for the funeral or what arrangements had been made with the funeral home. All he knew was that his favorite uncle, the only uncle he knew, was no more. And as much as Eddy hated the choices he had made which led to his death, he also knew that he was going to miss Tommy. When the body arrived at the burial hole in Lapeyrouse cemetery, some sweaty barebacked men were still digging the hole. The pastor and some sisters from the church, started up the singing of some hymns, *Amazing Grace* being an all time favorite.

The crowd from the funeral home had dwindled considerably but that was only because most were waiting for the food and drink at the church hall after the body had been buried. It would have been impolite to start eating before the grieving family arrived; still some heavy set women stood guard at the church hall over the pelau which was to be served on paper plates together with Chubby 'sweet drinks'.

Lystra collapsed when the first rock hit that wooden box with a loud thud. There was just something about that sound that could make a body sick to the stomach. When she came to, she continued her bawling right up until the last clump of dirt had been patted down over the grave. There were only a few wreaths - one from the church, one from Harry and one from the funeral home, but they were enough. In all of this Eddy was numb. In a zombie-like stance he stood expressionless, not crying, not speaking, not even to Lisa who had tried her best to console him. He felt a gamut of emotions from rage to guilt, from anger to sorrow to relief.

A few insensitive people who were there tried tactlessly to bring up conversation about the 'arrest' after offering their deepest sympathies. Eddy just ignored them. He had known shame and embarrassment like never before in the past two months. He had been called into the principal's office to discuss the matter and had received many an unkind glare, stare, taunt and scoff not only from other classmates at school but from teachers and students at Mr. Lee Wen's lessons also. But worst of all he had lost the friendship of Brian. And Soldier, who was his most trusted friend on the Beetham had died an ignominious death. Eddy did not know how much more he could take and although Lisa had been supportive, he wondered if she too had doubts about his integrity.

Tommy had so many dreams and plans, now he was dead; and for a brief moment, Eddy wished he could have been the one going into the hole in the ground instead of Tommy. Later that night after all the food had been eaten and everyone had retired, Eddy would make his way to the basketball court and ask for a 'piece' from a man called Froggie. Eddy had had one drink too many and had plummeted to the bottom of the sea of despair. Froggie was Cut Outta's sixth in command and had not been arrested the day the police made the raid because he was in San Fernando that day. A petty thief, Froggie had managed to escape the law many times over. Now he was the new man in charge since all the men ranking above him were being held in custody without bail.

"Nah whitey. Yuh young still. Every ting does come in a timing. Right now yuh on a hater scene. Tink bout wha yuh doin and if yuh still want check meh back tomorrow." Froggie had said in response to Eddy's request. It seemed odd to Eddy that a man like Froggie would dispense that kind of advice but many years later Eddy would thank the drug lord for steering him away from the path of destruction that night.

"He come from the Glo-ry
He come from the glorious kingdom

He come from the glory
He come from the glorious kingdom"

That weekend the QRC boy's choir put on their Christmas pageant. It was a resounding success and received rave reviews in the newspapers the following day. Sean and Alex had enjoyed every minute of their performance. In Alex, Sean had surprisingly found the understanding and rapport that his relationship with Brian and Eddy lacked. Sean hated being called a faggot but once he was with Alex he felt safe from the taunts and snickers. Alex somehow knew how to ignore the snide remarks of his classmates or give just the right reply that would allow him to be left alone. Nobody dared lay a hand on Sean Mathias anyway; all the boys knew exactly who he was and as long as they couldn't touch Sean, they wouldn't touch his new buddy Alex either. Besides, Christmas was in the air, Carnival was just around the corner and there were other more important distractions including end of term exams.

"Ah want a piece ah pork, ah want a piece a pork, ah want a piece ah pork for de Christmas" the Scrunter favorite rang out over the radio on Christmas Eve while Lystra cracked some eggs into a silver bowl. She had been trying in her own small way to put away the house with some pastelles, punch- a- crème and some fruit cake. She wanted to give Eddy a Christmas to remember. Meanwhile, amid the hustle and bustle of Charlotte Street Eddy was jostling with the mass of bodies hunting for a pair of earrings for Lisa and a pair of magnetic sandals for his mother. The array of smells,

colors and sounds awakened his senses. When he got home later that evening he would ask his mother's opinion of the earrings he had got for Lisa. "Hmm. Ah hope ah getting to meet dis Lisa gyul. She mus be real nice if she making you spen money yuh doh have," was all she would have to say.

Since Christmas Eve fell on a Friday, Lystra had planned to go to church that night for a special service instead of on Saturday morning. When she was all dressed around seven o'clock in a red long sleeve dress with matching shoes, she would turn to Eddy and ask "Yuh want to come with me chile?" Eddy who had been watching TV would at first decline but just as she was making her way out the door, he changed his mind, grabbed a t-shirt from his basket of clothes slipped on his favorite jeans and shoes and came outside ready to go. "Dem clothes ent looking too righteous fuh de Lord house yuh know but ah guess yuh go ha to go jus so." Eddy had not been to church since he made confirmation in the Cathedral on Independence Square almost four years ago, but he wanted to start the new year off right and if going to church would help to prevent some of the bad luck he had been having then he was all for that.

Chapter Eighteen
Unacceptable Behavior

"Oh the Love of My Lord is the essence
Of all that I love here on earth"

It was a quarter past eight and Lisa had just set her knapsack down between her feet as she joined the rest of sweaty worried girls in the late line. She had made a New Year resolution not to be late but it seemed that she had already slipped into her old routine one month into the new school term. She heard the shrill sharp voice of Sr. Monica over the microphone, making an announcement about something. Lisa didn't particularly care; she just hoped that Sr. Monica was in a good enough mood so that she would not have to receive her usual insults. In a few minutes, the shuffle of feet began as the students made their way to their classrooms after the morning assembly. She could see Sr. Monica's black veil swaying in the wind as she did her military style walk toward her office which was conveniently located near to the late line.

She glanced at the girls in the line and nodded in approval to the school prefect who had all the names of the girls who were late written down in a notebook. Lisa breathed a sigh of relief as Sr. Monica continued on her way but almost as if the goodly Sister had heard Lisa's sigh, she made an about face and looked at the late line again. "I thought I saw someone that looked like you, Mizz Williams, I just wasn't sure," said Sr. Monica as Lisa smiled coyly. "I would have thought that for the New Year you would be turning a new leaf dear but I can see that you are still stuck in the ways of last year."

Lisa didn't quite know what to say. There was nothing you could say really in response to Sr. Monica. She was not asking questions that needed to be answered, she was just making statements. "It would be good if you could take a page out of your friend Jesse's book and try to be more punctual but alas I fear it is too late for you." With those parting words Sr. Monica continued her stoic march but not before delivering a word of caution to another latecomer in the line. Lisa didn't ever mean to be late and sometimes she actually made it to school in the nick of time. Sr. Monica obviously did not know what it was like to live in the East and have to wait for half an hour for a bus route maxi taxi that had room for one, Lisa thought. If she left home at seven thirty there was no doubt that she would be late. Lisa had to leave home before seven o'clock if she was to reach to school on time and many mornings her bed sheets held her captive.

Now that Ted was gone, the place was a whole lot quieter. In his sober moments, he had pleaded with Vonetta that he would change and that he just needed a chance, but in Vonetta's eyes he had had one chance too many and the time had come for her to give Lisa a chance to have some peace and quiet. Lisa was glad that Ted was out of the house but for some strange reason she missed his presence. She had grown used to seeing a man around the house and although he had never been much of a father to her, Ted was the only father she had known for such a long time.

Lisa got to class in time for the first period which was Chemistry. She greeted Jesse with a smile but could see from her facial expression that something was wrong. "What's up Jess?" she asked. "Nothing, but I need to talk to you about something," Jesse replied. "About what?" Lisa hated waiting. "After school we'll talk," was all Jesse would say. "Mrs. Ramdhan isn't here as yet. Tell me what it is." Jesse refused and in a few seconds, Mrs. Ramdhan walked through the door to begin class. Lisa was perplexed as to what could be bothering Jesse that much but just assumed that it had something to do with Brian. Perhaps they got into a fight?

She knew that since Jesse's mom forbade her to spend Saturdays at Brian's house that their relationship had been limited to conversations on the telephone. Jesse had been fighting with her mother almost every day since then, but Ms. Janice would not budge in her stance. As far as Ms. Janice was concerned, A-Level exams were right around the corner and Jesse had no right to be focusing all her energy on boys instead of books. Even when Brian called and Ms. Janice felt the conversation had been going on for too long, she would give Jesse that look which meant "It's time to get off the phone now."

Jesse had begun to resent her deeply. "Ma the phone is on one way, we don't have to pay for the calls," she had argued one night after getting the eye. "Dat is not de point Jesse. So what, just because de phone on one-way dat mean yuh could stay up till three o'clock in de morning and talk away yuh life. No. Is eleven o'clock now, yuh on de phone since nine o'clock! Maybe Brian mudder ent care bout what time he study an what time he go to bed but you is my chile and dat phone is my phone an I have a right to say when yuh must come off it." Jesse had turned away and had mumbled something under her breath. "Doh grumble nuttin fuh me dere yuh know. Ah could cut de phone altogether yuh know. Me ent bong fuh phone an none ah yuh brudders and sistas does use de phone up like you. Dat is why it on one-way in de first place," Ms. Janice had retorted. The thought of not being able to speak to Brian on the phone anymore was not a pleasant one.

Outside of Mr. Lee Wen's classes which Jesse only attended once a week, Jesse did not see Brian at all. His body guards escorted him everywhere, so even when Jesse had suggested that they skip class and go somewhere, there was still the problem of getting rid of the guards. It was not until recess that day that Jesse confided her deepest and worst fears in a corner outside the Chemistry lab where there was very little student traffic.

"I think I'm pregnant Lisa."

"What! What are you talking about Jesse?"

"Could you lower your voice I don't want the entire school to know!"

"What do you mean you think you're pregnant? You have to have sex in order to get…." Lisa looked Jesse in the eye and Jesse's eyes said it all.

"Jesse you didn't. How? When? How come you didn't tell me anything?" Lisa was full of questions. That her best friend in the whole world had had sex and had not bothered to tell her about it seemed surreal.

"Look Lisa I didn't want to tell you because I was afraid of what you might think of me," said Jesse with head bowed. "Does anybody else know? Does your mom know?" Lisa was full of questions. "No. Only you. Who else do you think I would tell anyway?" Jesse asked almost surprised that Lisa would suggest it. "Oh my God! Are you sure you're pregnant?" Lisa asked her hand was over her mouth and her eyes were full of fear. "I don't know Lisa. I don't even know," said a terrified Jesse as the tears began to well up in her eyes. "I just know I missed my period last month and the same this month and this morning on my way to school I had to come off the maxi taxi so I could throw up," she said wiping away the tears.

Jesse having sex, getting pregnant, it all seemed unreal in Lisa's head. In fact the entire conversation seemed unreal. In Lisa's mind, if there was anybody who was supposed to have sex first it was supposed to be her not Jesse. Jesse was the less experienced more fragile person between them. She couldn't handle having sex far less getting pregnant. "But you don't even have a belly. You don't even look pregnant. Oh my God Jesse. You can't be pregnant. Maybe it's a hormonal thing. Remember that girl, Susan? She had some kind of hormone thing that made her miss her period all the time, maybe it's that. How many times did you and Brian…."

"Only one time"

"One time only? Well then there's no way," said Lisa convinced. "You can't be pregnant Jesse. Don't you have to do it several times?"

"I don't know Lisa. I don't know."

"Did you all use a condom?"

Jesse shook her head. "Did you tell Brian?" Lisa asked

"No, and I can't tell him just yet."

"What are you crazy Jesse!"

Jesse burst into tears and Lisa realized that she hadn't been entirely sensitive to the fact that Jesse was crying. She hugged Jesse. "I can't believe this is happening. This is not supposed to be happening to you," said Lisa as she allowed Jesse to soil her shirt with tears. Mrs. Tobias passed by and seeing the two asked, "Is everything Ok there girls?"

"Yes Miss. Today is the anniversary of the death of Jesse's dad and she's just feeling a bit down." Lisa said quickly in an effort to protect Jesse from the nosy Mrs. Tobias. "I'm sorry to hear that Jesse," said Mrs. Tobias as she gently rubbed Jesse's back. Mrs. Tobias had just started into a sermon on death and God's mercies when the bell rang to end recess. "Ok Jesse, I will remember to be praying for him today," she said as she ended the conversation. "Thanks Miss."

Jesse and Lisa walked back to class in a daze. Jesse stopped off in the bathroom to dry her face so that no one would be able to tell that she had been crying. Lisa was expressionless as a host of thoughts ran through her brain. Jesse was the most decent, most reserved girl she had known. How had Brian convinced her to have sex with him? How had Jesse had sex and not told her about it? If Jesse was pregnant what was she going to do? The idea of Jesse being pregnant seemed as absurd as the idea of Sr. Monica making Lisa the Head Girl. Jesse couldn't be pregnant. Perhaps she just had one of those hormonal problems, Lisa thought. Besides, if they only had sex one time it seemed impossible that Jesse could get pregnant after the first time. For the rest of the day, both girls were distracted and unable to focus. At lunch time though they would discuss the situation again.

"You need to get a test Jesse," said Lisa firmly

"You can't be sure unless you have a test done. Trust me my mother was pregnant and she did a test first, that was how she knew that she was pregnant. Until you get a test done you really don't know."

"I can't buy a pregnancy test, Lisa are you crazy!" said Jesse. Lisa knew that Jesse would be too ashamed to purchase one from the pharmacy. In addition, the community that Jesse lived in was so small, it would only be a matter of time before word got back to Ms. Janice that her daughter had not only bought a pregnancy test but was pregnant and having the son of whoever the rumor mongerer decided she was pregnant for.

"I'll get one then," said Lisa

"Are you crazy? Do you want to get in trouble?"

"I'll get it from one of the pharmacies on the Eastern Main Road after school. I'll go home and change my clothes so I won't be in uniform. That way I won't get into trouble." Lisa was determined to help her friend.

"I'm not sure but I think you have to do the test first thing in the morning when you pee Jesse."

"I'm so scared Lisa. I worked so hard around the house hoping to bring my period down and nothing happened. It felt like it was coming but it didn't come."

"Maybe it is still coming Jesse. Not to worry. You just have to do the test and that way you will know for sure whether you are pregnant or not and that way you will be able to relax if you aren't." Lisa was trying to be as supportive as she could be but the truth was that she was just as scared as Jesse at the prospect of her friend being pregnant.

"How expensive is it do you think?" Jesse asked as she began to hope that perhaps she really did have a hormonal problem.

"I don't know but I don't think it's that expensive. How much money do you have?"

"I have ten dollars for passage and only five dollars to spare."

"Don't worry I'll put some money in too," Lisa tried to smile and rubbed Jesse's shoulders. "Don't worry Jesse. You'll be alright."

"I feel so bad Lisa, so bad inside. I don't know what got into me. One minute we were kissing, the next we were naked. I didn't mean for it to happen. I feel like such a fool." The tears just kept rolling down Jesse's face.

"Don't cry Jess. It'll be ok. Trust me you are probably worrying for nothing," said Lisa as she tried to console her friend.

Lisa had been trying to keep a brave face but deep down she felt a whole range of emotions. She thought she knew Jesse. Jesse was her best friend, like a sister to her. How could she have had sex and not share such a significant life changing event with her? The Jesse that had had sex with Brian was not the Jesse she knew. But what had hurt Lisa the most was the fact that Jesse had kept such a secret to herself all this time. Lisa reflected on the many opportunities Jesse had to tell her and didn't. Although Lisa was glad that she was able to help Jesse now, she felt strange. Something in their relationship had changed, Jesse had not trusted her enough to share her deepest thoughts and experiences. Suddenly Lisa began to feel that she needed to begin holding back too.

The electronic gate opened as Sean Mathias pulled up into the driveway of the St. Clair mansion he called home. Alex was in the car with him. "This is a very big house Sean. It looks a lot smaller from behind the wall," said an awestruck Alex. "It's not bad but it takes a lot of time to clean. Thank God I don't have to clean it," Sean chuckled as he closed the car door. As he led Alex inside, he couldn't help but notice how impressed Alex was with the place, even though he had been over to the house before. Clay Italian tiles gave the garage floor an air of royalty and a stairway made of pure silver curled upward from the garage to the kitchen. Grey marble counter tops against a backdrop of stainless steel appliances, potted orchids, Chinese bamboo, and bonsai plants made the kitchen appear luxurious. A crystal chandelier hung over a huge teak dining table with seating for six and a black plush leather couch in the living room invited Alex to sit down. In a glass cabinet in the living room full of blue crystal, there were dainty little glass figurines and everything smelt and looked like something out of a magazine.

"Hi Josephine," Sean greeted the housekeeper of five years as he set his knapsack down.

"Hi Sean. How was your day?"

"It was fine thank you."

"Hello Alex. How are you?" she asked stiffly enough so that Sean could hear the disapproval in her voice.

"Can I get you boys anything to drink or eat?" she asked.

"Nah I'll help myself," said Sean as he reached into the refrigerator and grabbed two bottles of Smalta.

"I'll be in my quarters if you need me Sean."

"Thanks Josie"

Sean's room was not typical for a boy his age. In one corner he had a poster of rock star Prince with purple hair and a guitar in his hand, and in another, a picture of Boy George, looking like a girl with lipstick, blush, mascara and long braided hair. All the furniture seemed to revolve around a glass computer desk in the middle of the room. There was a wooden bookshelf in one corner with an assortment of books by English, American and West Indian authors. One entire shelf was devoted to National Geographic magazines and everything in the room seemed neatly put away and in its place.

"You can go ahead and check your e-mail," said Sean. Alex sat down right away and began to log on. "I am so stressed out with exams coming up so soon. You have no idea," said Alex without looking away from the computer. "I know exactly what you mean," Sean replied as he sat down at the edge of his bed. After he had finished his Smalta, he instinctively stood up and began to massage Alex's shoulders. Alex closed his eyes and relaxed.

Two hours later, Sean would give him a ride to his home at Coblentz Courts in Cascade. Alex lived with his mother and three other sisters. His father had died when they were all very young. Alex did not visit Sean often but on occasion, Sean had him over to the house. That night, Alex's visit would become the source of an argument between Mr. and Mrs. Mathias.

"We have to do something honey. You think I feel happy about this. I am just as upset as you are. I am just telling you what Josephine told me she saw and heard."

"I don't know which side of the family he would have got that from. I don't have anybody in my family like that." Mr. Mathias would look almost accusingly at his wife.

"Maybe we could take him to a counselor or something. I am sure this is a problem that can be fixed," said Marlene hopefully as she sat on the four poster queen size bed in her bedroom.

"I think we should send him away as soon as possible. He is a shame and embarrassment to the family. You think people are not seeing him outside. You think they are not talking about it already. Just now he will make news in one of those sleazy papers at the rate he is going. That is just the kind of thing people need to know about me," Damien Mathias steupsed.

"This is not about you Damien, this is about Sean. I say we take him to counseling."

"And I say we send him to Canada by his uncle. I think he will be a lot happier up there because obviously he is not happy here. I don't understand that child but I know he didn't get that from me."

"So who you think he got it from me?" asked Marlene indignantly.

Marlene and her husband for a large portion of the night went back and forth over the matter of Sean. Marlene had always thought he was a late bloomer but the evidence Josephine had repeatedly presented and the changes they had seen in Sean since his association with Alex, led them to believe that perhaps Sean was really attracted to boys.

Marlene had tried different ways to explain it away but it was undeniable that something was wrong and her husband did not have the patience to find the root cause. The following month and only a few months before exams, Sean Mathias was pulled out of school and sent away to a high school in Canada. Sean wasn't given much notice or opportunity to say too many farewells. He told Brian that it was because Trinidad was getting too dangerous and that his father was afraid that he would be kidnapped and no longer felt he was safe. Deep down Sean knew better.

On a sunny Sunday afternoon in January, Sean got on an airplane that was Toronto bound. Marlene, Sianne and Josie saw him off. Damien Mathias was at work. He had said his farewells the night before. Not a man to show much affection he had tried to joke about how many girls Sean would be able to hook up with in Toronto. "Alright son, you take care eh," Damien had said patting Sean hard on the back. It was the closest thing to a hug that Sean would get or that Damien had ever offered. As the Air Canada flight took off, Sean would recall the last conversation he had with his multibillionaire father and wonder to himself if his father was not directly responsible in some way for the way he felt about men.

"Ok, now, I read the instructions and what you have to do is pee in a cup and then put a little bit on this part here and leave it for a while," Lisa explained to Jesse. It was around four o'clock and Lisa and Jesse had taken a bus route maxi taxi after school and stopped off in Curepe. They both felt it would be better to do the test at Lisa's house because it was quieter and Lisa's mother would not be home. Even though Lisa was worried that doing the test in the afternoon instead of the morning might give them a wrong result, Jesse was too nervous to do the test without Lisa being present. "So how do you know if it's positive or not?" Jesse asked. "Well let me see here," Lisa turned over the box from which the pregnancy test had just come out. "If its two purple lines that means yuh pregnant and if its just one then you will be ok" said Lisa. "I'm so scared Lisa. I'm so scared."

Jesse's face was red. "Look Jess, no point in being scared before you know what the deal is. Suppose you getting all scared fuh nothing."

"Hmmn. Maybe you are right. Maybe it's nothing and I won't even have to tell Brian anything."

"Forget about Brian for now Jess, just go and pee so we could get dis thing over and done with" she urged. It was not that Lisa didn't like Brian, but she was angry that Jesse had chosen to leave him out of this part of the drama. Jesse had been worried sick and afraid while Brian was doing all the things he normally did. While Jesse was peeing in a cup wondering whether her life would be changed forever, Brian was probably at home watching TV. If Jesse was pregnant, Lisa felt that Brian ought to know right away so that he could do something whatever that something was. In a few minutes Jesse came out of the toilet with a styrofoam cup in hand.

"Ok so do you put the test in the cup or do you put the pee on the test?" Jesse asked. "I think the instructions say put a drop on this part here. Well yuh know what, let's just pour some on dis whole part just to be sure dat the whole area gets some. That way we could be a hundred percent sure." Lisa was hoping that the test results would be negative. If the results were negative, Jesse's life could return to normal and so could hers. She took the cup Jesse was holding, held it over the test in the wash basin and poured generously. "Oh geed!" Lisa exclaimed.

"What happen?"

"Some of yuh pee get on meh hand."

Jesse steupsed. "What happen yuh feel yuh hand going to rotten off ah what"

"I doh know. It might." Lisa laughed and so did Jesse. It felt good to be able to laugh in the middle of this unfolding drama. "So what now?" Jesse asked.

"Well yuh have to leave it for a few minutes, till the line comes up. I think two lines is pregnant and one line is not pregnant," said Lisa as she lay the test down at the side of the sink and washed her hands off with soap.

"So yuh just going to leave it there?"

"Well yeah. Yuh have to give it a few minutes Jesse. Come let's go outside because ah feel yuh go be watching this test too hard and dat might just spoil it." Lisa tugged on Jesse's arm and pulled her in the direction of the living room. Jesse sighed. "Please God; please don't let me be pregnant. I promise I'll never ever have sex again for as long as I live." Jesse closed her eyes and uttered out loud.

"For as long as you live Jesse! Don't you think that is a little harsh?"

"Not really. I don't ever want to go through this again, ever."

"You mean the sex?" asked Lisa

"No dummy. This that we are doing now. I don't know what I'll do if I'm pregnant."

"You're not pregnant Jesse. It's probably some hormone thing that you are overreacting about but on the subject of sex, you never did tell me how it was. I want to know all the details, did it hurt, did you bleed, did it feel as good as everybody makes it out be? C'mon tell me."

"Shouldn't the test be ready now Lisa?" asked Jesse as she made her way to the bathroom. "Hey wait" Lisa got up to follow her. "Aye that's not fair yuh know Jesse. I'm your best friend you should tell me these things. It's not....." Lisa stopped as she saw the expression on Jesse's face. She didn't have to ask. Jesse burst into tears. She cried and cried and cried until her face turned cherry red and her eyes were so swollen she could barely open them. "You'll be alright Jesse. We'll figure something out, don't worry."

But Lisa was worried; worried and scared. She knew Jesse's mom would not be happy if she got to find out but she also knew that her mom would not want her to have an abortion either. "Listen, you go home and rest Ok. Go quick before your mom start to think anything. Is already six o'clock. When you come to school tomorrow we'll figure something out." The next day when Lisa arrived at school, on time for a change, Jesse was not there. Lisa was worried about her friend and called her first thing after school. "What happened? How come you didn't come to school today Jesse?"

"Girl ah was too sick. Ah was sick really bad."

"Did you tell Brian?"

"Yes."

"What did he say?"

"He thinks I should have an abortion. He says he's not ready to have a child."

"What! He not ready to have a child. Is not him who have a baby in his belly yuh know!" Lisa was not satisfied with Brian's response.

"So what yuh going to do Jesse. What yuh want to do?"

"I don't know but right now I feel like I could keep it."

"Keep it!" Lisa was genuinely surprised that Jesse would be thinking that way.

"But Jess yuh have school, we have exams coming up. You can't take care of a baby now. Babies are expensive. My mom says a baby is like a money sucking machine. Yuh going to tell yuh mom?"

"I don't know. I was thinking that maybe I could convince Brian that we should have the baby and maybe we could get married after exams."

Lisa couldn't believe what she was hearing. "Jesse are you crazy! Do you think Sr. Monica will let you write exams in maternity clothes? How long do you think it is going to be before your belly starts to rise? I agree with Brian on this one. I think you should have an abortion. I can try and find out how too. My cousin Tricia had one last year. I dunno, I think she drank something like Guinness and eggs or something like that."

"I don't know if I want to do that Lisa. I mean this is a baby inside me. My baby."

"Well remember from biology class they say it's only cells dividing up to a certain number of weeks, so technically it isn't really a baby. How many weeks do you think you are?"

"I don't even know."

"Well I think we need to find out these things before we make a decision don't you think?" Jesse felt consoled when she heard Lisa use the word "we" almost as if she was the one that had got her pregnant. At least she knew she was not alone, even though the 'we' she felt needed to make the decision was her and Brian. Even though no decision had been made by the end of her conversation, Jesse thanked God above that she had a friend like Lisa that she could confide in. As confused and as troubled as she was, Jesse could not imagine how she would have coped without Lisa's help.

Chapter Nineteen

Something Ent Right

"Jesse ah think maybe tomorrow we should go to the doctor," said a concerned Ms. Janice. "Why yuh say dat Ma?"

"Well look at how yuh looking pale, pale, pale. Ah never see yuh looking so. One minute yuh good next minute yuh tired. Something ent right." Although Ms. Janice was a mother of five and had been pregnant many times over, not for one moment had it crossed her mind that perhaps Jesse was pregnant. "Yes an yuh see how yuh vomit up yesterday. Dat ent good neither. Yuh drink all de orange peel tea last night and yuh still feeling sick today. Could be one a dem stomach virus yuh get." Ms. Janice didn't have money to take her daughter to the doctor but she had a credit arrangement with the nearby Dr. Burrows.

Dr. Burrows had delivered all her babies and was the only doctor who would see her on short notice and with no money. It had been two weeks since Jesse discovered her pregnancy and she was getting sicker. There were no obvious changes as yet underneath her school uniform, however Jesse began tightening the belt around her waist so the weight she imagined she was gaining wouldn't show. Jesse in fact had not begun to gain much weight but every time she looked down at her belly, which was often enough, she had a sense that it was getting bigger every day. Now more than ever she was grateful for her folder, because she kept it armed in front of her like a body shield and it hid a large portion of her torso.

"I'll be alright Ma, is nothing." Jesse was not yet ready to have her situation revealed in the doctor's office, especially since she was still working on finding the right moment to break the news to her mother. "Ah still feel we should check it out Jesse." Ms. Janice hated to see her children ill. "Ah feeling a lot better than yesterday Ma. Wait till tomorrow nah an if ah still feeling bad well we could go but ah feel by tomorrow ah will be good," Jesse pleaded.

Ms. Janice knew that Jesse did not like going to the doctor but she felt that it couldn't hurt to wait till tomorrow especially since Jesse had said she was beginning to feel better. That night Jesse lay in bed and prayed that when she woke up in the morning she would not be feeling sick. She needed more time to formulate a plan, she just didn't know what the plan would be. When Ms. Janice was ready to leave for the market at 5.00 a.m. Jesse awoke as usual and seemed fine.

"How you feeling darling?" "Ma, ah feeling much better than yesterday," was Jesse's feigned response. Ms. Janice patted her daughter's head. "Ah make some pelau late last night so yuh could take dat fuh lunch," said Ms. Janice. After she bid her farewell the little yellow car made its way out of the narrow road in the darkness. Jesse watched the car disappear around the corner. She was feeling a bit nauseated but it would be a while before she actually came to vomiting. She began her morning routine of waking up the children for school.

Becca as usual always gave the most trouble to get up and get dressed. Jesse made some hot chocolate for everybody and warmed up some fry bake in the oven. Then she attempted to fry some eggs. Something about the smell of the frying eggs made her nausea worse and before Jesse knew it she was over the kitchen sink retching and throwing up. "Oh geed!" said Becca as she watched. "What happen to yuh Jesse?" Steve asked after she had washed the vomit down the sink and washed her face. "Aye yuh going to burn de eggs!" Steve attempted to finish working on breakfast.

Jesse sat down at the kitchen table too exhausted to move. Becca looked at her and screwed up her face in disgust. Jacob and Becca were play fighting with each other and seemed oblivious to what was going on, and Joan, the youngest of them all was standing at the corner of the kitchen table with her plastic bowl and spoon in hand waiting expectantly for food. Jesse knew she couldn't continue this morning routine for much longer.

By the time, Jesse had readied everyone and marched everyone off to school, she was so tired she had to take a taxi back home. She recalled Lisa's words the day before. "Jesse what yuh going to do with a chile? Yuh going to ruin yuh life. Yuh think you could just make a chile and do exams like normal? Think about what yuh doing," Lisa had pleaded. Perhaps Lisa was right Jesse thought. Perhaps she should just have an abortion but she had heard so much about abortion in school and how wrong it was and that it was killing a life. Jesse was afraid to follow up what she perceived to be one wrong act with another. But it wasn't just that, she loved Brian and this was his child; their child that they had made together and she couldn't bring herself to get rid of it even though Brian had begged her to.

"How could you do this to me Jesse?" an upset Brian had asked her. "You really don't love me do you." That had been the most hurtful comment of all. That he would even suggest such a thing to her was more painful than she could bear and though he would apologize for having said it later on she would never forget those words.

"Things real slow today eh," Ma Thomas said with a sigh. The sun was hot and the flow of customers through the Port-of-Spain market was at its lowest. "Is de time ah de year yuh know, people just pass out from Christmas an everybody saving money fuh Carnival. De sun hot too." Ms. Janice replied.

"Ay-ay, ah forget to ask yuh how Jesse shaping up for exam."

"Gyul, ah doh know yuh know. Yesterday she was sick an feeling weak. Ah tink she have a stomach virus or something. She waste one setta time on dat Chinee boy but ah tink ah put a stop to dat," said Ms. Janice wiping her brow. "Gyul dese young people nowadays not easy yuh know. Look ah have a neighbor dere whey ah livin. Is one piece ah girl chile she have. Dat chile I know is one quiet chile; doh give no trouble always in church wid de mudder on a Sunday. You know, a month pass an ah ent see dat gyul, next ting de mudder tell me is pregnant de gyul pregnant yuh know. Fifteen years old going Arima Senior Sec. Eh, now tell me what dat mudder coulda do again to bring up dat gyul right eh."

"So wha she do?" Ms. Janice asked

"Well she sen she by de fadder so he could talk to she an ah see she reach back home yesterday wid she belly rising. Steups. Sometimes ah does say de good Lord know why he ent give me no chilren in life," Ma Thomas concluded.

"Is a good ting yuh have a chile dat wouldn give you no stress like dat."

"Well gyul, de other day ah see she was acking up and giving me chat an ting but ah see like now she cool down. But ah had to put meh foot down wid she and de phone and wid dis going in people house every weekend. Ah tell dat gyul dat just because dem people rich, dat ent mean nuttin. She was only talking bout she Aunty Sally dis an Aunty Sally dat. Aunty Sally my eyeball. Steups. Ah want she to ask Aunty Sally to pay meh telephone bill. Dese young people doesn't be tinking sometimes yuh know, but ah glad ah put a stop to everything before tings start to get outta hand."

Ms. Janice wiped the sweat off her face with her hand and wiped her hands clean in her apron. "Ah jus doh know if she ready to get a scholarship gyul but ah saying meh prayers. As a matter ah fac, ah have to go up Monk St Benedict dis weekend an light a candle fuh each one ah dem children yes, especially she." Ms. Janice believed in going to Mount Saint Benedict for prayers and blessings. The home of the only Benedictine monks on the island was a source of peace for many people of all faiths and walks of life. Even if a body did not ascribe to the teachings of the Catholic Church, many a troubled mind found solace, and received enlightenment when looking out from the breezy vantage point of the monastery grounds.

For those who wished to pray, the church doors were always open and the monks were always willing and ready to listen to those who wished to unburden their souls. "Well jus say thank God yuh have good children who ent misbehaving yes gyul." Ma Thomas advised. "Dey not bad. Ah just wish Mr. GG was around to see how nice dey growing up. Especially Jesse. Ah only keeping meh fingers cross and saying meh prayers dat she get dat scholarship."

A little over a month after Tommy was buried. Lystra had received a new lease on life. In a strange way, although she missed him, or at least the Tommy she used to know, she was glad that he was gone; glad that he didn't have to lie on the streets like a jumbie, making fares with men so he could get a fix. He was in another place now, hopefully a better place and all Lystra could do was to pray for his soul. Her brothers and sisters in the Lord had rallied through and had really been there for her.

Every day now, Eddy would return home to find his mother, reflecting on some passage of scripture and trying to share some scripture verse with him. Eddy didn't mind it that much, he just couldn't handle the non-stop spiritual music in his head all the time. Morning, noon and night Lystra's radio station was stuck on a radio station that pelted out gospel music, preaching pastors and people calling in to give their testimonies. It was the only thing she would listen to and often Eddy would become irritated because sometimes he thought the preachers were talking a lot of nonsense. A lot of nonsense coming out of the mouths of born and bred Trinbagonians with American accents.

Although he had pleaded with her to reduce the volume on the radio or allow him to listen to some other music station, Lystra somehow viewed his defiance as "the devil talking" which only made Eddy more annoyed. Exam time was coming up and although he was glad that his mother was home more often instead of out on the streets of Port-of-Spain, his home environment was anything but conducive to study. Often he would find himself hanging out with Spranger or Uncle Tremble and the boys in front of Charlie's rum shop. It was only when Pastor Miller offered Lystra a job at his office answering the telephone that Eddy would have quieter nights.

Pastor Miller was a married man but he had been eyeing Lystra for quite some time. The opportunity presented itself for him to get closer to her when his receptionist left the job. Lystra was offered the job right away and although many sisters and brothers in the church questioned Lystra's suitability for the post, no one dared question the work of the Holy Spirit or the actions of Reverend Pastor Miller who was undeniably a man of God. Finally Lystra had the respectability that no foreman could ever give her. Head held high she walked to work every morning looking as spiffy as she could and invoking the envy of not only her neighbors but her sisters in the Lord who although smiling to her face and praising God's goodness in her life, commented behind her back about "how she reach so high up in de church already and she now get save."

Lystra was undaunted. In fact she had found working with Pastor Miller to be rewarding in more ways than one and for a moment Eddy began to believe that perhaps his mother had truly changed her ways, but when she began coming home late from work again with hair disheveled and smelling of sweat, Eddy knew that Pastor Miller was just another foreman of the spiritual kind. He knew his mother; she was saved yes but not about to change. Still he was grateful to all the nameless, faceless foremen. Their money over the years had put food on the table, clothes on his back and shoes on his feet. Eddy just wished that his real father whoever he was could have been one of them.

When Ms. Janice got home that evening from the market it was Becca that brought the news. "Ma Jesse vomit dis morning in de sink yuh know. It was gross." Ms. Janice was determined now more than ever that Jesse should go to the doctor. The possibility of pregnancy had still not entered her mind. She found Jesse in her bedroom lying down and sat on the bed beside her. "How yuh feeling love."

"I alright Ma, just tired."

"Well we going to have to go to de doctor tomorrow girl because ah doh tink yuh could have another day like dis," she said with an air of finality.

"No Ma. We can't go to the doctor yet."

"Why not Jess?"

Jesse was trying to find the words but she couldn't. She looked at her mother's face looking back at her, full of love and concern. How could she tell her mother that she had made a mistake; a huge mistake. How could her mother ever forgive her. Like a spring the tears welled up and Jesse's face became flushed. "Ah sorry Ma. Ah didn't mean to. Ah didn't mean fuh it to happen. It happen so fast and…" Jesse burst into tears and began sobbing uncontrollably as she held her face in her hands. "What happen Jesse? What happen?" Then, suddenly it all became clear to Ms. Janice. It was as if a light switch had been turned on in a dark room. Suddenly it all made sense. "Jesse doh tell me is pregnant yuh pregnant?" Ms. Janice looked bewildered at her daughter laying on the bed, hoping to hear her deny vehemently that it was so. Hoping to hear her say something like "Please Ma, don't be silly" in that know it all tone of voice, but Jesse never said it. She only shook her head and cried.

"Jesus Christ, look at meh crosses here tonight. Jesse is pregnant yuh pregnant fuh dat boy?" Jesse's sobs grew louder. Ms. Janice was bewildered as she looked perplexed at her child crying before her. "Lord farda in heaven help!" She put her hand on her chest almost as if she was trying to prevent her heart from jumping out of it. She remained there motionless for a few moments. Her heart was beating fast and the pain of what she had just learnt seemed to be real and moving from her stomach to her chest to her throat then to her eyes from which the tears began to roll forth.

"Jesus have mercy on meh," Ms. Janice uttered as she gazed upward. "Jesse de boy know?" Jesse nodded. "De mudder know?" "No Ma" Jesse said between tears. "Well dat mudder need to know right now. I did know dat boy was no good." Ms. Janice got up off the bed and marched to where the telephone lay in a corner in their tiny living room. Suddenly the thought of exposure made Jesse spring from her bed. "No Ma please. Brian will get in trouble. Please Ma, don't do it," her face was red and wet with tears and snat ran from her nose as she pleaded with her mother.

"Brian will get in trouble! Dat is what yuh worried about? Yuh whole life just get mess up by dis boy and dat is all you studying? Look gyul doh leh meh start on yuh." Ms. Janice was angry, hurt and disappointed. There was nothing Jesse could do, she felt her life unraveling before her very eyes, coming apart at the seams.

"Yes Goodnight Mrs. Chow Fatt, this is Jesse's mother calling. How are you?"

"Oh I'm fine thank you. How are you?"

"Not so good actually."

"Is everything ok?"

"Well not really. Yuh talk to Brian lately?"

Sally was becoming concerned. "Well yes, as a matter of fact he is home right now watching TV."

"Well he ent tell yuh dat he geh Jesse pregnant?"

"What!" Sally had exclaimed so loud that even Matt who had come home early that night, looked up from his crossword puzzle.

"Yes. Meh daughter pregnant fuh yuh son Mrs. Chow Fatt an ah think de only place dat coulda happen was inside your house."

"Now wait a minute now, hold on. Are you sure?"

"Sure about what? Dat she pregnant or dat yuh son is de fadder?"

"Mrs. Guevara I know my son. Are you sure that he is the father if Jesse is in fact pregnant?"

"Wha de ass yuh saying to meh tonight lady. Yuh tink my daughter is a jamète ah what. Yuh son is de first boy she ever know and yuh asking if he is de fadder? Look lady…."

"Now hold on Mrs. Guevara all I'm saying is that it is possible that…"

"Yuh trying to call my chile a ole ho is what you trying to say. Leh me tell yuh something. Dis chile coulda only get pregnant in your house by your son. An if she get pregnant in your house dat mean all de times when yuh did say yuh always home and yuh watching dem was a lie."

"Are you calling me a liar Mrs. Guevara?"

"Yes because dat is what yuh is. Ah shoulda never let my chile inside yuh house. Ah want to know what yuh son have to say bout dis and what yuh going to do about dis."

"I strongly resent your tone Mrs. Guevara, with all due respect I think you need to speak with Jesse again and find out which other house she has been frequenting. You have a good night." With a click of the telephone, Sally hung up. Matt, who had put aside his crossword puzzle was listening attentively to the conversation. "Did I hear right Sal? Is Jesse pregnant?"

"Yes and that was Mrs. Guevara on the phone ranting and raving like a wajang about Brian being the father."

"Are you serious?"

"Do I look like I'm joking Matt. She said Jesse is pregnant and Brian is the father and she wants to know what we are going to do about it."

"That's impossible. When would they have got a chance to even have sex? I mean he has people around him all the time now. That's just crazy."

"I know; that is exactly what I'm thinking. Maybe we should talk to Brian."

Before Matt had a chance to agree or disagree with that suggestion Sally was already calling him. "I think you should let me handle this Sally," said Matt but it was too late.

"Brian! Brian! Can you look here a minute please."

Sally was definitely ruffled now as she sat upright in her red satin night gown with her hair up in a clip. Brian came in a few minutes and stood in the doorway of his parents' bedroom, unaware of the conversation that had just occurred. "I just got off the telephone with Jesse's mom and she said something very disturbing Brian." Sally could see Brian was nervous already. "What is Jesse Ok?" he asked. "Oh yes, Jesse is fine, except that Mrs. Guevara says that she's …well pregnant."

"What!" Brian exclaimed almost as if he was hearing it for the first time.

Matt was silent just taking it all in. "Jesse pregnant! How?"

"Well she says you are the father Brian, do you know anything about that."

"Me. Ha ha!" Brian laughed in disbelief. "She said I am the father. Nah, nah that's impossible. How could I be the father? When would we have had a chance to do something like that?"

"Well that's the same thing I told Mrs. Guevara but she was ranting and raving about it so I figured I would talk to you."

"Well that's just ridiculous. Her mother kinda crazy though. Jesse always told me how her mother always was giving her a hard time. You see how much security I have now following me all over, even if I wanted to which I don't, when would I have the time to do something like that?"

"That is exactly what I thought Brian. Maybe you could talk to Jesse and ask her about this thing."

"Yeah and I spoke to her yesterday and she didn't say anything about being pregnant. That is weird." Brian shrugged his shoulders and shook his head perplexed. "Wow that is just amazing. Jesse pregnant. I can't believe that. Well I hope her mother finds out whoever the fella is but it isn't me."

"Ok Brian, that will be all," said Matt who up to that time had been silent.

"Ok" and with that Brian returned to his room.

As soon as Brian had pulled the door shut and left the room Matt spoke. "He's lying."

"What! How could he be lying?" Sally was perplexed that Matt would come to such a conclusion after such a genuine denial. "He's my son and he's a man and I'm telling you he's lying through his teeth."

"How do you know?"

"Trust me I know these things." It had suddenly dawned on Matt that his son was a man; a young man with racing hormones like any other teenager his age. "Think about it. A girl that you yourself told me Brian is crazy about who has been in the house several times is pregnant by some other fella and Brian is indifferent about it? Don't you think that's odd?"

Sally raised her eyebrows and seemed thoughtful for a minute. "Hmm well I guess he could have been a bit more upset and he seemed pretty cool."

"What if it's really his baby? Oh my God. This could ruin his entire life." Sally jumped out of bed now at the possibility that Brian could have actually had sex right under her very nose. "This would be all your fault Sal."

"My fault!"

"Yes, you were supposed to be watching them. I was never in agreement with the idea of that girl coming here in the first place."

The argument that ensued between Matt and Sally was short-lived because Matt left soon after for a drink at Smokey's and Bunty's. Sally worried and afraid that perhaps she had made a grave error, put on her bedroom slippers and made her way to her son's bedroom. The door was ajar and she could see him lying on his bed with his headphones on listening to music. She knocked gingerly and gently pushed the door. "Can I come in?" It wasn't really a question because she was already inside the bedroom. Brian sat up and removed the headphones. His eyes looked red and although his face was dry, she knew he had been crying. She sat on the edge of his bed and admired her handsome son. He had grown into quite an attractive young man. "I just wanted to talk to you for a minute," she started. It had been a while since she had had a heart to heart with her son. She had been so busy fussing over and about him since the kidnapping with security guards, therapy sessions and constant monitoring that she had forgotten that he was still a boy very much in need of his mother.

Chapter Twenty
A Mother's Love

"I just don't understand it Marlene" said Sally as she chewed on a forkful of sautéed vegetables in the air conditioned Sans Souci restaurant. "It's not like the girl's mother is happy about the pregnancy but she refuses to let her have an abortion and I'm sure by now its too late to do one anyway."

"I don't know Sal; if I were you I would offer her money."

"Don't you think I did that Marlene? I know it is going to cost us more in the long run if this girl has the baby. I mean its not just Brian's reputation down the road but she could try to stick us with more child support than needed. Who knows?"

"So why doesn't she want the abortion?" asked Marlene.

"Who the mother or the daughter?"

"Well both?"

"Well the daughter just loves Brian and somewhere I think in her head she feels that the baby will bring them closer together and Brian will eventually marry her and they'll live happily ever after. Well we both know that won't happen as long as I can help it. But the mother is going on about being Catholic and not wanting to take another life and I know for a fact she doesn't want her daughter to have this child," said Sally defiantly as she stabbed her fork into a cube of stewed beef.

"What does that have to do with anything?" asked Marlene not seeing the connection.

"That is exactly my point Marlene. I told her 'look I'm Catholic too but if it were my child I would do right by her', because unless God himself were coming down from above to take care of that baby there was no way she was having it."

"So what did she say when you told her that?"

"She just went on and on about how this was all my fault. But like I told her nobody put a gun to her daughter's head and made her take off her panties."

"Oh my God Sally you said that? You're positively awful!"

"Well it's the truth."

"So what does Matt have to say about all this?"

"He couldn't be bothered. He thinks we should just send Brian off to college after exams and allow everything to die a natural death."

"Do you really think they want money from you?"

"No. The daughter doesn't but the mother feels we should either take the baby after it's born or pay for the expenses. And I think she means for everything. You see why I was pushing for her to get rid of it?"

"Well didn't you say it's too late for the abortion now?"

"Yes I think so. She's almost five months already. Or is it six months....I'm not sure really but can't Senora Velasquez do something about a situation like this Marlene?"

"I doubt it Sally but you could ask her."

"Hmm, maybe I'll do that after lunch."

"What about Brian, how is he taking it?"

"I'm not too sure. He's not saying much, at least not to me. I know he feels something for the girl but I think he just feels a bit overwhelmed by the whole situation. I mean first it was the kidnapping now this. The poor boy has been through a lot this year."

"Poor thing" said Marlene who had just finished her meal and was wiping her hands in her napkin.

"But enough on that, I will figure something out. How is Sean doing?" Sally asked not wanting to seem too absorbed in her own affairs.

"Oh he's fine, getting ready to do his SAT exams"

"It was good that you were able to get him in a school right away. I agree with you and Damien, it isn't safe to have any kind of money in Trinidad anymore." Marlene had not told Sally the real reason Sean had been sent away and didn't plan on revealing the truth now either. "So he didn't have a girlfriend here at all?" Sally asked. Marlene was becoming uncomfortable and

Sally could see that she had hit upon a very sensitive note with her friend. "Sally, I hate to do like the Spanish but I really can't stay. Carnival time is the worst time for the business and its worse this year since Carnival is in the middle of March."

Marlene slid gracefully out of her soft cushioned seat and stood upright. She carefully leaned over, grabbed her black leather handbag and after giving Sally a farewell kiss on either cheek walked briskly out of the restaurant. Sally propped her chin in her hands. Maybe she would go to see Senora Velasquez she thought. More than one month after the discovery that Jesse was pregnant and that Brian was more than likely the father, Sally was in a dilemma. After many telephone conversations with Jesse's mother and even a face to face encounter at Ms.Janice's home with a bashful looking Brian in tow, she had found no resolution to the problem that Jesse's baby represented in her mind. What bothered her more was that Matt seemed unconcerned almost.

"So what if she has the baby and we have to help take care of it. These people aren't thieves you know, Jesse is a sweet girl that just made a mistake," Matt had said. Sally didn't see it quite like that. In Sally's mind, Jesse had not yet grasped the full depth of the power that she would wield once that child was born. Once Jesse knew what that power meant, all hell would break lose as far as Sally was concerned. There were only two choices: take the baby and raise it herself or forever be riddled with baby bills and dealing with Jesse or her mother. Neither option appealed to Sally. Even if she wanted to take the child, Jesse was not willing to give the baby up and the thought of raising her own grandchild seemed absurd. Matt seemed more comfortable with the latter option while Brian was clueless and ridden with guilt. It didn't seem fair to Sally that now that everything was finally coming together in her family life that this should come up to create more problems. She daintily wiped her mouth clean and made her way to the bathroom to freshen up. Perhaps she would go to see Senora Velasquez after all she mused. It couldn't hurt to try something.

"No Mrs. Guevara I'm very sorry but she will have to do her exams at another testing centre and she will continue to be expelled from school." Sr. Monica delivered her verdict with a stiff upper lip and a frown of disdain.

"Please Sr.Monica, it have any way. Ah mean Jesse is a good girl. Is just one mistake she make now and is really dat Chow Fatt boy and he mudder dat should be paying de price." Ms. Janice sat across the desk in a floral blouse and pleated navy blue skirt, pleading for her daughter to have a chance in the world. Next to her, Jesse sat shamefaced in a pair of track pants with an elastic waist and a tee-shirt. "This is very unfortunate Mrs. Guevara. Very unfortunate. However you must understand my position. I have to maintain a standard. What kind of example would we be setting if we allow Jesse to come back to school in her condition? She won't be able to wear the uniform with a belly. It wouldn't be right. I'm very sorry but she will have to do her exams at an external centre."

There was no swaying Sr. Monica and Ms. Janice was determined to walk out of that office with the few shreds of dignity she had left. Jesse's face was expressionless. She had missed a whole month of school already and now there was no way she could return. As much as she hated school and some of those stuck up girls in her class, she missed school, the routine of it at least. But most of all she missed Lisa and her life before her belly started to rise. She didn't know who had called Sr. Monica and exposed her but she suspected that it was Mrs. Chow Fatt because although her mother was disappointed and hurt by what had happened she was determined that Jesse should at least finish school and get her certificates.

In fact her mother had been more supportive of her than she had anticipated after learning of the pregnancy. "We'll figure something out Jesse. Yuh not showing right now really, just see if yuh could manage to keep going to school until ah figure something out." Ms. Janice had said to her; almost as if she could foresee that Jesse's expulsion from school was inevitable. Two months later when she could no longer tighten that belt around her waist and her rosy cheeks and expanding hips and backside began to raise eyebrows among the teaching staff; Jesse was called into Sr. Monica's office, expelled and asked to return with her mother. "Don't worry Jesse. You'll be alright. I hope yuh going to make me God mother yuh know" Lisa had joked in an effort to cheer her up. But Jesse knew there was no going back.

The rumors had been spreading in the school about her pregnancy. Sally told Marlene who told somebody who had a daughter going to St. Joseph's Convent. Whatever the length or direction of the grapevine, Jesse's pregnancy was something to talk about. The girls in her class whispered about it behind her back and even at Mr. Lee Wen's classes people knew. There Jesse no longer had the comfort of seeing Brian anymore since his parents had hired a private tutor who now taught him at home. It was mostly Sally's idea since Jesse's mother was behaving so 'classless and uncultured', she was convinced that the "fruit didn't fall far from the tree" and didn't want her son anywhere near Jesse.

The day Cindy Sawh snickered as Jesse passed by was the day Jesse decided that she could not go back either to school or to lessons. She took to her bed in tears that night but was back in class another day to hear the whisperings and murmurings. That her body did not lay testimony to the rumors going around until she had reached the fifth month of her pregnancy was indeed fortuitous considering that she was already three months pregnant when those two purple lines on the pregnancy kit sealed her fate.

As she walked out of the school gates on the day she was expelled, Jesse could feel the eyes of the girls from her class on her back watching her go. She didn't look back. She didn't want to. One brief moment, one bad choice, now she couldn't write exams in school. Her poor mother shamed and disappointed, Brian distant and aloof and Lisa struggling to be supportive at a time when Jesse wanted the earth to swallow her whole. Nobody really understood her she thought, not her mother, not Brian, not even Lisa although she admitted that Lisa did try. Jesse had never felt so alone in the world and as her body continued to change form both internally and externally, she sank into a pit of confusion, desperation and despair. By the time her mother had dragged her off to see Sr. Monica she had no pride left, no will to live, not even for the life she was carrying.

"Alright. Well yuh hear what Sr. Monica say, so ah will have to try to get you in a centre fas because exams is jus now," said Ms. Janice. As she and Jesse walked down Frederick Street. Jesse was silent. The sun was hot and Jesse's face and expanding nose glistened. She couldn't care less about exams or anything for that matter. "Alright well you go on home an ah will go back in de market and see if ah cyah make a sale today." Ms. Janice had told her when they parted at City Gate. Jesse nodded and held on to the railing as she tried to go up the long flight of stairs to get a bus route maxi taxi. By eleven o'clock Ms. Janice was back at her stall in the Port-of-Spain market. "So how it went," Ma Thomas asked. "Not good gyul, not good at all. Sr. Monica say she have to go to some external centre. Ah doh even know how to get Jesse in a external centre but ah going dong by Ministry of Education jus now. Ah jus say leh me pass and see how everything going here."

"Tings busy today gyul. Ah sell some eddoes and lettuce and some baigan fuh you. Look de change here." Ma Thomas reached into the pockets of her apron and handed the money to Ms. Janice who counted it right away.

"So what Jesse say gyul."

"She ent saying nuttin but ah know she feeling real bad an ah could understand why," said Ms. Janice as she sat herself down on her little wooden stool.

"Doh mind dat she go be alright. Ah just hope yuh could get somewhere fuh she to write she exam."

"Gyul when las yuh see Papa Netty pass through here?" Ma Thomas asked. She was genuinely concerned about the old drunkard. "Is a long time yuh know, ah think was last month yes. Ah hope he ent sick."

"Hmm. Ah hope not," Ma Thomas replied. The two women had grown used to Papa Netty's picong and taunts and although they didn't know that much about the man, they wished him no ill.

"So yuh heading off now Janice."

"In a little while. Ah just going to ketch meh breath a little bit first." The heat of the day and the difficulty of the mission she had tried to accomplish a few moments earlier had exhausted Ms. Janice. As she sipped on her little bottle of Chubby sweet drink, she tried to prepare herself mentally for her trip to the Ministry of Education in St. Clair. Her daughter had to write exams and there was no debating that in her mind.

All hopes of Jesse winning a scholarship for herself as a student of St. Joseph's Convent had been dashed. It was bad enough that her daughter was pregnant but at least she could get her certificates. After she had the baby, maybe Jesse could get a job and work for a while but Ms. Janice was not going to accept Sr. Monica's verdict lying down. Meanwhile on the maxi taxi going home, Jesse was in a daze. She felt as though a heavy cold rain was beating down on her shoulders. All the images of the last few months kept flashing back and forth before her as Sr.Monica's words rang in her ears like a death knoll. Her mind would fix on one image and then suddenly every thing would become a blur. Her heart was about to explode. Her brain was about to implode.

This was not her life happening. She saw herself looking down at herself and her life almost as if she was out of her body. When the maxi came to her stop at the Croiseé, something familiar about the place prompted her to get off. She could hear Lisa telling her that everything was going to be alright as she walked on autopilot to the taxi stand where she would fetch a taxi home. Then everything went blurry again. Mr. GG was talking to her and she wanted to talk back but she couldn't. Nothing was right, nothing made sense and Jesse felt as if she couldn't breathe, as if the air in her lungs was slowly being sucked out of her.

She put the car window down so that she could get some air and watched as the car zoomed past trees and houses and stores to enter the San Antoñio valley. Jesse wished she could be one of those trees, tall and aloof looking down on the people below scurrying around. How she wished she could escape from her life. By the time Jesse got home, she was exhausted. She needed to lie down, too many voices, too much noise. She could feel herself slipping away. "Not that way Daddy, this way," she scolded as she placed a fork on the dining room table on the left side. Then Jesse lay down and fell asleep.

Her condition would only worsen when she awoke and when Ms. Janice returned home to find Jesse talking to herself, no amount of slapping and throwing of cold water would help. "Jesus, Mary and Joseph deliver dis child," Ms. Janice wept. She shook Jesse and slapped Jesse and shook her again. Jesse was dead inside and out. She couldn't cry, or fight or struggle. She just was. For three days Ms. Janice stayed at home and tried to bring Jesse back to the land of the sane. She called the priest to pray on Jesse and got some women from the Catholic Charismatic movement to pray in the house so that the evil forces trying to destroy her child could be driven out. Jesse's condition remained unchanged. She still felt hungry and ate and drank and slept and went to the toilet when she needed to go but other than these activities, Jesse had abandoned all forms of normal behavior. She stayed all day in her room and played with her hair, talked to herself and pretended to be breastfeeding one of Becca's dolls. Some days she seemed fine until she would begin with her conversations. Eventually Ms. Janice took her to Dr. Burrows

"There must be something you can do doctor. Please ah beggin yuh." Dr. Burrows removed his pen which was fixed in his oversized afro and began to write on a little piece of paper. "This is a letter. You need to take Jesse to St. Ann's for psychological evaluation and possibly admission."

"What! I ent taking meh daughter up St. Ann's. She not crazy. She just under a lil stress. She just need yuh to give she something to help with de stress," Ms. Janice pleaded. "She pregnant doctor, she cyah make dis baby in St. Ann's!" A distraught Ms. Janice had said before leaving the doctor's office. She refused to accept that her daughter was mentally ill. She refused to believe that the stress of her life had been too much for her to bear. There was no history of mental illness on her side of the family, although she wasn't sure about Mr.GG's side. She would wake up in the morning with tears and cry herself to sleep. Why had this happened to her? Why now? Why had this happened to her child? Out of all the children in the world, God had to pick her child.

The looks of concern on the faces of her other children kept her going. Steve began to take on additional household responsibilities and began to act and behave like the man in the house, bossing Becca and the others around. For days Ms.Janice did not work and no work meant no money coming into the house. In the morning when she woke, she would ready the other children for school and leave Jesse sleeping. Ms. Janice listened to all who would advise her and tried a little of everything. Some said bathe her in bush; some said give a worming out; others advised that she needed to be born again. Ms. Janice cut some pieces of aloe from a plant in the yard, peeled off the tough green skin and tried to make Jesse swallow the bitter medicinal plant. Jesse would spit and fight her. It was useless.

When Senna pods, orange peel tea and all the bushes Ms. Janice knew would not work, Ms. Janice swallowed her pride, called Mrs. Chow Fatt and pleaded that Brian be allowed to talk to Jesse in the hope that hearing his voice might return her to the realm of the sane. Not even that seemed to work. Brian's conversation with Jesse seemed strange. It was as if he were speaking to someone he did not know.

"Lisa she behaving very strange. You try to talk to she nah, maybe she will remember yuh," Ms. Janice had pleaded before giving Jesse the telephone.

"Hi Jesse, how yuh going gyul?"

"Who is this?"

"Is Lisa, how yuh mean who is this?"

"Why yuh calling me? Ah didn't make the baby yet. Doh call meh until ah make de baby ok. Ah have to get ready now." Jesse hung up.

When she could no longer afford to stay at home and keep vigil with Jesse and the many people from the different churches who came to pray with her during the day and at night, Ms. Janice took Jesse with her to the market.

If she didn't speak or make any funny movements, nobody would know what was going on. But Ma Thomas was no fool, she knew something was awry from the moment she saw Jesse. Ms. Janice was forced to reveal the truth of the matter to her when Jesse began one of her conversations.

"Why yuh doh take she back to de doctor?"

"Ah take she to de doctor already. De doctor tell meh take she up St. Ann's."

"Ah cyah take Jesse up dere. Yuh ent see de kinda mad people dat does be walking out from up dere. Jesse not mad. She just stressed out. Is all this pressure dat just getting to she. My girl is a bright girl."

Ma Thomas felt sorry for her friend. She could see the pain in Ms. Janice's eyes and she knew just how much she was hurting under her iron fisted determination to see Jesse recover. "She go be alright. She just need some time." However Ms. Janice would soon discover that Jesse needed more than time.

Life had not been the same for Lisa since Jesse's expulsion from school. Suddenly Lisa realized that outside of Jesse, she didn't have any very close friends that she connected with in that way. There was nobody like Jesse at school or at lessons. No one as funny or as smart or as witty or as knowledgeable and naïve at the same time. When she visited Jesse at home, Lisa tried to talk to her and tried to find the Jesse she knew. Somewhere under that skull were the remains of her friend Jesse and how she wished she could reach inside that head and pull her out. It was no use.

Jesse recognized her and smiled but then turned to her new imaginary friends and continued her dialogues. Lisa never returned after that day. It had been too painful for her and had caused her to shed far too many tears on the way home. It would take her several months before she could refocus well enough to study for her exams. For Lisa, Jesse had died, except she was still alive.

By the time June rolled around, there were more exciting things in the gossip mill than Jesse's pregnancy by Brian Chow Fatt and her subsequent 'going off'. A-Level students had been dismissed from school around the first week in May to prepare for exams and had already received their CXC and A-Level exam timetables. Talk of graduation parties and dresses and dates were all the buzz for the Upper Six students and Form Five students getting ready for exams. Lisa, Eddy, Brian and the majority of their classmates were studying hard. Mr. Lee Wen held many last minute review sessions for students wishing to sharpen their skills in preparation for exams. Each exam whether it was a lab exam or multiple choice was critical.

Those aiming to obtain scholarships were pulling out all the stops. Jesse had wanted to be in that group. She had visions of herself winning a scholarship with her picture and her name in the newspapers. Her mother would have been so very proud of her. Brian had been able to catch up with his school work to some extent with all the private tutoring and was looking forward to the freedom that would soon be his once he began university. His father had connections in the Admissions Department and with most of the faculty deans at UWI, so Brian was certain of his spot there. He just wasn't sure about the course of study he wanted to pursue.

His mother had been suggesting that he consider some universities in England because his father had relatives living in Essex but Brian loved Trinidad. He loved his life in Trinidad and envisioned that his life at UWI would be even sweeter as Matt Chow Fatt's son. He knew he could get a lot of girls and he was even thinking of asking his father if he could get a new two door Mercedes Benz if he did well in his exams. However Brian's fantasy life at UWI would disappear one July morning when Sally announced to him that he was being sent to England.

"What! But I don't want to go there. I barely know my cousins there." Brian had protested. "Well now you will get a chance to know them better. Your father and I think it is for the best. You will have so many opportunities there." Brian didn't care about the opportunities. He had lost his best friend, his girlfriend, and now he was being made to leave the island he loved. There was no sulking, pouting or pleading that could sway his parents. Actually they had been thinking about sending him away as soon as exams were over. It was Matt who thought it would be a good idea to let him have a bit of a vacation with his friends before he went away. Brian had a whole new cadre of friends minus Eddy and Sean. Some of the friends hung around because they liked Brian and thought he was cool. Others were friends in order to be beneficiaries of Brian's generosity. Yet another group were friends just to be able to claim that they had a friend who was the son of one of the most powerful and most well known business men in the country. Whatever their motive, they came like hungry dogs around Brian shortly after Eddy's arrest and the rift that followed between the two boys and disappeared just as quickly after Brian's departure. News of Jesse's breakdown had hardly affected Brian's daily routine. "I always knew there was something wrong with that girl. She probably gets it from the mother poor thing," Sally had told Marlene over the phone. Brian couldn't understand it but chose to absorb himself in school work, friends and partying hard after exams.

The day before he left, Brian felt many mixed emotions. In a way he was glad to go, glad to get away from his parents, be on his own and make his own decisions. He thought about Eddy, Sean and Jesse. He had not heard from Sean since he left for Canada. He didn't hate Jesse but he wished he could talk to her. Wished he could tell her how sorry he was, that he never meant to hurt her. That he hoped she would be ok. The thought that she would be having his child while he was far away seemed unfair to both of them. Not that he wanted to marry Jesse. He couldn't now that she had lost her mind but how he wished he could turn back the hands of time. He wished that Saturday he had not felt so horny or been so anxious to be naked with Jesse. He wished she had not been so beautiful, so fragile, so vulnerable. Riddled with guilt and the knowledge that he might never see Jesse again, Brian closed his bedroom door that night and used his cell phone to dial that number he still remembered by heart.

"Hello, goodnight"

"Hello" Ms. Janice thought the person had been cut off and was about to hang up when the voice on the other end spoke.

"Goodnight Mrs. Guevara."

"This is Brian." Brian waited to hear her response.

"Goodnight" Ms. Janice sat down in her easy chair. She had lost the strength to be angry with the Chow Fatts or God or the world or Mr. GG. She was simply taking one day at a time. Her heart was a tender ball full of pain.

"I just called to say," he paused as the words got stuck in his throat. "I just called to say I'm sorry about everything." The tears welled up in Ms. Janice's eyes. "I never meant to hurt Jesse. I swear it. She is a good person and I never meant to hurt her. Could you tell her that for me?"

"Maybe yuh should tell her yuhself," said Ms. Janice as she looked across at Jesse rocking one of Becca's dolls on her lap.

"I can't. I just can't. I just wanted to say that."

"Well thank you for calling Brian."

"Goodnight Mrs. Guevara."

"Goodnight"

Later that night, in two different places, Ms. Janice and Brian would look up at the same starry sky with tears in their eyes and ask God different questions. Why is life so unfair? Why did Mr. GG have to die when he did? Why did this have to happen to my child? Why did Jesse have to get pregnant? Why are my parents sending me away? Why is it that Brian can continue with his life while my child has to suffer? Why poor people have to suffer so much? Why did things have to turn out this way?

The next morning while Ms. Janice was setting up her stall in the Port-of-Spain market, Brian would be fastening his seatbelt on a BWIA flight bound for

Heathrow International airport. Later that day, Ms. Janice and Ma Thomas would receive the news they had feared about Papa Netty. They had not seen him in at least a month. "Yes he dead last week Saturday yuh know, yuh ent hear that?" Kavita an Indian lady who sold Indian sweets and pies in the market informed them. "He didn used to live too far from me yuh know." Kavita was married to a black man and lived somewhere up on the Piccadilly. "Yes gyul, Papa dead. He had a lady used to come an check he in de night and cook for he an is she whey find he dead. Well ah figure she mus be take all whey he have in de house but he didn have much. De son making funeral arrangements for Wednesday. Ah talk to de son yuh know. He name Joseph. He have a big wok in town as some accountant something."

Kavita felt proud to relay the news to Ms. Janice and Ma Thomas. They didn't speak to her much. Kavita knew that they held a certain disdain for her. That she was able to give them valuable information about their friend Papa Netty made her feel very important. "Funeral is tomorrow morning about ten o'clock in de Anglican church. Anyway ah gone wid dat."

Ms. Janice and Ma Thomas thanked her as she left. "Well de ole man dead gyul. Ah wonder how ole he was?" Ma Thomas asked. "Ah dunno but ah sure hope de owner ah de rum shop sen a wreath cause wid de money he spend dere dey should pay for de whole funeral."

Chapter Twenty-One

It's a Boy!

"Hello, Mr. Chow Fatt."

"Yes, hello."

"This is Dr. Kissoon calling."

"Yes Dr. Kissoon."

"I'm just calling to let you know that your test results are back. So if you'd like to come down to the office when it's convenient…"

"Can't you give them to me over the phone?"

"Well I think it might be better if we spoke face to face."

"Doc you getting me worried now."

"Oh no. Nothing to worry about, I just think it would be better if you came in."

"I'm not dying right Doc?"

"No, no not at all" Doctor Kissoon laughed a bit nervously. "A man like you can't die yet." Matt smiled.

"Ok, I can make it around one o'clock."

"That's fine. Just let my receptionist Sherry know when you arrive so that I can see you right away."

"Ok Doc, see you then."

"Ok. Bye."

As Matt hung up the phone, he wondered what could be so important that Dr. Kissoon wanted to see him face to face. As long as he was not dying he would be fine but he was puzzled as to why Dr. Kissoon would not share his test results over the phone. Matt coughed. His fever had subsided but his cough was still there and at night he still had some difficulty breathing but all Matt needed to hear was that he was going to live. It had been months since he had heard from Priya. He had heard about her though; that she had a new boyfriend and that things were going well. Although he was jealous, he had been happy for her. He had his own stresses.

The police investigation into Brian's kidnapping had been going well until it seemed that some of Matt's business dealings ten years earlier with a Central businessman and former drug lord came to light. In those days business had not been so good for Matt and he sometimes needed loans. Big loans. He had repaid his creditor but years later when the man needed a large loan for his business, Matt had refused to help. He had no desire then to associate with men who were on the wrong side of the law. His former Good Samaritan did not forget Matt's ingratitude. "Neemakaram" was what he had called Matt.

Matt didn't care at the time but when it was learnt that there was a possibility that the man had carefully orchestrated the kidnapping using some hardened criminals from the Beetham, Matt was furious. That anger soon turned to fear when the police unearthed information regarding business transactions between the two men. Matt had to move quickly in order to prevent self-exposure. That kind of information in the wrong hands could ruin his reputation and in business Matt knew that his reputation was everything.

Money was the only silencing device he was prepared to use and use it he did. From the investigating officer down to the clerk filing the reports, Matt ensured that there was no chance his past dealings would come to the fore. Brian's indiscretions had been another cause for concern. Sally had been deeply troubled by the news of Jesse's pregnancy. Although she tried to dismiss it by casting aspersions on Jesse's character, Brian had told her the truth. It had hurt Matt that his son did not trust him enough to confide in him especially after the kidnapping. Now that Brian was gone, Matt had been able to get rid of the security guards and save some money.

Sally had tried to suggest that the guards stay on to guard her. Matt had scoffed at the idea knowing fully well the suggestion was another one of her attempts to get attention. He had been so busy with work and everything else that he didn't even notice that he had a persistent dry cough until one night he awoke unable to breathe. The following day he went to Dr. Kissoon for a check up. He was anxious to know what his test results would reveal and was at Dr. Kissoon's office in Woodbrook, promptly at one o'clock. What he would hear that evening would make him sick to the stomach.

"I sent the material we got in the bronchoscopy for cytological examination by the lab and the results came back today which is why I called you straight away," said a grave looking Dr. Kissoon.

"So what's the diagnosis? Do I have asthma?"

"No."

Matt let out a sigh of relief.

"Well unfortunately Matt you have PCP."

"PC what?"

"You have an infection called PCP which is short for Pneumocystis Carini Pneumonia."

"What the hell is that?"

"It's an infection of the lung which is what was causing the coughing and the difficulty breathing."

"What like pneumonia or something?"

"Yes."

"So do I just take some antibiotics for it?"

"Well not so fast. You see the reason I called you down here is because PCP is commonly seen in patients who are HIV positive. So I'd like your permission to do a blood test so that we can rule that out all together."

"What! AIDS! Doc I assure you I have no AIDS."

"I'm not doubting you but it's just that cases of PCP are extremely rare in non-AIDS patients. In fact I've never come across a PCP patient who wasn't infected with HIV."

"Nah, Doc, I don't have anything like that. I just need some antibiotics for the cough." Matt was a bit afraid. He had not told Dr. Kissoon about his indiscretions with Priya but he was sure she didn't have AIDS and he knew he couldn't possibly get it. He had used a condom almost every time.

"Look you are probably right so let's just do the test and be a hundred percent sure. I feel very strongly that we should do this." Dr. Kissoon urged. Those words, 'feel very strongly' Matt knew were loaded with concern. He thought for a minute. "Ok. Doc. If it'll make you feel better," said Matt.

"It will Matt." So Matt rolled up his sleeve and a nurse came in to take the blood test. He and Doctor Kissoon spent a few minutes after chatting about other man stuff like cricket and the recent selections of the West Indies Cricket Board. Doctor Kissoon gave him a prescription for the PCP to be filled, then Matt was off. Although he had tried to be cool in the doctor's office, he was deathly worried about what Dr. Kissoon had said. PCP? He had never heard of that one. This had to be an ordinary cold or something. He didn't have AIDS. The idea was preposterous. Priya was the only woman he had been with since his last medical and she was healthy. You could just look at her and see that she was healthy. She had a sexy body, curvy hips, she wasn't sick at all. Then Matt had a thought. Could Sally have been the one who was unfaithful. It wasn't too far fetched an idea he thought to himself. She had time, motive and a whole lot of opportunity.

But Matt knew his wife, she was too obsessed with him and their life together to do anything so crazy. Besides Sally was too scornful. She wouldn't have the guts to sleep with anyone she felt was beneath her and that ruled out a whole lot of people. Matt wondered if he was perhaps worrying for nothing. He decided to put the thought out of his head. And although he did contemplate calling Priya he knew he wouldn't know what to say after all this time. He would get the results in two weeks and the matter would be a non-issue. Later that night when Sally asked him what the doctor had to say about his cold he would brush it off. "Oh it's just a bad cold, I have to take some antibiotics."

"A cold had you not breathing?" Sally lifted her head from the Express newspaper she was reading. "Yeah. He says it could be allergies too but I'll live," said Matt as he sat down to watch the News At Ten on TV6 with a glass of scotch in his hand. "He's sure its not asthma?"

"Nah. It's nothing dear. Don't worry about it." But Matt was worried. Try as he might to put the doctor's words out of his head he couldn't. He only hoped that he was one of those rare cases of people who had PCP without having AIDS. He was too young to get AIDS in his mind and besides other than the cold he had, he felt fine. Matt felt he had at least thirty-five more years of good living left in him and a lot of unaccomplished goals.

"Everything looks good based on the ultrasound mam," a young doctor at the San Juan clinic told Ms.Janice. "I'm concerned though about your daughter's mental capacity to care for this child after it is born."

Ms. Janice helped Jesse button up the long maternity dress she was wearing before responding to what the doctor had said. "So de baby going to be alright?" she asked. "Well for now you daughter has a very healthy looking fetus growing inside of her."

"Alright well thanks doctor." Ms. Janice stood ready to leave. "There are medications that can help your daughter you know Mrs. Guevara," the doctor urged. "She is not in any mental condition right now to care for a child. Her condition could get worse. Do you think she even knows what is going on?"

"She know what going on doctor. She know it too much. Ah tell yuh already is just some stress she under. By de time de baby born she go get back good, you watch and see." Ms. Janice was still in denial. She marched Jesse out of the clinic and got in her car to head back to the market. Jesse was due any day now. Her belly had risen and her face, cheeks and nose had metamorphosized. The skin around her neck had grown dark and she walked uncomfortably under the weight she was carrying. Ms. Janice was neither looking forward to the birth of her grandchild, nor was she dreading it, she was simply preparing for it as best she could.

She had pulled out an old bassinet from one of her cupboards and had managed to gather up some cloth diapers and safety pins. Jesse's overnight bag for the hospital was packed and there were white baby vests and booties awaiting the new addition to the Guevara family. Ms. Janice had lost about ten pounds from the stress of the past months. Her clothes hung loosely on her body now that there was more space between the two entities. She had resurrected her sewing machine in an effort to make ends meet and had begun taking jobs sewing for neighbors in the area.

Burning the candle at both ends, Ms. Janice had struggled as hard as she could to put food on the table for her family and to shield the younger ones from the effects of what had happened to Jesse. More and more she began to wonder whether it wouldn't be best for her unborn grandchild to be taken care of by the Chow Fatts. Sally Chow Fatt could give that child so much more than she could and as much as she hoped and prayed that Jesse would somehow snap out of whatever she was in, Ms. Janice feared that if she didn't, taking care of a new baby would only make her condition worse.

Late one night, after everyone had gone to bed, Ms. Janice sat in the rocking chair in her porch and let the night air kiss her face softly. She could smell the freshness of the green grass glistening with dew and hear the night sounds of crickets and bugs and a cow mooing in the distance. The noises were like music, their melody golden. They comforted her the way a warm shower comforts the aching body of a construction worker at the end of a long day. Janice lost herself in the calm of the breeze and the sounds of the night as she rocked in her chair. Even the squeaks the chair made became a part of the melody. Then suddenly the melody was broken by Jesse's screams.

"Ma! Ma!" Ms. Janice almost fell as she ran to her daughter's bedside. Jesse was gripping her belly and bawling. Her bed was wet. Her water bag had broken several hours earlier when she went to the toilet but Jesse hadn't a clue that that was what had happened. "Oh God like Jesse making dis baby tonight. Becca run quick and bring dat white bag in my room in de corner." Becca who had aged considerably in responsibility since Jesse's illness promptly obeyed her mother's commands. "Come Jesse, come baby we going to de hospital ok. Take a deep breath. Yuh will be alright." Ms. Janice tried to change Jesse's underwear but she was moving about too much.

"Ok you will have to go just so yes."

"Ma. It hurting." Jesse cried. "Ok baby, it going to hurt. It supposed to hurt but yuh will be alright." Ms. Janice helped Jesse stand up and helped her to the car. "Becca stay by yuh sister till I come out side." A frightened Becca stood by the open car door and watched Jesse as she winced in pain. "Don't cry Jesse," she said as she rubbed the side of Jesse's arm. In a few minutes, Ms. Janice was dressed and ready to go. She hopped in the front seat. "Go back inside Becca and don't forget to lock the door. Steve, you in charge. Ah coming back jus now." And with a puff of white exhaust fumes the little yellow station wagon hurried down the bumpy road headed for Mount Hope Women's Hospital.

By the time Jesse arrived there she was fully dilated and ready to deliver. An intern on call in the emergency room checked to see how dilated she was but only because she was bawling so hard and so much. The doctor asked a few questions and instructed the nurses to have her taken up to the maternity ward. "Nurse meh chile meking a baby. Yuh want she make de chile right here?" Ms. Janice had pleaded when she realized that none of the nurses were paying any mind to her. "Oh gosh like dis girl ready to make de baby yes," said a plump nurse in a uniform that was too tight for her. "Take she up on de ward, I ent want no mess to clean up down here. Cross she leg tight. She ent making dat baby on my shift."

After the hospital attendants arrived with the gurney and helped Jesse on it, Ms. Janice attempted to follow her daughter.

"No mam you are not allowed into the delivery room."

"But is meh daughter. She not well."

"Mam, pregnancy is not a sickness. Just let us do our work," the burly nurse had said as she accompanied Jesse. "Ma! Ma! Doh leave me Ma!"

"Ah right here darling. Ah coming just now." Ms. Janice ran behind them with the overnight bag. "Wait she might need dis bag," as she handed it hurriedly to the nurse. The gurney turned the corner and Jesse's screams faded into the long corridors of the hospital. It was around three o'clock that morning that she would hear the news. "Mrs. Guevara your daughter had a boy; eight pounds nine ounces." A mixture of joy, relief, and sorrow flooded Ms. Janice. "A boy. A boy." She smiled, laughed and cried all at the same time. Mr. GG's first grandchild had been born.

Around ten o'clock a week later, Matt arrived at Dr. Kissoon's office. He was a bit irritated because Dr. Kissoon's receptionist had refused to give him the test results over the telephone. "Hi Doc. How you doing man?" Matt gave Dr. Kissoon a firm handshake before following him into his office. "Matt I wanted you to come down because I needed to discuss your test results with you."

"Doc you getting me frighten here now."

"Matt I have some bad news for you."

"What do you mean?"

"Your test results came back positive for HIV and your CD4 count is below the normal for an HIV patient."

"What! What you talking about HIV, CD4 what?"

"Matt I'm sorry but you have AIDS."

"No way! No way! You have to be kidding me!" Matt had sprung to his feet and was pacing.

"Matt I wish I were."

"There must be a mistake with the results doctor, maybe there is a mix up of some kind."

"No mix up Matt. The lab is very thorough."

"No Doc, that just can't be. I feel healthy I feel great. It was just this cold but I feel fine."

"Matt the PCP that you have is one of the infections that persons with AIDS commonly get. People who are infected with the HIV virus present differently. Fortunately for you, we were able to get the PCP in time. Unfortunately though you may be what they call a rapid progressor because…….."

"Wait doc, wait. There must be a mistake. I do not have AIDS or HIV or whatever the hell that blood report says. I am a healthy man."

"Matt it is only normal for you to feel angry right now."

"Normal? Doc I don't have AIDS!"

"Matt it will take some time for you to get used to the idea but I strongly suggest that you have Sally come down so that we can test her too to be sure that she hasn't contracted the virus."

"Sally? No Doc. Sally can't know about this. It would kill her. I want you to take another sample and test it again."

"Matt there really is no point in.."

"Do it Goddam it! I am not sick! AIDS is for homos. I am a married man. I have a wife and a son and a business. You can't be telling me now that I am going to die. Take the Goddam blood test again doc."

Matt's face was flushed as he looked angrily at the straight faced doctor. "Now Matt just calm down. We need to talk about treatment and quality of life, many people with HIV/AIDS are able to live well for a number of years."

"I can't be sick doc. There's no way." Matt was pacing up and down Dr. Kissoon's office again. "Look doc I have to go. I'll call you later when I calm down." And with that Matt stormed out leaving Dr. Kissoon speechless.

Matt drove around the Queen's park Savannah a couple of times then drove up to the look out on Lady Young Road where he parked his car and came out for a breath of fresh air. Could it be true? Could he really have AIDS? Matt thought about Priya. She was the only other person he could have got it from; or was it from a previous affair. Matt simply didn't know. He wanted to call her but he hesitated. He could see all the beauty of Port-of- Spain from where he stood. The buildings all seemed so distant and so far away. Matt watched as a few tourists purchased candied fruits and allowed themselves to be ripped off by a grey bearded strumming guitarist. He had to call her. Matt picked up his cell phone and dialed the number he knew by heart.

"Hi. Priya. It's Matt."

"Hi stranger. Long time no hear or see. I know you didn't call because you want to see me so what do you want."

"Priya I think you might have given me something."

"Something like what? A broken heart?" she asked in a sarcastic tone.

"I just came from the doctor's office and he's telling me I might have…."

"What Matt?"

"He's telling me I might have AIDS." Priya laughed. "Matt is this some kind of joke. Are you trying to find a way to get back at me?"

"Priya does it sound like I'm joking?" Priya could sense the fear in Matt's voice and it gave her a sense of power that she relished. "Well Matt, I really don't know what to tell you. That sounds absolutely terrible."

"Priya this is not funny. When last did you do an HIV test?"

"Please Matt. Don't make this my problem all of a sudden."

"Priya do you have AIDS?"

"Matt even if I did have AIDS which I don't do you think I would tell you? Now my advice to you is go talk to your doctor. He is the one you should be talking to not me. And here I was thinking you wanted to see me for old times sake."

"Priya please. I need to talk to you about this." Matt was perplexed and confused by the sheer callousness of a woman he once knew to be so sensitive and caring. "Matt I really don't have time for this. I'm sorry if you have AIDS but you need to talk to whoever else you were screwing when you were with me ok. In the mean time I have important matters to take care of so find some other sympathetic ear."

Before Matt had a chance to say anymore, Priya had hung up. Matt was in a daze. This could not be happening to him. He couldn't have AIDS. If he had AIDS then maybe Sally had AIDS too and if he didn't get AIDS from Priya did he get it from Sally? Matt managed to compose himself and go back to work that day but by four o'clock he was at Smokey's and Bunty's downing several strong drinks and contemplating suicide. He couldn't understand why Priya didn't even seem worried that she might have AIDS. About six months later he would understand when he read an article in the Business Guardian headed: "YOUNG EXECUTIVE DIES SUDDENLY."

"Priya Deoram, marketing manager of the Johnson Group of Companies, died yesterday at the St. Clair medical hospital after succumbing to pneumonia last week. Ms. Deoram who was one of the companies' top executives was admitted to St. Clair last week where she was diagnosed as having pneumonia. Director of the Johnson Group of Companies Marlon Smith spoke highly of Priya and added that the company has suffered a great loss. 'Priya will be sorely missed. She had a wonderful personality and was one of our finest managers,' Mr. Smith was reported as saying to the media. Funeral arrangements are yet to be announced." It was then Matt began to suspect that Priya had not been entirely honest with him. That perhaps she had known what her HIV status was all along and simply didn't care.

Chapter Twenty-Two

Aids is Not for Me

"His name is Brandon."

"What?" Ms. Janice turned around to face Jesse.

"I want to name him Brandon" said Jesse determinedly.

Ms. Janice was gently rocking the pink looking infant in her arms and showing him off to her cousin Barbara who had come up from Moruga to help Ms. Janice for a few days. "Is where yuh get dat name from gyul? We doh have nobody in our family with dat name Jesse," said Barbara. Jesse was silent and her gaze drifted off. She had been discharged from the hospital three weeks ago and was resting comfortably at home. Ms. Janice had been hoping for some change in her temperament after the baby was born but instead Jesse seemed to be getting worse. When the baby cried she would hold him carefully and breast feed him but when she was fed up of him nursing, she would pull him off her breast and leave him crying in the bassinet.

As much as Janice would implore Jesse to feed the child, Jesse would refuse once she was tired of him and so Ms. Janice had to resort to mixing formula and bottle feeding the baby whenever this happened. She was glad that her cousin Barbara had been able to visit. Barbara was short and slim and fifteen years younger than Ms. Janice. She was dark skinned with big strong white teeth and she kept her hair in a very low afro. Full of energy, Barbara got to work as soon as she arrived, cleaning the house, getting the children ready for school and helping Jesse with the baby. She was only visiting for a month but Ms. Janice hoped that in the weeks ahead she would be able to help her get the children and Jesse into a routine that would allow her life to return to some degree of normalcy.

"Brandon. Is a nice name Jesse. But you doh like Cecil? Like yuh uncle Cecil, remember him?" Barbara added seeing the look of concern on her cousin's face. Ms. Janice didn't like the name Brandon at all really. It was too close to the name Brian and as far as she was concerned, Brian was no father at all to this child. Jesse didn't respond. "Well Brandon isn't too bad a name. We might as well start to call de child something just in case he end up with a name like 'baby' or 'doo doo darling' because nobody know what to call him" said Barbara. "Things like dat does happen a lot in de country you know," Barbara advised. "Well we still have some time to get a good name," said Ms. Janice hastily. She was hoping that with time Jesse would change her mind about the name but she was wrong. Brandon Guevara would be the name that went on his birth certificate. Ms. Janice consoled herself that at least the child had her last name but it was a small consolation in light of the events that would soon follow.

News of Brandon's birth was not received well at the Chow Fatt household.

"She had a boy you know Matt," said Sally as Matt walked through the door.

"Who? What are you talking about?"

"I'm talking about Jesse. She had a boy."

"Hmmn" Matt grunted and headed for the shower.

One month after receiving his test results, Matt was still in denial. The doctors were all wrong. He had made Dr. Kissoon do another blood test and had obtained the same results. Still not satisfied he had gone to another doctor in the hope that the results would be different. They were not. Matt felt fine. He refused to accept that he was sick and chose to avoid the issue all together. Priya had denied being HIV positive but clearly she must have been. Matt wondered if he got it from Sally but confronting her would mean admitting that he had AIDS and he was not ready to do that. Instead Matt chose to go on living his life as if nothing had happened as if all was well with him physically. Every morning he got up, would examine his body in the mirror for scars or marks or anything that looked ugly or indicative of sickness. Matt was determined to keep living as long as he could.

At times he would become overwhelmed with feelings of guilt, regret, self- hatred and anger. Many times he would cry quietly in his car on the way to or from a meeting. Life was unfair. The world was unfair. He knew he had made mistakes in his life and had done a lot of wrong. He had cheated on his wife, neglected his family and been dishonest in his business dealings but most of his business associates did the same. None of these things he believed warranted the 'punishment' of AIDS and Matt honestly believed that God was finally punishing him. The punishment he felt was unjust, extreme and did not fit his offences.

He had never killed anybody or raped anybody. Rapists and killers, they should get AIDS not him, he thought. Angry with the world, with God, Priya, Sally and Brian, Matt started using sleeping pills to help him go to bed at night. He stopped having sex with Sally afraid that if she didn't have it he could give it to her but even more afraid that if she did have it, his could get worse if he had sex with her. There was a great deal Matt did not know about the virus that was destroying his immune system but Matt didn't want to know, because knowing meant admitting that he was infected and Matt was not about to accept the truth just yet.

"Don't you even care to hear your grandson's name?" Sally asked as she stood outside the bathroom door while he showered. "They named him Brandon. I kind of like the name. Although they left him with the last name Guevara. Chow Fatt would have been a much better choice if you ask me. But I guess they want to make a statement." Matt had not responded to a word Sally had said. "Are you even listening to me Matt?" "Yes Sally. I just have a lot on my mind." Sally was beginning to wonder whether she needed another trip to Senora Velasquez. News of Priya's death brought a sense of relief to Sally. In fact she had an even greater respect bordering on fear of Senora Velasquez, since she believed that the Senora had directly or indirectly brought about Priya's demise.

Knowing that Matt would no longer be tempted by Priya's existence anymore gave Sally hope that her marriage was well on the road to recovery. However, Matt's behavior seemed to be reverting and Sally did not understand why. "Well I wish I could see this gracious baby," Sally continued. "Just to be sure that he looks like Brian. Do you think we should tell him?"

"Tell who?"

"Brian. Do you think we should tell him when he calls this weekend?"

"I think he should know don't you?"

"No. I think he should focus on school. I don't want him feeling worse than he already feels about the whole thing."

"I think he has a right to know. He is the child's father after all."

Sally paused for a minute as she reflected on what Matt had just said. Her baby was a daddy. It seemed too incredible. Brian as a father seemed difficult to visualize. "Well only if he asks. If he doesn't ask I'm not going to tell him."

"He will find out sooner or later you know."

"Yes but there's time. Let him settle down first where he is."

Matt coughed as he emerged dripping wet from the shower. It was a deep rattling cough. "Matt that sounds terrible. That cold has been with you an awful long time. Don't you think you ought to get back to the doctor?" Matt entered a fit of coughing and his entire rib cage jumped up and down with each cough. "Honey I really think you ought to get yourself checked out again. You're tired all the time and you have all those night sweats…" said Sally as she laid her hand on his wet back. "You've even lost a couple of pounds, I can tell."

"I'm fine dear. I'll be fine." Matt felt as if he didn't have enough air in his chest after the coughing fit had subsided. He needed a new prescription for the drugs that Dr. Kissoon had recommended to him but he was ashamed to go back to Dr. Kissoon's office. He had cursed Dr. Kissoon out the last time he was there when he received the second positive set of test results. Dr. Kissoon was not just his doctor but a long time family friend and Matt was embarrassed when he considered that he had called Dr. Kissoon the "son of an illiterate cane cutter from Chaguanas." He could feel his body weakening everyday although he managed to get up each morning and head off to work. But the cough was coming back and with it, periods when he had difficulty breathing. The following day when Matt took in with a fit of coughing and had trouble breathing during a meeting, his associates rushed him to the hospital.

"Matt's where?"

"In hospital. What happened?"

"Oh my God. I'll be right there."

Sally hurried away from the House of Beauty in Long Circular Mall where she was getting her nails done and drove as fast as she could to St. Clair Medical. There, doctors were trying to clear Matt's airways so that he could breathe. Sally had called Dr. Kissoon while she was waiting to let him know what was going on and Dr. Kissoon who was also attached to St. Clair Medical had cancelled his afternoon appointments in order to be of assistance to one of his best clients. "Has Matt spoken to you about his condition?" Dr. Kissoon asked Sally when he arrived. "What condition?" Dr. Kissoon could tell that Sally did not know what he was talking about. "I'll need to talk to Matt first. I spoke to him before but he wouldn't listen."

"Doctor what are you talking about?" Sally was confused and perplexed. The thought of her husband dying was even more chilling than the thought of a divorce. When she was finally let in to see him, Matt looked exhausted and pale with a tube around his nose attached to a respirator. "Matt darling. I'm here." She patted his forehead dry with a handkerchief she had in her hand bag. "Doctor his skin is so cold," she said as she turned to Dr. Kissoon.

"Hi Matt." Dr. Kissoon spoke softly as Matt looked up with the eyes of a child unable to speak or to move he was so weak. "Like you trying to scare all of us." He joked. Matt could barely muster a smile. "Maybe its time we talk about that thing we were talking about the other day don't you think?" Matt nodded. "Can

Sally stay or you want me to come back later?" Matt
nodded again. Sally was wondering why Dr. Kissoon
would come at a time like this to discuss business
matters. She found it rude and insulting and was about
to suggest to Dr. Kissoon that he come back later when
Dr. Kissoon asked her to sit down. "This is about you
too so I'm glad both of you are here." Dr. Kissoon shut
the door to the bedroom.

"Sally, Matt came to me a few weeks ago when this
cough started and I diagnosed him as having PCP."

"What's that?"

"It's short for Pneumocystis Carini pneumonia and
is a fungal infection of the lung most commonly seen
in AIDS patients."

"What does that mean doctor? Is he going to be
alright?" It never for a moment entered her mind
that her husband, Matt Chow Fatt, business tycoon,
multimillionaire, could have AIDS.

"Just a minute now Sally let me finish."

"Ok"

"I gave Matt some drugs to help with the PCP and
then we did a blood test. You see PCP is one of the
end stage manifestations of AIDS patients and Matt
doesn't appear to have had any other symptoms up to
this point. Maybe he did but just didn't bother to check
but he could just be a rapid progressor and …."

"Doctor, I don't understand what you're telling me.
Just break it down. What are you trying to say?"

"Sally, Matt has AIDS. He was in fairly healthy
condition at the time he was diagnosed although I can
see that things have got a bit worse." Sally didn't hear

past the word AIDS. She swore the room shook at that very moment. She got up from the chair she was sitting on and her eyes fixed on a poster on the wall displaying the organs of the body. She began to cold sweat and her whole body began to tremble as she took in deep breaths. Sally could hear the hum of the air condition unit in the room almost as if it were right inside her ear. Her lips became dry and her face went ghostly pale.

"Doctor what are you saying? Is Matt going to die?" asked a trembling Sally. "Sally we all have to die at some point. There are a lot of AIDS patients who go on to live for a number of years before dying. Unfortunately Matt's immune system is severely weakened and unless he overcomes this bout of pneumonia I'm afraid his prognosis is very grim."

Sally could not believe what she was hearing. She felt an instant pain in her stomach and in her head, as if someone had kicked her to the ground. She looked into Matt's eyes. She could see that he was trying to say "I'm sorry" with them. "I suggested to Matt some weeks ago that you have a blood test done and now I'm suggesting to you that you have one done right away. If you would like I can have one arranged for you first thing tomorrow morning at my office, but the sooner you know what your HIV status is the better prepared you will be to deal with it." Sally didn't know much about HIV except that it killed you and that homosexuals and promiscuous people got it. How then was she, a woman who had never been unfaithful to her husband and who had only ever had sex with one man her whole life suddenly become a candidate for HIV? Her senses were numb.

"Look, I know you two will need some time alone to talk about all this so I'll leave now. Matt is in good hands here but I'll come and check up on him tomorrow. He's stable now but once he can get over this episode he should be alright. Sally was glued to her seat. Her lips were dry and her eyes icy as she looked straight at Matt. "How could you do this to me Matt? How could you? I swear to God if you've given me this thing. I'll kill you, you nasty son of a bitch. How long did you know huh? How long? All this time you were screwing around with your woman you had that nasty disease and you knew it. I hate you! I hate you!" Tears rolled down Matt's cheeks but he could not say a word. He closed his eyes. "What have I not done for you Matt? What have I not done for you? You disgusting animal." Sally had begun to raise her voice without even realizing it.

Suddenly the door squeaked open. It was Lue-Ann. Sally turned her face away in order to compose herself. "Hi Sally. I came as soon as I heard," said Lue-Ann. "Hi bro. How are you?" Lue-Ann continued. A short light skinned woman in a pale blue blouse and navy blue skirt followed Lue-Ann through the door. Sally was furious that Lue-Ann would bring a non-family member in to see her husband at a time like this. Wanting to stay but not being able to control her emotions. Sally waved a weak goodbye, only for Lue-Ann's benefit and left the hospital immediately. "AIDS! If Matt had it he must have got it from that nasty Priya. Damn him. Damn them both." Sally thought on her way home with tears rolling down her cheeks. She was numb with pain. "I can't die now. I'm still young, I have to see Brian finish school and marry a decent woman. Matt can't die. He just can't."

Sally drove along the Western Main Road in a haze of mental turmoil. The doctor's words played over in her head. She tried to remember how often Matt had used a condom in recent months. There were a few times when he hadn't. "Oh God" Sally put her hand to her mouth. The thought of having AIDS, the thought of dying, what would people say if they knew. What would Marlene think? Sally could barely keep her hand on the wheel as she drove home. So many thoughts racing through her head. Senora Velasquez had not warned her about this. Matt dying of AIDS. He was so young. It seemed too incredible to be true. They couldn't both die. He was the wrong one, not her. He was the one who had broken their marriage vows. She shouldn't have to pay the price for that. Sally would not rest until she knew whether she would live or die.

As much as she trusted Marlene, she was afraid to share this information with her. She needed someone to talk to, someone who would understand. Later that night in tears she called Dr. Kissoon. She stayed on the phone with him for almost three hours. Early the next morning he would take a sample of her blood, recommend her to an excellent psychiatrist and give her a one week prescription of Valium just to help her sleep at night. The valium she would take but she refused to make an appointment with the psychiatrist.

Everyone knew Matt she thought and Sally was too ashamed to relieve the burden of her soul to anyone, not even if they were bound to confidentiality by law. As far as Sally was concerned, confidentiality about these matters in Trinidad society was a myth.

"What did you get?" Lisa asked excitedly.

"You tell me first," said Eddy

"No I asked you first. Come on tell me."

"One A and three B's. An A in Math and B's in everything else."

"Wow, Eddy that's great. Congrats."

"I thought I had done worse. I guess it's not too bad. What did you get?"

"One A, two B's and one C. I got the C in Chemistry. I always hated that subject. But I got an A in Math."

"Lisa that's real good." Eddy hugged her. They had just met at Excellent City Centre after collecting their grades from school. Collecting their grades had been an odd moment for both of them. With Brian and Sean gone and Jesse out of school, Lisa and Eddy were glad that they still had each other. "We should celebrate," said Lisa. "I agree" said Eddy. "Freedom after seven long years of torture and stress."

"Yippee! I can't believe it. I can't believe I'm finished with school. No more getting up in the morning and being late. No more Sr. Monica harassing me."

"Now we just have to get jobs" said Eddy.

"Yeah I know. But for today we can celebrate. Let's get some ice cream, on me," said Lisa as they stopped in front a little pastry booth in the mall.

"I'm not complaining," Eddy smiled.

"Do you have any idea where you want to work Lisa?"

"I don't know, but I was thinking I might try to get a job in the bank or something. Those bank girls always look so good and professional in their uniforms. I just don't know if I'll get in. What about you?"

"I dunno" said Eddy taking a lick of his ice cream cone. "I think I want to go to university to study law or something like that but for now I'm actually thinking about joining the police service. I can't afford university now anyway."

"You a police officer. Ha. Now there's a thought." Lisa giggled

"What's so funny?"

"I just can't imagine you in a police uniform. Oh my God, women will just be throwing themselves at you."

"I don't need to have on a police uniform for that Lisa. Women are throwing themselves at me right now."

"Please!" Lisa steupsed.

"No really. I mean this one girl just bought me ice cream and I didn't even have on a uniform."

Lisa laughed and slapped Eddy playfully on the shoulder. Despite everything he'd been through from last year till then, Eddy had managed to pull through. Even when he had his low moments, he somehow managed to pick himself up by the bootstraps and keep at it. It was one of the qualities she loved about him the most and just one of the many reasons why she envisioned her future with him. They both wished that

Jesse and Brian were there to celebrate with them. Lisa wondered what Jesse was doing at that very moment. "You know we should go visit Jesse and the baby some time Ed," said Lisa. The two were walking hand in hand on the way to City Gate. "Yeah. It would be interesting to see how Brian's child would look. Imagine he's not even around to see his own son. That's just terrible."

"You know what's terrible? Jesse being a mom and not being able to take exams. Jesse was the second brightest girl in our class you know. I'm sure she would have got a scholarship if they had just let her take exams. That Sr. Monica. I hope she pays for her sins."

"You really don't like Sr. Monica eh Lisa."

"Eddy you have no idea. You should try being a St. Joseph Convent student for one day, and then you'll understand."

"I would love to as long as I get to see what you girls do in the ladies room."

"You're so silly Ed," Lisa giggled

"What? No really. I always wanted to know why it takes so long to freshen up."

The two jumped in a maxi taxi heading East. They were going to catch a movie in Palladium cinema in Tunapuna. Movie Towne was always too expensive for them. Now that they knew each other better and it was just the two of them, they felt comfortable to go to the cheap cinemas where the patrons cursed out loud and smoked marijuana at the back. Those were the cinemas they had gone to before they met each other anyway. Now there was no need to pretend.

Chapter Twenty-Three

When the Roles are Reversed

"Oh God Jesse! Jesse! What yuh doing girl!"

Barbara had only been gone a week when Ms. Janice found Jesse huddled in a corner on the ground. Brandon was out of his bassinet on the kitchen floor naked, bawling and exercising his two month old lungs. Ms. Janice scooped the baby off the floor and looked at Jesse bewildered. "What happen Jesse? What happen?" she asked. Jesse was nervously shaking her legs tucked into her chest and wringing her hands. "Becca! Becca! What happened?" Ms. Janice was shaking the baby in her arms as she stared at Jesse. She knew that Jesse was not getting any better although she wanted to believe that she had seen some improvement in the time that cousin Barbara was visiting.

Ms. Janice turned around to face Becca. "Becca what happen? Ah thought yuh was supposed to be watching

Jesse and de baby!" Ms. Janice yelled. "Ah was watching dem. Dey was good and den ah just went outside for a little while. Ah dunno wha happen Ma." Becca said in her defense. Becca had been playing outside in the yard with Joan and Jacob and had followed their mother inside as soon as the car pulled up like young chicks followed a mother hen. "Ah thought ah tell yuh to watch Jesse fuh me eh. Look Brandon was now on the floor. Ah tired talk to you Becca. Ah tired talk." Ms. Janice had not been thinking when she released the backhand slap that connected with the side of Becca's face. Becca's cheeks stung and a spring of water burst forth from her eyes. "How long dis child was lying here eh? How long?"

"Sorry Ma," Becca whimpered. The now eight year old had been forced to become an adult overnight and her spirit still yearned for playful days with her older sister and younger siblings. Ms. Janice hastily prepared a bottle of formula for the infant and stuck it in his mouth. She looked at Becca's reddened face and disheveled hair. She looked just like Jesse when Jesse was that age. Becca was still a child. Still a baby. Ms. Janice overwhelmed with guilt by what she had just done spoke softly to Becca who was still standing there as if waiting for another blow. "Ok Becca. Just go back outside Ok and give me a chance here." Becca left the room with Joan and Jacob in tow.

More and more the idea of having Mrs. Chow Fatt take Brandon was beginning to appeal to her. Even while Barbara stayed with them Ms. Janice was slowly beginning to realize that she could not cope with Jesse

and Brandon at the same time. Becca's school work
was beginning to suffer and Steve had come out of
school and started to work in a nearby mechanic shop
to make ends meet. Jesse had got worse after the baby
was born and there was no denying that. She seemed
more and more distant and less collective. She wasn't
remembering as much as before and she was becoming
more detached from Brandon. She had stopped breast
feeding him so that now he was completely on formula.
But worse, she rarely wanted to hold the child. Ms.
Janice knew she had to do something but the idea of
giving her grandson away to a stranger seemed so cruel.
"Well if yuh really look at it. She is he grandmother
too yuh know," Ma Thomas had advised her. "Gyul in
your old age with all dem children you done have so
late already, you cyah be taking care of no baby." Ms.
Janice was torn but a few days later what she would
witness would confirm her decision in her mind.

"Good news Sally. Your test results are negative for
HIV"

"Oh thank God" Sally breathed a sigh of relief. She
sat across the desk from Dr. Kissoon and made the sign
of the cross. "Thank God!" Sally had had a torturous
two weeks waiting on the results of her blood test. The
worst part about it was that she couldn't even talk to
Marlene about what was going on. Afraid and unable
to confide in anyone, Sally turned to God and Senora
Velasquez. She had asked the Senora if she cured
terminal illnesses like cancer and the like. She was
not about to let Senora Velasquez in on her turmoil.
"Si, Si, You want cure. I give cure for everything," the

enthusiastic silver haired lady had told her. "But cure for sickness es mucho dinero."

"How much Senora?"

"Ten thousand dollars. Cancer is a big big sick, es mucho dinero. Take plenty time to cure cancer, mi hija," Senora warned shaking her head. Sally was desperate but opted instead to take her chances first with the prayers she was familiar with before putting ten thousand dollars in Senora's soft money hungry hands. "My cure very good mi hija. For you I drop price to nine thousand. Cure is muy bien. No cure like that in Trinidad, only Venezuela." Senora Velasquez spoke confidently. She had built a strong clientele in Trinidad and was now experiencing much better fortunes than she was in her home country. Sunday Catholics and non-practising Christians were her best customers and although Senora Velasquez tried to convince Sally in vain, she felt certain that Sally would return. Sally went instead to a Catholic book store and purchased a novena book to St.Jude the patron saint of hopeless cases.

She had cried her eyes and her heart out the night after Dr. Kissoon first spoke to her. When Matt was ready to be discharged from the hospital two weeks later, Sally was hesitant as to whether she could live in the same house with him. A febrile, pale looking Matt was brought back home in a wheel chair with a long list of prescriptions and a huge medical bill. He had got over the worst part of the pneumonia but doctors had said that his prognosis was poor and that he didn't have very long to live. Sally wasn't sure whether she hated

Matt more than she wanted him dead. She wasn't even sure if she wanted to touch him. She was simply glad that she was going to live and that God and St. Jude had spared her life. The thought of becoming a widow was frightening to her. She knew herself only as Mrs. Chow Fatt, wife of business magnate Matt Chow Fatt. Outside of that, who was she really? It was a question she didn't have an answer for and one that she was now being forced to think about. "Just leave the wheel chair right there," she said to the ambulance attendants that brought him in from the hospital.

Sally had prepared a room for Matt downstairs. It was actually Rosita's old quarters. She moved Rosita to Brian's old bedroom and put Matt downstairs in Rosita's self- contained unit. She had purchased several bottles of bleach and several boxes of disposable gloves and adult diapers for the home attendant she had hired to take care of him. The woman whose name was Donna was as unattractive and as wiry as a coat hanger and just the type of woman Sally wanted to care for a man like Matt in his condition. She was his wife alright and like a good wife she took him back and had someone care for him but as far as she was concerned, Matt was a dog for what he had done to her and God was punishing him for his sin. He would die like a dog in his own house if Sally could help it. She felt he should be grateful that he had a roof over his head and a bed to lie in at night. Rosita was given strict instructions not to attend to his needs if he called and he was not to have any visitors. In fact Donna and Rosita were to have no interaction at all since Sally did not want the germs Donna was being exposed to, to be transferred to Rosita.

"Yes, Lue-Ann, it's a very rare type of pneumonia. He really can't have anybody see him at all, because they'll bring germs from outside and that could trigger it again."

"But can't I even…"

"No Lue-Ann. Sorry. I have to run now. Maybe we can talk later."

Sally was reveling in her new found power. Even Lue-Ann had to listen to her now. Matt was at her mercy and for the first time ever, Sally was calling the shots. Matt's right hand man and business partner Alan had spoken to Sally and was given free reign to make the decisions that Matt would usually make. Alan was to meet once a week with Sally to let her know what was going on with the business. Although Sally couldn't understand many things, she trusted Alan implicitly. She had told him that Matt was dying of cancer but Alan had heard the rumors. Trinidad society was just too small. That was the acceptable version of a reality that she was not at all prepared to deal with. Alan had visited Matt about two months after his discharge from the hospital but was too shaken to visit him again. The thought of his former partner reduced to a mass of sore ridden flesh hanging on bone was simply too much for him to deal with.

Matt's brothers and sisters were very concerned that Sally would not allow them access to their brother but presumed that it would only be for a short time. Two months into his return home however, they would begin to get much more aggressive and Sally would be forced to let them see their brother's condition. "How could you have him like that Sally. He needs to be in a hospital. What kind of a monster are you woman! I'm calling an ambulance right away!" Lue-Ann had screamed at her when she first laid eyes on her brother. "He has AIDS Lue-Ann."

"What! That's impossible."

"Yeah. Why do you think he looks like that? Your brother was having an affair didn't he tell you. I know how close you two were. That's what he picked up. I just thank God he didn't give it to me."

"An affair! What nonsense! Not Matt. He would never do that. If anybody was having an affair it would be you." Lue-Ann was horrified by her sister-in-law's remarks.

"Excuse me? You know what. This is my house and I will not have you disrespecting me in my house so get out."

"Sally, Matt needs..."

"Get out! Miss holier than thou hiding behind that big crucifix on your neck. Saying all those prayers. What are those prayers going to do for Matt now eh? You and all your holier than thou friends. Who the hell are you to judge me? Get the hell out my house! Get out! " Sally was screaming at the top of her voice. She didn't care if the neighbors heard. She didn't care if Matt heard. As far as she was concerned Lue-Ann had no right to tell her what to do with her husband. She was the one married to him. Who was Lue-Ann? Did she know what it was like to love a man and have him reject you in every possible way? Did she know what it was like to know that your husband was coming home late, because he was having sex with another woman over and over again? Did she know what it was like to smell the scent of another woman on your husband? Did she even know the smell of sex? Who the hell was Lue-Ann to tell her anything about her husband and about what she should and shouldn't do?

"Sally listen please. If my brother has AIDS and I doubt very much that is the case then we can take him overseas. We can get professional care for him. The doctors said he has pneumonia. Pneumonia can be cured." Lue Ann was trying her best to get Sally to see reason.

Sally laughed for a little while, much to Lue-Ann's dismay. "You're such a fool Lue-Ann. Your head is so stuck up in the sky talking to God in your own little bubble that you don't even know what is going on around you. You think pneumonia has Matt looking like that? Pneumonia could have a man looking like that and smelling like a cesspit like that. Not even the drugs they have him taking are helping him now." Sally steupsed. " You know, you think you are so much better than me. You and all Matt's family think he's so much better than me. You think I don't know what you all say about me behind my back? Well guess what, I didn't give Matt AIDS. He brought this on himself. Matt has AIDS and he's going to die! He's going to die you hear that! Your precious Matt is going to die! So unless you plan to raise him from the dead like Lazarus I think you better get the hell out my house."

"Sally please let's…."

"Get out bitch!" Sally screamed. That Sally had used such a foul word to describe her was a little too much for Lue-Ann to bear. She turned and with a sigh slammed the door shut behind her. Sally hit the shut door hard with her fists and began to cry. "Why Matt? Why? Oh God why me?"

Matt barely had enough energy to talk and a bout of retinitis had left him blind in one eye but his hearing was still good. For the most part, his new nurse kept him clean, ensured that he ate and took his medication and would tell him a little about who she saw coming through the front gate. Donna was not allowed upstairs at all. Sally was afraid she might bring some of the AIDS in the house. In the earlier stages of his illness, when he had just come home, Sally would dress up in clothes that she intended to throw in the garbage and would put on gloves and a cloth over her face, then put plastic bags on as much of her body as possible just to pass by the door and look at him. She looked quite a frightful sight indeed. Needless to say her attire for these rare visits to her husband did not instill confidence in his nurse. But Donna was experienced and the money was good, so she gritted her teeth and wiped up his vomit and all his other bodily emissions reminding herself constantly of her pay check at the end of the week. She worked from Monday to Saturday with Sundays off.

Although Sally had contemplated having someone come to take care of him on Sunday, she decided against it and so, on Sunday Matt was basically on his own. Donna was instructed to leave a few milk drinks by his bedside with some crackers and snacks to carry him through the day. If he had strength to feed himself he would eat. If not he would starve. On Monday morning Donna would be greeted with a room smelling stink of pee, vomit and feces and the pus from the sores that started to ooze from all over Matt's body. When the sores began to appear, Sally no longer visited. The sight and the smell of them made her sick to her stomach. In a matter of months, Matt had whittled away into skin and bone and seemed no longer human.

At first, Dr. Kissoon paid one house visit, no charge. At that time he had advised Sally that she needed to get more light in the room for him and gave her advice on other things. He promised to visit again but whenever Sally called he was always very busy. Then she stopped calling. Like a corbeau circling its half dead prey, Sally was waiting for Matt to die. She was too numb with pain to cry any more. Crying? No, the time for crying was past. Sally was bitter and angry. After all her efforts, all the money she put into Senora Velasquez' pocket to get Matt back from his mistress, he had almost killed her. She imagined herself in his shoes, lying there helpless, smelly and soiled and dying. The thought that she could have been that way was infuriating enough. That Matt would have been the one to get her sick made her see red every time she thought about it. As far as Sally was concerned, Matt had got what he deserved. In four more months she was due for another blood test to be certain that she didn't have the virus. At least that was what Dr. Kissoon had told her but Sally wasn't worried about that. She knew God didn't want her to die yet.

She had been faithful all this time, that's why God had spared her life she thought.

"Oh God Jesse! Jesse! Jesse what you doing to the child! Ms.Janice bawled as she hurriedly snatched her grandchild away from his mother.

Brandon was crying loudly and there was bright red blood spouting on to the pale skin of his arm. "Jesse what wrong wid yuh! Yuh going to kill dis child!" Ms. Janice screamed as she wet a wash rag with cold water to wipe the blood. Jesse flung the razor blade she had in her hand to the ground and began to cry. Brandon's diapers were soiled and the blood was flowing on to them. Ms. Janice wiped the blood off his arm and looked at the cuts Jesse had inflicted. They were just two it seemed and not too deep. All the while Brandon was bawling and wriggling his little plump body in her arms. "Oh Lord Jesus! Oh sweet Jesus" she cried as she opened her medicine cabinet and pulled out some plasters in a box with one shaky hand while the other clutched Brandon tightly.

She lay Brandon down on the kitchen table and placed the bandages over the cuts carefully. "Doh cry darling. Doh cry baby," she said as she rocked him back and forth the way most mothers do. The tears were rolling down her face as she comforted him. She pulled a baby bottle full of formula out of the refrigerator, emptied its contents into a pot and lit the stove under it all with one hand. Becca had been watching TV with Joan and Jacob and Ms. Janice had been making dinner when she heard Brandon crying and felt prompted to look in on him only to find him bleeding. Ms. Janice knew she couldn't continue like this. It had been too much for her. The cost of taking care of a new baby was too much of an additional expense. She had lost money at the market and was barely making ends meet. Ms. Janice had reached the end of her rope. She knew what she had to do.

That night she put some warm clothes on Brandon and rocked him to sleep in her rocking chair. "Yuh grand pappy woulda love to see yuh boy," she whispered down to him with tears in her eyes. "Yuh have a nose, just like him." She took Brandon to bed with her and gave Jesse some Tylenol PM to help her sleep. The next morning Ms. Janice made breakfast readied everyone for school. Steve looked like a man in his coverall heading off to work but Ms. Janice knew he was still very much a boy. She dropped everyone off to school around eight o'clock, gave Brandon a bottle and took him with her for a walk.

When she got home, Jesse was still asleep. Ms. Janice found the telephone number for Mrs. Chow Fatt in a little pocket book she had in her handbag. "Jesus please gimme de strength. She looked at Brandon gurgling and making cooing noises in the bassinet, which she had put in the living room earlier that morning. Then with a heavy heart she picked up the handset of the telephone.

"You want to me to do what?"

"I want you to come for Brandon," said Ms. Janice almost inaudibly.

There was silence on the other end of the telephone.

"I thought the last time we spoke you made it clear that you wanted nothing to do with me or my money. What happened?"

"Is Jesse. She not well. She not well at all and ah cyah take care of him and meh udder children at the same time. Is so hard fuh me." Ms. Janice voice crackled as she tried to hold herself back from crying. "Ah cyah do it. Ah cyah do it. Ah doh want to put he in de orphanage dat is why ah call yuh. Ah know yuh had said yuh woulda take him if we doh ask for money. Ah did never want yuh money but ah want him to have a good life. He is a sweet baby. A nice baby. He look a lot like yuh son." Sally was speechless. She could hear the desperation in Mrs. Guevara's voice. True she had offered to take the baby but that was when she thought Mrs. Guevara and her daughter were gold diggers trying to cash in. When Mrs. Guevara had told her off and refused to ask for money, Sally thought she had managed to score a double victory. Now Mrs. Guevara wanted her to raise this child she wasn't even convinced was fathered by her son. "Mrs. Guevara. I have a lot of things going on right now you know."

"Just take him fuh a week. Please. Yuh could always make up yuh mind after dat. Please. Ah fraid something bad happen to him."

"What do you mean?"

"Jesse not well ah tell yuh. She not treating de chile right and I not here all de time to watch what she doing to him. Ah jus doh have de energy." The thought of having a chance to spend time with a baby that was possibly her grandchild in the midst of everything that was taking place with Matt seemed to appeal to Sally. At least if nothing else she would have a chance to see what the baby looked like. She could divert some of her energies into taking care of him. She remembered how cute Brian was as a baby and how much she enjoyed hearing him gurgle and coo when he was five months old. "Ok. I'll take him for the week and we'll see how that goes. But I'm not promising anything" said Sally sternly. "Alright. Thanks a lot eh," said a humbled Ms. Janice.

"Where do you want me to meet you?"

"If yuh come dong in Port-of-Spain Market and come thru de gate facing de transport division, ask anybody fuh Ms. Janice and dey will send yuh by my stall."

"You're taking the baby to the market?"

"Yes. Ah accustom bringing him. Sometimes whole day he does be wid me."

"Ok well I'll see you there."

"If yuh come by twelve o'clock dat go be good."

"Ok then. Goodbye."

Sally was horrified at the thought that a baby would be exposed to the kind of germs the market harbored. She blamed that on Ms. Janice ignorance and lack of education.

Later that morning Sally sat in the back seat of the Volvo with two stuffed toys she had picked up in preparation for his arrival, while her driver, walked through the crowded market in search of Ms. Janice and the baby. "You is wid who?" Ms. Janice asked the stranger.

"So why Mrs. Chow Fatt ent come out de car." Ms. Janice steupsed.

"Look just watch meh stall a minute," she said turning to Ma Thomas. Ms. Janice picked up a blue bag packed with baby things and followed the driver with Brandon in her arms over to the parked car where Sally was. She knocked hard on the heavily tinted glass window. "Hello" The knock on the window had startled Sally. She wound the glass all the way down.

"Hi. Mrs. Guevara? Oh my goodness, he is absolutely adorable." The moment Sally laid eyes on Brandon, she knew without a doubt he was her son's child. "He's a good baby. He don't give no trouble at all." Ms. Janice said. "Yuh will love him."

Sally was in awe at the sight of this fat cheeked child who bore such a startling resemblance to her son. She reached her hands through the window to hold him and Ms. Janice placed him slowly and with a heavy heart into her arms. "Oh my goodness and he is heavy. Look at those cheeks," said Sally. Almost as if he was aware that he was the star of a show, Brandon gurgled and cooed and sucked his little hands. "Well dis is de bag wid de tings he like." said Ms. Janice "Ah have diapers in dere and some other things. Ah put meh number on a piece a paper if yuh need to call me fuh anything." Even though Sally knew that she would not be using anything from the bag. She signaled to the driver who promptly took the bag from Ms. Janice's hand.

"He is so cute." Sally couldn't get over how cute he was. Ms. Janice stood there as if waiting for something.

She wanted Sally to ask her when to feed him, how to burp him, whether he cried before going to bed, what his favorite lullaby was but she never did. "Mrs. Chow Fatt. I think we are in a bad spot here. We have to move," the driver said as he got in the car. "I will call you if I need to," said Sally as she started to put the car window up. She was afraid of breathing in too much of the market air.

"Bye bye darlin. Bye bye pumpkin," Ms. Janice blew kisses to her grandson as the car window went slowly up. The minute it was up, the car zoomed off. Brandon was gone and Ms. Janice was left with a pain in her chest. "He in good hands now Janice. Dey will take good care of him." Ma Thomas had tried to console her. Ms. Janice knew she had made the right decision. She just wondered if she would ever see him again and worried about how Jesse would react when she realized that her child had been taken away from her.

Chapter Twenty-Four
Unexpected Fortunes

"Aye hi" Lisa hugged Eddy who had just come out of a St. James taxi that stopped to let off passengers on Woodford Square. "Were you waiting long?" he asked. "Nah just a few minutes." It was 4. 30 on a Friday afternoon and as usual Port-of-Spain was abuzz with people going to their favorite, Friday evening hang outs or just heading home after a long week of work.

"You ready?" asked Eddy.

"Yeah" Lisa looked sharp in a pale green linen skirt suit that complemented her shape, with a black pair of pumps and a matching handbag. The two got in the backseat of the taxi, feeling lucky to have stepped into a taxi that only needed two more passengers. "How was work today?" Lisa asked.

"Ah not bad. I think I'm finally getting used to dealing with miserable customers and my boss was in a good mood today so it was cool. How about you?"

"I dunno. Bank work is not as glamorous as people make it out to be. I had to do filing all day today. It was very boring."

"Well that's because you're new. They always give the new person some thing they don't want to do."

"I guess. But I was hoping that I'd be doing something different by now."

"Maybe in a few months. Not to worry."

"By the hospital please driver. Take for two." It only took them a few minutes to get there. Eddy handed the driver a five dollar bill and opened the car door.

"I'm glad you came with me Ed. I think I would have been scared to come here by myself," said Lisa as the taxi sped off further up the St. Ann's Road.

"I never came in here before you know. I never had a reason until now," said Lisa in a low voice. The St. Ann's hospital was not anything like mental hospitals they had seen on TV. The security guard stopped them and asked about the purpose of their visit. "Go straight up those stairs there and talk to the person at the desk," the overweight guard directed. They obliged. "Jesse Guevara….Hmm leh meh see what ward she on," said the hairy faced woman. "Ok yuh see dem stairs dere, just go straight up and turn right. It's the first door on yuh right."

Lisa's grip on Eddy's hand became tighter as they walked up the stairwell. "Shouldn't some of these people be in restraints? I mean how come there are so many people loose?" Lisa was genuinely scared.

"Not to worry. They cyah be more crazy than me," Eddy said with a wry smile.

"This place smelling stink Ed. You not smelling it?"

"Yes but ah trying to ignore it so try yuh best to not remind me ok."

Lisa's hand was over her nose now. They pushed open the ward door and were greeted by women of various ages, all without restraints and busy doing various things. Then they saw her. In a pale blue night gown with hair all neat and pulled back looking as peaceful as an angel. She was sitting on the side of her bed with her legs down looking out the window. Lisa looked at Eddy and hesitated a bit. He gave her a gentle shove on the groove of her back. Lisa walked toward Jesse with her heart beating so fast and so loudly she thought everyone could hear it.

"Hello Jesse" said Lisa as she stepped cautiously forward. Jesse turned to see her. "Hello Lisa" she said with a stoic expression on her face. "You remember me. I thought you wouldn't remember me," said an amazed and excited Lisa as she got closer. Lisa was getting ready to sit on the bed beside Jesse when Jesse spoke again. "Don't do that. I don't like people sitting on my bed. They scare away the babies." Lisa seemed confused. "Ok. No problem" Lisa took a few steps back again.

"Aye Jesse remember Eddy?" Eddy who had been a little way off began to approach.

"No."

"Don't you remember Eddy, Jesse? We used to be in class with Mr. Lee Wen together, remember Mr. Lee Wen?" Jesse who had been looking at Lisa all the while suddenly turned again to look out the window with an expressionless look on her face. Lisa looked at Eddy not knowing what to do. "I brought you this card Jesse. For your birthday." Lisa offered her the card hoping she would take it. Jesse was silent and continued to stare out the window. It was while Lisa was setting the card down on a stand near to Jesse's bed that she noticed the pieces of bandage around Jesse's wrists.

"Jesse. Jesse." Jesse would not answer. "Ah leaving the card here fuh yuh ok." It was hard for Lisa to see her friend like this. They had been through a lifetime together, shared so many dreams, and experienced so much as friends. Jesse was her best friend in the whole world like the sister she never had. She wasn't supposed to be visiting her here. They were supposed to be coming from work and making plans for the weekend to go window shopping for jeans and shoes on Frederick Street. The kind of stuff working girls fresh out of school on a tight budget do. There was so much more of life Jesse had not seen. So much more of life Lisa wanted to share with her.

"Yuh scaring de babies away Lisa. Doh do that." Jesse steupsed and looked straight at Lisa. "I'm sorry Jesse. I'm sorry." Lisa's eyes were full now. Jesse began to wave her hands in front of her face as if she were chasing flies away. "I'm so sorry Jesse." Lisa wanted to say how sorry she was that things didn't work out between her and Brian; how sorry she was that Brandon had been taken away from her; that she had attacked Ms. Janice with a butcher knife and left her no choice but to bring her to this smelly hospital full of crazy people; how sorry she was that she hadn't been there for her; how sorry she was that she didn't beg Sr. Monica to take Jesse back to school; how sorry she was that she had been able to do her exams and go on with her life while Jesse's life had stopped.

"Let's go Lisa. Ah don't think she up fuh company right now," said Eddy. The truth was that he was becoming more nauseated by the smell as time progressed and a bit afraid of some of the other women on the ward. The woman on the bed behind him had just squeezed his buttocks and grinned back at him. Lisa stepped back a bit, not wanting to leave but realizing that it was pointless to stay. "Bye Jesse. I'll come again another time ok." Jesse was still flailing her hands in the air, striking out at invisible flies. Eddy tugged a little harder on Lisa's sleeve. "C'mon Lis."

Lisa wiped the tears from her eyes and waved one last time to Jesse in the hope that she would wave back. She didn't. As they walked out of the hospital Eddy stared into the faces of some of the men and women he saw and wondered what made a man or woman go insane. He wondered what the story behind each face was: a broken marriage perhaps, the death of a child, drugs. And what determined the threshold for each person. The point beyond which they could take no more. His mother loved to say "God doh give yuh more than yuh could bear." He wondered whether in the cases of the men and women he saw if God had perhaps made a mistake. He thought about his uncle Tommy and about Jesse. God surely had made mistakes there. Or maybe it was that people weren't strong enough; that somehow it was predetermined who would be able to cope with the stresses of life and who wouldn't. If that was the case then Lisa was strong and so was he. That thought made him feel good inside.

"You Ok?" Lisa hadn't said a word since they got into the taxi he had flagged down. "I'll be fine."

"You know what you need. A Carib."

Lisa barely smiled. "What are you planning on getting me drunk and having your way with me?"

"No. But yuh cyah blame a fella fuh trying."

She nudged him in the ribs and smiled. "What am I going to do with you Eddy Torres?" she asked playfully.

"Love me that's all. Love me till the day I die," he whispered in her ear.

Lisa steupsed then smiled up at him. Eddy smiled back but he was serious about what he had just said. He had big plans for the two of them and he hoped she felt the same way too. She did.

Somewhere on the other side of town, Sally Chow Fatt was having lunch with Marlene at the Sans Souci and showing off the new stroller she had bought for her grandson renamed Brian Chow Fatt Jr.

Somewhere down town in Port-of-Spain market, Ms. Janice was receiving the news that she had inherited a large sum of money from Papa Netty's estate and needed to go in to the offices of Jones and Morgan to hear the reading of his will.

Somewhere further uptown in Woodbrook, Sally Chow Fatt's blood test results had come in and Dr.

Kissoon was wondering how he was going to break the news to Sally. How he was going to tell her that she was HIV positive.

The lives of these two women from two different worlds were about to change dramatically and somewhere in the realm of the spiritual both of their husbands smiled and praised God for his goodness.

THE END

Glossary Of Terms

Word	Meaning
Ah	I, of, a - depending on the usage. E.g. Ah get ah hand ah fig (I got a hand of fig)
Ahready	Already
An	And
All skin teet is not a grin	Not every smile is a genuine one
Allyuh	All of you
Ay-Ay	Sort of exclamation or form of salutation; may also be used to express anger
Aye	Salutation; Can be used when greeting someone or trying to call someone who is far off
Bacchanal	Confusion
Bayrum	Alcohol based liquid with medicinal properties. Used to reduce fever, it is often sapped on the forehead or body
Bazodee	Confused or disoriented

Beh-Beh (Bèbè)	stupid
Betta	Better
Brudder	brother
Bulling	Act of sodomy
Buss	Burst
Buss a lime	The act of hanging out and having fun with friends
Baigan	Eggplant
BWEE	BWIA – British West Indian Airways
CEPEP	Community Environmental Protection and Enhancement Programme
Change	Money
Chile	Child
Chilren	Children
Chinee	Chinese person or anyone with mixed Chinese heritage
Coke	Cocaine
Cole	Cold or Flu
Coo Coo	Popular dish made with cornmeal and ochroes
Cut Arse	beating up

Couyah (Couyon) Mouth	Way of fixing one's mouth in order to ridicule or point to someone
Creole	Term used to describe people of African, European, or mixed Afro-European descent. Usage varies
Cyah	Cannot
CXC	Caribbean Examination Council
Dan	Than
Dat	That
De	The
Deep- Freeze	Another word for freezer
Dem	Them
Den	Then
Dere	There
Dese	These
Dey	They
Dis	This
Doh	Don't
Doh dig ah horrors	Never mind that/Not to worry
Dong	Down

Doo Doo	Sweetheart (term of endearment)
Doubles	Popular East Indian delicacy made with curried chick peas and commonly eaten at any time of day
Dougla	Person of mixed East Indian and African heritage
Dread	Another term for friend
Eh	Huh or What? Used at the end of a threat or request. May also be used in place of ent
Ent	Isn't that so?
Fack	Fact
Fadder/Farda	Father
Fas	Fast
Fella	Fellow
Firs	First
Force Ripe	A young person or child who tries to behave or dress much older than their actual age
Fraid	Be afraid of
Fren	Friend

Frennin	Being friendly with
Fuh	For
Funny	Another way of saying uncomfortable. E.g. Ah feeling funny
Gaping	Act of staring and scrutinising members of the opposite sex
Geh	Get
Gimme	Give me
Grong Provision	Term used to collectively describe yam, eddoes, potatoes, sweet potatoes
Gyul	Girl
Ha	Have
HELP	Another way of saying AIDS
Ho	Whore
Inspec	Inspect
Jamète (jamette)	Prostitute
Jerry Springer moment	Moment of drama
Jus	Just
Ketch	Catch
Ketching Power	become possessed by evil – to appear to becoming so possessed

Ketch a glad	To get happy about something all of a sudden
Kill yuh nose	A way of describing something which smells deathly stink
Las	Last
Leh	Let
Lil	Little
Lookin	Looking
Lotta	Lot of
Maco	To mind someone else's business
Mama Man	Man who is too dependent on his mother
Maljoe	Blight or bad luck
Marrid	Married
Mash	Get Away (term used to chase dogs away)
Meh	My or me
Mehself	Myself
Mine	Mind (but can also be used in the correct way)
Mudder	Mother
Nah	'no' or 'please' – varying usage.E.g. Doh do dat nah! or Nah man.

NALIS	National Library and Information System Authority of Trinidad and Tobago
Navel string	Remnants of the umbilical cord
Neemakharam	Ungrateful person
Noting/Nuttin	Nothing
Obeah	Caribbean version of witchcraft with roots in African sorcery and rites
Ole	Old
Outside woman	Mistress with whom a married man has a relationship
Outside child	Child born to an outside woman
Panty man	Man who is considered too weak to be considered a man
Paranderos	Men and women who go house to house singing parang songs around Christmas time
Parang	Spanish style songs, sung at Christmas time in Trinidad

Paratha	Roti that has been shreded
Pardner	Partner
Pelau	Popular rice dish made with pigeon peas and chicken or beef
Peppah	Pepper
Phoulorie	Tasty Indian delicacy made with flour and split peas
Picong	Teasing between friends
Piper	Term used to describe a drug addict
Pong	Pound
Putting Away	Cleaning of one's house usually done at Christmas time
QRC	Queen's Royal College
Raggedy	Tattered, broken down
Red Ting	Term used (mostly by men) to describe a woman of mixed race and light complexion
Res	Rest
Riding Out	Leaving a place, usually after a party
Rum-bud	alcoholic

SAT	Scholastic Aptitude Test
Seer Woman	Obeah woman – woman who deals in obeah
Sell water	Water believed to have power to increase the sales of the object on which it is sprinkled
Setta	Set of
Small Ting	Another way of saying "no problem"
Snatty Nose	Snot-nosed
Sorf	Soft
Spitty	Covered in spit
Steups	Noise made when one sucks one's teeth. Used as an expression of anger, disappointment or unhappiness
Stinkin	Stinking, Dirty
Sweet Drink	Soda
Sweet Talk	Use charming words to win a woman's heart
T & TEC	Trinidad and Tobago Electricity Commission
Taking Wood	The act of having sex with a man
Tanks	Thanks

Tief	Thief (noun) or Steal (verb)
Tie Yuh Foot	The act of casting a spell on someone in order to gain the love of that person
Ting	Thing
Tink	Think
Too Bad	Very (e.g. the orange is sweet 'too bad'; this means the orange is very sweet) Also means plenty of something
Udder	Other
UWI	University of the West Indies
Village Ram	Womaniser in a small village
Wajang	Wild, loud and uncultured individual
Waste ah time	Good for nothing or waste of time depending on the usage
Wasn	Was not
Wat	What?
Whaz de scene	What's up?

Went off	To become crazy or insane
Wha	What?
Whappen	What happen?
Whey	Where or that, depending on the usage
WICB	West Indies Cricket Board
Wid	With
Wok	Work / Put down a wok - to do the job of beating up or killing someone
Woulda	Would have
Yampee	Term used to describe the mucus that appears around the corners of the eyes after sleep
Yuh	You or your
Yuhself	Yourself
YTC	Youth Training Centre (prison and training centre for adolescent law offenders)

About the Author

Beverley-Ann Scott was born and raised on the island of Trinidad and Tobago. She grew up in Marabella and attended St. Joseph's Convent San Fernando and St. Stephen's College in Princes Town. She later went on to obtain her BSc in Information Systems and Management and worked in the banking and business sector for many years prior to deciding to pursue a career in medicine. For over five years she worked as a part-time and later full-time journalist with Catholic News, a local Catholic weekly newspaper. She is currently finishing medical school at a university in the Philippines. Although this is her first work of fiction, expect to hear more about this budding young author who has made an appealing and refreshing entry into the world of Caribbean fiction with her novel The Stolen Cascadura.

CPSIA information can be obtained at www.ICGtesting.com
Printed in the USA
LVOW130735270213

321814LV00001B/1/A

9 781434 332875